Praise for

Named one of the Best
(So Far) by
Named a Best Book of 2023 (So Far) by Cosmopolitan
Named a Best Book of Spring 2023 by *Esquire*
Named a Most Anticipated LGBTQ+ Book of 2023 by
BuzzFeed, Electric Literature, and *Them*
Named a Most Anticipated Book of Spring &
Summer 2023 by *Bustle*
Named a Most Anticipated Book of 2023 by Our
Culture, Yahoo!, *The Millions, Literary Hub,* and *Spy*
Named a Most Anticipated Debut of 2023 by
Debutiful and Goodreads

"At heart a love story, *Dykette* seductively examines themes like queer nonconformity and its place in a heteronormative world."
—*W*

"A fascinating look at queer couples and how things like gender, sexuality, age, and even horniness can affect everything about a relationship." —*Cosmopolitan*

"[A] biting tale of two young queer couples who go upstate with an older lesbian couple . . . Plenty to cringe and laugh at."
—*Rolling Stone*

"If you're in the mood for a sexy novel that explores the messiness of queer relationships, *Dykette* should be on your list."
—*The Advocate*

"*The Big Chill* goes gay in Davis's raunch-com about six queer Brooklynites spending the holidays at a Hudson farmhouse.

Come for the sometimes-riotous relationship drama, stay for the myriad cultural in-jokes." **—Electric Literature**

"There's a whiff of *Who's Afraid of Virginia Woolf?* in this wry, horny battle-of-the-lovers, and also the sensation of piecing together some gossip on Instagram. *Dykette* makes a strong case for mixing goofiness with sexiness in contemporary fiction." **—Bustle**

"*Dykette* takes on desire, debauchery, and destruction through a distinctly queer—and propulsively entertaining—lens." **—The Millions**

"[A] sexy debut novel." **—Nylon**

"Through Sasha, Davis constructs a field guide to queer dynamics, making sharp observations about generational divides, the butch/femme dynamic, and what it means to perform your gender or sexuality (as exemplified by an explosive plot about performance art). You won't soon forget Sasha, nor any of the other larger-than-life Brooklynites in her cohort." **—Esquire**

"This deeply smart, original, and funny debut novel has permanently shifted my understanding of the relationship between honesty and performance." **—Marissa Higgins, *The Millions***

"*Dykette* is a riveting and often darkly funny novel that accurately examines New York queer culture with an insider's authenticity." **—Bust**

Dykette

A Novel

JENNY FRAN DAVIS

A Holt Paperback
Henry Holt and Company
New York

Holt Paperbacks
Henry Holt and Company
Publishers since 1866
120 Broadway
New York, New York 10271
www.henryholt.com

The Library of Congress has cataloged the hardcover edition as follows:

Names: Davis, Jenny Fran, author
Description: First edition. | New York : Henry Holt & Company, 2023.
Identifiers: LCCN 2022052741 (print) | LCCN 2022052742 (ebook) |
    ISBN 9781250843135 (hardcover) | ISBN 9781250843128 (ebook)
Subjects: LCGFT: Queer Fiction. | Lesbian Fiction. | Novels.
Classification: LCC PS3604.A96223 (print) | LCC PS3604.A96223
    (ebook) | DDC 813/.6
LC record available at https://lccn.loc.gov/2022052741
LC ebook record available at https://lccn.loc.gov/2022052742

ISBN 9781250843173 (trade paperback)

Our books may be purchased in bulk for promotional, educational, or
business use. Please contact your local bookseller or the Macmillan Corporate
and Premium Sales Department at (800) 221-7945, extension 5442,
or by email at MacmillanSpecialMarkets@macmillan.com.

Originally published in hardcover in 2023 by Henry Holt and Company

First Holt Paperbacks Edition 2024

Designed by Gabriel Guma

Printed in the United States of America

1 3 5 7 9 10 8 6 4 2

The faggots have the routines of community and the rhythm of the streets to live by: visiting, lunches at small cafés, late day tea, walks, accidental encounters, organizing, issuing manifestoes, putting on plays, changing lovers, shifting alliances and living arrangements and gossip, endless gossip. . . . They find routines in their collective lives and turn them into rituals. They created the ritual of the brief encounter, the ritual of dying love, and the ritual of outrageousness.

Larry Mitchell,
The Faggots & Their Friends Between Revolutions

PART ONE

Minx

In gliding state she wins her easy way:
O'er her warm cheek and rising bosom move
The bloom of young Desire and purple light of Love.

Thomas Gray,
"The Progress of Poesy"

You're a Mean One, Mrs. Grinch

ᘓ ᘔ

TUESDAY, DECEMBER 24

The only thing Jesse wanted for Christmas was a nude photo of Sasha as the Grinch, so Sasha was writhing in a virtual thatch of green fur generated by her iPhone, naked in an empty claw-foot bathtub, her right thumb hovering at the ready over the camera button and her back arching pornographically, her left calf draped over the edge of the tub and her right toe crooked skyward with balletic aspiration. She was a busty Jewess masquerading as a lissome green creature, which was probably why she couldn't get the picture right, no matter how artfully she twisted. When her face looked hot, her tits came out lumpy, and when her body looked acceptably supple, the filter distorted her facial features into a mess of plush green fur and digitized eyelashes.

It was thankless work. Sasha grunted in frustration each time another terrible photo appeared in her camera roll. But she contorted anew, refocused the phone on her face (now visibly strained with determination), and humbled herself before the technology of the day—which everyone else used for purposes mundane and mercenary, but which Sasha was using for the highest purpose: that of seduction. The Grinch filter jumped to life in holographic patches.

Sasha and her iPhone wrestled for control of the image. Cotton-candy plumes of lime-green hair haloed her pink cheeks, swaying as she twisted her neck. Her nose blunted into an Anglo-Saxon snub dyed a shade deeper than the rest of her silky swirls of facial fur. It was the kind of nose she'd so often wished for growing up, but she saw now that it was all wrong on her face—a snub nose made her look asshole-ish, elitist. Glittering, bitter emerald irises ringed beefed-up black pupils, darting furtively in a milky bath of computer-generated sclera. Tangled green bushes replaced Sasha's own dutifully threaded eyebrows. She smiled to reveal long, mossy teeth.

Besides the buttery eyelashes fanning the cartoon-princess eyes, it would be crazy to call this monstrous face "feminine." But somehow the effect was beautiful in its hallucinatory sway. It produced an image that was visionary rather than literal, a trancey interpretation of what "woman" might mean in a blurry sense. Mediated by the Grinch filter, Sasha's face was steely, its aspirational wickedness intercepting a darling, doe-eyed inno-cence. She pursed her scaly lips, cocked her furry jaw.

She looked really hot. It made sense that Jesse was horny for the Grinch. She—the Grinch—was a villain, a minx. The story of the Grinch was ultimately the tale of a cunt with a growth mindset. It was the story of a heart that could—and would!—swell to three times its size by the story's end. Jesse was horny for the Grinch's bitchiness, but also horny for the Grinch's redemption. Yes, her boyfriend was horny for the Grinch's peregrination.

She typed the words *come back to me* in white font, mas-saged the text down to its tiniest possible size, and implanted it, subliminally, in the gleam of the Grinch's pupil. *I want to be better for you*, pleaded the big emerald eye. Inspired by her own virtue, Sasha contorted herself into the acrobatic shape of an exotic frog, making sure her ankles—her two best features—glistened daintily.

The bathroom was flooded with the soft light of a custom-made feat of industrial lamp design. Gays hated overhead lighting; Jules, their host and the house's owner, had let the original ceiling fixture dust over, taped down the light switches. It was certainly possible that under fluorescent bulbs, the green of Sasha's fur would not have shimmered so.

Jesse's interest in the Grinch had something to do with the color green. Jesse had recently given her a green-and-pink Vivienne Westwood orb necklace for their one-year anniversary, along with a limited-edition Kylie Jenner eyeliner (called "Kyliner" and accompanied by a glossy note from Kylie herself) in Grinch green. All of the kitchen tools back in Jesse's Brooklyn apartment were green: cheese grater, knife, teakettle. Most of the furniture, too, including a Realtree camouflage love seat that Jesse had upholstered that fall. Green succulents on the coffee table and a huge metal cactus with prickles to hang their keys and Sasha's headscarves. Green bottles of vermouth on the bar cart and green-and-white vintage YSL towels in the bathroom, which Jesse had got from working on a set. And, for the holidays, three tiny green stockings on the defunct fireplace, each embroidered in Jesse's hand with a different initial: *S.* for Sasha, *J.* for Jesse, and *V.* for Vivienne, Sasha's black pug. And Sasha always wore a bootleg green Chanel ribbon around her neck or in her hair, its tendrils curling around her shoulders or between her collarbones. Today the ribbon sat in a loose knot around her neck. On her phone screen, the ribbon flashed in and out of the frame, the filter unsure how to Grinchify it.

Sasha stretched out her legs and arms in the bathtub and let her phone rest on her stomach. Vivienne, who had been sleeping on the plush bath mat, lifted her head to lick Sasha's dangling wrist, and Sasha massaged Vivienne's shiny forehead. The blood rushed through her vascular highway, her heart pounding out an uncertain rhythm. She put one leg on either side of the tub, like the woman in her favorite birthing video. This was unsexy of her, to flash herself at the ceiling. But her Grinch face had unlocked a feral rush. She imagined eleven tiny green pups suckling at her green teats while Jesse waited anxiously at her side, peering from time to time to see if a tendriled green head was emerging yet from her furry green crotch.

Jesse was in the bedroom next door to the bathroom, on the phone with Faye the psychotherapist. Though it was their first afternoon in Hudson, and technically they were on vacation, Jesse had forgotten to cancel before Faye's forty-eight-hour cancellation window, so she'd excused herself from the rest of the group for the fifty-minute phone session to avoid paying Faye's cancellation fee. Sasha's phone read 3:23, meaning that half an hour of Jesse's therapeutic hour remained.

She aimed the phone at her tits with newfound motivation. The filter's touch was less artistic with the body than it had been with the face. The color it cast over Sasha's flesh was nauseating, the nipples sprouting pathetic tufts of kelly-green fur. Jesse would think bristly nipples were hot, so she snapped a half-hearted picture, but the image on the screen horrified her, and she deleted it quickly.

As she contemplated her next pose, she realized that she could hear scraps of dialogue from Jesse's therapy session in the bedroom next door. Actually, once she really began to pay attention, she heard Jesse's voice on the other side of the wall ringing with sharp clarity, her words crystallized in such a way that attentive listening became unnecessary.

Sasha placed her phone facedown on the edge of the tub and sat up very slightly, her tailbone pressed to the ceramic basin like an ear to a door. Stock-still, she brought a hand up to her face, caressing her cheek, which sizzled as she listened. Jesse was slandering her!

"Sasha says she was put on this earth to be kissed, cuddled, fucked, admired, adored," Jesse was telling Faye. "But all she does is take my love and affection; she never gives it back to me."

Jesse then alleged to Faye that since Halloween, Sasha had been consistently cold to her, that Sasha's gaze was totally devoid of care. In Jesse's estimation, Sasha struggled to show love regardless, but since Halloween, Sasha had become exasperated and irritable, snippy and impatient.

"Sasha *flinches* when I try to kiss her," Jesse was saying. "Like I'm a pervert. Is it stupid that I love her? Is it stupid that I love someone who makes me feel like that? It feels pathological, to be this pathetic dope who keeps loving someone who flinches away from me."

A small, shocked laugh rose in Sasha's throat. Jesse wasn't speaking with malice. There was no performative gloss to these statements, the way there would have been if Sasha were talking to her own therapist. Jesse sounded sad and guileless, and was documenting for Faye the shape and size of that sadness.

Libel! Sasha thought. Though she wasn't actually sure where the lie lay, Jesse tended to speak with an assumed neutrality that cloaked her own bias. Of course Jesse's charges lacked context, a bigger picture—they lacked Sasha's side of things.

There was a pause, Faye's turn to speak to Jesse through a pair of wire headphones.

Jesse took a deep, raggedy inhale. "How does it feel in my body?"

Sasha imagined Jesse's body scan. Jesse's lungs were unclogged, unburdened by the confession. Her heart bursting with righteousness, her sturdy quads twitching against her track pants with the inertia of Faye's affirmation. Her gut whirling, as usual, with anxiety. Sasha welled with guilt and grief. She pictured Jesse's colon clamped and twisted like a crushed plastic bottle. Poor thing—it was easy to feel sympathy for Jesse's colon.

Sasha stared down at her naked body. Her stomach bunched into two thin and discrete rolls of fat, one just under her ribs and the other above her crotch. She pinched them together like lips. *Fuck this*, the lips said. She tried to force the two rolls of fat into one unified stomach pouch, but a faint line remained where the skin had become accustomed to bunching when she sat. She grasped at her flesh until the skin began to tenderize. She pressed her boobs together to make a cushioned plate of armor on top of her racing heart.

"It feels like I'm starving for love, and she's feasting on it," Jesse continued. "She's a glutton, and she gives so little—she withholds it from me because she can tell how bad I need it. She's punishing me."

Sasha bristled at *glutton*. But she did know what Jesse was talking about, as far as the flinching was concerned.

A few weeks before, on hiatus from her literature PhD program in Rhode Island and back in Brooklyn for Thanksgiving, Sasha had been standing at the stove in Jesse's apartment, making rice. Jesse had come up behind her and grabbed her around the waist. For the first thirty seconds of the embrace, Sasha was grateful for the touch, which meant that Jesse still wanted her. (Delusional, Jesse would have argued here, because she'd never stopped wanting Sasha.) But then the feeling of Jesse's hands was off-putting, too tight, like a sports bra. She felt bloated and repulsive. She shook the hands off her, writhing away from Jesse's grasp and grabbing both of Jesse's wrists tightly in her fists, saying only that she didn't want to burn the rice.

Jesse had looked wounded, hands hanging limp in the air. Sasha felt guilty, so she released him. Instantly, the hug was not what she wanted—it was too desperate, too gratifying for Jesse. Jesse had flooded the hug with significance that Sasha hadn't intended; the hug was beginning to make promises that she couldn't keep—nightly hand jobs, a shared bank account, unilateral exoneration. As soon as Jesse began to caress her ass and nip at her neck like a happy puppy, Sasha reverted to her closed-off, looking-away thing. Jesse hated this more than anything else. Sasha made her body go slack and unresponsive and willed Jesse to notice, to attend to the difference, but he did not. Jesse was too hungry for Sasha to notice that the thing he wanted had disappeared. Her heart was pounding like a bloody dolphin heart. Jesse's mouth was on hers, fruity and metallic. His body tight against hers, firm bound chest pressed to her. She almost gagged on the tongue. She focused somewhere behind Jesse's head and counted to twenty. She understood that she had already ruined everything. All there was left to do now was let out a few groans, maybe a couple of soft yelps. Jesse snaked a strong, eager hand into her underwear, and she knew that she was closed, a tight, wet spiral clenched shut. When Jesse pressed on down eagerly, like her kittycat was a buzzer at an apartment building aglow with a hot party, Sasha let out a quick, involuntary growl.

What had come to her mind was literally that line from Barthes: *Does it still count as sex if someone dies?*

But she had not died, not yet, and as soon as Jesse announced, "You're closed, baby, open up," she knew he was going to coax her open. It was demoralizing to be loved so much when you were so mean. She focused on loosening.

"Come on," Jesse urged. "Can I come inside?"

"No," Sasha said weakly.

Concentrating hard, the rice bubbling on the stove and frothing onto the burners, Sasha relaxed her muscles until Jesse was able to slip a finger inside of her, and then another finger, until she was truly being fucked. Jesse's fingers slithered inside her with greater force, a hangnail battering her G-spot.

Aww, she'd thought, Jesse. A sweetie, someone who loved her, someone she loved back. She didn't have to reject this love or be so suspicious. She felt herself soften. She made the noises she knew Jesse liked, some benevolent mews. But the truth was that she liked pretending, it was what she had always done, crying out and letting her breath suck in and out of her in short, raspy puffs until Jesse believed he had made her come; she could even tremble her legs in mockery of coming, relax her whole body as though with relief. She couldn't believe that some straight girls made such a big deal about never faking it, like faking it was anti-feminist. Faking it was easy and fun. She sighed cutely into Jesse's sweaty hairline for good measure.

Sasha liked her body better upright. Her stomach was not flat, admittedly, but standing up, it could be believed that she had once possessed abs, and had only very recently lost them. Standing, she could focus on a few key features that she didn't mind: visible kneecaps, tits jammed into attention in a 32F bra, manicured fingernails—black gel acrylics this season, coffin shape—with well-tended cuticles. Standing, she could imagine that she was Jessica Rabbit, breasts heaving against a pale pink twin-set and a miniskirt cinching a twenty-inch waist, creamy arms hinging at lethally sharp elbows. Lying down, as she was in the tub, she felt like a fleshy skirt—her tits pooling at her sides like melting heaps of buttercream frosting.

"Maybe I can explain it like this," Jesse was telling Faye. "I was walking with Lou a couple weeks ago, and they were saying something about how being the lovesick dopey guy is fun, for a while. Y'know, the chase. But what's more fun is being lusted after. Lou wants to make someone else feel desired, sure, but they *also* want to be the person someone else, like, sacrifices their pride to pursue."

Sasha's constricted throat let out an ugly hack. Was Jesse implying that Sasha didn't lust after him? What Jesse didn't seem to understand was that his desire to play captive, dog-house husband, and Sasha's desire to play queen—each committing to the game until there was a chance of a winner and a loser, then upsetting the balance before there could actually be one—was a bond reliant on both of their participation. Without it, one of them would always be marooned, a pathetic dope.

Jesse told Faye that he'd asked Lou if their new girlfriend, Darcy, was that person for them—someone who made them feel as desired as they made her feel. Without hesitating Lou had said yeah, of course she was. Jesse reported to Faye, voice breaking, that upon hearing Lou's answer, he'd felt almost envious.

A violent, sour swirl of rage gathered in Sasha's abdomen at the annoying hiss of Darcy's name. Darcy and Lou were not yet in Hudson, but suddenly she could feel them leering at her from behind the plush cotton towel hanging on the opposite wall. She collected her body into a ball and rocked back and forth, a restless catatonia grinding her vertebrae like bulbs of garlic.

Jesse was, now doing some sort of guided meditation with Faye, lost in a reverie about the early days of his and Sasha's relationship. How Sasha would scratch Jesse's whole body with her long nails until Jesse came from pure anticipation. How Sasha bought a nursing corset whose cups unhooked to reveal her creamy tits, hanging like storm clouds from which Jesse could suckle fresh raindrops. How Sasha would leave sweet notes and weird gifts—a Skittles brand candle, a tiny taxidermy mouse, an iridescent button—when she'd left Jesse's apartment at dawn, which was what she thought girls were supposed to do.

Now Sasha was intent on punishing Jesse for something that Jesse hadn't even done. Sasha's delusion, Jesse called it. Her fantasy.

Sasha felt, for a moment, dizzy. Then, just as quickly, the anger deflated like a broken blister, leaving her flapping open, waterlogged and bilious. A spasm of sorrow. Her tailbone ached against the porcelain tub. She bit down hard on the inside of her cheek, loosing a hunk of flesh that she swallowed unceremoniously. She clutched at the porcelain walls of the bathtub. No, she thought, no, no, no, this isn't happening, it can't be happening. I can*not* have let things get this bad. As much as she hated Jesse in that moment, she hated herself more for prompting this bitter version of him. She'd defeated him, emasculated him.

She was willing to believe the worst about herself—eager, even, to do so, lapping up the insults like a thirsty dog. Hearing the vilest things about herself satisfied the evil part of her that ached for recognition. She could have climbed out of the tub and scrambled downstairs to safety, she knew. The problem was that now, as always, she didn't want to stop listening.

Things were wrapping up. The following week's appointment was being confirmed, the final affirmations stated, Jesse reminding Faye that they'd be in Hudson for another week, guests of Jules and Miranda, before returning to Brooklyn. Sasha hurled her phone down on the shag bath mat and pulled on her underwear, dressing quickly in an oversized pink satin dress and black tights.

ᘉ ᘐ

In the kitchen, their queer elders bent around the wood-topped island like members of a summit, both pitched forward on their elbows. Jules Todd, prime-time news anchor for the liberal channel, scribbled on a legal pad. Vivienne sat heavily at the feet of Miranda Saraf, a licensed social worker and Jules's partner of five years.

"Mommy is your world," Sasha reminded Vivienne softly, bending to bury her face in Vivienne's neck scruff. She didn't use baby talk with Vivienne; this would degrade them both.

"She's so perfect," Miranda sighed, reaching out to massage Vivienne's velvety ears.

Vivienne lapped gratefully at Miranda's right eye.

It was well documented in human-interest profiles about Jules that she preferred male dogs to bitches and, though she was in between dogs right now, had a propensity for bigger breeds like sheepdogs. Regardless, both Jules and Miranda had taken a shine to Vivienne.

"Let's think this through," Jules was saying. The refrigerator doors were flung open, and the nearly empty shelves gleamed under the fluorescent bulbs. "We have plenty of condiments, including two types of mustard and a big thing of fish sauce—I had a Thai cooking craze this fall—and half a bag of semisweet chocolate chips. We'll want a case of seltzer? And some bagels for the morning, yeah?"

Seltzer, Jules was writing. Then she added *bagels, cream cheese,* and, after a moment's pause, *tomatoes.*

"Jesse doesn't like raw tomatoes," Sasha said.

She made herself focus on the words Jules was writing. Her eye caught the word *limes,* and she forced herself to trace each pen line with her entire soul, trying to lull herself into a stupor.

"Cooked tomatoes are okay, though, right?" Jules was saying. "Like in a tomato sauce?"

Footsteps sounded on the stairs. Sasha's heart hammered like an old, sad engine. Jesse appeared in an aquamarine hoodie and loose white denim pants. Sasha trembled with desire and sweet sadness. But she stayed where she was. She had to be strong about this. She had to be smart.

"Tomato sauce is fine," Sasha said.

"Hey," Jules said, nodding to acknowledge Jesse's arrival. "Also, what do people like in their coffee?"

"I'm a half-and-half guy," Jesse said, heaving Vivienne into her arms as though nothing was wrong. She didn't touch Sasha during the transfer of the dog, just hooked her fingers under Vivienne's armpits and pulled.

"Would it be okay if we got a thing of oat milk, too?" Miranda said. "Sorry to be a pain."

Miranda was now turned toward Jesse, still massaging Vivienne's buttery ears, her thin fingers rubbing precise, dime-sized circles.

"Let's make sure we get the barista blend," Jules added.

When Jesse laughed, Miranda said, with the tiniest edge of defensiveness in her voice, "It's not *such* a big deal, but the normal oat milk doesn't mix in very well. The barista blend is creamier."

Oat milk, Jules wrote. *B. blend.*

"I added limes, too," Jules said, transparency important to her. "For the drinks I want to make."

"What about snacks?" Miranda fretted.

"If they have those Firehook crackers, let's get them, those are great," Jules said, writing it down. "With a smear of goat cheese and some quince jelly? Perfect."

She pressed her fingers into the shape of a b-hole and then kissed the finger bundle before releasing it.

"Nuts, maybe," Sasha said, but she had long since dissociated. "Chips. Fruit."

Cara Cara oranges. Quince paste.

"Lou likes fish," Jesse said, and Jules wrote it down. "They made me this really good tilapia one time. I wonder if they'd make it for us one night."

Darcy and Lou were aboard the Amtrak; someone would have to go retrieve them shortly.

"What does Darcy eat?" Miranda asked.

"Anything." Jesse's eyes shone at Darcy's dietary flexibility. "Well, maybe just write down 'pink things.'"

The out-and-out nerve of "pink things"! This was, of course, a reference to the performance that Jesse and Darcy would be livestreaming from Jules's backyard sauna later that week—it was to be a pink wonderland, bimbo heaven. Sasha wanted to break Jules's pen across her knee. But now Jules was writing, with a bemused smirk, *pink things*, and Sasha could only growl softly.

Mom, Vivienne's wet marble eyes pleaded, *simmer*.

"What, like raspberries and bubblegum?" Miranda asked, smiling.

"She has a sweet tooth," Jules confirmed, also eager to show off her knowledge of Darcy's palate, though they'd met only a few times, adding *(sweet)* to the final item and capping the pen with a flourish.

The grocery list done, Jules and Miranda tag-teamed a fast tour of the farmhouse. Sasha was in a fugue state, but the tour managed to hold her interest. From the outside, the house was painted a stylish, if unusual, matte black and set off from the road by a concerningly slim margin. And inside, it had— besides the commercial-sized kitchen with a massive sink and water that went from freezing to scalding in three seconds— two massive living rooms, each roughly the size of Jesse's one-bedroom apartment in Brooklyn, outfitted with cashmere blankets, wood-burning fireplaces, and wicker furniture covered by sheepskin throws, all of which you could tell were bought not secondhand but tags-on new from artisans in Ireland and New Zealand.

When Jules and Miranda were staying at their apartment in Park Slope, they lent the house to various friends of theirs, always free of charge. These friends, Jules explained, had begun a tradition of leaving behind whatever odds and ends they couldn't finish as a sort of treasure hunt for their hosts to discover upon their departure. And so the kitchen had accrued an eclectic mix of edible ghosts from gays past: graham cracker–flavored beans in the coffee grinder, calcified veggie burgers in the freezer, artisanal herbed popcorn in the pantry, half-eaten packages of beef jerky in the drawers, cans of diabetic cat food lining the bathroom shelves. There was a slippery and steep staircase without a banister, so narrow that you could catapult yourself down, arms outstretched, while safely wedged between the two walls.

Jules and Miranda wanted to model what was possible, to present a future that Jesse and Sasha might strive to emulate—in turn reaffirming Jules and Miranda's own choices. The tour was partly informative (this is where to find aspirin and extra toilet paper; here is where the recycling piles) but mostly an opportunity for Jules and Miranda to assert their dominance ("ass their dom," as Sasha and her best friend, Sylvie, habitual abbreviators, referred to this sort of older-lesbian flex).

It seemed to Sasha that Jules and Miranda saw themselves as ambassadors of adult lesbianism, a world in which Sasha and Jesse were positioned as fresh-faced initiates. In this way, each couple helped to bolster the other's vision of itself. It brought Jules and Miranda joy to direct and produce the ten-day getaway in their stately farmhouse, to think of themselves as benevolent queer elders (though they were not so old, only long-domesticated and homo-normie in comparison to Jesse and Sasha's yearlong relationship).

But—and this was not to be understated—it also thrilled Sasha and Jesse to consider themselves among the chosen by these successful older gays, to tell friends that they were spending the holidays at a "friend's place upstate" and then reveal, via pictures of the sauna and the estate on Instagram tagging @TheRealJulesTodd, that they were relishing in the privilege of their adjacencies. The foursome enjoyed a symbiosis that struck Sasha as entirely lovely.

Rows and rows of cookbooks, contemporary novels, and memoirs filled the built-in shelves, highbrow mainstream titles, the types of books that appeared on top-ten lists at the end of each year. The plentitude and popularity of the books made Sasha feel unreasonably lucky, as though the books were hard to come by; like it was a luxury to treat yourself to the best-sellers and buzzy books, ones that normal people read, instead of the weirdo pulp books she found on eBay. For some reason she'd subjected herself to obscure literature, which she believed herself to enjoy, but seeing the titles in the Hudson farmhouse made her wonder if her taste was a sort of self-punishment. It had simply never occurred to her that she, too, could buy these bestsellers. The way popular art repelled her was part of how she conceived her singularity, her outsiderness. Of course she wanted to read these books, everyone did. But she was afraid of what she might discover in them—that they were better, deeper, more deserving of attention than anything she might find in the margins of the internet or might herself create. That they were popular for a reason.

The dining room featured a full bar with a sophisticated array of gins and rums in all sorts of flavors, like walnut liqueur and black cherry rum—Jules was an amateur mixologist—and Jesse complimented Jules on her selection of liquor. Jules complained that she was an alcohol hoarder, loathe to throw away even the crustiest, most bitter bottle.

"Can you teach me how to use brandy?" Jesse asked.

Jesse aspired to be a Renaissance butch. He was always picking up new trades and skills: gardening, upholstering, sewing, plumbing and electricity, glass-blowing, leatherworking, carpentry. These skills did come in handy at work; Jesse worked as a film and television set decorator, where he was often asked to install a vintage medicine cabinet or mend a wig. At Jesse's question Sasha experienced another pang of devastation. Sasha didn't enjoy learning new things because she felt twisting, impatient rage whenever people explained things to her, so instead she'd spent her life identifying the few things she was good at and privately becoming better at them. It was shameful, weak-willed. She thought about being better, about taking up mixology or woodworking, and puffed up a little with determination.

In the upstairs bathroom there was the claw-foot tub. The ceiling sloped down so low and so abruptly that standing up from the toilet too fast could result in a concussion. Sasha could barely hold eye contact with the bathtub, whose shiny silver knobs gleamed at her with taunting recognition. The bathtub likely still held her smell—the porcelain streaked with nervous sweat and sullen discharge.

Vivienne whined at the bottom of the staircase, and Miranda scampered downstairs, hoisted the dog up into the crook of her arm, and then rejoined them.

"We'll have to really watch her on the staircase," Miranda said. "Her paws are so slide-y on the wood."

When Miranda released her, Vivienne trotted into the biggest bedroom, which she no doubt assumed was theirs. Bedroom 1 had an ornate four-poster bed, crumbling golden wallpaper, and creaky scuffed floors. This was actually *theirs*—Jules and Miranda's—they told Sasha and Jesse sheepishly, because it was so much nicer than the other two. It included a glamorous bathroom with the house's only shower ("You can use it anytime you want") and a green Victorian daybed with a tasseled bolster pillow arranged against the window. Jesse and Sasha recalled Vivienne from the hanging tassles, which she was now mouthing like a seal, eyes abulge. It was Jules and Miranda's house; of course they'd taken the nicest bedroom. But their weirdness about it produced a twinge of discomfort that flitted momentarily between the two couples.

"Look," Jesse said in a low voice when Jules and Miranda had already left Bedroom 1. There was a huge vibrator—a pale blue Le Wand—plugged into an outlet by the bed, resting on the nightstand. Sasha was sure she'd never seen a vibrator that big, and it filled her with both slight scorn—didn't they know that they made tiny ones now?—and slight envy—how extravagant!

Pale blue was an eye-roll color for a vibrator, like choosing the white KitchenAid mixer (stationed in the kitchen) and the oiled bronze bathroom hardware in deference to the predetermined palette of adult life. And there was something a little smug about the vibrator's prominent place in the bedroom.

It was possible that they'd simply forgotten to put it back in the drawer after their last fuck. But Miranda and Jules had spent the past week in Brooklyn, driven Sasha and Jesse up to Hudson that morning. Had the vibrator been plugged in like this all week, awaiting their arrival? Or had Jules and Miranda snuck upstairs during Jesse's therapy session and Sasha's bathroom photoshoot? The vibrator didn't look wet, but of course Jules and Miranda, self-described neurotic freaks, would have rinsed off and dried their vibrator immediately after use to thwart the growth of bacteria. Sasha let herself smile at Jesse in response, grateful for the moment of perverted curiosity between them, and ducked out of the room behind him.

Bedroom 2, across from Bedroom 1, was the second-nicest bedroom. It had a saggy queen bed covered in a plush white comforter, a few yellowed patches at the bottom that everyone pretended not to notice.

"We figured this one would be for Darcy and Lou," Miranda said, and that was that, which struck Sasha as slightly unfair, though she knew the gracious thing to do was to step aside and yield to the absent couple. Jesse noted that Lou would love the frosted glass sliding doors of the closet, and that Darcy would appreciate the mangled mannequin slumped in the corner of the room.

Miranda shut the door to Bedroom 2 with discretion.

That left Bedroom 3 to Sasha, Jesse, and Vivienne. They were the youngest couple and the least impressive, perhaps on their way to something-ness but perhaps not. Bedroom 3 was closest to both the bathroom and the stairs, and it featured a painting of a horse with a large penis. It also had sheer curtains that Sasha and Jesse both vocally appreciated. The nice pale yellow color! Big windows faced the street, providing the inhabitants of Bedroom 3 a clear view of whatever was happening on the road outside and giving the cars driving along the road outside a clear view of whatever was happening in Bedroom 3. A Subaru trundled down the road, its radio audible from the house.

Miranda and Jules explained that they were in the process of moving their lives upstate, having lived primarily in the Hudson house since the summer, though they'd spent the past week in the city dealing with some pressing matters around their apartment and one of Miranda's patients, who was being—and here Jules began to circle her pointer finger by her head to signal *crazy* until Miranda knocked it away with a twitchy smile—*difficult*.

"We're realizing we're recluses," Jules said. "The city stresses us out."

"What about—you know—the news," Jesse said.

"The shed in the backyard should do the trick once I get a guy up here to help me with my setup," Jules said. "I'll still go to Manhattan a few times a week, but that way I can broadcast from there when I don't feel like commuting."

Jules and Miranda exchanged a look that suggested there might be more to this narrative, but then Jules was waving them all back downstairs, continuing to chatter as she brought up the rear, her house loafers slapping down the steps.

The lengthy explanations about their living situation reinforced the feeling that Jules and Miranda were not really their friends. Friends didn't need updates like these; with friends you lived in hilarious mundanity. The tidy way the information was presented was the way Sasha might've delivered an update on her studies to an aunt: neat and cheerful, sanitized of conflict.

In truth, the two couples hardly knew each other. They'd met Jules and Miranda at a Kentucky Derby–themed party at a bar on the Lower East Side that past May. Over the course of the race and the upset afterward—Country House, a 65–1 long shot, claimed the title after Maximum Security outpaced the competition and was disqualified—Jules and Miranda had plied Sasha and Jesse with mint juleps, macaroni and cheese balls, and deep-fried broccoli sloughing flakes of salt-and-pepper tempura. At the end of the evening, swaying with drunkenness, they'd exchanged phone numbers and vowed to keep in touch.

"I was thinking we could do the interview here," Jules said softly to Sasha, gesturing to the closed door of Miranda's office. "Whenever you're ready, of course. No pressure."

Sasha had pitched a profile on Jules to her department chair as a piece about queer domesticity, which she promised she'd attempt to publish in a prominent literary magazine. She planned instead to pocket the four hundred dollars that she'd been awarded. A fair trade, since she did more than her share of unpaid labor for the department as its only hot graduate student.

Sasha agreed that the office would be perfect for the interview.

Her interest in Jules had precisely nothing to do with her area of graduate study, which was on the concept of the feminized miniature—shrunken objects, small spaces like sickbeds and dollhouses, petty ephemera. Sasha was proposing the possibility of a femme narrative theory vis-à-vis the feminized miniature: stories that were gossipy, speculative, concerned with minutiae. Sasha had devised the idea to write about Jules after Jesse passed along the invite, figuring that she might as well enter the week with motivations of her own.

Sasha fervently wished that this cultural history of the femme already existed so that she wouldn't have to be the one to write it. It was very embarrassing to be the one writing about femininity. Femininity was obviously an indication degraded as trivial by the culture. But worse, the discourse *surrounding* femininity was degraded even further than the thing itself as shrill and annoying. She felt a lot like Nabokov, actually, who famously said he wrote a book with no other purpose than to get rid of it.

༄ ༅

Jules and Miranda huddled in the corner of the kitchen, discussing something in low voices as Jesse and Sasha gathered themselves to go collect Darcy and Lou from the Amtrak station. Other obligations had kept the third couple in the city until later in the day. Jules bent down to kiss Miranda's forehead, and when Miranda looked up at her, the sunlight caught her eyes, illuminating her searching look. Jules mouthed *I love you* into Miranda's face. In moments like these, Jules had a very sexy caretaker vibe. Sasha's kittycat tingled. She dumped some kibble in a Tupperware for Vivienne and filled a bowl with cold water. She felt around in the pocket of her pink puffer for her gloves.

"Ready?" Jesse asked, brandishing the key fob to Jules's Prius.

They were to take the Prius to the station while Miranda and Jules went for groceries in Jules's old Toyota, which was kept permanently upstate. Vivienne snorfled anxiously when she saw Sasha and Jesse leaving without her, but from the window they watched her settle into Miranda's lap on the couch with a Greenie.

Sasha and Jesse got into Jules's car. Jesse revved the Prius to life with a fuel-efficient purr. Sasha didn't have her driver's license, so Jesse drove them everywhere.

"Hey, pretty," Jesse said to Sasha as they inched backward onto the road.

So the plan, Sasha thought, was to pretend as though everything was normal?

"What?" Jesse said, though it was clear he wasn't really curious why Sasha was unhappy. Sasha ignored him.

The sun was just beginning to set, turning the sky a pinky-orange that Jesse was obsessed with. He kept asking Sasha to take pictures of it from the front window as he was driving, and Sasha obliged angrily; she didn't identify with the impulse to capture the sunset, or any natural beauty. She snapped a few quick pictures of the sky, without making sure the lighting was good or the view through the dirty window was clear, and air-dropped them to Jesse before slipping the phone back into her coat pocket.

She debated saying something to the effect of *I heard your therapy session*. But then it would be over so quickly, and the outcomes so predetermined: Jesse's apology or else a big fight; Jesse's denial or else loads of lesbian processing; Jesse's righteous indignation or else the awful feeling of having wounded a sweet creature. The lack of her own innocence weighed heavily on her. Her passive invasion of Jesse's privacy was nonetheless invasion, and there was no doubt Jesse would see it that way, too. Jesse, who thought reading a partner's diary or looking through a partner's phone was sociopathic. But all was fair in love and war. A girl had to be a detective in matters of the heart.

No—she would sit on the data, delighting in the information, and then later use it to her subtle advantage. This was the only way that she could get ahead of it; this was the only way she could make it make sense. She would determine when the *punctum* would occur—the moment of piercing focus that would sharpen the next ten days into one distinct memory. *Sasha* would detonate the bomb. She would do this by collecting and strategically deploying intelligence.

She allowed herself another moment of gleeful withholding. Of course Faye had lapped up the dirt on Sasha. Early on in their relationship, a year prior, Jesse had pulled up Faye's headshot online to show Sasha Faye's big green eyes and shaggy red hair. Her lips were pushed together, suggesting that while she was smart and opinionated, someone who would take a stand when push came to shove, she was also informed by a practice of nonjudgment. Sasha had felt, for a second, jealous. She'd felt preemptively cheated on, though at the time she and Jesse were not yet monogamous.

"She's pretty," Sasha had said in response to the picture. And then: "I think she'll be perfect for your transference."

Jesse had laughed and assured Sasha that in real life, Faye's roots were growing in mousy brown.

Watch out for Sasha's High-Femme Camp Antics, Faye had warned Jesse the previous winter, when Jesse told Faye about Sasha's trick of never wearing her glasses in public so that she would always be squinting sexily and needing assistance to find her way around. Or her habit of responding, whenever someone asked her where she'd bought something, with "Thanks, I got it in Europe."

"What did she mean by that?" Sasha had asked.

"She said that what we're most attracted to is also what might hurt us most," Jesse had said, smiling with half her mouth.

"So you should be careful," Sasha said.

In the static white noise of the car, insulated from the frozen blur outside, Sasha reached out and touched the back of Jesse's head, where his hairline met his neck.

"That feels nice," Jesse said.

The opening flourishes of Van Morrison's "Brown Eyed Girl" came from the speakers.

Jesse was focused on the road ahead of them, so Sasha turned her phone away from Jesse. She was supposed to be taking a social media break, and she'd been good about staying offline in the past couple of weeks, but the rush of serotonin that came from opening the app made her quake. First she checked up on her favorite wedding planner. Not much was new—few people got married over the holidays, but there was one wedding around Thanksgiving between a bottle blonde and a software engineer. Sasha watched their wedding video on low volume so Jesse wouldn't suspect. There was so much to learn from straight culture.

She navigated to Darcy Jankovic's profile, her number-one recently searched profile. Darcy—Lou's new girlfriend, of artsy-elite, Slavic-vibes internet fame—was currently working at a Lower East Side atelier called waïfhewn that sold waif-hewn pants and beaded purses for a couple hundred dollars apiece. Her most recent pictures were of the monochromatic Stella line, slim red pants with plastic cutouts on the butt cheeks.

Darcy's handle was @reality___cheque. She had just over ten thousand followers and a blue check next to her name to signal that the account was really hers and not an imposter's. Darcy's trendy clothes, thick, glossy hair, and Slavic features produced a gestalt effect of beauty. This enraged Sasha, who believed herself to be more beautiful than Darcy, if you took each feature separately and rated them against each other. Sasha looked like Emily Ratajkowski, if EmRata were a size 10. Yet the sum total of Sasha had the effect of being less hot than the sum total of Darcy. And you had to consider people holistically, because that was how the world perceived them. This was what she found most repulsive about Darcy—how Darcy made her, Sasha, feel misunderstood. Darcy's look tainted hers by virtue of Darcy's very existence, and so Darcy was her natural enemy.

Just before the pants, the last few pictures on Darcy's Instagram were:

1. From December 2: Darcy sitting on a plush white bed (unmade), wearing a baseball cap with the word *DADDY* printed across it and a sheer nightgown, her perfectly round tits poking through the fabric. Sasha zoomed in on the image and made out two fleshy mounds topped with nipples that looked, to her eye, like Hershey's Kisses—they struck Sasha as avoidantly, rather than securely, attached to Darcy's breasts. The attachment style of Sasha's own areolae was decidedly secure.

In the picture, Darcy is taking a mirror selfie, and she's pursing her lips in a way that's supposed to look self-awarely seductive, like she's making fun of herself for trying to look "sexy" but also insisting that she *does* look sexy, though you can't accuse her of trying because she's already made it clear she isn't, or is, or whatever. The photo is edited so that she has two sets of eyes, one set of eyes photoshopped under her real ones. Darcy and Sasha were both five feet and seven and a half inches tall, but Darcy was the type of five-foot-seven-and-a-half who would round up, referring to herself as an angular five-eight, while Sasha was the type of five-foot-seven-and-a-half who would swear under oath that she was five-seven.

2. From November 12: Darcy sitting on a pink tuffet, cross-stitching the missive *slut !!* onto a pillow. She's mid-stitch, concentrating on her work, making sure to tilt the pillow just enough for the camera to capture her progress. She's wearing an ostentatious prairie dress. Her thick, furry ankles are stuffed like dirty sausages into athletic socks and big white sneakers. Her glossy black hair is piled on top of her head in a big nest, tangled but somehow also clean-looking. Her arms are slender, taut. Full, pink lips stretch from one side of her face to the other, a plump Cupid's bow at the center. Her lips are her best feature, and lips are more visible than ankles.

3. From October 3: Darcy reclining on an examining table, white paper crinkling around her, long legs splayed open, a peach emoji shrouding her crotch, wispy, pubic leg-beard giving the peach a fuzzy halo. Her hair—again tangled, dirty-clean—is splayed out against the fake-pillow portion of the examining table. She looks freshly fucked by a dyke gynecologist's speculum. The location tag: Callen-Lorde's Brooklyn location. The caption: *Pussy Doctor Nancy says I have the lowest iron levels she's ever seen but she also told me she studied with Foucault in Paris in the '70s so she's my new #shero ???*

Of course the note was about having low iron—hot girls were anemic now. At the bottom of each picture, where it was announced who had liked the photo, was Jesse's handle, an artifact from zealous days at lesbian college. But Jesse's name was accompanied by hundreds of others; there was nothing original about Jesse's admiration of Darcy's image or the accompanying caption. Jesse was simply following along with what was expected of him—to fall in line with the rest of

the recognizable handles by double-tapping the picture of
Darcy. Jesse's like alone would never be enough to sanction
the photo, just as the absence of Jesse's like would never be
enough to make the picture flop. It was the cumulative effect of
the likes, the buildup, that mattered. Jesse's like was a small but
mighty link in the great chain of endorsement.

Jesse was chattering on about different types of dykes as different types of dairy or non-dairy milks.

"Okay, so I'm all Midwestern milk-fed with my half-and-
half, and Miranda and Jules are barista-blended," Jesse said as
they drove past frozen fields.

Sasha dragged a long black nail along the icy window, drawing a circle and another overlapping circle. A Venn diagram.
That used to be a thing they did—identifying objects, outfits,
and songs that were "center of Venn," rare things that they both
wanted to incorporate.

"That moment when they were whispering was *so* oat," Jesse
went on. "What do you think they were talking about?"

"Not sure," Sasha said.

"What type do you think Lou and Darcy would be?" Jesse
asked.

"I am so sick of dykes-as-milk memes," Sasha said.

"Are they coconut creamer?" Jesse mused. "Definitely they'd
be something *luxe*."

Jesse's pathetic valorization of Lou and Darcy annoyed her,
just as Sasha's reverence for Jules and Miranda annoyed Jesse.

"Part of me feels like they'd be non-dairy," Jesse suggested,
"but I can also see them being just a few drops of the most
sumptuous, fattening cream. Like, just a few drops."

Sasha put a finger to her lips, and Jesse went quiet.

There was a brick building just before the train tracks.

Jesse slowed the Prius to a crawl as she rolled down Sasha's window, sending a gust of freezing air into the car. Sasha immediately jabbed the window button to roll it back up.

Tucked in the doorway of the brick building was a silhouette holding a shiny black duffel bag, its polyester sheen glinting in the setting sun. A woman—Sasha immediately identified her stature and posture as Darcy. Her arm began to wave at them apprehensively, as though not yet sure that they were her ride. Jesse cranked down Sasha's window again and called out, "Hey! Darcy! Lou!" and finally Darcy came into full view. Sasha pushed the window up again. Jesse didn't notice.

Darcy had the proportions and the gait of a charmingly clumsy Borzoi. She was almost pigeon-toed but not quite. Instead she walked with her knees banging together, expensive patchwork jeans swinging neatly around her long, skinny legs, a short buttery puffer closed tight at her neck. The shoes were caramel-colored leather Margiela tabis, the split toe evoking bare labia. A trendy designer bag swung around her arm.

You're just trying to be on-trend, Sasha had accused Jesse more than once. Jesse also coveted trendy bags by the new "it" designers, those Adidas-collab track pants everyone was wearing, and bought Crocs just as soon as they made a comeback— but it was people like Darcy who created these trends. Sasha didn't know where Darcy's money came from, but she knew intuitively that Darcy was rich. It was probably family money, because Darcy wrote bad poetry and peddled ugly stitched creations. She didn't have a real job, even, besides helping out at the atelier. Jesse used to judge these layabout types, until he started to idolize them.

A caramel-colored Louis Vuitton (fake-chic) headscarf cradled Darcy's hair as she came into full view, knotted neatly under her chin, and she was smiling a big, warm grin, lips plush against her shiny white teeth. She rapped merrily on Sasha's window, startling Sasha, and then let out a laugh that sounded bright through the glass. Finally Darcy went around the car to get into the back seat.

Sasha sank down in her seat as Lou emerged from the shadows. Lou was one of Jesse's close friends. Someone whose gentleness and affability she didn't know if she could really trust. Lou had a real job. They were a small-business owner, ran a design-oriented home goods shop in Bushwick. But Sasha was unsure if Lou's niceness was a facade. Fuckboy behavior often lurked beneath a deceptively chill surface; it was how fuckboys got away with being fuckboys. By being the nice guy, the easygoing guy, they wielded their power, which could also be thought of as their unflappability, instigating more and more mania in those they fucked and fucked over. That was why Sasha feared breezy people like Lou. The calmer and nicer they were, the more loud and hysterical she became in protest. She felt huge around Lou.

Lou wore Carhartt pants and a thin deer-print puffer over a thick hoodie pulled down around their ears and forehead to shield them from the fierce cold. The puffer was Burberry—there was a rubber logo saying as much attached to the left breast. Lou was Black and tall and lean, a few inches taller than Darcy. The puffer was hot of them, one of those rare designer items that Sasha had never seen before. Lou grasped Sasha's hand through the half-open passenger-seat window, which Jesse had once again cranked down, and they squeezed out a hello between them. Sneakers that had once been the domain of dorky elementary-school boys, ugly ones, but ones that Jesse would believe were cool because now they'd made a comeback, adorned their feet; Sasha had seen Jesse searching for similar styles late at night, comparing prices on Farfetch and Grailed.

Lou liked Sasha—they'd always been kind to her, taking an avuncular interest in her studies and noticing when she'd cut her hair or done her nails. Lou respected Sasha's femininity by playing up a chivalrous butch persona—someone who'd help her climb over a felled tree in the park or offer to help her carry a package down the stairs to their apartment, admire her Barbie manicure and gush over a new piece of jewelry, their style and keen artist's eye understanding immediately what was special about this or that object.

Jesse and Lou were a dyke duo that they joked was akin to *Gossip Girl*'s pretty-boy Nate (Lou) and stocky, eternally horny Chuck (Jesse). They'd often go to the Frick or the Met on weekends and share a steak at an Upper East Side restaurant at eleven in the morning, calling their escapades "lost weekends" and taking pictures of close-up sections of spice-rubbed meat, inevitably decorated with edible flowers Jesse stole from Central Park.

Sasha watched from the passenger seat as Lou and Jesse hugged before loading the bags into the trunk.

"Hey, cutie," Darcy sang to Sasha from the back seat.

Sasha twisted around to look at her. They'd met two or three times over the course of the past year, and each time Sasha doubted that Darcy remembered her from the previous meeting. She was a floater in Darcy's vision, attached to her tenuously through Lou, her guy du jour, and through Jesse, the friend whose status was cemented by Lou's admiration and who Darcy was eager to impress just enough to win Lou's approval but potentially no further.

"Hey," Sasha said.

Darcy's face gleamed rosily from the cold, her headscarf slipping to the side and the knot drifting toward her right ear.

The seat belt clicked closed and in a flash of apparent annoyance Darcy yanked the whole headscarf apparatus off her head.

Lou got in the back seat beside Darcy, and then all the car's
orifices were sealed; the four of them stewing in the hot air
thrumming through the Prius's vents. When Sasha looked
back again, as Jesse peeled out of the train station and headed
in the direction of the house, Darcy was speed-texting, her
nails clacking against the screem. Lou was gazing out the window, hands shoved in the pockets of their puffer.

Jesse turned on the radio, and Fleetwood Mac's "The Chain"
crackled forebodingly out from the speakers.

Listen to the wind blow, watch the sun rise
Run in the shadows, damn your love, damn your lies

When they pulled into the driveway, the sun was hanging
low in the sky, casting a plumy pinkish-gray haze onto the house.
Darcy began snapping pictures of the sunset.

The chorus picked up, and Lou sang along with Stevie
Nicks: *And if you don't love me now, you will never love me again.*

෬ ෨

After grocery shopping with Miranda, Jules had changed into
black Champion sweatpants, the logo against her upper left
thigh, which was a sexy look for her, and an oversized plain
white long-sleeved T-shirt that was uncomfortably erotic for
Sasha to behold. It was the sort of getup Sasha liked Jesse to
wear, simple and masculine, and she felt an unsettling, yet
unsurprising, twinge of attraction to Jules. What Sasha liked
so much about Jules was her large size and her straightforward

butchness; those two things combined made her feel safe with Jules, secure in her girlhood. In recent years, it hadn't made sense for Sasha to describe her attraction in any way besides "into butches," or even—if she was feeling cheeky and provocative— "straight for butches." Sasha simply wanted to press her body against Jules's and to feel Jules's body push back.

As Jesse unloaded groceries, Sasha found herself wanting to harbor the heat from Jules's crotch against her abdomen, like she had when they'd hugged goodbye, both drunk, after meeting at the Derby party. Sasha routinely dreamed about Jules touching her. She was more bothered by the attraction she felt to Jules in real life than she was by the sex dreams. The touch in her dreams was always light and not strictly sexual, as though Jules had enormous strength that she was holding back because she didn't trust herself not to attack Sasha like a wild animal.

"That cardinal we saw at the train station made me think of this," Jesse said, taking a break from the groceries to pull something up on her phone. Sasha hadn't seen a cardinal; she didn't notice things like birds singing or the moon changing shape in the sky.

The image was one Jesse and Sasha had seen at a craft fair months ago and joked was a portrait of them: a naked woman behind a huge red butch bird. In the painting, the woman is trying to spoon the bird, her legs wrapped around the bird's tail as though she's rubbing her kittycat against it. Half of her face is visible, one arm, one leg, a slice of her hourglass waist and hips. Sasha smiled despite herself, remembering the way they'd stood in front of the image together, giddy with recognition.

Sasha had told Jesse that she'd be so annoying as a big butch bird. "You'd be taking forever to build our nest, and I would say, *Jessebird, does every stick need to be* exactly *the same size?*"

"Yes, Sashabird, it does," Jesse answered. "And you'd be that naked woman trying to spoon the big red butch bird, always trying to get your arms to fit around his wings."

Now Sasha leaned into Jesse and let herself be hugged, both of them pressed up against Jules's granite countertop. Jesse understood her. Jesse understood that she was the woman in the image, a pretty girl whose bad attitude could be mitigated only by attention. On the phone with Faye, Jesse had dabbled in hyperbole, yes, but only because she'd been frustrated. Sasha was a special girl, but also a difficult one; it was good for their longevity that Jesse had Faye—to vent, to express himself. Sasha remembered the testiness between Jules and Miranda as they'd been getting ready to leave for the train station—the moment Miranda had spat, *I just—I just.*

She had long thought of Jesse, who'd existed on the outskirts of her social nexus since moving back to New York after college, as a subterranean bachelor, a set decorator and part-time jewelry designer. She lived in a Bed-Stuy basement apartment that took up the back room of the dyke barber Cate Campos's salon with an obese tuxedo cat named Batwoman. She was broad-shouldered and had short, thick hair and a stick-and-poke tattoo that spelled out *DYKEBALL* over her left rib cage. She would cock her head to the side in disbelief or in attraction, it was hard to tell; she was calm, always, hard to rile up or startle, which fed Sasha's sense that she could ask for anything and Jesse's reaction would be casual, as though Sasha were just asking to borrow some toothpaste. Jesse reminded her of Jordy Rosenberg's narrator in *Confessions of the Fox*, the guy who describes himself as having this "shameless, gross vibe" that makes women uninhibited to ask for anything they want to do or get done to them. Jesse had this too. Nothing was hotter to Sasha than shamelessness and perversion. A guy who couldn't control himself was great, but a guy who would good-naturedly go along with whatever gross thing you wanted—that was the highest of the high.

Sasha wondered, while Jules and Miranda gingerly lifted bunches of kale and heads of garlic out of the paper bags and tucked them into the vegetable drawers, about Jules's steadfast love for Miranda. It was a love that existed more fully in her imagination than it did anywhere else, a love that fascinated her, turned her on, and bothered her, made her jealous, angry, crazy, rapturous.

Sasha was learning that Miranda carried an air of quiet judgment, was always closer at hand and more firmly within earshot than you expected, and had a mischievousness about her that made you feel like you shared some funny secret. Miranda Saraf was two years Jules's junior at thirty-eight, a psychotherapist who specialized in anxiety, eating disorders, and trauma. Miranda presented as caring and responsible, a general baseline of goodwill, but at the same time always a little bit distant, wearing no makeup and a slight smile.

Today she'd dressed in loose oatmeal linen pants and a black cashmere sweater. She was a classic low-femme small/medium. The sort of petite Sasha envied, a few inches shorter than she was—Miranda was probably five-four or five-five—and with narrow shoulders that always had something draped around them—a blanket, a scarf, Jules's arm—to keep her warm. Her parents had come from Iran as teenagers in the 1970s. Her family was Jewish, Sasha knew from the podcast Miranda hosted with another queer Brooklyn analyst. The show was called *Two Bad Therapists*, and the two of them—Miranda and her friend/cohost—often talked about the gaffes they made with patients (names changed and identifying features concealed) in an effort to humanize and demystify the therapeutic process.

Less therapist-as-oracle, went the tagline, and more therapist-as-human.

The podcast was philosophical and intellectually rigorous and for it Miranda assumed an academic accent. She discussed the intersections between psychotherapy and things like prison abolition and anti-capitalism. She was interested in expanding understanding of intergenerational Jewish trauma beyond the Ashkenazi experience. Her smallness and her seriousness were intimidating to Sasha, who was neither small nor serious. If Sasha was to be trapped in a room with one other person on the trip, Miranda would be with whom it would be hardest for her to make conversation. They occupied two totally different planes of existence, Miranda grounded and sense-y, whereas Sasha was frenetic and dissociated, believing that emotional presence actually ruined most things.

The open floor plan allowed Sasha to surveil the other two couples at once as everyone milled about the downstairs: Jules and Miranda were establishing themselves as the conventionally and aspirationally successful power couple (Jules's aggressively welcoming posture, Miranda's stilted hostess position), while Darcy and Lou effortlessly revealed themselves to be members of Brooklyn's late-twenties/early-thirties artistic elite whose hotness and coolness had to be carefully modulated so as not to overwhelm the room (Lou's jovial yet undeniably cool hedging, Darcy's self-assured way of dropping her objects onto every available surface while apologizing for having brought so much stuff).

Lou traveled like an itinerant gym teacher, complete with a mesh sports bag filled with a tangle of purple and yellow pinnies, a couple pairs of soccer cleats, and a gym-class parachute.

"This is sexy," Jesse affirmed, beginning to unfold the tightly bundled parachute.

"Hey, hey!" Jules cried when Lou tossed a soccer ball onto the floor. She bounced at the ready like a Wii avatar, then geared up for a cartoonish kick, withdrawing a big foot as far as it would go. Sasha instinctively braced for impact, but naturally Jules lightened up at the last minute, punting the ball just a few inches across the wood floor. Vivienne shot like a rocket out of the way.

"Nice footwork," Lou said charitably.

"How's the biz?" Jules asked Lou while emptying a bag of corn chips into a bowl.

Lou's sexy artisanal home goods store had been featured in *The Cut* and *Vogue* and mentioned twice in the *New Yorker*'s Daily Shouts.

"Pretty good," Lou said modestly. "We can't keep up with the demand for cutting boards this season."

Lou designed multicolored speckled resin cutting boards that had become, in the past year, a requirement of every trendy Brooklyn apartment.

But everybody was featured in *Vogue* these days! It wasn't like it was 2000. A frenzied spirit seized Sasha. How could people go on using the same standards of success from twenty years prior as though nothing had changed? And, crucially, how could she herself ever reach these outdated standards? Sasha's heart began to race faster thinking about the actual irrelevance, yet enduring status, of *Vogue*. She gulped down some seltzer from a random open can on the table.

"Oh, I wanted to show you guys," Jules said, moving toward the glass door that led to the backyard and swiping its sheer curtain to one side. "Across that little creek it's way flatter, perfect for practicing. Maybe we could even organize a little three-on-three at some point."

Jesse and Lou were co-captains of the new lesbian soccer team in Brooklyn that Jules Todd had attended once or twice that summer, appearing sporadically as though in a movie cameo, scoring a few goals and completing a few virtue-signaling assists before ducking out. Jules had taken a liking to Jesse and Lou, two enterprising young dykes in whom Jules no doubt glimpsed a younger version of herself, over post-practice drinks in October.

"I haven't had that much fun in forever," Jules reminisced about her afternoon playing soccer. "It got me thinking— seriously—about how you two can capitalize on this."

"It's not really about the money for us," Jesse said.

Jules gazed down at Jesse with slight contempt.

"That's fine, then. We don't need to talk about it." Jules pulled the curtain closed.

"We just mean that we don't expect to make any money for a while," Lou mediated. "Or ever."

"There will come a time in your life when money means more to you than it does now," Jules predicted and though they both nodded solemnly, Sasha felt Lou and Jesse holding back laughter.

Sasha began taking out the ingredients to make pizza dough. She'd promised pizza for dinner, and it would take an hour for the dough to rise. She worked quietly, measuring flour and yeast and warm water. Within a few minutes, everyone had dispersed. Lou and Darcy were in one living room, curled up together on the sectional sofa in front of a muted TV show or the news, Sasha wasn't sure which, and Jesse was on her phone in the other living room, deep in a text conversation with a work prospect. Jules and Miranda were still puttering over the groceries in the kitchen near Sasha, organizing bags of chips and spices.

For a few minutes the three of them didn't speak. Jules and Miranda were pretending not to notice Sasha, or they were all pretending that they were so comfortable around each other that they didn't need to acknowledge one another's presence. It was hard to tell.

"Need any help?" Jules said, seeing Sasha struggle to get the dough to coalesce.

"Can you make me a drink? Please?" Sasha begged.

"*Cock*-tails!" Jules enunciated. "I'll get to work."

As Jules deliberated over her bottles of fancy liquor, Miranda poured herself a glass of seltzer and settled on the couch by Jesse with a book—a tame trauma memoir from a few years back that Sasha hadn't been able to get through—leaving Sasha and Jules in the kitchen, silently at work on their respective projects.

Sasha's dough was finally coming together. She tossed some flour on the kitchen island and kneaded with all her might, stretching it with her palms then crumpling it, twisting it over to start the process again. The dough, warm and soft and sticky, reminded her of a morning breast. She spread more flour over the mound, and then more, trying to focus on channeling ancestral instinct into her hands. This motion was soothing, the pressing and smashing and regathering; though she noticed her heart was still racing so fast that she could barely catch her breath, making her light-headed.

"Fuck" came Jules's groan, followed by a trembling thud upon the counter.

The ice in the freezer had solidified into one enormous glacier, dulled and scissored with scratch marks from the food

traffic above it. Jules peered morosely down at it. In order to
crush it into pieces, Jules mused aloud, she'd need to put it in a
canvas bag and smash it with something really heavy.

"Do you have a canvas bag?" Sasha asked, still kneading.

"No. Fuck."

Jules wiped her phone screen on her sweatpants and googled
furiously for subsitutions for canvas.

"What about a linen pillowcase?" suggested Sasha.

Jules looked up at her blankly, as though unhearing, but
then said, "That's perfect. I'll go grab one."

Jules shot upstairs and returned with a beige pillowcase, and
Sasha watched with satisfaction as Jules brought down a massive vegetarian cookbook again and again on the glacier like a
bludgeon until the block splintered into hundreds of small ice
sculptures, crowding Sasha's workspace.

"What's that noise?" Lou called from the living room.

"Jules is speeding up global warming," Sasha joked, and they
all laughed merrily at Jules's antics. A cozy sense of goodwill
suffused the house, the sun fully descended and the fire crackling. The lack of natural light awakened in them a survivalist
camaraderie, drawing them closer in spirit.

As afternoon became night, the group settled into a quiet
rhythm. Jules used the splintered ice to make cocktails—blood-
orange negronis—and Jesse volunteered as waiter, presenting a
glass to Miranda in her reading nook, two glasses to Darcy
and Lou, cuddled up on the other couch and half watching a
dumb Christmas movie, and a final glass to Sasha, distracted
by periodically checking the rising dough and slicing onions
and olives for toppings.

"This is a sort of twist on a classic negroni," Jules explained
to the group with a pedantic smile. "Instead of orange, I used
pomelo."

Sasha took a sip of the drink, which for all the hype around Jules's mixology tasted like a basic cocktail.

"Thanks, Jules," Darcy called over from her position on the couch, nestled in Lou's armpit, and Jules beamed.

Sasha beckoned to Jesse, but it was Jules's eye that she caught. Jules started to walk toward her, surprised yet pleased at being summoned, but Sasha waved her away, using her words this time: "No, I meant Jesse."

Jules nodded dramatically, of a scorned waiter. "Ah, yes, madame wants the *other* boy."

She appreciated Jules's butch-on-butch use of "he" for Jesse, though Jules herself was a standard Gen X she/her, like Abby Wambach or Lea DeLaria. Sasha was reminded of the way Maggie Nelson wrote about her partner Harry Dodge's butch-buddy film, *By Hook or by Crook*. In the film, Harry and Silas Howard call each other "he" and "him," but the outside world—cashiers, bank tellers—calls them "she" and "her." The goal of this, Nelson wrote, "wasn't that if the outer world were schooled appropriately re: the characters' preferred pronouns, everything would be right as rain. Because if the outsiders called the characters 'he,' it would be a different kind of he."

What did Sasha need to say to Jesse? Nothing, she just wanted him close by, to do small favors for her, to handle the hot bowl that held the rising dough and touch her neck.

She'd certainly tortured Jesse enough at the beginning of the relationship: asking Jesse questions like *Would you have left your ex for me?* at three or four in the morning; exaggerating the side effects of her antipsychotic so that she was constantly flushed, stumbling, dizzy, blind, in need of Jesse's steadying hands on the sidewalk; calling Jesse her boyfriend and using "he" pronouns to discuss him with her friends; being cruel about other women's looks if she was jealous of or threatened by them, calling them potato-faced, log-like, animatronic; seeing Jesse's recent ex, Ruth, at a Friday-night screening of *Booksmart* in Cobble Hill and dissolving into giddy hysterics with her friends; taking a series of covert pictures of Ruth and *her* friends in the row behind Sasha and her friends; firing off a picture to Jesse—Ruth's face foregrounded by a pretty sliver of Sasha's own—as she'd walked back from the subway late that night, taking care to send the crop that most distended Ruth's features. The picture had been out of bounds, Jesse insisted.

"Can I Cum Inside?" Sylvie had laughed when Sasha told her about the sex game she made Jesse play in those early days. "Cum like *C-U-M*?"

During this telling, Sasha and Sylvie were at their favorite nail place in Brighton Beach. Sasha's manicurist, Ivy, was trimming and moisturizing her cuticles. Sasha was getting her classic Barbie French acrylic manicure: light pink base with a hot-pink, shiny tip instead of the traditional white-tipped, tan-based French. Sylvie had started getting Barbie French manicures, too. Lots of hot girls had. Sylvie's nail technician, Evelyn, was polishing Sylvie's left pointer finger with the light pink base coat (she had strong nails, which she chalked up to being on estrogen, and always preferred natural to acrylics).

"Jesse's sports-gay thing—related to your father being a coach?" Sylvie had theorized, her right hand still soaking in a bath of toxic fluids. "Daddy teaching you how to 'make a pass.' Coach's daughter is, like, forbidden fruit ripened under the light of the heteropatriarchy. You are the goalie of your own pussy. And she's looking to score. Can I Come Inside is nothing but a bad game of soccer."

Sasha's father taught tennis, a sport in which the net was to be avoided, so she wasn't convinced by Sylvie's mixed metaphor, but she smiled politely at her friend's analysis. A former highly ranked player, her father worked now as a pro at a country club on Long Island in her parents' suburb, teaching little boys and girls how to smack their raquets against those horrible yellow balls. Sasha's older sister Natalya had been good at tennis as a child, but Sasha remained comically bad—at first sincerely, and later spitefully—and rarely made contact with the ball.

Sasha had watched Ivy hunt through the box of fake nails to find Sasha's size, Sasha's fingers soaking in a warm, fragrant bath of chemicals. Her fingers were tiny, requiring the narrowest talons. Ivy set aside two nails for each finger.

❧ ❧

Everyone, including the pug, took a smoke break before dinner, but Sasha stayed inside to keep an eye on the pizzas in the oven. Lou's back was to Sasha, flanked by Darcy and Jesse, each of whom Sasha could see in profile. It had since been explained that the deer-print jacket they wore was from a creative partnership between their store and Burberry for the brand's FW2019 collection. They'd acquired the jacket in anticipation of 2020, which on social media they'd termed the Year of the Deer (and which had attracted a sizable following, with people—mostly Lou's friends and admirers, those who wanted to be like Lou—buying deer-print comforters, scarves, and the like). It was cool to be a quasi-furry now. Deer print was the weirdest animal print but also the perviest; for Halloween Lou had painted their tan hound dog (left behind this week in Brooklyn with a sitter who needed holiday housing in the city) with white flecks to look like a fawn.

From Sasha's vantage point, only the funny line of fake fur cascading down the back of the jacket was visible, beginning at the base of their shaved head and ending just above their Carhartts. The sky was gray, the ground speckled with patches of brownish green between mounds of dirty snow, and the narrow river crisscrossed the property in winding, lovely black syrup. Vivienne was frolicking in a patch of weeds, dashing from plant to plant.

Jules and Miranda were seated in the two metal chairs opposite one another, and so she could see them both in profile—Jules's big glasses magnifying her left eye, the wind sweeping through her short salt-and-pepper hair; Miranda's slim frame huddled in a big plaid puffer, her dark hair secured in a low bun and her eyes, ever conscientious, darting toward Vivienne from time to time to make sure she was safe.

They looked, from a distance, like five best friends. They were passing the joint among themselves, smoke escaping from their mouths as they puffed and talked, talked and puffed, in an endless rhythm. The glass door was almost completely soundproof (the wind took care of the rest), so Sasha couldn't hear anything they were saying, though Jules and Jesse would occasionally erupt into audible laughter, the noise so quiet and muted that Sasha urged to turn up the volume on the porch scene as if on a remote control.

Watching the five of them from her perch in the kitchen, the one-way mirror into this fivesome, Sasha was able to scrutinize Darcy in peace.

Jesse and Darcy had met on Halloween, at the launch of Darcy's book of poetry. The party was filled with the initiates of a particular inner circle in which everyone either was gay or looked gay and administered drugs from canisters. The party was in Williamsburg, at a club called Aphrodite's. Shiny stilts hoisted up glimmering legs in fishnet stockings. A semi-famous radical cellist carried a cloud of pink cotton candy. Zebra-print wallpaper gleamed under the strobe lighting, music pulsed out of the speakers in bilious waves. Darcy showed up late and then milled around the party like a goddex, her face aglow against the screen of her iPhone.

To the party, Jesse had worn his dark hair slicked back and satin gentleman's pants. He stood off to the side to text Sasha, who was stuck in a late-night Shakespeare seminar in Rhode Island, about the party. The texts came back to her now, as though scrolling across Jules's teleprompter.

A hot writer, for once
I love her
She looks extremely sexy
Kind of like you—
Bombshell

Miranda took a single puff of the joint and then waved it away each time it subsequently came back to her in the rota-tion. She looked freezing—it was twenty degrees out—despite the thick, luxurious hand-knit scarf circling her head; she burrowed into the scarf so that eventually all Sasha could see were her eyes, the tops of her ears, and a patch of shiny black hair. In the distance was the house's crowning glory, its sell-ing point: the sauna, a long wooden barrel in the far corner of the backyard that was, as the story went, just big enough for six people—provided that those six people were comfortable enough with each other to press sweaty thigh to sweaty thigh, damp forearm to damp forearm.

To keep warm on the porch, Darcy was now jumping around, dancing and laughing. She was shaking her plump butt without an ounce of self-consciousness. Flailing her arms, shimmying. Jesse was watching Darcy dance, and her face was luminous with something that Sasha could only identify as *pride*. Sasha knew enough to recognize that the thing about inner circles was that they didn't really exist unless you were on a college campus or in a small city. In truth, the rings weren't concentric at all, but overlapping, with a thousand centers. And whenever you found yourself creeping closer to a center, you'd realize that there was an even smaller band within it, a tighter knot less penetrable than the surrounding one.

Finally, the five of them came inside, windswept and red-cheeked, shaking off their layers.

"Dinner in ten," Sasha announced like a hag, slinking back into the kitchen with self-loathing.

Jules and Miranda excused themselves to go change for dinner. Sasha turned her attention toward Lou as they and Darcy made their way into the living room and retook their spots on the couch, nestled in each other's crevices. Jesse was among them, too, but separate from the fusion of Darcy and Lou, which had hitherto been separated just once, during the car ride. They radiated a halo of honeymoon-colored light, flush with new love.

Lou was being how Lou always was. Easy to talk to, with a booming laugh and a winking smile. Tomboyish—and something of a Gay Mayor type, too. Funny, quick-witted in that way you only encountered in queers who were so cool that they didn't even need to act mean or tough anymore. It was like these queers had ascended to andro-Nirvana, where everyone could finally just chill out and be nice to each other.

Lou and Darcy's list of mutuals was endless. They were still in that stage of a new relationship where mutual connections were delightful to discover, though in truth their relationship had been preordained by their twin social royalty. It was not surprising that they knew the same people; these people were the reason that Darcy and Lou were now dating. Sasha kept an ear trained on Darcy and Lou's conversation as she got to work setting the table. Jules and Miranda descended, slightly spruced up for dinner and aglow with the second round of cocktails, joining the others in the living room.

It was embarrassing to admit, Lou was telling the group, self-assured and self-effacing at the same time, but they were a starfucker. Everyone laughed good-naturedly. Lou was being funny while also flattering Darcy. Darcy was *ahh*ing and *nooo*ing as Lou smiled around their theory about their own starfuckery, Jesse chiming in, saying, "No, actually, you *do* do that," and Jules and Miranda chuckling with the tiniest bit of discomfort, probably because they weren't a hundred percent sure what *starfucker* meant.

Sasha in fact knew from Jesse that Lou dated troubled, successful women; they were good at tending to anxiety and ego and creative genius. They had, for a long time, dated a well-known producer named Emily, who had an anxiety disorder that prevented her from leaving her apartment except to go to the dry cleaner's.

"I make things," Lou was telling Miranda, who'd asked something along the lines of, *Remind me what you do? Like, your day job*. "And I just opened a storefront in Bushwick. It's luxury artisanal items. Home goods and gifts, mostly."

"They sell ceramic mugs that look like Greek deli cups," Darcy said, shaking out her hair and fluffing it around her shoulders.

Lou laughed. "Sure, but also big epoxy clocks with signals instead of numbers, and foam lamps, and little ceramic trucks." Lou paused. "I'm the one who makes the trucks, I should clarify—I have a bit of a thing for trucks."

Darcy affected an impressed expression. She hadn't known this; it was a hot, getting-to-know-you moment, an opportunity for Lou to impress her and for Darcy to gasp and coo. This prompted Lou to show her pictures of their tiny totemic trucks, iridescent red and green-and-pink camouflage, all based on trucks they'd seen parked around Brooklyn.

"I put them on Craigslist as a joke, under 'cars,'" Lou said, this time with a hint of embarrassment (the detail was dorky?). "People ask if the radios work, about the safety features, everything. And what's funny is that everyone thinks they're the first ones to make the joke, asking about the dimensions of a ceramic truck. But everyone seems so genuinely happy with themselves that I always end up trying to make them feel funny, treat them like they're special."

"That's heartening, that people haven't become so jaded and humorless," Darcy sighed.

"On Craigslist, at least," Jesse put in.

Darcy turned back to Lou, earnest and direct, matter-of-fact, in their face: "So you're an object perv."

"I'm into ambiguous objects," Lou said, waving their hands in jagged juts to evoke ambiguity. "Objects that either have two purposes or an unclear purpose, or objects that conjure unclear and conflicting emotions—object that mean two things. I dunno—it's kind of hard to explain."

"No, I get it," Jules said, nodding.

"So, like, a toilet brush that's shaped like a cherry? The ones that are always being advertised to me on Instagram?" Miranda offered, laughing a little.

"Exactly!" Lou's tenor and expression, so genuinely delighted, lifted Sasha's mood. "That's exactly it, yeah."

The banter was hypnotic to Sasha, like listening to a play or a podcast about how to flirt. She drifted over to the couch. She couldn't stay away; she was like a moth to a flame.

"So how do you know each other?" Miranda drew a line in the air with her finger connecting Darcy and Sasha. "Because of writing stuff?"

"Us?" Sasha asked.

Darcy shrugged. "I've known Sasha awhile."

Awhile was a generous characterization, Sasha thought, but she didn't contradict Darcy.

"And you?" Another finger-line, this one between Darcy and Lou. It was uncool to ask explicitly how people knew each other (if it wasn't obvious to you, that meant you weren't really integral to this world), but Miranda was forgiven for it because she was earnest and slightly older.

"We've actually known each other for seven years," Darcy laughed.

"I was at NYU while she was at Bard," Lou cut in.

"And then our paths kind of kept crossing?"

"Art stuff," Lou elaborated.

Darcy again turned the conversation back to herself and her own "type," as if she was reciting a charming monologue: *I don't usually date babies. Babies have intimacy issues. I like to date people who are already in love with me.*

Sasha excused herself to check on the pizza. The cheese was bubbling and had acquired a crispy brown film in certain places, glistening where she'd drizzled the surface with olive oil. Smears of burrata had melted into creamy circles nestled within pockets of tomato sauce. It was almost ready.

In the background, Lou was describing an essay they were working on for an anthology one of their friends was editing for Nightboat about "the pathetic genre."

"The pathetic is always kind of sexy," Lou said. "That push and pull."

Sasha waited until the last possible minute to beckon them into the kitchen for dinner. They took their places around the big oak dining table and marveled at the pizzas, three steaming orbs set between the Gothic candlesticks that Jesse had found in a closet and lit. Vivienne settled herself on a fur pelt at the far end of the table. Everybody cooed. Jules took a seat at the head of the table, and Miranda sank into the seat to Jules's right. Darcy came next; Lou sat at the other head of the table. Sasha sat next to Lou, and Jesse arranged himself between Sasha (on her good side) and Jules. As they sat down to eat, having already watched them outside, separate from her, it was easy for Sasha to simplify their roles. To make them into caricatures. If Jules and Miranda were their Hudson king and queen, the ever-so-slightly staid matriarch and patriarch tasked with keeping everyone in line, then Darcy and Lou were their sexily unorthodox prince and princess, the ones who were naughty and subversive, but still royals, next in line for the crown. Jesse and Sasha were like a pair of low-ranking nobles, a duke and duchess from some far-out kingdom lusting thirstily for their share of the family jewels.

Everyone tucked into the pizza with verve, emphasizing how good it was in a way that made Sasha question if it actually was, pulling apart strands of cheese with their fingers. Libations were flowing—wine, beer, hard seltzers, ginger-flavored kombucha. In the background, Jules's record player cranked out Mariah Carey's Christmas album. Sasha ate one piece of pizza, and then another. She stroked Vivienne's velvet forehead, fed her chunks of cheese. She snuck a look at Jesse, willing her to notice.

ᖈ ᖇ

Her only "thing" is that she's into sex, Sasha had rage-texted Sylvie the night of Halloween, while she watched Darcy Jankovic read on the Aphrodite's Instagram story in a loop. *Like that makes her cool or something.*

Sasha was powerless. All she could do was cast aspersions that made her sound like a prude. Like that made her original or something.

When she'd gotten back to her apartment in Providence on Halloween and found that Jesse had not texted, she'd undressed, stood topless in front of the bedroom mirror, shoved her tits up with her left forearm, and snapped an angry picture of her reflection.

Fuck, Jesse replied to the photo an hour later.

Sasha waited, but no further message followed.

All he said was "fuck," she seethed to Sylvie after forty-five minutes had passed.

Probably he's so turned on, Sylvie texted back, charitably, from her own bed in Brooklyn, *and that's why.*

But Sasha knew that wasn't why. Jesse no longer loved her as much as he once had, and this was because of Darcy. The only proof she needed was in the text messages he had sent her. The way he showed his love for her was by simply saying so. It always had been that way, and by saying very little he was announcing, however tacitly, his dwindling interest.

"You fucked her," Sasha had accused the following weekend, when Jesse came to visit her in Providence and was anchored onto her hip bone, Sasha's preferred sexual organ.

"What?"

"You fucked her," Sasha repeated. "And there's going to be hell to pay."

"Fuck," Jesse groaned. "Tell me again."

"Hell to pay," Sasha growled.

"What kinda hell?" Jesse managed, still humping her hip bone, eyes shiny with the promise of future sexual favors.

"You think I'm going to let you Come Inside again?" Sasha taunted. "Are you stupid? Or high? You knew what you had. You thought with your big, hard dick instead of your tiny brain, and you fucked her, and now it's all gone. Me and Vivienne, you'll never see us again. You'll have to start from square one. All alone. Is that what you wanted? Tell me, was it worth it?"

Jesse grunted, coming. Sasha had affirmed his manhood in two ways: first by implying that he was the type of guy who could sleep with anyone (essentially a panty-dropper), and second by saying that he had a big dick.

"You fucked her because you *wanted* to," Sasha insisted quietly, even though Jesse was now silent and slack against her chest.

"Because I wanted to," Jesse acknowledged gamely, legs quivering with the effort of reaching his pelvis up to Sasha's hip bone.

"I'm your girl?" Sasha pressed.

"You're my girl. I didn't fuck her. I love you, my love."

Sasha could feel herself grasping at the circumference of the thing she wanted, its vague shape fuzzy and slippery and formless. She needed reality to underpin the performance of anger.

Because she was so angry! What she wanted was for Jesse to not just play along with her anger, but actually mean his contrition, take responsibility for some of Sasha's rage whether or not he'd done anything material to cause it. What she wanted was for Jesse to have fucked this other bitch, whoever she was (because at that point Darcy was just an image), to have really deceived her and betrayed her in all the ways she enumerated during sex. Otherwise, if it remained baseless, her rage was just pathetic.

The Real Real

ৎ৵ ৵ৎ

Sasha did her morning skin-care regimen while trying to remember every detail of her first date with Jesse the previous December. More specifically, she was trying to remember how she'd felt about Jesse back then, Jesse who at that point was, impossibly, a person she did not yet know. For the first few months of their courtship, Sasha had trouble integrating all the different Jesses that she experienced: in-bed Jesse, sidewalk Jesse, restaurant Jesse, social-group Jesse.

That fall, newly single and angular with heartbreak, Sasha had posted a spate of thirst traps with the express purpose of ensnaring a five-nine butch named K. But instead of K, she'd hooked Jesse, an acquaintance she vaguely knew from college who responded to her pictures with fire and pink bow emojis. Jesse's open appreciation for her was sweet, so she invited him to the all-night festival of ideas and reading at the Brooklyn Public Library with fledgling expectations.

As she went through the motions of her morning routine,

Sasha realized that she'd been doing this very routine for years—since before she'd even met Jesse. Her face was older than her relationship. This also meant that it was the same face Jesse had seen a year prior on the steps of the Brooklyn Public Library. But there was an uncanniness to the face that gleamed back at her in the mirror of Jules's bathroom—she could never see herself as Jesse saw her; anything she imagined Jesse saw was just an approximation, a flipped image.

Her makeup routine was focused on producing a dewy, fresh-faced look that could be either dressed up (for a party or event) or down (for class, or an intimate dinner party, or an evening in). After cleansing with her face wash, formulated in a Palo Alto lab specifically for her skin tone, skin concerns, and the water hardness of her zip code, she moisturized with an SPF-laden rosy beauty balm, digging a fingernail into the jar and smearing it across her cheekbones, twisting her lips into a kiss to make sure she was glowing from every conceivable angle. Next she rubbed a gelatinous glob of Milk makeup grip primer onto her face. Then came a thin application of Maybelline BB cream/8-in-1 skin perfector, followed by a highlighter stick that she again swiped across her cheekbones and under her eyes (dewy was the name of the game), and a bit of blush, which she rubbed into the highlighter until she was a glowing, flushed doll. She liked to look like she was running a mild fever.

She applied a low-key cat-eye with her felt-tip Zuzu Luxe eyeliner, flicked her eyelashes with the rubbery pink Benefit roller mascara, and blinked a few times to make sure there were no clumps. With a wand of clear mascara she combed her eyebrows into neat arches, smacked on a sheen of pink lip stain and then, for good measure, a swipe of gold-tinted lip gloss. The final step was to spritz her whole face with Milk makeup grip spray (at a safe distance of about half a foot away from her face), eyes closed, to set the whole thing in place for the day, and then rub a drop of Chloé Eau de Parfum on her wrists and behind her ears.

The night of her first date with Jesse, Sasha had decided to do a little extra—a pinker lip under the sheen of gloss and more rouge on her cheeks and the tip of her nose (as though she'd been sun-kissed in that dreamy '90s way). At the library, there were hordes of people in geometrical coats and bright yellow tights and severe little haircuts. Almost everyone was carrying a small notebook. It was very hot. Sasha's upper lip immediately beaded with sweat, which she knew would compromise the integrity of the BB cream. She blotted her philtrum with the sleeve of her cashmere cardigan (shrunken, and buttoned just one button, stretching over her boobs).

Jesse and Sasha weaved through the crowds of people, managing somehow to stay together. Sasha was growing sweaty and disoriented, thirsty for water. There were espresso machines at every turn. It was too late for coffee—midnight—but Jesse got to work preparing herself a paper cup of espresso. Sasha watched the process, transfixed and high: the stream of watery coffee, the thin trickle of milk collecting into a foamy scrim, the whirring machine finishing off with a self-satisfied *huh*. Jesse making espresso was sexy because machines and their handling were sexy.

The conference-room-turned-virtual-reality-room on the library's third floor was cavernous and mostly empty, a few plush chairs arranged in a semi-circle, paintings of men on the walls. An androgynous video artist arranged Jesse and Sasha in two of the chairs and gave them each a pair of blocky black goggles and white headphones. The artist told them to press play, and the experimental virtual reality experience, called *Nevaeh (heaven backward)*, began. They rose above a vast ocean, breaking through the clouds. Ladybugs began to fall from the sky, crashing into the water, little legs flailing; this they observed from above. The sky opened into a gleaming palace of storybook creatures and vaguely Greek divinities. They laughed and spun in their chairs, soaring through their virtual galaxies.

Behind the VR goggles, Sasha thought of something she'd learned in an undergrad philosophy seminar. The Greek philosopher Zeno had a paradox called the paradox of the grain of millet. The paradox states that a single grain of millet falls silently, but a thousand grains of millet make a sound when they fall. Hence a thousand nothings become something. An absurd conclusion but nonetheless true.

In the Prospect Heights diner afterward, where they shared a plate of Jell-O, the TV had been set to the liberal channel.

Jules Todd delivered the news with good-natured ferocity, her hooded butch eyelids painted with blue eyeshadow to appease viewers, laughing to herself as she detailed the current administration's failures as though its stupidity was beyond belief, though at the same time the whole point of her segments was that it *was* to be believed, that this all made perfect sense, that they were traveling along a predictable axis of history through which there was no free will and no original behavior.

Blocky subtitles flashed across the bottom of the screen of the TV:

> WHY WOULD AN AMERICAN PRESIDENT
> ASK VLADIMIR PUTIN FOR DIRECTION

Why *would* an American president ask Vladimir Putin for direction, Sasha mused to herself, unless the motive was sinister, the tyrants in cahoots? Jules was instructing Sasha to look for hidden clues, to pay attention, to think critically; she noted this somewhere deep in the folds of her brain, to be *smart* about things rather than so fucking stupid, as she tended to be. Hers was a stupidity she'd tried to reclaim as radical naivete, approaching the world as though wholly new to it—a sense of being Amelia Bedelia, refreshingly literal and sexily oblivious. But oblivion was out, it didn't work anymore. Being smart was in.

"She's my exact type," Sasha had slurred in a stage whisper. They were drunk on the flask Jesse had smuggled into the library for their virtual reality experience.

Jesse said, "Ha. Jules Todd is so—I don't know. Dorky."

"She's butch and sexy," Sasha had argued, aware that she was also describing Jesse, who wore her short hair greasy and pushed back. And then, to buy an extra dose of credibility: "I know her."

That was an overstatement, but nonetheless true.

"How come?" Jesse wanted to know.

"Lesbians in Media conference," Sasha said.

"Is that what you are?"

"No, I only went to cruise."

Jesse laughed.

"She was the keynote speaker," Sasha insisted. "We said hi in the lobby."

"Question," Jesse said. "I know my hair is in a Bradley Cooper phase right now, so you'd never be into it, but when it was buzzed last year, was I far enough into your butch brackets to be considered hot?"

Sasha narrowed her eyes.

Jesse reached up and pulled her hair back.

"Better?" she asked.

Sasha wanted to say, *Yes, better,* but she was aware that she could not tell Jesse what she preferred yet, just as Jesse was not allowed

to tell her Jesse's own desires; this was the game, they were entitled to their desire but not yet entitled to express it openly.

"What's your type?" Sasha asked Jesse.

"Minx," Jesse said, raising her eyebrows.

She was describing Sasha, but only because Sasha had
already described her. Everything they would say to each
other that winter was precisely meted out in order to remain
in kind and not in excess of the other; for one of them to be
in excess of the other would have been nothing short of a
humiliation.

Jesse pushed her Jell-O around the bowl with a long, silver
spoon. Sasha chopped her American cheese omelet with the
side of her fork and trundled a hunk of egg and cheese over to
the pile of ketchup.

Early the next morning, in Jesse's dim bachelor pad, Sasha
secretly approached the square for February 14 in Jesse's small
calendar and drew in faint pencil—Jesse was in the bathroom—a small heart followed by the word *Sasha*.

The winter of their courtship, Sasha spent a long time in the
upstairs bathtub in her parents' Long Island house. She'd been
recovering from a cyst on her tailbone. The cyst became infected,
then abscessed, and then it was removed in an operating room
under general anesthesia. When she came to, she had a walnut-
sized hole to the immediate left of her tailbone. The surgeon
had stuffed her walnut-sized hole with packing gauze that was
meant to be changed twice daily. At the time, Sasha was working as a copywriter for a fashion company and had been given a
week off to heal, so she'd decamped to Nassau County for some
TLC. Twice a day, she climbed into a bath filled with Epsom
salt and gingerly pulled a rope of packing gauze from her hole.

After the bath, she lay prone on her childhood bed while her mother forced fresh gauze into the hole with a pair of tweezers, sealing the area with a medical-grade bandage.

Because of all the baths, she found that she had plenty of time to practice her lines for when she was finally healed and able to fuck Jesse.

Soon you'll be able to do whatever you want to me, but in the meantime, I want you to ask me over and over again if you can Come Inside. *Each time you ask, I'm going to say* No. *When you can't stand it anymore, and you absolutely must* Come Inside, *you're going to force your way inside anyway. Okay, go.*
Can I Come Inside?
No.
Can I Come Inside?
No.
Can I Come Inside?
No.
Please Can I Come Inside?
No!
Can I Come Inside?
Tell me why you want to Come Inside.
I want to Come Inside. Let me Come Inside.
You can't Come Inside.
Please let me Come Inside.
No.
Can I Come Inside? Can I Come Inside?
No! No!

In the bath, she'd taken hold of the tip of the bandage, detached from the putty of the wound and floating outside her body like a limp tail in the salty water. She pulled gently, but nothing happened. The pain was impossible, enormous. She pulled harder. The rope, when it emerged, was coated in bits of debris that resembled white asphalt, slimy and swollen with brown blood and bathwater. The coil was at least two feet and had been stuffed so tightly into the hole that it was wrinkled like a shirt that had been lost in a drawer for years.

The bathtub at Sasha's parents' new house on Long Island was much different than the one in Jules's bathroom, the one she'd humiliated herself in the previous afternoon and that now loomed in the mirror behind her dewy face. Her parents' tub was pleased with its commitment to suburban comfort—insulated knobs, a smooth ledge for balancing razors and shampoos. The Hudson tub, on the other hand, reveled in its smug impracticality, the bronze knobs scalding to the touch, the curved edges fickle hosts for an iPhone or a mug.

༄ ༅

"But you guys are babies!" Jules was protesting to Jesse as Sasha descended for breakfast, pucking a fried egg onto Jesse's plate. "You're, what—twenty-five?"

She said twenty-five like it was the same as seventeen, or twenty-one. Sasha pointed out that Jesse would turn twenty-six the following month, but Jules waved the comment away with a yolky fork. She was eating quickly, making a little sandwich with her thick cut of sourdough and her over-easy egg, smearing ketchup on each bite before forcing it in her mouth. She chewed quickly, expediting eating so that she could keep talking. Miranda was beside her, bundled in cashmere, bleary-eyed and nursing a coffee.

"Babies!" she insisted.

Sasha didn't know why Jules was so hyped up. She didn't remember ever discussing their ages, though it was unspoken common knowledge that she and Jesse were much younger than Jules and Miranda. Wasn't that the reason Jules and Miranda wanted to fuck them?

"Babe, can you lower your voice?" Miranda said, sliding two aspirin toward her mug and swallowing them both in one big gulp. "I'm hungover."

Jules had been up since dawn, banging around the kitchen. The noise had woken Sasha up and prompted her to sneak out of bed, preening in the solitude of the bathroom. The evidence of Jules's morning run was all over the house: headphones askew on the kitchen table, a sweaty Under Armour shell draped across a chair, running shoes jumbled at the base of the stairs.

Sasha rapped her acrylics impatiently against her mug of black coffee, and Jesse placed the oat milk that Sasha had requested in front of her. "Here you go, princess."

The thrill of seeing Jules in the morning—the rumpled sweatpants, the sweaty hairline, the deepened lines around her eyes. Though Sasha had already done her routine, she let the feeling of intimacy, however false on her end, ignite inside her, extending from her abdomen to her hands, which she wrapped around the mug of coffee while staring into its murky dark pool. The night had been restorative for her and Jesse. They'd slept well despite everything, the quiet of the country lulling them and Vivienne into a dreamless stupor. Sasha had even felt close enough to Jesse to slide Jesse's hands into the warm spot between her thighs (her *polkeys*, her grandmother used to call her own warm spot in Yiddish when Sasha was a child) as they'd fallen asleep, him spooning her. She'd woken up with his finger inside her, Vivienne sandwiched between them, her velvet head so sweetly on top of Jesse's. Vivienne's lovingness called Sasha's own into being, loosed something in Sasha's armor.

"Oh," Jules said, observing their interaction over the oat milk. "*Oh*."

"What is it?" Jesse laughed.

Jules waggled her eyebrows suggestively. She was aroused by the thought that they'd had sex in Bedroom 3—of course she was. Jesse grinned at Jules. Sasha felt like a rare pearl, a prize. She pursed her lips into a smirk, shifting her eyes demurely toward her fried egg. She was glad that Darcy and Lou were still asleep. With just Jules and Miranda and Jesse, she was the obvious princess.

"Babe, could you grab me the paper?" Miranda asked, oblivious to the butch moment Jules and Jesse were enjoying. She shrugged off a layer of cashmere. "First I'm freezing, and now I'm all sweaty from the fire."

"The Change," Sasha said.

Indeed a fire was blazing in the brick fireplace of Living Room 1, sending currents of heat flowing into the kitchen. Under the cashmere robe, Miranda was in an artist-edition T-shirt through which Sasha could see her nipples. Her hair was wet and springy from a morning shower, and she was sipping coffee out of a Veselka mug, tapping her chipped red nails against the ceramic absentmindedly. The mugs in the kitchen all bore the names of New York brunch-crowd favorites: besides Veselka, there was Saraghina, Peaches, Hart's.

Jules hopped up obediently from the table, sprinting to the doorway, and returned with a blue plastic bag. She slid that morning's *New York Times* beside Miranda's plate. It narrowly missed toppling her coffee mug.

"M'lady," Jules said, like a rough-around-the-edges butler.

Miranda laughed. "Jesse is a positive influence on you," she observed, sliding her eyes over to Jesse. Sasha was proud that Jesse was the prototype of a good boy, a role model to boys even older than he.

"Baby, baby, baby, don't say that!" Jules sipped manically at her glass of orange juice. "I've always been chivalrous."

Miranda smiled at her sideways, a private moment between the two of them. Sasha welled with the urge to burst it.

"Do you guys still have S?" Sasha asked.

"*Ess!*" Miranda crowed, getting a kick out of Sasha.

Jules let out a vague whimper, and Miranda's eyes didn't lift from the style section. Jesse put a palm on Sasha's thigh under the table, as though rewarding her for her journalistic probing and/or her audacity, and tickled her through her nightgown, making her flinch with pleasure.

"Well, we're old," Jules said.

Sasha sensed that that would be the end of that for now. But the pale blue Le Wand!

"I'm going to make us hot chocolate," Sasha announced. "Isn't that what they do on Christmas morning?"

Having never experienced a true Christmas morning in her childhood, Sasha was determined to do everything right. To breakfast, she'd kept on her sheer pink nightgown and styled it under a white beaded robe that clattered onto the table every time she reached from something or gesticulated. She felt it carried Anglo-Saxon drama that was appropriate for the occasion, especially when she stood, as she'd done upon arriving in the dining area, facing the fire, forcing the light to illuminate her lingerie-clad form (black lacy bra and matching underwear) underneath the sheer gown. She'd done this for Jules's benefit, mostly, standing with her back to the room and her front to the flames, letting their heat lap at her naked flesh.

She tousled Jesse's hair as she got up to make hot chocolate. Jesse smiled up at her with love eyes.

Vivienne scampered into the kitchen after her, and Sasha furtively scooped a pile of the diabetic cat food into Vivienne's bowl—couldn't hurt. Vivienne was looking particularly chunky. Out the window, the morning was gray and calm, a flurry of snow beginning to coat the ground. She loved winter. The ground was frozen, the sky calm, the sun rare. She got to work boiling milk—whole milk; this was no occasion for oat—and rummaging around for the tin of Ovaltine she'd clocked during yesterday's house tour.

There was so much dailiness to fill—hours and hours of it. And it was only the first full day. Cooking for six made Sasha feel like a Russian housewife. She leaned into the Soviet thing; it was trendy now—her father born in Kyiv in 1965, followed by her mother in Leningrad in 1967, each decamping to Brighton Beach as children. She'd packed in preparation to flex her Ashkenazi heritage: the sheepskin coat, the glitzy-glam earrings, the pale green rabbit fur Ushanka hat and matching hand muff from her favorite designer knockoff place in Brighton.

She assembled six mugs on the counter, rotated twelve pieces of toast in the four-slot toaster. This all contributed to a feeling of domestic abundance, that romanticized thrill of feeding hungry mouths.

She carried two mugs into the kitchen. When she placed a random diner mug in front of Miranda, Miranda's phone, which was lying faceup beside her plate of eggs, suddenly jumped to life. Miranda flipped it over before Sasha could see the notification. She set the other mug beside Jesse.

DYKETTE 67

"What were we talking about?" Miranda asked.

Jules took another bite of her open-faced sandwich, considering.

"Perfect hot chocolate," Jesse praised.

"Need help carrying the rest?" Jules asked, flexing her forearms and biceps against the table to announce her willingness to rise.

"I'm okay," Sasha said.

As Sasha turned back to the kitchen, Miranda flipped her phone around to the faceup side. She pressed her finger to the touch ID of her phone, the screen showing a text conversation that consisted of paragraphs of text—gray boxes that kept, as Sasha watched with fascination, getting pushed up to make way for new ellipses and chunks of writing from the sender. She'd never seen anyone go off quite like that via text. Sasha couldn't make out what the words said, only their volume, which filled her with a sense of dread. She stepped into the kitchen.

"This swan maple syrup is great," Jules said from the table as Sasha gathered the remaining mugs. "Who found this?"

Sasha set a mug down in front of Jules and then retreated to her own seat. Miranda was trying not to look at her phone, but the messages kept popping up on her lock screen. Sasha's eyesight wasn't good enough to make out any of the words, though she squinted subtly anyway.

"I did," Jesse said. "It's hot, right?"

Jules nodded, sliding the bottle over to Jesse, who poured a little bit into her coffee.

"The thing about sex," Miranda said suddenly. "It's normal to go a few weeks, or even months, without it."

Sasha said, "Like, that's how long your patients go?"

She was obsessed with Miranda-as-therapist, wanted to

know the names and biographical details of Miranda's clients, even if they weren't famous (and Sasha was fairly sure that at least a few of them were).

Miranda nodded noncommittally, like she didn't want to give too much away.

"Gays or straights?" Jesse asked.

"Both." Miranda's tone was casual. She wasn't looking at Jules.

Sasha was overcome with the sense that if she and Jules were together, if they were to have an affair, they'd be all over each other, unable to stop fucking. She imagined them in the shower, Jules's body much bigger than hers, pummeling her into oblivion in a sudsy wonderland. She saw foamy scrims of soap, all her orifices clean and slippery. The two of them wet and slide-y, silky nets of soap shifting between them. Because the relationship would not be the one she had with Jesse. With Jules, she would be constantly aroused, not just sometimes, when Jesse caught her in the right mood. She and Jules would reach for each other in the night. They would press their bodies together at any chance they got. The fantasy was fleeting and casual. Sasha refocused on her breakfast, which was growing cold.

There were footsteps on the stairs, and an amoeba comprising Darcy and Lou emerged, entangled in each other's formless postures. Vivienne jumped down from her fur pelt on the dining table, using Sasha's lap as a step, to greet them.

"Hey, cuties," Darcy said, sleepy-sexy, reaching down to pat Vivienne.

Darcy was wearing a white waïfhewn T-shirt airbrushed with a muscular torso, quilted blue abs detailed on the fabric. On the bottom, ass-embracing gray sweatpants slung low around her hips.

Sasha sucked in her breath. The thing about Darcy was that

she was weird in a mechanical way, one that followed all the rules of contemporary weirdness without being odd in a generative manner (which was to say *actually weird*). You couldn't be *actually weird* and still be palatable to that many people.

Lou was in the baggier equivalent of Darcy's sweats and a loose yellow T-shirt. The two of them separated to find spots at the table. Darcy tousled Jesse's hair, just like Sasha had done, on her way around the dining table. Jesse looked up, eager, until he noticed Sasha glaring at him, at which point he turned back to his eggs. His vanity usually charmed her—the way he rubbed gel into his hair incessantly, pulled everything out of his closet while trying to devise an outfit—but the thought of Darcy's approval meaning something to him made her sick.

"Merry Christmas," Lou yawned.

Jules struggled to her feet and dutifully padded over to the kitchen in her daddy slippers to get Lou and Darcy mugs of coffee.

"Sasha made hot chocolate, too," Jules called from the kitchen. "Anyone into that?"

Darcy and Lou looked at each other. "Just coffee for now, yeah?" Lou called back, and Darcy nodded.

"Anyone else feeling really hungover this morning?" Darcy asked. Her hair was lank around her face, yet somehow still silky. She leaned her elbows on the table and pitched herself forward, eyeing the spread of toast, eggs, potatoes, and pancakes on the table with a grimace. "I can't look at all this food."

"I can't eat this early, either," Miranda said, eyes on her paper.

It was true; Miranda's eggs were untouched, though Jules had served them to her in the way she liked—scrambled, with a smattering of parmesan cheese grated over them.

Sasha shoved her nearly empty plate of food closer to Vivienne so that Vivienne could finish every scrap.

"Thank you, love," Darcy croaked as Jules set a mug in front of her. Her gratitude was overblown, designed to make her appear sympathetic and worthy of being constantly served.

"Sugar and cream," Jules announced, satisfied with herself for remembering how everyone took their coffee.

"And for you, no sugar, just milk," Jules said, sliding a mug over to Lou, who quietly accepted it and began gulping the coffee down, eyes fixed on Miranda's discarded real estate section.

The sweats that Lou wore were actually nothing like the sweats Jules wore, the longer Sasha examined them—Lou's were Eckhaus Latta, expertly tailored, blue and orange stitching down the sides, acquired at a sample sale that fall; Jules's were Champion, befitting her old-school (Jules was born in 1979 in northwest Washington, DC) butch haircut and biceps, with bleach stains around the crotch that Sasha imagined were streaks of dried semen. Her kittycat puffed.

"Weeks to *months*," Jules repeated absently, as though just hearing what they'd discussed minutes earlier.

Jesse was wearing a wrinkled button-down over an oversized white T-shirt, long olive sweat shorts, and thick athletic socks. Her hair was flopping around her face; she hadn't yet fixed it with gel. There was a tiny crust at the edge of her left eye. Sasha picked it off and fed it to Vivienne, whose eyes almost bulged out of her head with glee. They called eye goop—their own and Vivienne's—a delicacy, because it was her favorite thing.

"My best friend at Barnard was the head of the Barnard Asexuals—the Aces, they were called," Miranda said.

"No way," Jesse said.

"Her name was Blanche," Miranda said with a little laugh. "I loved her."

"Asexual name," Darcy mused.

"I feel like Blanche is a sexy name," Sasha countered. "It's very *Valley of the Dolls*."

"I don't mean that the name Blanche itself is unsexy," Darcy clarified. "Just, like, it's the name that an asexual would totally have. Asexuals have hella dramatic names. Also, like, a lot of the time asexuals actually *enjoy* sex."

She was such a know-it-all contrarian, always needing to situate herself in opposition to Sasha—to assert herself as the more woke one. Sasha knew some asexuals liked sex! She was the one in the gender studies PhD program. Sasha forced out a conciliatory giggle that she made sure was threaded with malice.

"You sleep okay?" Jesse asked Lou, jostling Lou's shoulders. "You seem out of it."

Lou shook their head. "Anyone else hear the squirrel in the ceiling? There was a scampering sound above my head all night."

"Fuck," Jules said. "We've had that problem before—though not usually this far into the winter. Maybe I'll get on the ladder later this afternoon."

"Jesse can help," Sasha offered, and Jesse explained, "She likes when I'm handy."

"I kept thinking it was going to bust out of the wall and land on us," Lou was saying, but Darcy shrugged. "I didn't hear anything."

Sasha imagined the two of them in bed together, barely two months into their relationship. They were fucking, of course—probably nightly. Sasha imagined Darcy's hands around Lou's muscular legs, Lou's head pressed between Darcy's slender thighs. She bet Darcy's pussy tasted like a corn chip. Lou wouldn't mind that. She wasn't turned on by the idea of the two of them having sex. Darcy had begun to actively repulse her, and she'd long ago forced herself to get rid of any attraction she would've otherwise felt toward Lou because of Lou's brotherly friendship with Jesse.

Sasha used her pinky nail to deposit some undissolved hot cocoa mix into her mouth.

"What's going on in your phone, baby?" Jules asked Miranda, who was again puzzling over her phone screen.

Miranda bared her teeth like a Dobermann, shaking her head with slow disbelief. Everyone watched her try to craft a narrative out of what was going on. "This patient," she ultimately said.

"The bad one?" Jules tongued some syrup off her lip knowingly.

Miranda grimaced, vaguely assenting.

Sasha wondered what made her patient bad, other than the paragraphs of text. Bad patients were different than Bad Therapists (the conceit of Miranda's podcast). What made a patient bad instead of simply "challenging"?

"It's *Christmas*," Jules complained. "Can't he give it a rest on *Christmas*?"

This was the first time Jules had acknowledged the holiday, invoking it to voice her opposition to the bad patient, to advocate for some respect and propriety. Everyone laughed, in on the joke.

Sasha lifted Vivienne onto her lap.

"I made Jesse wait to fuck me," Sasha announced.

"See, I'm bad at that," Darcy said, scrunching her nose up.

Sasha ground her teeth into her tongue. *I'm bad at that*. A humble-brag.

"I tried to do that," Darcy continued with an air of alluring vagueness, "but the truth is I'm so difficult in other ways that I feel like I need to have *something* going for me. And honestly, that something is usually just being an easy lay."

Darcy was referring cagedly to a situation she'd gotten herself into that fall, a situation in which she'd "been difficult" that most of the table already knew the details of. Jesse and Sasha knew the story through Cate Campos, Jesse's landlord and the notorious butch barber-bachelor whose heart Darcy had recently shattered. Jules and Miranda, who ran in the same middle-aged dyke friend group as Cate, had also heard the story from Cate. Because history is written by the victor, Lou had told Jesse a cherry-picked version of the story, too, which Jesse had breathlessly relayed to an aggravated Sasha.

Darcy could call herself difficult, a cunt, a bitch, but she wasn't; that was the point of Darcy, that she was easy in all ways—easy to bed, socially easy, blessed with an interpersonal facility that Sasha lacked.

But it was also her easiness that got her into that trouble with Cate. Cate was the founder of T's in Bed-Stuy, which had for the past decade been the premier spot for queers to get their hair cut. Cate's own hair was short and simple, salt-and-pepper in the way Sasha loved, and she always reeked of that lovely barbershop smell of glossy product.

Cate had pursued Darcy on Instagram while Darcy was beginning to make Lou's acquaintance and strike up a flirtation with them.

All Cate had been able to talk about that fall, when they'd burst into Jesse's apartment unannounced to rifle through their potato chips and drink their seltzer, was Darcy—Her Royal Hotness, Cate called her. Jesse hadn't had the heart to tell Cate what she knew about Darcy and Lou, so Jesse had played dumb, and later, when she'd told Sasha, they both felt gross about their perceived complicity.

The official goss was that Darcy and Lou had fucked in the bathroom at Colina Cuervo while their mutual friends brunched on buttermilk pancakes and empanadas. Jesse was protective over Cate, whose longest relationship in all her forty-eight years had been about two years, so she'd chosen to withhold this information from Cate—but it had come out anyway; their world was small, and Cate's circle was large.

To no one's surprise, Darcy broke things off with Cate soon after the brunchtime liason came to light. Cate had been irate—Cate, who had sent gifts to Darcy's apartment all fall, Cate who had fancied herself Darcy's gateway to the upper echelon of the dyke elite (or at least the fifty-year-old set, which in dykeland was the hottest of the hot). Cate had asked for everything back and summarily stricken Darcy's name from an upcoming photography show featuring Cate's haircuts (Cate was planning to cut Darcy's hair before the split and feature the haircut in the show, natch).

Some gifts, of course, could not be returned: the specialty fig jam, the candied nuts, the fresh flowers, the squares of orange-infused dark chocolate. Other things could: vintage photographs from Cate's collection, family heirlooms like a set of brass rings. Cate had some family money, but most of what she had (e.g., the designer bag Cate had swiped for Darcy while doing hair for the company's ad campaign) were gifts from friends. And for that reason, Cate had made it out that Darcy had betrayed *the entire community*. She was slowly rehabilitating her public image, and the week upstate with Lou would prove to everyone that they were serious, meant to be.

"We never even fucked," Darcy was saying to reiterate the absurdity of the gifts Cate promised her.

The fetishization of the older-younger couple in lesbian relationships in media confounded Sasha. Not that it wasn't hot, but it wasn't at all common. It was just the Eileen Effect—Eileen Myles being the canonical older-butch dyke always dating a twenty-two-year-old pale waif, and that becoming the standard in a vacuum of representation. Everyone was simply ahb-*soos*ed with it.

There was a lull in the orbit of Darcy's story, which had saturated the dining room table with chuckles and mirth at Cate's expense. Sasha decided to jump in.

Sasha's own difficulty, she explained as Jules poured her a fresh mug of coffee, had always been wrapped up in the sex itself—she was not withholding with gifts or time or any of that, gave objects freely, fell headfirst in love, but she guarded her body—her actual body, her flesh, her titties and kittycat—from outside view as though they were sacred documents locked in an ancient library.

"I know," Miranda said in a self-consciously light tone. "I read your article!"

Sasha noticed that her generous pour of barista-blend oat milk was beginning to settle. She was titillated by Miranda's acknowledgment, and also petrified. Earlier that year Sasha had sold an essay about the fable of the girl with the green ribbon around her neck to a prominent literary magazine. In the essay, she'd identified the act of wearing a green ribbon around one's neck—as the girl in the fable does—as the ultimate high-femme performance. She'd also explored her own erotic, aesthetic, and political decision to symbolize those "high-femme camp antics" that Faye described, playing femme-fatale dating games by wearing a green Chanel ribbon tied around her neck, or at the center of her middle part, or as a streaming ribbon down her ponytail, both to mark herself as Jesse's girl and to announce herself as fragile, a thing that could be harmed.

There was something about a high-femme vulnerability, the

performance of softness that she was trying to assemble in the essay. She'd reconceptualized the relationship between Jenny, the green-ribbon girl, and Alfred, her ribbon-horny husband, to theorize that lesbian gender was about the sensuous promise of destruction and the unwieldiness of desire that had no place to go, and could not be sated, so had to get materialized in this disturbed fashion. She'd discussed Cherríe Moraga's metaphor of femme-as-turtle, too, a turtle flipped on its back, fleshy underside exposed. This was what it meant to flash one's green ribbon, to flash one's pink belly: to bare the ways in which you were totally destructible, and ultimately powerless.

The essay had, to Sasha's surprise and dismay, gone semi-viral on Twitter, with two distinct camps emerging. One claimed that she was wretchedly anti-feminist for wearing the green ribbon (it was a quasi-chastity belt, they accused, a "deranged misunderstanding of femme camp" that manifested as an "apologia for lesbian abuse" or, more vaguely, "toxic behavior"). *Free Jesse!* the Twitter trolls had crowed. Others called her "immature," which Sasha couldn't help feeling was a keenly tragic missing of the point. The other camp—mostly, to Sasha's relief, made up of fellow girl weirdos—understood that Sasha was playful, engaging with persona, being *funny*. It was funny! This was all fucking funny!

Oh my god SASHA, Sylvie had texted her at the height of her Twitter scandal. *You're internet-famous for being a nightmare!!*

When she'd insisted that Jesse go on Twitter to defend her honor, Jesse had spent hours writing rebuttals to the comments only to be woken up the next morning with seemingly hundreds of angry queers mocking Sasha, Jesse, and even Vivienne (!). Subsequently, they'd both decided to do a long social media fast. Jesse had in fact forbidden Sasha from checking Instagram or Twitter until at least February.

"High-Femme Camp Antics," Jules intoned, intentionally high-pitched and singsong, shimmying her shoulders with a chuckle. Sasha's gut churned. Jesse, though, smiled proudly.

"So iconic," Darcy praised absentmindedly.

It was easy to forget that Darcy had *liked* what she'd written, so much so that she was developing a performance based on Sasha's essay. In real life, Sasha's presence disappointed Darcy, making Sasha constantly aware of the distance between her actual self and the persona she'd cultivated in the essay.

❧ ❧

At noon they were still at the kitchen table, on their third cups of coffee and now talking about the afterlife. They'd taken turns disappearing from the table to go freshen up and get dressed. Sasha, already freshened up, had dressed in black tights, a felt houndstooth dress, and a matching felt bucket hat.

Sasha announced that Jesse wasn't allowed to remarry if she died. If she did, Sasha would come back as a ghost and kill the mistress in her sleep, a feat she'd perform in her ghost outfit. In moments like these—detailing the ghost murder, slitting the mistress's throat and then taking Jesse by one hunky arm up to heaven—she felt herself verging on some manic performance, a delirious whim that forced her to embody a hyperbolic persona with lots of attitude and gesticulation.

Darcy cocked her head in disbelief. Sasha wondered if she'd taken the high-femme camp antics a step too far, but Miranda laughed, and Sasha figured that if Miranda—eternally correct, emotionally responsible Miranda—thought it was funny, it couldn't be so bad.

"What's your ghost outfit?" Lou wanted to know.

Sasha explained that one's ghost outfit was her best outfit

from her time on Earth. This was a concept she'd ripped off from *Vanderpump Rules*. It was the only outfit you'd get as a ghost, so it would have to be both stylish and functional. Hers would be her Hello Kitty corset and her red Adidas by Fiorucci miniskirt.

Jules said, with a sly smile, that she'd love to see Sasha in that outfit, and Jesse, not getting that he was supposed to be threatened, planted a big kiss on Sasha's soft cheek.

"And in the winter?" Lou countered, like Sasha knew they would.

"Ghosts don't get cold."

"Okay, but what if you died, like, tomorrow," Darcy said. "You wouldn't want Jesse to spend the next, what, seventy years of their life alone, would you?"

Why wouldn't she want Jesse to spend the next seventy years mourning her?

"I'll paste your picture onto a Popsicle stick and carry it everywhere," Jesse promised.

Sasha's palms twitched with sweat. "You'll delete everything else, right?"

"What, like nudes?" Darcy laughed.

"Everything is tasteful," Sasha insisted to the group, though no one seemed concerned, then turned to Jesse: "Just promise me you'll delete them."

"I bet it's just titties," Darcy sighed.

"Sasha worries about people turning her image into porn," Jesse explained.

"That's not the way it works," Darcy said. "But in Europe everyone's tits are always out anyway, so that's probably why I don't worry about that stuff."

"Stone bitch" was the phrase that came immediately to

Sasha's mind, after Leslie Feinberg's seminal novel *Stone Butch Blues*.

Tell us more, Darcy, about how European you are. Tell us about the way the Croatian sun roasts your shoulders, tell us about your love of canned fish and the girl you'd kiss for practice at your German primary school.

Sasha had been performing this act of possessiveness not for Jesse's benefit, but for Jules's. Jesse had picked up something that did not belong to her, that wasn't *for* her, and Sasha fought the urge to take the whole thing back. Yesterday's overheard therapy session with Faye battered at her sensibilities again after having lived somewhere subdued in her veins for the previous sixteen hours.

She felt her muscles stiffen, her smile go slack. She was transforming into a cunt. A mean girl. It was like her hero Chris Kraus says in *I Love Dick*: "The only thing I can do is tell the dumb cunt's tale."

The only thing she could do was tell the dumb cunt's tale. Wherever Sasha went—including this trip upstate, even—her alienness was key to her belonging. This was what it had always meant to her, being gay. Her whole life, she'd known how to weld herself into a viable alternative to the popular thing. She wasn't a nice girl, but she wasn't a mean girl, either. Someone had once told Sasha that she wasn't hot enough to be this crazy. But that itself was an unfair construction—you didn't have to be hot to be crazy; you had to be hot to be mean. Being cruel, a cunt, was one of her modes, just like being sweet. But at the dining room table in Hudson, faced with an amalgamation of dykes whose slight differences were not always parsable, she didn't quite know what that alternative thing was, what precisely was needed. If it wasn't meanness, and it wasn't niceness, what was it?

"Sasha," Darcy said after Miranda had collected their breakfast plates. Lou and Sasha were stationed at the sink, Sasha washing and Lou drying. "Can I go through your suitcase? With your supervision, of course."

Darcy longed to take some cottagecore photos in Jules's backyard, and Jesse had teased some of the garments Sasha had brought upstate as possibilities. The thought of Darcy wearing her clothes filled Sasha with terror and pride. A big part of her value was in the wardrobe she'd curated—and not even in a shallow way; these were the objects she'd hunted and bargained for and waited patiently to go on sale.

"Yeah," Sasha said. "Once we're done with the dishes."

"Where is everyone?" Lou asked, wiping dry the inside of a mug with a dishrag.

Darcy shrugged. "Miranda and Jules are reading, I think, and Jesse and I are going to get started on planning our little *projet*." She pronounced it in the French way, *projjjay*. "Which is why I wanted to look through your stuff."

"That sauna thing?" Sasha asked, trying not to visibly shudder though she was overcome with revulsion by a soggy piece of omelet clogging the sink's drain.

Darcy nodded, her eyes shiny.

"You guys can go," Lou offered, taking Sasha's spot in front of the sink filled with steaming hot water. Darcy planted a kiss on Lou's cheek, and they let out a sound that was like, *ahhhh*.

Upstairs, Jesse was in Bed 3, scrolling through her phone. She jumped to attention when Sasha and Darcy marched in. Sasha unzipped her suitcase while Jesse and Darcy watched. Jesse was, unfortunately, notorious for signing on to set-design and film half-baked projects—*projets*—like these, and over the course of their relationship, this tendency had caused not a small number of disagreements and resentments. But Sasha had promised Jesse that this time she'd at least feign support for this particular project ("Imitation is the sincerest form of flattery," she'd patronizingly reminded Sasha more than once), so Sasha graciously lifted her clothes one by one out of the suitcase.

The red velvet fringed pants.

The nursing corset.

The reworked Adidas corset.

The peacock dress, a few errant feathers fluttering down from the full sleeves.

The fur-and-pearls collar.

The white feathered angel wings, four feet long and four feet tall, with flexible bands to attach around the wearer's shoulders, accompanied by a fluffy white halo-headband.

The blue and brown camo shirt, cut from a thrift-store dress.

Darcy marveled over each new thing, even though as a brand-whore herself she had every coveted designer item of the past five years, most acquired at the dead of night on eBay. Darcy cared more about being on-trend; Sasha cared more about being rare. Ultimately, Darcy selected the black Adidas corset and the pink fishnet tights, over which she wore a sloppily stitched-together Vivienne Westwood Anglomania piece that featured a ribbed pink miniskirt affixed with a long satin tail.

"Swish, swish, bitch," Darcy simpered, staring at her reflection in the mirror. At the end of the tail was another little ribbed bit that Darcy expertly affixed around her ankle, like a female Poseidon. Sasha had never worn the thing—she'd tried it on when Jesse wasn't home and didn't like the way it stretched across her hips.

"The *wings*," Darcy kept saying, greedily pawing through

the suitcase though she'd already selected an outfit. "We absolutely need to do a photo shoot in the snow with these. Snow angels!"

Sasha was slightly ashamed to admit, even just to herself, that she'd brought the wings to Hudson in part to please Darcy. In fact, as Darcy marveled at Sasha's items, Sasha felt herself teem with pride; she was being confirmed or anointed, or maybe coronated. There was a degree of undeniable pleasure; there was also a stitch of anxiety.

"Are you actually going to turn the sauna on for this performance thing?" Sasha asked.

"It's warming up right now," Jesse said. "The goal is to get it just hot enough so that she's sweating a little, but not so hot that the equipment gets damaged."

Sweating into Sasha's clothes, she meant. Jesse's *cause célèbre* was initiating a lesbian sauna culture to rival that of gay men's bathhouses.

"Or that Vivienne can't breathe," Darcy said, not reassuringly, pulling the pink and beige fabric of the Westwood piece more securely over the tights, the long tail piece flapping cartoonishly against her legs. She preened in front of the mirror for a few seconds, shifting this way and that.

Sasha froze, her heart constricting. "Vivienne is part of this?"

"We were going to put her in the collar," Jesse said, brandishing the fur collar. "You said that was okay."

"I thought you were kidding."

Jesse looked concerned. "Why?"

Darcy looked away.

"She's a *pug*," Sasha said. "Pugs are brachycephalic."

Darcy assured Sasha that the sauna wouldn't be hotter than a summer day.

"Summer is too hot," Sasha said. Her heart was the size of a quarter. "Vivienne gets too hot, we don't take her outside in the summer."

Darcy scowled at her. "Ninety degrees, tops."

"*Ninety?*" Sasha imagined Vivienne gasping for breath, pawing at the sauna door while Jesse focused the camera on Darcy's naked body, Vivienne smudging a desperate line through the steam on the door, Jesse and Darcy having S. Vivienne wasn't supposed to *be* outside on a summer day for more than a few minutes, she wanted to reiterate, especially if it was nearly ninety degrees, but she didn't know how to without provoking Jesse and providing Darcy with more evidence that Sasha was a loser.

"Eighty-five?" Darcy negotiated good-naturedly.

Jesse asked Sasha to please chill. "I know how to take care of her."

Sasha suppressed a growl. *No you don't*, she wanted to say, though it wasn't quite true.

"And the ribbon?" Darcy said quietly to Jesse, redirecting the attention back to her body.

Sasha instinctively clutched at her green Chanel ribbon, affixed to her ponytail, as though Jesse might rip it off of her and give it to Darcy. But to her relief, Jesse went into her own suitcase and began rummaging around. She'd brought an entire duffel of props. It was mostly filled with objects rather than clothing. She rifled through silk cherry blossom branches, cherub figurines, and plastic gems before pulling out a ribbon.

It was a cheaper ribbon than Sasha's, though both were fake Chanel. The ribbon that Jesse produced was *clearly* a fake. This was an imitation ribbon, whereas Sasha's ribbon was an homage ribbon, a ribbon with a commitment to brand fidelity. Sasha breathed a short puff of relief. The ribbon that Darcy would wear was glossy and thin, in a green both deeper and less luxe than Sasha's. Sasha didn't know where Jesse had found it. She hoped it was on the street, in a gutter.

The ribbon was about one's desire to know—the anxiety around not-knowing, and the sadness of knowing. It was an ode to the stony lez ribbon femme who makes her guy so horny and anxious for her that he ends up killing her. The performance was inspired by the green-ribbon story vis-à-vis the treatment of the girl with the green ribbon in Sasha's essay. *She's a fan*, Jesse had told her as they'd packed for the trip, transparently stroking Sasha's ego. *She wants to be your friend; she's inspired by your work.*

Jesse handed the counterfeit ribbon to Darcy. Darcy tied the ribbon around her neck, giggling at her reflection in the mirror above the dresser. Sasha's mouth was so dry that she found it difficult to swallow.

Later, from Sasha's vantage point at the kitchen window, she could make out the vague shape of three figures in the sauna: Jesse struggling with the camcorder, pressing this button and that; Vivienne perched obediently on one of the wooden benches, the pearls on her collar gleaming, her vagina suctioned to the wet wood; and Darcy in bits and pieces, a flash of green at her neck, the swoosh of the Westwood tail fluttering in the humid air. After a few minutes the door had steamed up, and Sasha could no longer see anything.

Sasha pulled her laptop out in Bedroom 3 and logged in, her fingers instinctively scuttling across the keyboard.

Footage from the night of the party showed Darcy on her knees in high-femme drag, juggling a thick microphone and a copy of her book. She pantomimes sucking the mic like it's a dildo, the microphone's wire tangling around her knees. Darcy, positioned halfway down a long staircase, gyrates in her pink lingerie slip as she chants lines of her poetry.

We'll work when we're dead!
We'll work when we're dead!
We'll work when we're dead!

Sasha peeked over the top of her laptop. A white truck high-tailed down the road, tightly hugging the curve. For a second she was convinced that the truck would hit the front of the house. She sucked in her breath, bracing for the impact. When it safely passed, she ran to the bathroom and looked down at the sauna, the wooden barrel of it surprisingly small. She still couldn't see Vivienne or Jesse or Darcy. Reassured, she returned to the Safari browser.

The week after Halloween, *The Cut* ran an article about the debauchery that had ensued after Darcy's reading. The journalist's first-person account of the night described the drug-fueled after-party at Darcy's Crown Heights apartment as "reeking of sex."

The Twitter fallout from the party, which Sasha followed closely, had—predictably—two sides: those who criticized the party itself and those who took issue with the *coverage* of the party. The Media, that eternally available and defenseless enemy.

The boring people—liberal squares, conservative squares, it didn't matter—responded to the hedonistic absurdity of the party, but this perspective was essentially prudish nonsense and not worth too much consideration.

The critics of the coverage interested Sasha more. They responded to how the article—which valorized Darcy and her friends, breathlessly reporting a night of radical debauchery in the style of a smugly alt tabloid—made frivolous the subversive potential of the party: its unapologetic queerness, its celebration of sex and sex work, its anti-capitalist thrust.

This party honestly seems so exhausting, in a boring way, someone on Twitter complained.

Sasha was riveted by the charges of mundanity. Classifying something as dull and boring was the quickest way to strip it of its majesty, positioning the wielder of the "boring" charge as eminently more fun and spontaneous than the wannabes so eager to indicate the fun they were having.

Perceptive readers had picked up on the party's insistence of its own weirdness, and the way that that insistence made the party seem boring. The accusation of boringness was easy to lob and difficult to actually imagine, given the pictures. Even Sasha knew that the party *hadn't* been boring—these internet commentators felt, like she did, excluded. She scrolled through the pictures on the bed in Bedroom 3. She'd seen them many times. She navigated to the video the club had posted on its Instagram page that night.

As she always did, she held her pointer finger down for a still picture of the entire crowd so that she could parse it for an image of Jesse. She scanned for a wide-legged stance, broad shoulders in a teal puffer, the tousle of thick hair. But she couldn't find him no matter how hard she searched. It was almost like he had not been there at all. There was ample evidence of Darcy's presence only—Darcy in a gauzy dress with nothing underneath except for a pair of Hanes underwear, its ass scrawled with hot-pink letters tracing the word *BIMBO*.

The film was knotted and mangled, implying absolutely gleeful chaos. There was a big cake, pink buttercream oozing down its sides. Darcy sank into the cake, deeper and deeper until she was separated from the ground by only a thin layer of frosting. Everybody screamed. In the last few seconds of the video, guests reached for hunks of the smashed cake with their hands, smearing pink streaks across the club's floor and their faces. For a second, the camera caught Lou's face beaming under the strobe lighting, reminding Sasha of the internet's smug, gossipy associative logic—its femme sensibility! She'd have to write that down—insistent on forging connections between everything so that any two names, any two places, were linked only by a matter of how many times you clicked.

In early November, Darcy had needed a set designer, a props guy; Lou knew just the person. Soon, Jesse and Darcy were collaborating to scheme up a performance, Darcy's ploy to up the ante on the Halloween party. Darcy's latest piece would center the pursuit of becoming a frill, a ruffle, an object of accessory status. When Sasha's green-ribbon essay was published a few weeks later, the performance abruptly changed course. Darcy had finally found the source material she'd been looking for.

As though to make it up to her, this dangerous affiliation drawn between Darcy and Sasha, Jesse had, in recent months, become even more obsessed with regaling Sasha with found objects, accumulating a cadre of mini things in a shrine in the Brooklyn apartment: tiny wooden doll chairs scavenged from Brooklyn's thrift shops, tiny bows made of berries and flowers from the trees in the neighborhood, shards of glass from Riis beach.

But Jesse was finding pink things for Darcy's performance, too—discarded acrylic fingernails, silk headscarves, old tubes of lipstick, and velvet pillows in that particular shade of pink that could be described only as "baby."

On Instagram at least, Sasha could most accurately describe Darcy as "slutty baby." Her eyelashes were fluffed and flayed with mascara, her lips were puffed outward like a strange fish's, and her angular jawbone intercepted a long, slender neck. There was a freshly scrubbed quality to her that made her look both cleaner and more squalid than Sasha. Sasha gleaned the relevant biographical details from Google searches and social media.

Born in 1990 in Zagreb, Darcy was a blend of her mother's Yugoslavian gravitas—though Sasha couldn't ascertain the exact breakdown of post-1992 nationalities represented in Darcy's lineage, her Instagram showed photos of a family estate on Croatia's Dalmatian coast and a severe Slavic mother—glossed over with a luster of Berlin cool (her family had relocated to her father's native Germany in the aftermath of the Yugoslav Wars, where she'd lived between the ages of two and twelve) and finished off with a thick Rolodex of Los Angeles connections (the Jankovics decamped to Los Angeles in 2005, enrolling their daughter in Hancock Park's elite Marlborough School).

Despite the money flowing through Darcy's biography, the patchworked foreign childhood, ambiguous accent, and Yugoslavian birthplace meant that Darcy's generational trauma was more accessible than Sasha's, and also that she had a maddeningly cute, mysterious accent whose flavor was a little sibilant Slavic and a little *Deutsch* and a little California Valley girl. All of which, taken together, meant that Darcy was winning their undeclared Eastern Euro girl rivalry.

Sasha stole another glance out the window.

She tried, virtuously, to put herself in Jesse's designer-collab sneakers. His excitement about being involved in this project could be fine—Darcy was an exciting person, a shiny person. But her boyfriend was turning into Darcy's—what were people online calling this sort of pathetic guy?—*simp*, a guy who does way too much for the girl he likes. Sasha loved Jesse's simping for her; she could not abide his simping for another.

Yes, unfortunately she hated this other woman more than she could ever hate her boyfriend, for no other reason than that she *loved* her boyfriend, who in turn owed her his loyalty, and not the other woman, from whom she expected neither love nor devotion. And Jesse's devotion was not ordinary, not transferable—it was custom made for her, designed to fill every one of Sasha's concave places.

Sasha tried to let the envy of Darcy and longing for Jesse flow through her like a river, neither rejecting nor judging the emotion. It was something Faye had once suggested to Jesse, but like most such advice she found it totally useless.

୧ ๑

Just beyond the front door, Jules accepted a massive cardboard box from a vendor, whom she thanked profusely and slipped a fifty-dollar bill. Inside the box were seven robust bundles of radicchio, big leafy roses grown in northern Italy, harvested and delivered within twelve hours.

"Literally so beautiful." Jesse aimed his phone at the radicchio roses.

Jules pulled a leaf from a pale green rose of radicchio, its thin skin streaked with pink capillaries. She crunched down on it.

"Bitter," she praised. "Perfect for my Caesar."

In the group chat established before the trip to Hudson, one of the things they'd agreed on was the need for a theme night—a reason to dress up, to get into character. Jesse suggested Italian American Christmas, and everyone agreed that it seemed fitting; the cultural moment was one of bingeing

Sopranos reruns on Netflix and leaning into *Jersey Shore* nostalgia. But because none of them had actual Italian heritage (besides Jesse's Sicilian great-grandfather, who'd converted to Judaism and changed his name to Oscar Pearlstein in order to marry a green-eyed Polish Jewess), they consulted the media.

Darcy had prepared the meatballs late that afternoon, after the sauna run-through, and was now making the sauce. She began by prying open big cans of crushed tomatoes and sizzling onions and garlic in the biggest saucepan in Jules's kitchen's repertoire. Then, unsatisfied with the size of the saucepan, she'd switched over to a cauldron, delicately placing the meatballs into the bubbling sauce on the stove to marinate with a slotted spoon. There they bubbled, pink-raw and dotted with herbs, like dirty snowballs.

"Can Vivienne have some?" Darcy asked Sasha, gesturing to a piece of meat that had detached from its ball and was braced against the side of the stove.

"Of course she can," Sasha said, flicking the chunk of meat onto the floor. Vivienne lapped it up eagerly, waited for more. When Darcy wasn't looking, Sasha gouged a chunk of meat out of another meatball with a spoon and pushed the mangled meatball under the surface.

Sasha got to work crafting a tiramisu, pouring a shallow bath of Jules's rum into the leftover morning coffee and ripping open the package of ladyfingers. She creamed the mascarpone and the sugar to assemble the dessert, dipping each ladyfinger in the alcoholic coffee for exactly fifteen seconds and then laying it gently against the layer of cocoa powder she'd sifted into the pan.

She was working overtime to establish herself as the housewife of the trip, to earn her keep by setting out the snacks and sponging the table after every meal. Darcy could make the sauce, sure, but Sasha was the one who would shovel the leftovers into Tupperware containers at the end of the night.

Once the tiramisu was chilling, she poured the rum-laced espresso into a few miniature mugs, as a sophisticated touch, and handed them out to Jesse, Miranda, Jules, and Lou, who were catatonic on the couch in front of the TV.

They sniffed the mixture suspiciously before setting their small mugs down on the coffee table, promising Sasha that it was delicious, but they'd drink it slowly over the course of the episode. Worried, Sasha asked if anyone wanted creamer to soften the taste a little, and Jesse said that would be good, so she returned with the coconut creamer from the Hannaford run and poured a little bit into each mug. "That's better," Jules said generously, dutifully finishing her cup.

The Real Housewives of New Jersey was playing. The Italian American stars had returned to the homeland. Satisfied, Sasha sat down to watch. The curly-haired Italian American princess and her family were in Milan. They were shopping. They were eating Italian food and squawking at all the pigeons. The episode didn't hold Sasha's interest. Watching someone else shop depressed her. She returned to the kitchen to start on the eggplant parmigiana, which required an hourlong process of salting the eggplant, breading it, frying it, and then baking the entire dish.

A few minutes after five, the sauce ready on the stove and the eggplant parmigiana bubbling in the oven, everyone emerged downstairs in their Italian American Christmas outfits. Lou was dressed in an approximation of Furio from *The Sopranos*, with a vintage Armani suit jacket and shearling loafers, while Sasha channeled Carmela Soprano in a leopard-print top, pink track pants, and strappy vintage Prada heels.

Darcy had gone the futchy '90s-Marisa-Tomei-meets-*RHONJ*-season-1-Teresa-Giudice route, in a swirly navy suit jacket and assless leather chaps, under which she wore a pair of tiny black underwear. Jesse and Jules, meanwhile, had both gone for a Guido look, though they'd navigated to two separate poles of the Guido aesthetic: Jesse had the slightly prissy, muscle-bound, gym-tan-laundry look popularized by *The Jersey Shore*'s Pauly D, while Jules had dressed as a greasy and buff mobster in a white ribbed undershirt and baggy trousers, hair gelled back into a severe helmet. The kind of straight-shooter who wasn't afraid to get his hands dirty; this guy dipped comfortably under the greasy hoods of both cars and clits.

It was Miranda who surprised them all, emerging from upstairs after they'd assembled in the kitchen. She'd dressed as Adriana La Cerva of *The Sopranos*. From bottom to top, she wore: black stilettos which elevated her to a teetering five-eight; a tiny miniskirt that showed off her supple calves, slender thighs, tiny waist, and slim hips; and, perhaps most shockingly, on top, nothing but a thick leather belt wrapped tightly across her small breasts, heaving them up into two ample, rounded muffin tops pressed together in a remarkable crease of Italian American décolletage.

"Hello, boobies," Jules drooled, sidling up to Miranda and kissing each tan muffin top with maestro energy.

She'd teased her hair into a puffy, curly mane and applied a smokey eye with an expert's sense for shading.

"Fuck," Darcy said. "You look *good*."

"Adriana?" Lou asked.

"Call me Rosa Complicata," Miranda said.

"Those are gorgeous," Jesse supplied. "They're a Gallica rose variety. Very healthy roses."

"*Luhv* the wifebeater," Sasha praised Jules.

"Undershirt," Jesse corrected. "We're calling it a ribbed undershirt now."

"Ugh, seriously?"

"Yes, seriously!" Jesse planted a wet kiss on her cheek.

"Whatever, social justice warrior," Sasha said, smizing at Jesse.

"I'm not an SJW!" Jesse insisted. "I just don't think we have to say 'wifebeater.' It's gross."

Sasha experienced a surge of tenderness toward Jesse, who had once cried from guilt after accidentally dropping a bedazzled swan figurine on Sasha's head.

"You should do that with your boobs," Jesse said to Sasha, with some awe in her voice, and Sasha acquiesed politely while privately noting that there was no way in hell a flimsy belt would ever be able to hold up her tits. "Boobs out for Italian Day."

They stood, stiff in their costumes, around the table to feast. Sasha gestured at everyone to sit.

"Enough of that," Sasha said. "Stop hocking my boobs."

Jesse produced her Dysphoria B Gone herbal tincture, an amber vial gifted to her by one of Lou's vendors, and squeezed a droplet under her tongue.

Sasha thought of the abandoned Grinch nude. And the libel Jesse had spewed during yesterday's therapy session. She looked down onto her plate, which contained a heaping serving of eggplant parm and a pile of plain spaghetti.

"If I'm butter, if I'm butter, if I'm butter, then he's a hot knife," Jules crooned, harmonizing with Fiona Apple's "Hot Knife," which played absently on the record player in the corner. She had started drinking just after breakfast.

"If I get a chance, I'm gonna show him that he's never gonna need another, never need another," Lou, a Fiona Apple fanboy, responded good-naturedly.

"Wait, is there any way we could support you? In taking your top off?" Jules offered Sasha naughtily, belatedly getting into the game.

"Babe, she said that's enough," said Miranda the futch interpreter.

"Abbondanza abbastanza!" Jules gesticulated.

"What's that?" Jesse asked.

"Enough abundance," Jules translated. "It's like: we have what we have; what we have is plenty; and so we have everything."

"That's really nice," said Sasha, meaning it.

"I'm a hot knife, I'm a hot knife, I'm a hot knife, he's a pat of butter," Jules trilled softly, tucking into her spaghetti.

Before they could finish dinner, Darcy whipped out her camcorder and insisted on doing a series of photoshoots and videos: Vivienne with the eggplant parmigiana, Jules and Jesse grinning and holding a platter of spaghetti and meatballs like dynastic Italian American restauranteurs (father and son, maybe, or older/younger brothers). Darcy directed Sasha to plunge her heel directly into a meatball that had fallen on the floor, and Darcy filmed as the meatball broke apart, Vivienne lapping up the crumbles of meat, bits flying out of her lips and coating her chin.

"Ew," Sasha said, prying off the heel to rinse it off in the sink.

The last set of portraits to be taken before dessert were the family pictures: Darcy had a vision of them arranged in different permutations in front of the big fireplace. First she went by couple, posing Miranda with Jules; and then Sasha and Jesse—Sasha with an arm on the mantel, Jesse crouched beside her, and Vivienne sitting sloppily in front of them, tongue out, thirsty from the meat.

Darcy asked Jesse to take the picture of her and Lou, and in it she grabbed Lou's waist from behind like a deranged prom photograph. Once Jesse got the shot, she began humping Lou's ass jokingly, and even Sasha, in that moment, was alarmed by the extent to which she found Darcy sexy—the way her calf twitched, the un-self-conscious way she gyrated her hips—and her movements stirring.

"Brothers!" Darcy called, done with her humping. Lou and Jesse gamely approached the fireplace and posed fraternally together while everyone laughed.

Darcy took father-and-sons photos of Jules, Jesse, and Lou next, forcing Sasha and Miranda to pose as "the Mob wives." By this time Sasha was furious that her tiramisu was getting warm on the table, but she gritted her teeth and complied. She needed these pictures to come out well. She didn't want an unflattering image of her to exist on Darcy's camcorder.

"BRB, making these into porn," Darcy trilled.

"Give me more!" Jesse coached gruffly from the sidelines like a field hockey coach. Sasha angrily angled her body this way and that while Miranda stood stiffly beside her, smiling lightly, having no idea how to embody *Mob wife*.

The last photo, set on an iPhone timer, was of all six of them, plus Vivienne, in the familial recreation they'd fantasized for the house: Jules as stolid patriarch and Miranda as maternal matriarch; Jesse and Lou as their boys, good-natured brothers; and Sasha and Darcy as their wives, feuding sisters-in-law who had it out for each other.

"Merry Christmas," Darcy said, laughing and burping at the same time.

It occurred to Sasha that maybe it was weird they were all

here instead of with their families. But of the six of them, Jesse, Sasha, and Miranda were Jewish; Jules was a WASP from Washington, DC, whose parents took an annual Mediterranean cruise this time of year (they weren't close); Lou's family was California communist-atheist (*Your parents are, like, Leninists*, Sasha once overheard someone say to Lou); and Darcy was Eastern Orthodox, meaning her Christmas wasn't until the following week, fashionably late and, she assured them, more fun and elaborate than the Americans'. She'd be flying back to Los Angeles for her mother's annual party.

The movie they decided to watch before bed was not one of the Italian American classics they'd been floating (*The Godfather*, *Rocky*, *My Cousin Vinny*). The Italian American moment had passed, everyone slumped onto the couch to digest the carb-heavy meal. Jesse made the executive decision to put on *Boys Don't Cry*, the 1999 Americana drama starring Hilary Swank as Brandon Teena and Chloë Sevigny as Lana Tisdel, while everyone else scrolled on the phones they'd left in the couch cushions before dinner, catching up on texts and Instagram stories.

"Tell the story of the dress," Jesse urged when the movie began to play. "Sasha *has* Chloë Sevigny's old dress," she added.

Usually, Sasha's favorite thing was Jesse bragging about an object she had. It made her feel not just like an accessory, but like something even fringier, an *accessory*'s accessory.

"She gave it to you?" Miranda's eyes, scrubbed clean of Complicata's makeup, were wide.

Sasha told her no. "I wish. I just bought it."

"You've seen it," Jesse informed them. "She wore it to the Kentucky Derby party last May."

"How much did it cost?" Jules wanted to know.

"That question is femmephobic, Jules," Darcy fake-lectured in what Sasha took to be a mild imitation of Sasha's own voice (as though that were an argument she would ever make!).

The dress was made by Comme des Garçons and The RealReal verified the dress as having belonged to Chloë. Sasha never saw it in the store. The experience of encountering it online was almost more special because of the big bold letters, the self-conscious fangirling of the announcement.

It was dark red, thin wool, with big black hearts all over it. Midi length, crew neck. The midsection was cut out, strung together with ruched leather strips at the waist, so that your abs, if you had them, showed through. The RealReal listed it as extra small, a US 2. Chloë's size. Sasha had been too scared to measure herself and confirm that the dress wouldn't fit, so she didn't, banking on the dress's stretchy material. In the days after ordering, she kept revisiting the page to go over the listing details.

Fabric: 100 percent wool; combo 95 percent polyester, 4 percent nylon, 1 percent polyurethane.

Condition: Very good. Slight fading at underarms; light wear throughout.

Sasha believed in the transformative power of objects. Material things were important. She had known Chloë's height—five-eight—and her weight—130 pounds—not to mention her bra size (34B)—for years; knowing celebrities' measurements had become a party trick of hers, and Chloë's measurements were among the first she'd committed to memory.

How did Sasha love Chloë? Let her count the ways. Chloë Sevigny first appeared in *Kids*, Larry Clark's film about New York and HIV, and became a muse at the elite fashion house Miu Miu; she interned at the now-defunct magazine *Sassy*, precursor to Tavi Gevinson's *Rookie*, in the early '90s, when she was seventeen. *Our intern Chloë has more style in her little finger* . . . one photospread was captioned, the spread featuring Chloë in all sorts of funny hats; in one photo she wears a short black dress and sheer black tights, her thin legs pressed together; she's identified as an It Girl. In *The Last Days of Disco* she is Alice, a stylish publishing employee entrenched in the world of early 1980s disco, and most importantly she is Lana Tisdel in *Boys Don't Cry*, with long red nails and an FTM boyfriend whom she loves so, so much.

There she is in *Boys Don't Cry*, singing karaoke in an oversized T-shirt and jeans at a seedy rural Nebraskan bar in the mid-'90s. Brandon Teena is new to town. At the karaoke bar, on that still night, nobody knows about the violence that will eventually unfold—the murders of Brandon, who is trans; along with his friend Phillip DeVine, who is Black; and a woman. Three unthinkable murders, a hate crime that will inspire this movie (though the movie elides the detail of Phillip). But here, in the Hudson house, it's still the beginning of the movie, the promise of love is still alive. In the bar, there's just Chloë and two of her small-town Nebraska friends sadly singing "The Bluest Eyes in Texas" on a Friday night. Everyone is a little drunk, a little sloshy. Brandon watches Chloë as a country girl named Lana, a girl with a severe side part and big blue eyes. He sees the sadness hot on her face, the moodiness, the sweetness.

As Brandon and Jesse and Jules and Miranda and Darcy and Lou and Sasha looked at Chloë Sevigny's sad singing face, Sasha sensed that she—Chloë—was the only woman alive who was ever this loved.

"Every so often I try to find a video of the real-life Lana," Sasha said. "But I can't even find a picture."

Darcy pulled one up quickly on her phone, revealing that

Sasha had been speaking hyperbolically. There was one unsatisfying photo of Lana online. Everyone took a turn looking at it.

"Huh," Jules said. "She doesn't have quite the star power of Chloë."

"I feel like that's just the nature of Chloë playing you," Sasha argued. "You'll always pale in comparison to her, but the comparison itself is flattering."

Darcy fast-forwarded through Brandon's rape because no one wanted to see it. They were all still scrolling on their phones, though, so it wasn't like they were paying that much attention to that scene anyway. Darcy's finger on the fast-forward button was performing her aversion to the rape; she fast-forwarded out of principle, not real pathos.

Chloë was a sort of insider object among Jules, Miranda, Sasha, and Jesse. Sasha wondered if that was why Jesse had chosen this movie. After meeting Jules and Miranda at the Derby party, the four of them had staggered drunkenly over to the Performance Space for the after-party of a gala Chloë Sevigny had hosted.

The party was crammed with New York's artistic queer elite, A-listers Sasha didn't recognize but definitely knew were famous, a well-known DJ here and a famous sculptor and dance artist there. Some people were in extravagant costumes, and so was Sasha; Sasha was dressed as a straight-woman movie star; she was gender-bending, whether an observer would have appreciated it or not. Her hair was in a little bun at the middle-back of her skull (like a straight woman), a few tendrils artfully separated from the bun and curling around her neck (again, like a straight woman).

Before the party, Sasha had only seen Miranda and Jules sitting down, in the context of a straight bar. Everything was different at the Performance Space. Jules was talking to a semi-famous dyke DJ with a thin mustache that they stroked compulsively. Sasha saw that Miranda was donning, underneath the cardigan she'd been wearing at the chilly straight bar, an emerald green dress with buttons proceeding diagonally down her chest, stopping at her left hip bone, which jutted out from her body and made a neat tent in the fabric of her dress like a tiny erection. Her face was round, with sharp cheekbones, a tight dark bun at the nape of her neck (like Sasha's, but the lesbian version with off-kilter placement). Big brown eyes with long eyelashes, set deep within her cherubic face, and sexy dark bags under her eyes alongside the beginnings of crow's feet near her temples. She was juggling two very full cups of wine and a silver wallet. Her nails were short and unpolished.

She was, in a word, melm.

Melm was a term Sasha used to describe a certain aesthetic among women in Brooklyn and other places like it. Melm was normcore, kind of, but with a flash of inspiration, a speck of luminosity that still maintained a self-conscious gesture at messiness.

At first she'd thought that the word must already exist, and that it was probably of German origin. Something akin to the Danish word *hygeelit*. When she googled the word *melm*, she was pleased to see that it, too, was Northern European—Dutch, rather than Danish—meaning dry earth or thin sand.

Melm was those girls who stood in line for coffee or whatever scrolling their phones with a chewed thumbnail bearing a chipped manicure (Sasha called this a *stubicure*—melm 101), most of their hair corralled into a cloud scrunchie, platform Skechers, a sheer blouse over a white bikini top, argyle socks in gym shoes even when no exercise was to be done, denim skirts from France worn a touch too long, weird stretchy tube tops, baggy button-downs over loose gray jeans. Melm was feminine, sure, but it was styled to keep something messy. Anachronistic but not twee. Melm girls were named Nicole and Emily and Isabel.

The only mention of the word *melm* Sasha could find online was an old Urban Dictionary entry, dated July 3, 2003: "The coolest thing ever. You cannot even compare to its coolness." That seemed right to her, actually. The reason you couldn't compare to its coolness was because melm was something you recognized after the fact, not something you intended to produce. Melm was tonal, aesthetic. It wasn't so much the content of the look as much as how one felt glimpsing it. At the after-party, Chloë Sevigny was lingering in the corner, a beautiful wallflower dancing intimately with a female friend, their bodies interlocking and separating as fluidly as cells dividing under a microscope. The way her body moved, intertwined with her friend's and on its own, was like nothing Sasha had ever seen before—sexy and confident *but also* girly, *but also* butch.

Chloë was hilariously wearing the inverse of Sasha's own dress (Chloë's old dress—and so by the associative property, Chloë was wearing the inverse of her own old dress): a black minidress with red frilly hearts everywhere, white fishnets on her legs, and white fishnet gloves threaded with red ribbons.

Sasha shuffled nervously in her wool dress that had come directly from the closet of Chloë Sevigny, one of Jesse's hands at her back. Sasha was wearing a dress Chloë had thrown away, while Chloë was wearing the updated heart dress, this season's hearts. She had upgraded her look. Sasha was there to stand as a delegate representing the 2016 Chloë, while Chloë was being the 2019 Chloë. Sasha was to stand on the side of history, to represent the past. Sasha was there to demonstrate the very spirit of *vintage*. She was unsteady on her feet, flushed and a little drunk, watching Chloë dance. People came up to her and

she engaged them, then released them back into the swamp of
the crowd.

Jesse kept telling Sasha to stop staring. But she couldn't; she
was spectacular, and Sasha had, while watching Chloë, lost
all sense of herself. She was a lifelong starer. It was generally
accepted that the one who stares is uncool and the one who is
stared at is cool, but Sasha didn't feel uncool staring at Chloë. She
felt instead profoundly lesbian, seen-by-butch, seen-as-femme.
Maybe a better word for it was *dykette*, containing both the
butch's gaze and the femme's stare—because, of course, they're
looking at each other. It's not a stare from below, the lesbian
stare, but a pure wanting, a desire whose direction is always in
flux. Finally, Chloë made a move. She bisected the room, coming directly into their path. Jesse and Sasha both froze. They
didn't know how to handle themselves; Jules and Miranda, who
had once provided cover and camouflage, were gone, getting
more drinks or using the bathroom; and Chloë was walking
right toward them. Sasha and Chloë made eye contact for one
harrowing moment. Chloë did not indicate that she recognized
her old dress. To own so many things was actually to own very
few things; to have so much was to really have very little.

Later that evening, Jules and Jesse bonked heads while bending
simultaneously to examine the expertly sewn crotch panel of
the famous lesbian DJ's pants. They laughed about it for a long
time, the four of them—not including the DJ, who left shortly
after to play their set.

"Babe, I'm tired," Miranda told Jules.

"We're leaving for Hudson in the morning," Jules explained
to Sasha and Jesse.

"Do you have a place up there?" Sasha asked.

"Oh, yeah, we love it up there," Jules said.

"Our place is"—Miranda performed the gesticulations of the desperate—"well, it's kind of a mess at the moment."

"It's a real fixer-upper," Jules said, and Sasha pictured insulation bursting from the floorboards.

"That's nice, though," Jesse said. "To have a place upstate."

"Ha, yeah. If you guys are looking for a winter getaway . . ." Jules let the end of the sentence dangle. It was one of those things that wasn't actually meant to happen, an invitation extended out of obligation and etiquette. It turned out that the alleged shoddiness of the house was, like many other things, just Jules's self-effacing figure of speech.

ৎ ৯

The six of them watched the sex scene from *Boys Don't Cry*, the one where Brandon and Chloë fuck by the river, reverently. In the scene, they are kissing by the river and Brandon takes off Chloë's bra, revealing her puzzle-piece vertebrae. He lays her down in her washed-out jeans and there is a dark mole just above her left nipple, he rubs her breasts and her back arches, showing off her rib cage. The scene transitions quickly to him going down on her—he's still fully dressed in jeans and a button-down—and all you see is Chloë's ecstatic face and her arched back, her two silver cross necklaces at her collarbone, she is coming, she is gasping with pleasure. Brandon comes up to her mouth, kissing her again. He undoes his jeans and before she can see anything he slips his cock into her, and she moans again, throwing her head back, and then there is the crucial moment: the top of Brandon's button-down gapes open and Chloë peers into it. She sees his binder and his chest squeezed into it, she is confused for a second, she is pulled out of her ecstasy, and then she understands and is transported back into her ecstasy; she understands all this, not in a cliché trans-exposure way— "discovering" Brandon's assigned sex and "knowing everything" about him; it's not like that at all—but rather in the same way she is pleasured by this information, turned on by it. It's an existential understanding that says, I knew Brandon was this beautiful creature already, and I love it. She pulls away from him, understanding her role as a dykette, which is to know all of this and to love it. She sits up, still topless, and her long red nails venture exploratorily to Brandon's jeans-clad crotch, rubbing it gently, and she smiles. She smiles because she loves him and what he is, and she smiles some more, because she knows that this is her role, she knows all this and this is why she smiles.

Sasha was just like Lana; could Chloë know from Sasha's gaze that this was existentially true, that they were two of a kind? It troubled Sasha that Chloë could not know this, that there was no way to tell her beyond staring at her last May.

What does it mean to know or to feel who someone is, Sasha wondered while staring at Chloë, both Chloë's face on the screen and, in her mind's eye, Chloë's human face from the after-party.

"It's just us now," Jesse had said after Jules and Miranda made their getaway from the after-party, and Sasha looked into Jesse's face. It was just them now. All night, Sasha had looked away from her, and she was surprised to see that Jesse was still there, as though wholly unchanged.

The credits were rolling now, the music swelling up and up and up. Darcy made a flippant remark about how poorly the movie had aged, but Lou fought back good-naturedly while Sasha shook Jesse awake so they could make their way upstairs.

"I thought it was going to happen tonight, for some reason," Jesse muttered as she galloped sleepily up the stairs.

"What?"

"You know. With Jules and Miranda."

She didn't want to admit it aloud, but Sasha had felt that way, too, when they'd watched the Chloë sex scene. She'd felt the heat of Jules's sweatpants-clad leg besides hers, and the swampy energy radiating off Miranda's body, hot with angst around her relationship. Miranda's dissatisfaction throbbed like a wound in Sasha's crotch.

But noticing all this wasn't cool, not really, Sasha thought as she drifted off to sleep. What WAS cool was simply to LOOK cool, like Chloë did, and BEING cool to the core was really just LOOKING cool to the core, and what WAS cool was, like Darcy, being a METAPHOR for coolness, what WAS cool was ACTING cool, and THIS was the tautology of coolness.

She wondered, as she often did, if Jesse knew this, too, or if she alone was burdened with the true knowledge of Darcy's allure. Sleeping beside her, mouth open, snoring in rhythm with Vivienne, Sasha noted that Jesse looked none the wiser.

PART TWO

Princess

I like their lady horse swagger,
after winning. Ears up, girls, ears up!

Ada Limón,
"How to Triumph Like a Girl"

Venus Envy

༄ ༄

JULY 2019

Sasha loved drama and she loved shiny things, and so on special occasions, she was penetrated by a pearlescent dildo. The dildo, named Pearly, protruded from the stiff ornamental heart at the crotch opening of a leather harness that Jesse made during an experimental leather-crafting workshop at Lou's luxury gift and home goods shop.

Sasha spent years of her life administering blow jobs in a condemned dog park after dark, and so Pearly, whom Jesse wore with the sort of sophistication she admired in butches and found lacking in men, felt to her like a major improvement. Besides, Pearly was pretty. It was flecked with specks of glitter that caught in the light and shimmered, iridescent, under a slick of lube.

What had made Jesse's leather-crafting workshop experimental, Sasha wasn't so sure, although she happily entertained visions of Jesse skinning a beast with her bare hands and scraping fur from flesh with a switchblade and bloody, dexterous fingers. She liked, especially in those early months, to think of Jesse as a hunter, pummeling her with big muscles, ferocious with desire for Sasha's flesh.

Jesse said that everyone in the experimental leather-making workshop had commented on her harness's heart, calling it "so romantic." That made Sasha proud—proud that everyone had been discussing it and, by proxy, her, and proud that the discussion had invoked Jesse's love for her. Jesse had spent hours bent over her tools, breaking her back with the labor of it, hammering and shaping and pressing her whole body weight against the tools to slice the swaths of leather. Jesse was devoted enough to use her muscles—the embodiment of devotion, its physicality undeniable—to demonstrate her commitment to Sasha.

"This is an act of sweet imagination," says the femme in *Stone Butch Blues* who teaches the butch protagonist how to use a dildo. It's a hot scene, the femme coaching the butch to Come Inside and fuck her—she teaches him the right pace, the right pressure, the right way to lock his hips against hers. In the end, she comes, and they are both happy.

The day after the leather-crafting workshop, Sasha had let herself into Jesse's apartment with the Hello Kitty key Jesse had made for her at the local Ace Hardware. She liked following Jesse around hardware stores in those days while he shopped for bolts and wrenches and paint swatches, and he'd recently surprised her by presenting the key during checkout. The key was the wrong shape for the clerk's machine, but he got it to work, and now Sasha had a hyperbolically large bright pink, red-bowed key that she stuffed into her wallet with the smug authority of a live-in girlfriend.

That afternoon, the leather harness lay in a heap on the kitchen counter. Inelegant, like Jesse had dropped it from a great height. Silly as it was, Sasha was scared to touch it. She didn't know what went where; she didn't pay attention to things like that.

But she worked up the nerve to arrange it the best way she knew how. There was the big leather heart, where two of the three leather straps came together, facing out, shielding the wearer's crotch in a false demonstration of demureness.

Sylvie, always on call for news like this, came over to the apartment posthaste to examine the harness. She screeched at its heft, held its weighty Vegetan in her hands.

"Sasha! He loves you!" Sylvie screamed.

"I know." Sasha beamed.

Sylvie stepped tentatively into it, and they both shouted with wicked delight at her deviance until Sylvie took it off. Sasha bragged to Sylvie that everyone else in the experimental leather-crafting workshop had made mundane leather accoutrements, like leashes and collars—standard BDSM fare that was fun, of course, but hardly required the dexterity and creative vision of a strap-on heart harness.

Yes, it was the vision that Sasha loved most of all. The way Jesse had pictured, in the stuffy workshop, the leather crotch that would bear itself against both of their pubic bones once Pearly was fully inside.

Jesse tanned the harness in the hot summer sun for a few days after until it achieved a look of oldness, and then flung it over a big fake white flower in the corner of her bedroom, where it stayed for the next month, untouched, straps straddling the big petals, heart facing out.

At the lesbian beach volleyball tournament on Fire Island, they saw a sun-leathered butch lumbering across the sand with the gait of a beleaguered high-school field hockey coach. They saw fog so dense that they couldn't make out the mainland from the bay. They saw people swarming the dock where ships came into Cherry Grove with their hands cupped above their eyes, shuffling uncertainly toward the ferries when they disembarked. Among them an ancient couple, two women with bandages flapping open on their chins, doddering their walkers down the boardwalk to the beach. They saw pierced and ringed nipples and low, pendulous breasts.

People staggered across the sand holding red, white, and blue piña coladas, a drink that Jesse and Sasha later split 70/30. Sweating lesbians, some lithe but most robust, raced up and down the beach chasing volleyballs. The balls smacked on their forearms and down over the net on their palms, popping on their finger pads as they set the balls gently into the air. *Uhh!* they grunted. *Bump! Set! Spike!*

To the beach, Jesse wore a shirt from a thrift store that said *Real Men's Wear* and vintage board shorts, mustard-colored with swirling brown designs.

"What're those?" an elder dyke asked Jesse on the ferry above the roaring engine, and Jesse said they were random vintage.

"From the seventies," Sasha put in, because it was what she said when she didn't have another answer.

Another ferry seatmate with the trappings of a designer (shaggy hair, nose ring, popped collar) cut in to correct Sasha.

"The graphic design technology on the shorts wouldn't have been available in the seventies," she lectured from behind her '80s wraparounds. "It's nineties-*doing*-seventies."

Sasha was too sun-high and breezed-out to care about botching this piece of fashion history. She fixed her gaze at the shore from behind her own sunglasses (slightly dented red Armani). She had on a red rubber Adidas by Fiorucci skirt and a sparkly cheetah-print bathing suit top whose straps dug into her shoulders, leaving red welts that she'd need Jesse to rub out later that night. She had selected this swim top because Natalya commented that the orange bathing suit top she'd originally tried on in the dressing room at Tokio7 looked like it was struggling—suffering, really—to contain her breasts.

"Burdensome knockers" was Natalya's swift assessment when Sasha tried on the bathing suit.

"Fuck," Jesse said, eyes spiraling with desire when Sasha had reported this. "'Burdensome knockers.' I want to be burdened by your knockers."

Sasha too wanted Jesse to be burdened by her knockers, withstanding the burden like a big cat pacing herself over the carcass of a gazelle.

Exciting news! LezVolley posted on its Instagram the morning of the tournament. Pictured was a bottle of Bumble and Bumble hairspray foregrounding a beach, gay pride flag fluttering in the breeze. *All players will get @bumbleandbumble surf spray bottles in their welcome packages—so they can avoid the "hair struggle" of spending 5 hours on the beach of Fire Island!*

Sasha wasn't sure why hair struggle needed to be in quotation marks, as though it was a euphemism for something else, something distinctly lesbian and probably sinister. In fact, everything about the tournament was extremely literal, and exactly what they'd been promised: lesbians playing volleyball on the beach, lesbians swimming, and lesbians spectating. After a few hours on the island, after they ate their picnic lunch on the beach and settled in to watch the teams warming up, Sasha's thick hair had whipped around the sand and salt-filled air so much that it was coarse as a felt blanket. Literal hair struggle, no quotation marks needed. But Jesse kept telling her it looked sexy.

"Volleyball is such a femme sport," Jesse observed.

Jesse was at that time in a short-lived LHB (long-haired butch) phase, though she would never have used Bumble and Bumble hairspray no matter the length of her hair. She wore her chin-length strands greasy and pushed back, only using a fancy yet butch combination shampoo and conditioner ("for men") that she'd gotten from a set.

"Tell me I look sexy with my hair pushed back," Jesse said sometimes, pseudo-quoting Aaron Samuels from *Mean Girls*. On cue, Sasha would reply, "You look sexy with your hair pushed back."

But once, a few months before the tournament, Jesse had found a ponytail holder with a long blond braid affixed— some sort of child's Disney Princess costume. She'd tied it to her low butch bun and left it dangling down her back for a fashion event. Sasha hadn't liked the braid, told her in hushed tones as models in terrycloth dresses pranced around a Lower East Side playground, that it made her look like a pedophile, a comment that had mired Jesse in gay shame and for which Sasha had to apologize not once but twice at Mission Chinese afterward.

The real reason Sasha didn't like the braid was that it reminded her of something she herself would have worn—was she jealous of the braid, resentful that Jesse had found it first?

"Just look at Double Zero," Jesse was saying as they watched the tournament, to prove her point that volleyball was indeed a femme sport.

They fixed their attention on Double Zero, a member of the team I'd Hit That. True to her name, she was a blond-cheerleader

type in tiny pink spandex and oversized tinted sunglasses that
somehow stayed on her head even as she spun and slid.

Sasha was a puddle in Jesse's lap. She was getting severely
sunburned, yet because of the fog she felt cozy and swaddled
in warmth. She nuzzled her face into Jesse's neck. It smelled
like fish.

Double Zero was surprisingly deft on the court despite her
prissy looks, fastidiously monitoring the out boundary and racing toward balls that lay inside the court's bounds. This was
impressive—her "hustle," as Jesse called it.

"Do you think she's hot?" Sasha asked, lazily swiping her
hands across the sand to dig a moat around the two of them.

Jesse reminded Sasha that she didn't like blondes.

There was an attractive couple a few feet away from them
on the sand, and Sasha began to study them: the long-legged
dykette in a *Baywatch* red one-piece and her sinewy LHB girlfriend, setting up camp with the beachside bells and whistles
of the truly prepared: a beach umbrella, foldable chairs, a cooler
filled with beer and seltzer.

The long-legged girlfriend was putting on a show, shrieking
and running around with her limber legs, collapsing from time
to time on her girlfriend's lap. Sasha glared over at her, unable
to work up the energy to be actually angry. The LHB tried to
get her girlfriend to sit still, shushing her, but she struggled
and thrashed, and then she was off running again, toward the
water, her screech vibrating like a siren as she got farther and
farther away.

In the distance, a different tall butch, this one in red sneakers, sat pensively facing the water, in clear defiance of the volleyball games. They were disengaged from the championships
in such a way that suggested antipathy rather than ambivalence,

like maybe they'd been ousted from one of these teams, or their enemy had just won a match.

"Don't go," Jesse pleaded suddenly, returning to an argument they'd been looping through, but there was a self-aware futility to this request. The plan was in motion, the Providence apartment rented, the courses selected.

"It's only a few hours on the train," Sasha said.

"Five years! Or six!" Jesse recited.

Sasha would only be on campus for two of those years, she reminded Jesse. But Jesse valued instant gratification.

"I'm going down to the water's edge," Sasha announced, struggling up on the sand and turning toward the water.

She trekked across the rolling beach hills, arriving where the ocean lapped at the shore. It was cooler here. She stared out into the sea, keenly aware of the long-legged, red-suited girl by her side. She stole a glance at her compatriot: a lumpy, sexy nose; bronzed shoulders with a tight bicep; moderate mounds of breasts straining gently against the fabric of her red bathing suit (30B or, in the spirit of generosity, 32C).

The *Baywatch* girl was splashing around in the froth. She was having so much fun totally alone. But she wasn't alone, not really. Sasha moved slightly to the left to avoid getting wet.

"Sah-ree!" the girl called over to her.

It was then that Sasha noticed the girl's left hand. The shimmering orb of the engagement ring, a rock affixed to a thin band. Her nails weren't polished, but they were neat, with a little bit of white showing at the ends. Not dirty, not particularly clean.

Around Sasha's other side—her bad side, she fretted—the angsty butch in red sneakers appeared. The three strangers were flashes of red strobing on the beach: Sasha's skirt, the girlfriend's bathing suit, and the butch's sneakers.

"Hi."

Sasha turned toward the butch on her left. Their face was streaked with the fine lines of early middle age, soft in the way Sasha found comforting.

"Hi," Sasha managed.

She waded prettily into the Atlantic ocean. The water was choppy and cold as it rushed in from the foggy horizon. She could only stand it for a few seconds, crashing around her hips, before retreating to the shore.

"Oh, god." The butch was staring at her.

"What?"

"You have—you're—"

Sasha looked down. She'd worn her Thinx period underwear into the water under a pair of mesh spandex and now a trickle of watery blood slid down her leg.

Sasha laughed mightily, swiping away the blood with her palm, and the butch laughed, too. The girlfriend splashing in the froth looked over to see what was going on and said, "Oh my god, do you need a tampon or something?"

Arms protectively encircled Sasha's waist. Jesse had come up from behind, stalking the sand so quietly that Sasha shrieked. Sasha pointed out the remains of the trickle to Jesse, who said she wanted to lick it up, and suddenly they were back on, back in the game.

"You were almost shark meat!" the *Baywatch* girlfriend screamed over to Sasha.

Emboldened by Jesse's presence, Sasha called out to the girlfriend, "I like your ring!"

She bounced giddily over, the tops of her small boobs jiggling wildly.

"It's silly," she said, sticking out her left hand so that they could get a better look at it. "But it makes me happy."

Her girlfriend, the LHB manning their towel and snacks atop

the sandy hill, waved gaily at them. The other butch looked down at the sand and shuffled away, defeated.

Jesse told a story—primarily to Sasha, but also to the long-legged girl still within earshot—she'd read about sharks. A group of rich people were tasked with transporting a friend's yacht from Maryland to Florida in the 1980s, when a severe storm made the yacht capsize miles from the Atlantic coast. Luckily, the friends were able to take shelter on a small life raft. They lingered there, hungry and thirsty, for days. One man had suffered injuries in the accident and bled continuously into the bottom of the boat, under which a group of sharks was silently congregating. One man went mad and announced that he was going to get some beer. He jumped off the side of the boat. His friends heard him being devoured by the sharks for about twenty minutes. The man with the injured leg died of blood poisoning. Another man said he saw sand and was going to swim to the shore. He jumped off the boat, and his friends listened to *him* get eaten alive by the sharks, too. Just as the two remaining survivors were gearing up to eat their dead friend, they were happily rescued. The story was in the news again because it was going to be made into a TV film for Shark Week.

"I hope you know I won't accept a generic ring," Sasha joked to Jesse as they walked along the beach.

Jesse agreed. She said that she was going to fashion a ring with the help of a lesbian gem-cutter she'd heard of in New York. She suggested a rose quartz heart with a tiny blue star to complement her dyke-jock anklet tattoo, and to pay homage to the Buffalo butch-femme community in their favorite ethnographies.

Sasha's ex, threatened by the loose friendship she'd had with Jesse before they started dating, had once said that the two of them were *almost like soul mates*. On Co–Star, they were a perfect match in every single category—love, intellect, aggression—except for their basic identities. Sasha's sun sign was Gemini, and Jesse's was Pisces.

"It's hotter this way," Jesse said after they'd finally worked up the nerve to look at their charts together.

"You should always be fundamentally incompatible with your boyfriend," Sasha theorized, manufacturing relief.

As Sasha continued to free-bleed, Jesse stooped to pick up her hundredth purple shell for her large collection of shells and buttons.

As they marched down the beach, waves lapping at their feet, Sasha composed a song to the tune of Carrie Underwood's "Before He Cheats" about Jesse sleeping with other women when Sasha started graduate school:

> *Right now, he's probably brewing her some fruity little seltzer*
> *cuz she can't drink dairy*
> *Right now, he's probably lying on her small boobs saying, "I*
> *wish you were Sasha"*
> *Oh, but she don't know . . .*

Here she made her hands into claws and widened her eyes, reaching a fever pitch. It was a reference to the times that Sasha had scratched Jesse's entire body with her long fingernails, leaving marks that made Jesse's soccer teammates wonder what she'd been up to at post-practice sauna sessions.

It made Sasha sick to think of Jesse being as fundamentally incompatible with someone else as he was with her—him being marked by someone else in the way she'd marked Jesse, retracing the lines she'd already traced.

The purpose of the song had been to satirize the inevitable, to make it funny. They were scared of what would happen when Sasha went three hours north to study bimbo literature. But as they sang, over and over again, in a tone-deaf monotone as they stalked the beach, Sasha felt sick to her stomach. She made Jesse promise not to use Pearly on any other women, people Sasha referred to as "conquests," like Jesse was a missionary or a crusader.

Sasha focused on a couple cheering from the sidelines, a woman shaking blue-and-pink pom-poms with the meaty hand of her girlfriend, potbellied and bronzed with a blond fur pelt atop her head, clamped around her neck.

"Of course I won't," Jesse said. "You're my one and only, Sashabird."

But she was too good at playing along, that was the problem. She never knew how much of the joy they experienced was material and how much was fantasy. That had always been the problem and would always be the problem.

That night, back in Jesse's apartment, their skin was hot to the touch. Jesse peeled off her shirt, revealing red shoulders, picked Sasha up, and carried her into the bathroom. She placed Sasha on the sink, against the mirror, and left her there. Sasha's sunburned back twitched with pleasure against the cool glass. When Jesse came back into the bathroom, she'd inserted Pearly into the leather strap. The heart covered her crotch. "If I can't make love to you, and I can't fix what hurts you, then where's my butch magic?" the protagonist asks a femme in *Stone Butch Blues*. "I want to plunge you," Jesse said, and Sasha thought, *Like a toilet!* Jesse sucked at Sasha's neck, sore and red from the burn, sliding her tongue over the tendons. Her hands were everywhere, pushing Sasha's tits up and squeezing them so hard that she cried out, part from pain and part from pleasure, and she grabbed Sasha's waist, finally kissing her mouth, first hard and then soft, filling her mouth with her tongue. Pearly was pressed against Sasha's thigh, digging into the muscle. Jesse pushed her legs apart and slid her fingers into Sasha. "You're so wet," she said, like it was funny, how did you get so wet?

"What do you want?" Jesse said, and Sasha said, "Everything, now."

It was almost like they were soul mates, Sasha reasoned, but not quite and that was the important thing. Jesse slowly eased Pearly in, that initial almost-hurt and pinch, and then began pumping her in and out, the vibrator making a sound like a motor chopping through waves. In and out she went, rocking her hips against Sasha's, her body against the mirror.

While Sasha rinsed off in the shower and Jesse sat on the toilet watching, Jesse said Sasha's sunburn was very sexy. The parts of Sasha that had been covered were much paler than the ones left bare, so it was almost like she was clothed and naked at the same time, like she was wearing a skin bikini, the teenage-boy fantasy of a stripped *Baywatch* girl in Sasha-bird form. And Sasha faced the hungry pervert who was set to devour her, just like a thing to be fucked, just as she'd already been fucked by the sun.

Arm Candy

ço ço

Jesse had taken to gluing Sasha's fake eyelashes onto his chin. It was a triumphant but humble suggestion of a beard, the approximate shape and size of Jesse's masculinity, and much cheaper than testosterone. That morning, the beard glistened under Hannaford's artificial yellow lighting. They already needed more bread and fruit, so Jesse had volunteered to go to the grocery store this time. Sasha said she'd keep him company.

Hannaford turned out to be a well-stocked grocery, serene and empty the morning after Christmas. The two of them spent close to an hour under bright lights debating the merits of Cara Cara oranges versus blood oranges, red tomatoes versus yellow, Parmesan versus aged Asiago, brioche versus bagels, basil versus mint, and mint chocolate chip Klondike bars versus Oreo ice cream sandwiches. Jesse and Sasha approached each other with a performative politesse that felt like a relic of their courtship.

"I love salt," Darcy said when they returned home, lifting a jar of gherkins from the teeming paper sack. "Anything pickled or briny, I'm *hella* addicted."

True to their shared California roots, Darcy and Lou both punctuated their speech with the word *hella*, a truncated Bay Area term for *very* or *a lot* initially coined by Oakland rapper Keak da Sneak in his 1996 track "Ring It." Despite having lived in New York for six and ten years, respectively, Darcy (who'd come of age in SoCal) and Lou—born in Oakland in 1989— clung nostalgically to *hella*.

Jesse had picked out things that were intended to please Sasha, either because of their kitsch—she selected a box of snowflake-shaped Cheez-Its, for example, and gravitated toward items with nostalgic appeal, like Babybel cheese wrapped in a wax ball and Froot Loops—or its bougie, novelty appeal (a sixteen-dollar jar of Vermont-tapped maple syrup, fancy balsamic in a glass bottle shaped like a deer). Jesse made everything nice, was the type of guy who'd bring fresh dill to a picnic to sprinkle over store-bought hummus. The gesture made Sasha ache with love. But Sasha couldn't help remembering that Darcy would also love Froot Loops (now Darcy was gushing over the box), given her taste for artifice. Who was Jesse trying to please?

Lou came over to help unload the groceries, and Darcy turned her face to snicker up at Lou. The diminutive nose, the strong chin, the tall and lovely forehead. She noticed Sasha and Jesse watching and drew her body toward Lou, enveloping them in the process so that the two of them turned away together, like they were on the same rotating stage.

Sasha had put the groceries on her new credit card, which had a four-hundred-dollar monthly spending limit; she was trying to build her credit so she could eventually buy her own studio or one-bedroom apartment in north Brooklyn (which, at her current income rate, would take about twenty years). It was a room-of-one's-own urge, and of course she felt properly conflicted about property ownership in gentrified Brooklyn. At the same time, she was hemorrhaging funds in rent every month in Providence. Darcy and Lou each immediately sent Sasha $22.50 on Venmo, one-fourth of the cost, which Sasha transferred to her checking account to avoid feeling like she'd spent such a large sum of money. For his part, Jesse had recently bought her expensive fondue at the Standard and was excused.

Sasha wanted—nay, needed—to appear authentically Russian, a wife from the cold climate of the old country, and show that the food of her childhood was as exotic as that of Darcy's so she was making pierogis and a hearty borscht for lunch. Lou helped her cut precise rounds for the former and fill them with a creamed mixture of potato, cottage cheese, and caramelized onion. Lou worked with the steady hand of an artisan, obsessed not with uniformity, but with making sure each pierogi featured a unique scalloped edge. Jesse's family, third-generation Chicago Polish, had bourgeois cravings for fancy restaurants and nice hotels, but Sasha's family had retained their peasant tastes even as their lifestyle had upwardly mobilized from a two-family in Brighton Beach to the house on Long Island purchased when Sasha was in college.

The meat-eaters—everyone but Sasha and Miranda—had marinated an impressive lamb shank and adorned it with dried herbs and pomegranate seeds. A crock of labneh acquired from the fancy grocery store in Hudson and a bowl of onions caramelized in a full stick of butter, glistening in their fatty bath, complemented the Russian–Middle Eastern meal. Usually dinner was when they feasted, so it was a zing of luxury to indulge like this over lunch. Vivienne had been placed on a sheepskin on the big mahogany dining table and was sleeping in between bites of flatbread, which Sasha had held one by one on the stove until they were greasy and crisp on the outside, soft and chewy on the inside.

Over lunch they talked about nothing; they'd been in Hudson long enough to have stopped speaking in generalities, in recaps of time between their last encounters and this one, and started speaking the language of a shared mundanity— things that happened to all of them, suddenly more or less communally.

While Sasha and Jules cleaned the kitchen, Jesse and Darcy went to work in the sauna to rehearse for the show on Monday (an objectively creepy day to produce pornography). Sasha, undone as she'd ever been, hauled her grief-heavy body around the sink and the countertop while she sponged, imagining what was transpiring ten yards beyond the kitchen.

Darcy was definitely languishing on the ground, naked and sweating among her pink things. The glistening sheen over Darcy's body was definitely making Jesse's groin ache. She stewed and puttered around for a couple of hours, tried to read, tried to write. Nothing worked.

Only two months earlier, Jesse had presented Sasha with a teeny-tiny glass pink pacifier he had found on the sidewalk and attached to a thin gold chain.

"A necklace for my baby girl," Jesse said. Sasha let Jesse secure it around her neck, on top of her green Chanel ribbon.

"Not for her?" Sasha narrowed her eyes and pursed her lips, peeking down at the pink object.

"Of course not," Jesse said. "You're my baby, not her."

"But will I always be? We won't become one of those couples who gets divorced?"

"Of course not."

"How do you know?"

Jesse *shhh*-ed her, and sang out with levity: "We'll always be young, and we'll always be in love."

What even is the "dirtbag left," Sasha complained to Sylvie, curled up with her phone in the living room during the dull hour before dinner. It was a question that had been bothering her. She didn't like not understanding things; she just liked pretending she didn't understand them.

It's the leftists who are into being funny and offensive and hot, Sylvie replied instantly. *Marxist in a funny way. They're like all trying to be the new Kathy Acker.*

She called Darcy a "manufactured woman," testing out the phrase, but Sylvie wrote, *No, I actually don't think that's it.*

I don't think that's what you hate about her, actually, Sylvie continued after a beat. *You don't hate me and my fake tits and perfect pussy. And you don't hate yourself for all your aggressive styling. All women are manufactured.*

This was true; she was obsessed with the feminized minutiae, and what was Sylvie talking about if not that exact thing?

Of course, Sasha hastened to reassure Sylvie. *I don't hate you, I love you. It's not about the procedures or the surgeries. What I hate is her beauty, her* appeal. *Actually I'd hate it more if it were "all natural." What's so gross about her is how she was born with it, for the most part. The enhancements are the* most *palatable aspect.*

Sasha tried to explain that she felt she must see everything Jesse saw, that they needed to see Darcy's naked body together, as though they shared an entire nervous system, the same pair of ocular nerves and the same brain. Any image he saw must be flipped into Sasha's own brain. There was both no way around this and no way to make it happen.

When Jesse had come into the house after the sauna rehearsal, Sasha had been happy to see him and touch him—relieved to feel his damp skin through his white T-shirt, press her flat knuckles against his hot pink cheeks, wrap her arms around his sticky trunk, grasp his sweaty hair. She'd been eager to tell him about what she'd been thinking about and working on with Sylvie and feed him a chocolate snickerdoodle cookie, the fun treat she'd made while waiting for him to come back. But Jesse's eyes were bright and shifting around the room, distracted; he'd come from having a great time with someone else. Even as she'd hugged him she had felt the tension in his body, his wanting to pull away and shower upstairs.

Now, though the real Darcy was only a few rooms away, Sasha stared at a picture of Darcy in a popular Brooklyn club that featured a wide glass balcony, on which Darcy stood in a matching rose-colored bra, underwear, a silk lingerie robe. Someone had captured her from below, a chain choker glowing around her neck. Darcy had captioned the photo *Welcome to hell*.

Sasha read in her neurotic styles workbook that the terms *paranoia* and *projection* are often used interchangeably. This made a lot of sense to her and seemed pretty obvious. Since the fall, she had experienced a rage that was not blind but all-seeing, miraculously vivid. Now she found that she was able to transcend her own individuality—to see what Jesse saw, to know what Jesse knew.

Sasha and Jesse had once promised each other that they would be absurdly honest with each other, honest even to the point of vulgarity. And honestly, she knew that Jesse wanted to touch Darcy's body, wanted to handle it like a sponge. What he wanted to do was fuck Darcy, because to fuck Darcy would be to travel beyond the dimension that Jesse and Sasha inhabited together, to fuck Darcy would be to be transported out of a love dimension and into a feral one, to fuck Darcy would be to reduce himself to a preverbal state that lacked consciousness and dabbled in the divine.

Sasha was deep in thought, eating from a bag of vegan Cheez-Its on the couch, when Darcy appeared in the doorway.

She held out the box to Darcy, who said, "Oh, thanks, I love fake food."

Sasha gave her the whole bag of them, handing them across the arm of the couch with ceremony. Sasha wanted her to take them just as she had taken Jesse, and she craved for Darcy to see her generosity; there was something thrilling about handing things over to this woman, who already had so much—everything, it seemed—and making a show of depleting Sasha's own resources.

But then, after accepting the snack, Darcy was not looking at her anymore. She was distracted by a tangle in the fringe of one of the blankets tossed over the couch; their interaction had ended. Her ears were small and red, facing the other direction, her shiny hair in a little clips-and-bobby-pins style Sasha would never have thought to attempt.

❧ ❧

After dinner, light fare of leftover focaccia dipped in the dregs of the tomato sauce, Lou and Darcy retreated to Bedroom 2 while Sasha and Jesse busied themselves cleaning the kitchen, silently wiping down the tables and rinsing the dishes. Jules and Miranda went to wheel the trash to the curb and carry the flattened cardboard boxes and empty La Croix cans they'd accumulated to the recycling.

Outside the window, a husky voice on speakerphone was trying to sell Jules Todd a miniature horse. The horse in question was a mini pony named Pistachio, who had been rescued and was now looking to be rehomed after some storm damage had been done to the horses' sanctuary.

"You should buy the horse sanctuary," the voice was saying in an insistent, buoyant way. "I'm not saying you have to be responsible for the whole horse sanctuary, but it would *definitely* be nice for you to be around horses."

Jules was acquiescing, but noncommittally, in a way that was engineered to assure this person that she was perfectly capable of buying a horse farm in Nashville if she wanted to, but the issue was—and here she lowered her voice conspiratorially— they were trying to have a baby, and so the horse would be a nonstarter, even though of course Jules loved horses. The other voice loudly assured Jules that horses and babies got along just fine; they loved each other, in fact. Nashville was the perfect place to raise a kid *and* to own horses.

When Jules came back inside, she was still holding the phone up to her mouth, smiling and rolling her eyes.

Who is it? Sasha mouthed, and Jules said, "Hold on, Cate, just one second."

Sasha should have recognized the voice. Her accent was flat and Midwestern, comfortingly provincial. Sasha inhaled, as though she would be able to smell Cate's barbershop scent over the phone.

Jules was telling Cate that she had guests, and that—here she lowered her voice—Darcy and Lou were among them, though she was reasonably sure that they'd retired for the evening. Cate loudly assured Jules, her voice crackling confidently over speakerphone, that she was quite over the whole thing and had recently begun seeing a couple new people, Jules said, "Okay, well, I've got to go—we'll catch up next weekend, yeah?"

They were old friends, Sasha understood, and that meant that there were old feelings of competition that they elicited in one another: two butches in their forties at the center of the same inner circle, one who owned a home in Hudson and was planning on parenthood—an expressionless Miranda trailed Jules—and one who had a timeshare in Fire Island and lived in a studio apartment above her Fulton Street salon. The butches had chosen different paths but longed to see their reflections in the other. Each guy symbolized to the other both the path not taken, the path avoided—for Cate, the path avoided was facile domesticity and mainstream fame, and for Jules it was a tapestry of short-term lovers knit together into some approximation of a love life, lesbian mayor status, and a floor full of bleached hair shorn from various lovers' and friends' scalps—but also the path that could have been, the path that was still in the periphery, still somehow, by virtue of an old friend's having chosen it, an option.

Jules hung up the phone, and her body visibly flooded with relief. She hurtled toward them like a bowling ball, thrashing against the counter and ricocheting forward. She hugged them both at once, and Sasha felt tiny and dizzy in her generous wingspan, pressed into Jesse like cubes of ice in a tumbler.

Sasha always loved when Jules hugged her—big hands, big arms, solid trunk and legs.

Tonight? Sasha asked Jesse telepathically, but Jesse didn't respond.

Jules released them from the hug and got to work boiling water for tea.

Jesse and Sasha were pawns in the older-butch competition of whose burly cardinal wing they'd be swept under. Sasha trembled, feeling like cool plastic between the older butches' fingers. Cate had sheltered Jesse by letting her live in the back half of her studio for cheap, but now Jules was hosting them for the holidays, along with Cate's sort-of ex, Darcy, and the one who'd taken Darcy from Cate (Lou). In this moment, Jules had the upper hand, the greater sway over the younger generation. To retaliate, Sasha knew, Cate was trying to sell Jules on the idea of a horse farm and keep her at a distance, to remind Jules that she was only two to three life choices away from being a guy who left the city to have a kid.

"Anyone know of someone looking to buy a horse?" Jules was saying. "Cate sent me a picture of Pistachio, and she's super cute. Surely someone in our circles needs a mini pony?"

"I need a mini pony," Sasha said. "I'll take her."

"Sold," Jules said.

"I have a patient who's writing her dissertation about horse girls," Miranda said, glancing over at Sasha. "I wonder if they'd be interested. I can ask."

Sasha, hoping to get lucky: "Is that the patient who keeps texting you?"

Sasha wasn't sure where Miranda's boundaries lay in terms of disclosing information about her patients, but she was sure that whatever they were, Miranda would be clear about them.

Miranda shook her head. "That's someone else." To both Jesse and Sasha, she said, "I'm navigating—there's been a difficult patient."

"They're trying to cancel Miranda," Jules said wryly. "For being 'biphobic.'"

"Aren't you bi?" Jesse asked Miranda.

They moved into the living room and sat down on the couches.

"I guess," Miranda said.

"Have you ever seriously dated a man?"

"A couple."

Jules bristled visibly, but Miranda pressed on: "One of them even recently agreed to be our donor. How's that for biphobic."

"Oh!" Sasha had grown gleeful. "Are you trying to—?"

Miranda sighed a world-weary sigh. "I froze my eggs a few years ago, but they say you have a higher success rate if you freeze embryos. I didn't know that at the time, of course, so I'm essentially paying rent for those little guys to live in an industrial freezer awaiting their uncertain future."

Miranda divulged that the previous weekend, she and Jules had FaceTimed with Fernando, an old ex of hers who worked in the archives at UCLA. He'd agreed to be their donor, but tentatively—that he'd have to talk it over with his partner, who might take a while to warm up to the idea.

"No self-respecting straight girlfriend would agree to that," Sasha sighed.

Miranda, ruefully: "Well, we're at the whim of an oral historian, so who knows."

"A *baby*," Sasha said. She still couldn't believe it.

"Wow!" Jesse said. "But when?"

"Maybe imminently," Miranda said, swirling her drink around in her glass. "I don't want to be an old mom."

She was about thirty-eight at the moment (born in 1982 in Teaneck, New Jersey), meaning that by the time she got pregnant she'd be thirty-nine or forty. When the baby was twenty, she would be sixty and Jules, sixty-two. That seemed okay to Sasha, whose own parents were very young—they'd had Natalya, now a therapist, and then Sasha in a span of fifteen months during their early twenties. She peeked over at Jules, whose face was like a mask. None of the dynamic mannerisms or showy expressions that usually dominated her face. Sasha's heart twitched with fear.

"Realistic Mommy," Jesse joked.

"Do you think you could raise a boy?" Sasha mused.

"Well, who knows what they are, really," Jules said from behind her flesh mask in a way that struck Sasha a bit defensive, as though Sasha didn't agree that gender was a construct.

"Right, but a little boy with a little penis," Sasha said.

Miranda said she thought little boys were cute at the same time Jules said, "Honestly, I don't know that I'd know what to *say* to a little boy—" and then stopped in her tracks. They stared at each other.

A current moved between Jesse and Sasha.

Do you think they want to fuck us?

Yeah, definitely.

Now, though?

Not sure—awkward.

"Don't you feel like you were a little boy, though?" Jesse said to Jules. "Maybe it would be easier."

"Kids are fucking expensive," Miranda said, setting her drink down on a coaster on the side table, as though this were the last, definitive word on having children, and despite the fact that she was the one who had initially voiced a desire to mother.

"You have to think of each one as a half-million-dollar investment," Jules said, good-naturedly taking up the other side of the argument, "that will probably never pay off, but at least you get someone to take care of you when you're old."

"Realistic Daddy," Jesse said, laughing, and Jules laughed along somewhat uncomfortably.

"Who's going to take care of you when you're old?" Jules was looking at Sasha now with eyes black and watery, and Sasha looked to her left and right as though there were someone else Jules might be addressing.

Jesse supplied, maybe just to ease the tension, that she knew people who had signed up in shifts to give the famous lesbian filmmaker Phoebe Livingston sponge baths when she was dying.

"So you think you'll have a band of young devotees to take care of you?" Jules asked, still disarmingly good-natured.

"Well, I don't know," Jesse said. "I hope so."

"What about when they have partners to take care of, though? And kids?" Jules pressed.

"I definitely want kids," Sasha clarified, so Jules wouldn't think this was her fantasy, too.

"Being partnered doesn't necessarily mean there's someone to take care of you," Miranda argued airily.

Jules let out a frustrated scoff.

"I just mean like, what if the other one is *also* sick and disabled?" Miranda said.

There was a moment of silence while everyone solemnly pictured the hardships faced by a couple of two elderly, disabled lesbians unable to care for each other in their old age.

"Sure," Jules allowed. "No system is perfect."

ରେ ରୁ

After brushing her teeth and washing her face, sobering up considerably, Sasha settled in Bed 3 with her book. She was reading *Reverse Cowgirl*, a sort of anti-transition narrative in which McKenzie Wark pays studious attention to being fucked, isolating being fucked into the sort of rare hyper-focus that made the words *fuck* and *fucking* sound strange when turned over in Sasha's brain while reading.

"Before someone even tries to fuck someone else, at least according to McKenzie Wark's utopian dream," Sasha told Jesse as Jesse scrolled on her phone, "they will first have to learn how to be fucked."

Sasha liked the high status that Wark awarded to sensation, to the *feeling* of being fucked. Sasha found it rare for a writer to describe both the feeling and the concept in the same breath.

In Sasha's previous relationship, there had been no leather harness or pearlescent dildo. Her ex had fucked her well but sometimes reluctantly or haltingly, and she'd always have to ask if she really wanted to be doing it.

"I want myself to go away," Wark complains to her lover. "Just hold me now. Make me go away."

"I love that," Sasha said to Jesse. "I love the idea of really *feeling* your own annihilation."

"Usually you're so horny for the concept, though," Jesse said, easing another droplet of Dysphoria B Gone under her tongue, "and for you it's less about the sensation itself. You're so into the setup."

"Kay," Sasha said.

She closed the book, sliding her finger into it to mark her place.

"Once," Sasha told Jesse, "when I refused to go fetch a bowl from the kitchen, my ex said, 'I thought you wanted us to have strict gender roles: I'm the man and you're the woman.'"

Fetching was butch, but kitchens were femme. Clearly, as Sasha now explained to a nodding, drifting-off-to-sleep Jesse, Sasha did not want strict gender roles so that she would have to climb out of bed and fetch a bowl from the kitchen. She wanted strict gender roles so the ex would protect her, provide for her, and wear men's clothing.

Back then, they were passing through liberal arts school, where everything existed in miniature, dioramic as it was picturesque: the thin girls blowing bubbles on a sloping hill, playing with dolls and taking Advanced Fiction Writing; the couples using their parents' money to rent apartments in rambling wooden buildings; the people writing at their computers in tiny thesis carrels, fucking each other in dormitory rooms, and producing zines at breakneck speed. The miniaturization of it all, living in a fake neighborhood, had made Sasha feel deserving, or maybe the word for it was entitled. It made her feel entitled to ask for what she wanted, which in those days was for her ex to change, to better suit her desire. This expectation still warped Sasha's perception. It wasn't about her ex at all, but an entitlement native to Sasha—a private shame, to be sure, but a belief that what she wanted was what she deserved.

Wives and Girlfriends

 confetti

They lay in bed until Vivienne was whining at the edge of it, her haunches poised to be airlifted down to the cold wooden floor. Sasha pulled on a housecoat that was sewn from old towels in different shades of pink and snuck downstairs with Vivienne a heavy load in her arms, praying that no one would be awake yet. But of course Jules was in the kitchen, pouring water from a huge liquid measuring cup into the top of the coffee maker with studied focus.

In moments like these—standing face-to-face with Jules in the morning, her hair a nest and her mouth dirty with sleep, crust in Jules's eyes and dark circles peppered with tiny white dots underneath—she understood that her alternate life, the one in which she was Jules Todd's girlfriend, the girlfriend of a *celebrity*, was not actually so different than her current one.

Because the first time she'd seen Jules in real life, Jules had been a celebrity, not a friend. Sasha had cruised the 2017 Lesbians in Media conference on the Lower East Side, where Jules was the keynote speaker. She had her sights more modestly set on the dorky, crew-cut butches she hoped to seduce in order to add a few notches to her belt (she'd only slept with a handful of people) and maybe even do some networking with the Condé Nast cohort, snag some free makeup.

As soon as she got to the conference room in the hotel, checked in at the front desk, and tucked her identification tag into her purse, a lesbian in media asked Sasha about the pattern of her skirt.

"It's not Pucci, is it?"

Sasha replied that she didn't think so. "Just some random vintage from the seventies." (In those days, she didn't own any Pucci.)

"Are you sure?" the woman pressed. "It really looks like Pucci."

Jules's speech at the conference began with the straight-forward tale of her rise. This was to be expected; dykes loved logistics. Jules explained, aided by a barebones PowerPoint, and wearing what Sasha had to assume was a Bindle & Keep suit (a bespoke lesbian suit tailoring business Sasha had just learned about and was now obsessed with spotting in the wild), how she'd been living with friends in a big, drafty house in western Massachusetts to get her bearings after breaking up with her college girlfriend and subbing for her friend's radio show. Sasha took notes lackadaisically, not because she wanted to emulate Jules's career but because she was interested in the idea of the "substitute," an idea that she pondered vis-à-vis its relationship to surrogacy (another practice that had always fascinated her).

When Sasha came to after her surrogacy-induced dissociation, Jules was telling the audience about how the newly retired liberal news personality Michael Lewis—rumored to be gay, though this was never confirmed—began to push for Jules to get her own show. Jules was pacing around the stage like this was a TED Talk, gripping a microphone in her left hand. Then she was joined by an interlocutor, a bisexual *New Yorker* writer who parried thirstily with Jules Todd.

This interlocutor sang Jules's praises, sparing Jules the embarrassment of listing her own career highlights. The reviewers loved her. They called her a tiger, funny, good-spirited, a star. They called her dynamite, whip-smart, uniquely engaging. She wasn't running a typical, dryly liberal show; her show was progressive, startlingly original. It really made you think about the heart of the country's issue in a way that was accessible to both Clinton- and Obama-loving liberals and the rangy, leftist-progressive-socialist types who were cropping up as millennials came of age.

Jules Todd straddled the line, everyone said, and now the interlocutor bragged, between the old liberals and the young leftists; she struck an appealing middle ground that aspired to bridge the gap between two generations of progressives. And while there was the usual online hate—homophobic screeds from right-wingers, disdain from Bernie Bros (Jules was for Hillary, even though she obviously had some qualms about her), and dismissals from younger, more radical podcast hosts and indie news hosts—there was also a massive fan following of converted conservatives and steadfast progressives alike. There was also Jules's personal life, an "out" lesbian with a "long-term partner." The interlocutor called this "visibility," a word that everyone loved then.

The PowerPoint flashed to Jules's first public appearance with Miranda at a GLAAD awards ceremony from the previous year, Jules in her velvet blazer and Miranda in a pale blue silk slip dress, her hair knotted in a lopsided chignon at the nape of her neck. When Jules won the award, the interlocutor gushed, she'd thanked Miranda in her speech, and by the next morning their relationship was public, noted briefly in the

New York Daily News and accompanied by a picture of the two of them, Miranda teetering in her pale blue heels and arranged protectively around Jules's bulky arm.

As a newly minted liberal arts grad, Sasha was supposed to appreciate the work that Jules had done but ultimately—because Jules was not adequately radical or, more simply put, just too old—discard her as "heteronormative," or even Lisa Duggan's term "homonormative," another much-beloved charge in 2017 that as far as Sasha knew just meant "gays behaving like straight people by being domestic."

There was the ideological problem, sure, of aligning oneself with straightness and its attendant bad stuff, but Sasha now, upstate and three years out of school, wanted to believe that you could be domestic and boring in a way that was less trad-wife and more cozily basic.

Because here was the thing: Miranda *was* kinda basic. No-frills. Melm. As they sipped their coffee quietly, Sasha studied Jules more closely than she'd allowed herself to in person. Even though Jules had branded herself as aggressively butch normcore—that day she was wearing a rugby shirt, loose jeans, and her big blocky glasses—you could tell that she was attracted to the shininess of the Brooklyn hipster girls like Darcy in the same way that a rodent was attracted to a gleaming piece of trash on the train tracks. But when it came down to real attraction, Jules had that dyke-from-the-suburbs thing for a basic femme-y girl. Ultimately, Sasha was too glittery for Jules.

So did all this mean that Jules just wanted to date a straight girl? Or maybe a culturally straight girl, a girl whose only non-straight thing was that she was actually gay? Was Jules to blame for the rapid mainstreaming of gay culture, with her appreciation for basicness?

We're experiencing a schism in queer culture, Sylvie once explained to Sasha, *between earnestness and snark*.

Sasha thought as she watched Jules paw through the *New York Times* that like many gays before her, Jules's public prominence assumed the entire burden of a cultural movement.

When Miranda came downstairs in a bathrobe and wet hair, with big dark circles under her eyes and a weary smile, Sasha felt nothing but goodwill toward her.

"Hey," Miranda said, a therapized maturity edging into her voice. She brought a hand to her face and pushed back a hank of hair. "I think I'm going to spend the day getting some work done. Would you let the others know when they wake up?"

"Of course," Sasha said.

Miranda set up her work station in the study on the first floor, by the downstairs bathroom. Sasha had peeked in that morning to see a no-nonsense cherry-stained desk, an ergonomic chair, a slim MacBook computer, and a stack of yellow legal pads, the top one covered in scrawling black pen. She wondered what work Miranda had to do when she wasn't actively talking to clients—insurance paperwork? Monthly statements? Rereading the notes that she'd taken earlier, if therapists even did that? Did each legal pad correspond to one of the clients she'd be talking to that week?

Sasha's sister, Natalya, was a "bad therapist" who had just finished her social work degree—bad as in, she freely discussed the ridiculous things her clients said, only without using their names. Natalya complained about her unshowered, depressed patients stinking up her couch and shared the juicier details of her patients' love lives. She wasn't a therapist because she wanted to help people, she said; she was in it for her own curiosity, which she prioritized satisfying above anything else and which she was most proud of about herself—her endless need to know. Finding things out and seeing what might happen if she did or said certain things was a salve for her.

Sasha doubted that Miranda was the same type of therapist as Natalya, so whenever Natalya and Natalya's profession came up Sasha tried to keep things vague. Natalya was straight, slim-hipped, and fratty and had gone to Dartmouth, where she'd been a beer-pong champion and the source of the men's rugby team strep throat epidemic of 2014. They looked a little bit alike, Sasha and Natalya—dark hair, big deer eyes, round face—but styled themselves so differently that most people didn't realize they were related.

Besides, Miranda was famously trauma-informed, specializing in queer issues and anxiety disorders. On her website, she discussed her areas of interest, which included feminist psychoanalysis, women's issues, and innovative approaches to talking about body dysphoria. In fact, Sasha was fairly sure that Miranda was friends with Jesse's therapist, Faye. That bitch.

രു ൔ

Jules also wanted to get work done that afternoon, and had phone calls scheduled throughout the day.

"Let's check in about how everything's going later, yeah?" Jules asked, laptop tucked under her arm.

"What, with soccer?" Jesse asked.

Jules cocked her head. "Yeah. I wanted to talk through a few suggestions. If you're still down."

"Cool," Lou said.

"I mean, only if you want to," Jules said.

"Of course, Dad," Jesse answered.

"Respect your elders!" Jules rapped the back of Jesse's head, and Jesse's face betrayed a moment of concern.

Jesse drove Sasha, Darcy, Lou, and Vivienne to Kaaterskill. When they pulled into the parking lot, there were almost no other cars there, and they decamped giddily from the Prius, Vivienne sprinting through the frozen grass and trotting into a pile of a previous dog's shit.

Lou and Jesse started kicking a soccer ball around the grounds, before the winding trails through the woods began. Darcy joined in here and there, when the ball flew toward her, but mostly kept her distance.

Vivienne dashed from Jesse to Lou and back again, trying to pounce on the ball. She kept missing, tripping over her paws, and even when she did manage to pounce on the ball in such a way that it stayed still under her paws, she didn't know what to do with it—giving a wide-eyed, startled look and then hopping away, letting the ball roll toward someone else.

Sasha had a show-ponyish personality and a glossy mane, so naturally she'd been eager, the previous summer, to dress in a short black-and-white-striped skirt, a small top, and platform heels, strutting onto the field with two flags from the equipment dyke, waving them mildly in the direction of the team she preferred (the one with the hotter players). She'd done stints as both a cheerleader and a sensual referee for Jesse and Lou's soccer team.

Feeling close to Darcy in their mutual exclusion from the soccer playing, Sasha told Darcy about her longtime dream of being the house mother for a fraternity of butches. She would tenderly kiss each drunken butch forehead after a night of debauchery, get up early to make the butches aeropress coffee (which she'd learned was the preferred method for butches), and even teach them to fuck with dildos like the femmes do in *Stone Butch Blues*. She'd be a full-service house mother, she said. All the better for their electra complexes.

"We should do it," Darcy said. "Start a frat house. I wanted to be in a fraternity so bad in college."

"You did?" Sasha couldn't really tell if she was kidding or being serious.

"Yeah, but instead I just fucked all the sorority girls," Darcy said. Sasha didn't doubt it was true (Darcy could be a womanizer, a femme-for-femme Casanova; this much was well documented), but she sensed that Darcy said this for her own benefit—and maybe Lou's, as they were within earshot—rather than Sasha's. It was part of Darcy's never-ending, continuous narrativizing of her own life: the crazy people she'd fucked or dated, the art she was making.

"In England," Darcy Anglo-splained, "the wives and girlfriends of famous footballers are called WAGs."

Of course Sasha knew what a WAG was. She reached to show Darcy her soccer ball necklace, a relic from the 2005 FIFA world cup that she had secured around her throat that morning. She'd found the necklace on eBay, and it shipped from Japan. Its little crystal pentagons gleamed as she turned it in her hands.

"Ooh," Darcy said. "Can I try it on?"

Proud and only a smidge unwilling, Sasha took the necklace off and reclasped it around Darcy's neck.

"Now I'm a WAG," Darcy tittered.

Wasn't she one already? Sasha could never tell if Darcy's imitation of Sasha was flattering or condescending, like dressing up as Sasha was a cruel joke.

Sasha complained loudly that she was no longer able to feel her fingers.

"Join us!" Lou called out.

They squared off—Sasha, Jesse, Lou, and Darcy, Vivienne still dashing from foot to foot, nearly getting drop-kicked—and kicked the ball around in a way that resembled more of a game. Tacitly, Jesse and Sasha were competing against Darcy and Lou. Jesse passed Sasha the ball, and Sasha punted it in a random direction, where it was intercepted by Lou and shuttled to Darcy.

Darcy wore fashionable, high-heeled Pucci boots that Sasha thought might have impeded her ability to play soccer, but she was coordinated enough to manage it. Every time she kicked the ball, she let out a little giggle, like she was surprised at herself, even though Darcy was at heart a jock—she posted pictures of herself in old soccer uniforms from time to time with a caption like, *i was a gay child ~!*

In Sasha's experience, many dykettes prided themselves on knowing nothing about soccer. Their bit was ignorance, charming innocence—the way they'd cock their heads and say points instead of goals, exaggeratedly unable to tell who was on what team, loudly ask what had happened when the stadium erupted in cheers. This naivete was, Sasha knew, *out*. Jules Todd had decreed it resolutely during her segment the first time she'd talked to Sasha on the TV, when she was at the diner with Jesse. Being smart was in. Being attentive and sharp was in. Bimbo was okay, but you had to have a brain, too. Pretending to be dumber than you were was worse than useless. It was embarrassing.

The struggle of the dykette for Sasha was that she wanted more than anything to be noticed. Recognized. Not even as gay, really—just as pretty. Or as literally anything. But it was also her biggest fear, being scrutinized. Attention was the mechanism through which she would be exposed. Exposed as what, she didn't really know. When a third-grade bully had taunted her, calling her a lesbian and saying that all lesbians were ugly (and so therefore, by the associative property, Sasha was ugly), her mother had hastened to reassure her that that wasn't true—that some lesbians were pretty, like for example her colleague Jean at the hospital. Sasha could be a *pretty* lesbian.

But being a pretty lesbian was like being the woman in the image Jesse had shown her early in their courtship, the naked woman trying to wrap her arms around a big, red, butch cardinal. She, like Sasha, was afraid.

Darcy was able to play in her Pucci heeled boots, but Sasha kept sliding around in her hot-pink Coach ones, so she retreated to the sidelines. When Sasha had acted as the Dyke Soccer sensual referee, she would whisper "That's *out*" sadly to herself, holding the flags aloft even though no one really cared anymore.

Without fail, Sasha felt stupid during those games, tall in a way that was readily apparent and not the much trendier petite. She was flashy, desperate. She was a mistake, a big and useless doll. Jesse wanted her to go away, too. She wished she could go away from her own self, but there was, as always, nowhere to go, no ledge to climb up on. Dykes on the bleachers behind her could see up her short skirt and feast their eyes on the cellulite dimpling her upper thighs and ass, now covered mercifully by her snow outfit.

They decided to take a walk into the Kaaterskill woods. Their lungs were thrumming with cold air, fingers and toes long numb and lost to feeling. Weirdly, they paired off initially not as couples, but as Jesse/Darcy and Lou/Sasha. Darcy was telling Jesse about someone she'd dated in Berlin a few summers back.

"We'd be in bed together, and he'd be angstily smoking a cigarette, like, 'I have to admit that I'm thinking about my ex again, and you deserve my full attention, Darce'—he called me Darce! Darcy is short enough!—and I'm like, 'Emmett, that's un*toward*! You actually *don't* have to tell me every time you think about your primary partner, who I happen to know is both prettier and richer than me!'"

Sasha lingered behind Darcy and Jesse, eavesdropping. Darcy was doing more self-mythologizing, self-narrativizing.

"He has a total Madonna/whore complex," Darcy went on, "I think because his dad was the love of his mom's life, and he died out of nowhere, at age forty-two, on a bike ride, no underlying heart conditions or anything—it makes me feel so bad when people die that way, exercising, because it's something I never do and it's so noble of them to do it for their health, and what do they get? A *heart* attack—but anyway, the mom never got over the dad, she dated a few guys since, and so the model that Emmett got from his mom was that a woman should be absolutely devoted to one man. It's something that scares him, because even though it's better to have loved and lost than to never have loved at all, he's seen his mom's heartbreak and wants to avoid her fate. He thinks the way to do that is to either use women for sex *or* to become so obsessed with them that they can never be real to him. And all *I* wanted, of course, was to get fucked two, maybe three times per month. It was a classic situation of misaligned needs."

Darcy's boots poked little holes in the icy snow in her wake as she monologued, Jesse nodding at every word. Sasha, Lou, and Vivienne lingered behind them, close enough to catch the smell of Darcy's perfume scarfing through the air and step on the holes that her boots created. Over the past few days, Sasha had been endeared to Lou in small moments, and she imagined—perhaps delusionally—that they had some sort of alliance in the face of Darcy and Jesse's intense and burgeoning friendship.

"Hey." Lou flashed their phone over at Sasha. The screen showed an expensive set of lingerie, a complicated outfit of twisting bands consisting of a bottom, a top, garters, and a collar. Sasha clicked through the images passively.

"Nice," Sasha said.

"For Valentine's Day," Lou said in a low voice, jerking their chin toward Darcy.

"I mean, she'll look great in it. She looks good in everything."

Sasha was trying to remember that her greatest power was her discretion—like a Brighton Beach lingerie shopgirl, the way she could cut you down with the twitch of her eyelid.

"Picture this," Lou said. "I see her rocking the strap on the underwear pulled up above the waistband of a pair of low-rise jeans, or a looser trade pant."

Jesse would probably love it if Sasha dressed like that.

"Mmm," Sasha said.

"Should I just do it?" Lou's finger hovered over the checkout button.

"Wait, what size do you have?" Sasha asked, because she was a glutton for punishment.

"32C, I think, for the bra? The rest is S/M/L, so I'd get, what, a small?"

Sasha advised, "Go with 30D. Darcy's really tiny. And the smaller the band size, the more ample cleavage you get."

"Thank you, thank you," Lou praised. "There—it's ordered."

They came to the frozen waterfall, and Jesse repeated the statistic, which they'd overheard in the grocery store and repeated often over the past few days, that one stoned teenager flew off the precipice per season. The falls were frozen in a massive, static drip, a magnificent drop. The air whipped around them as they snapped pictures from their perch on the wooded path, the overlook surrounded by a thin wooden barrier at the bottom of an icy hill.

Vivienne's paws slipped around the ice as she tried to keep up, and Darcy scooped her into her arms.

"Oh, honey," she cooed, stepping down the hill leading to the observation deck to get a closer look. But she lost her footing and her legs shot forward, rendering her horizontal in the air for a couple of seconds as she teetered, almost levitating, before succumbing to gravity and crashing down the hill on her back. She shot like a bowling ball down the hill. For a split second, as they watched, there was quiet.

Then, all at once, the volume racheted up: Vivienne screeching as she and Darcy careened toward the drop-off, Darcy's high-pitched cry for help as she and Vivienne began scrambling on the ice to avoid the direction of the gorge, the awful sound of nails and claws against the frozen ground, the screech of puffer jacket and snow pants skidding against the ice.

Sasha shrieked and covered her face with her gloved hands. Everyone else lunged forward uselessly, as though to help Darcy and Vivienne. Darcy's body practically bounced on the ice as her limbs flailed, trying to right themselves. She twisted onto her hip, latching onto a rock wedged in the ice just as she was about to crash into the flimsy wooden barrier, and at the same time somehow lobbed Vivienne heroically upward into Jesse's waiting arms.

When it was all over, Darcy lay in a heap at the base of the hill, on the observation deck, like a pat of cold butter, her creamy jacket crumpled up to reveal a slice of skin on her lower back. Vivienne snorted with manic distress in Jesse's arms.

The violence of her movements had made everything wrong: One of Darcy's acrylic nails was impaled in the icy snow, and one of her feet was now clad in just an athletic sock. The only casualty of the fall was her left boot, which had shot off her foot and tumbled down into the abyss, landing in the icy rock pile below with a muted thud—more of a tap, really, but with an echo.

Jesse and Lou ran after Darcy, Vivienne, and the detonated Pucci, shuffling quickly but carefully in their grippy boots as they navigated down to the scene of the accident.

Lou whisked Darcy to her feet and grabbed her close. She mewed softly into their puffer like a wounded kitten.

Sasha grabbed Vivienne from Jesse and clutched her so tight that Vivienne let out a choked grumble.

"Are you *okay*?" Sasha asked Darcy.

Darcy removed her head from Lou's chest. "My ass hurts. Everything hurts."

Jesse and Sasha peered over the observation deck. The view made Sasha dizzy, and she took a step back.

"You saved Vivienne's life," Sasha said, amazed.

"Look at the drop," Jesse marveled, almost reverent, still standing by the thin wooden barrier.

The chasm encompassed the area of a small town, a whole concave glowing world like one you might pass while driving along a highway at night. Flanked by 260-foot walls composed of craggy rocks dripping with thick bundles of icicles and perfectly formed peaks of snow, it culminated in a blue-black layer of iced-over river punctured with boulders. The waterfall itself had become a taut, glazed ribbon parachuting from the top of the observation deck to the river in perpetual descent. Smaller rocks dotted the surface where the frozen fall encountered the petrified river. Nestled in the depths between two of these smaller rocks was the boot, one black suede toe and one brightly colored swath of swirling fabric barely visible.

"Hooooly shit," Sasha whispered. "The shoe."

"I wish there was a way we could get it," Darcy said, her voice shaking.

"I guess we could very carefully climb down the other side . . ." Lou strategized.

"A better bet would be to send a drone or something," Jesse pontificated. "Something with forceps that could dip down and get the boot like a claw."

"Like the arcade game!"

"Well, yeah, but it would have to be bigger—like a huge claw crane."

Lou asked, "You know anyone with one of those?"

"Jesse is cherry-picker certified," Sasha bragged.

"There *is* someone I could maybe call . . ." Jesse rooted around in his puffer pocket for his cell phone.

Darcy laughed hysterically, manically, softly to herself. Sasha caught her eye and laughed too—*Our crazy boys!* The confidence had been stripped from her face; her expression was set not in its usual mask of composure and awareness of its own perception, but rather in a new expression: fear. She was pale and shaking, and for the first time, Sasha could see that she was struggling to pull herself together, to downplay the accident, to brush off the way she was hurt.

"Really," she said. "I'm fine. Those boots were getting gross anyway. Don't worry about it."

Lou kept asking if she'd hit her head. Darcy reiterated that she'd fallen on her ass. She laughed uncomfortably, bending at the waist as though to prove that she was still just as flexible as before. With Darcy squared away, and acting right as rain—to save face? To be a hero?—everyone worried about Vivienne, huddling around her. Sasha was relieved; she needed everyone to assure her that Vivenne was going to be fine.

"Are you sure *she* didn't hit her head?" Sasha sniffed, and Jesse came to hug her from behind. "I shouldn't take her to the vet?"

Darcy seemed relieved, too, focusing on Vivienne.

"I spared her the worst of it," she promised.

Darcy appeared in Sasha's periphery with her mouth turned down, her hands shaking in the pockets of her puffer, her sock foot balanced on top of her boot foot to avoid stepping down on the icy snow.

"Babe, get on my back," Lou insisted.

Vivienne's tail was between her legs, and she was trembling. Sasha buried her face in Vivienne's cold, velvet ear.

"My baby," Sasha wailed on a loop. "My poor girl. My baby. My poor girl."

"I'm okay," Darcy said. "If I can just get someone on my right side, to—?"

Jesse obeyed, taking the crook of Darcy's arm to bolster her like a crutch.

"C'mon." Lou crouched down in front of Darcy, gesturing that she should jump aboard. Jesse hoisted her onto Lou's back, which required him to grab her around the waist.

As they made their way out of the frozen forest, Darcy reached over from her perch on Lou's back to stroke Vivienne. "Poor thing," she said, regaining some of her composure. Sasha knew she was about to say the socially in-step thing, the thing that would serve to narrativize the incident and place it firmly in the realm of the social.

"We are trauma-bonded now," Darcy decided, smiling.

ৎ ৵

On the drive back to Hudson, Lou played the radio so low that it was impossible to make out any of the song lyrics. The sun was beginning its descent, and the bare trees glowed red in the thin gloaming. In the back seat, Sasha pressed her numb hands to the heating vents.

Sasha was still stiff from the fright of seeing Vivienne almost career off the cliff. She clutched Vivienne to her chest, Vivienne's piglet noises in her ear.

Darcy was eating a stale, half-frozen donut. The donut was Oreo-flavored, with cookie crumbles that kept spilling into Darcy's lap. When she was done, she brushed the crumbs unceremoniously onto the floor of the passenger seat and tossed the cardboard box in the back seat.

Lou began to drift over to the right, where the freeway led to an exit ramp.

"Are you seriously pulling over right now?" Darcy asked Lou.

"Yeah," Lou said.

"Here?" Darcy whipped her head toward Lou's side to make sure there was nothing Lou was seeing that she couldn't.

They were on the highway.

"I *hurt*," Darcy insisted. "All over."

"The sunset!" Jesse chimed in. "We haven't really seen it yet."

"We see it every night," Sasha said. "Can we just go home?"

Lou was commandeering the vehicle toward the overlook.

"I have a special idea," Lou insisted. "I think it'll cheer you up."

Darcy, annoyed: "I think what would cheer me up is going home and getting in the bath."

"I promise," Lou said. "Do you trust me?"

A current of frisson short-circuited between the new couple.

"Fine," Darcy relented.

"Yay!" Jesse said.

"Vivienne needs to get home, too," Sasha said. "She's starving."

Lou parked at the single space at the overlook and left the ignition running.

Jesse aimed his phone at the sunset, zooming in and snapping.

The sound of the trunk popping.

"You're getting *out*?" Sasha yelled.

Lou flashed her a smile in the rearview window before opening the driver's door.

"I'm so sorry to do this to you, Sasha, but yeah, we're getting out."

Darcy groaned as she opened the passenger door, hovering gingerly above her car seat while grabbing the side of the car. From the back seat, Sasha watched her hobble to the front of the car, where she paused, leaning on the hood with a moody expression dimming her face.

Lou appeared from the trunk with Sasha's massive angel wings and matching halo in tow.

They'd taken the costume from Sasha's luggage—or else Jesse had given it to them?

Jesse jumped out of the car without a glance toward Sasha, who seethed as the three of them marveled mutedly, through the thick windshield, at her wings. They were going to leave her and Vivienne in the car while they did whatever it was they planned to do. She wrestled her wet gloves onto her hands and gathered Vivienne in her arms. Viv groaned in protest as Sasha heaved the two of them out of the car.

Since the sun had all but gone down, the only light they had was a flashlight that Lou carried, pointed determinedly down into the snowy path before the four of them. The overlook wasn't a very long strip, so it could only be several more paces before they reached their destination. Sasha waded furiously through the snow a few steps behind the rest of them. Around Lou's neck was their notoriously fancy camera. One of Darcy's arms clutched Lou's waist. In Darcy's other arm were the angel wings, which bumped against Lou each time Darcy almost slipped. On her head, the halo perched confidently, bobbing with each step she took.

Darcy and Lou were like Teflon in their newness. They'd escaped the indignities of the trip so far unscathed, without a scratch on their surface. They luxuriated in the first bloom of love, laughing about the drama rather than being burdened by it; they could think of themselves as separate from the psychodrama of the Jesse/Sasha and Miranda/Jules dynamic.

They'd been fucking every night of the trip, Sasha decided, probably sometimes for multiple hours a night, and they were sure that they could be heard, but they didn't care. They were nonstick. They couldn't imagine any remark failing to slide off them, couldn't imagine any wound surviving the night.

"Here good?" Lou was asking.

"This was your idea? A photo shoot?"

Lou thrust their arms out. "It's gorgeous, no?"

"Sure." Darcy unfolded the wings carefully and slung the straps around her shoulders, fluffing them out so that they reached their maximum size.

They all stood in front of her. Sasha found herself involuntarily agape at the sight of Darcy in her (Sasha's!) angel regalia. The wings' heft, their height, their power—could not be overstated. She was a snow angel, having finally achieved the balance she was always after, splitting the difference between being excessive and being understated; the wings both dwarfed and exalted her actual size. Under the wings, she wore her long cream puffer coat and white iridescent snow pants. One Pucci boot, one sock foot. Sasha thought about taking a picture herself, ashamed at her impulse to docment this image on social media, tagging @reality___cheque. But she'd left her phone in the car, leaving only Jesse and Lou to memorialize it.

Lou took a knee on the snow and began adjusting their camera's lens. Darcy stood stock-still under the weight of the wings, a single highway light illuminating her frame from behind.

"All right," Lou said. "Ready."

Darcy turned her back to Lou, showing the wings in their entirety. She swiveled her neck around, tooching her booty (a skill she'd no doubt picked up, as Sasha had, from cycle 18 of *America's Next Top Model*, back in 2012) and smizing (cycle 12, 2009). Lou held the flashlight with one hand and the camera in the other. They snapped a few pictures, consulting the LCD display after each. Everyone was quiet. Sasha and Jesse stood huddled together against the cold like mourners, Sasha permitting an arm around her waist, Vivienne peeing quietly in a snow bank nearby.

"You look incredible," Jesse said.

"Are you serious?" Sasha asked.

"What do you mean?"

The anger welled up so quickly in Sasha's throat that all she could do was mime rage, gesticulating in the dusky air until Jesse lost interest and turned away from her.

"So hot!" Lou called out. "Turn around and try more of a pose, maybe?"

"Yeah, cock your hip to the left a little bit more," Jesse suggested.

Darcy did as she was told, but her eyes betrayed boredom.

"Butt!" Lou cried out, and Jesse followed suit: "Butt!"

This was good-natured, and engineered more for Darcy than for them: Darcy's "thing" was showing her butt as much as possible; the boys were only helping her stay on brand.

Darcy turned obediently, letting out a weird cough-laugh as she did so, but didn't pull down her pants.

"Butt?" Lou asked, crestfallen.

"I'm good," Darcy replied. "We can go now."

"The black and blue of your bruise will pop against the snow," Jesse observed.

"I'm okay," Darcy said.

"Do you want to get any facing forward?" Lou asked.

"I think we've probably got the shot," Darcy said.

The mood had shifted almost imperceptibly. Darcy's eyes were like an overly buffed surface—dead, dull, not shiny. The corners of her mouth twitched unhappily. She was embarrassed, Sasha understood. Or annoyed? Either way, Darcy reminded Sasha of herself when she was mortified—politely chipper, passive-aggressively menacing. Why didn't Darcy want to show her ass as she had so many times before? Did it hurt?

"Will this work?" Lou tilted the screen of the camera toward Darcy to show the image, which they could all see was incredible. She was glowing, surrounded by trees draped in ice and a world of snow.

"Thanks," Darcy said. "These are great. We can go now."

"What's wrong?" Lou asked.

Her ass hurts, Sasha wanted to translate. *She doesn't want to show it to you right now. You're looking at a girl who has sold herself as someone who will always show her ass but in this moment doesn't want to, so let's go the fuck home.*

"Nothing." Darcy stepped out of the wings and folded them, tucking them under her arm. "I just want to go."

"You okay?" Jesse was saying.

"Let's go," Sasha said. "Can't you see her ass hurts?"

Darcy glanced at Sasha coolly, her expression was inscrutable.

"IT'S FREEZING, AND I WANT TO GO HOME NOW," Sasha tried again.

"Wait," Lou said. "Look."

There was a deer, absolutely still, standing a few feet away from them. They could make out the deer's rib cage rising and falling with gentle breaths, the watery gleam in her eyes. The deer, Sasha thought, lets us identify with the hunter and the hunted. She was so beautiful that for the first time Sasha half understood the desire to shoot her and kill her, so that they could approach her in the woods and carry her wounded body away.

☙ ❧

"How's the Grinch nude coming along?" Jesse asked. They were thawing in Bedroom 3, their outer layers blanketing the floor, lying against the comforter in their insulated shells and long underwear. The vent above the bed cranked out puffs of hot air, making Sasha's armpits tickle with sweat.

Sasha said it was going. The edges of Darcy's annoyance had rubbed off on her; she wanted to go under the blankets with Vivienne and not be observed.

"Don't worry about it," she said.

"Really?" Clearly Jesse thought she was being coy, and Sasha softened.

"Yes."

She admitted that she was having trouble capturing her whole body because of angles.

"What if I take it for you?"

This was exactly against the point of the nude—which was for Sasha to be exposed to the ugliness of her own body alone and to capture the one instant, through a series of tricks of light and angles, in which she looked beautiful. The point was for her to do that labor; that was the present. Having Jesse take the photo was ridiculous.

"I want to," Jesse said. "Let me do it."

Sasha would regret it, but she took our her phone and opened Instagram, selecting the Grinch filter and fluffing out her hair in a halo of green sworl. She handed the phone to Jesse. Then she slipped off her top layer of clothes, leaving on her bra and underwear, and arranged herself prettily on the bed with a good-natured grumble.

When she cast her gaze upward, toward Jesse, Jesse had a look on his face that Sasha had rarely seen. A look of astonishment, of absolute rapture. The look struck Sasha as unadulterated, unprocessed and unmediated by Sasha's own presence in the room—because instead of looking at her, Sasha, Jesse was gazing into the phone—perhaps at a picture of her, one she hadn't yet vetted.

"What?" Sasha asked, pulling the blankets up around her tits, self-conscious.

"Wait," Jesse said, still looking at the screen while coming to sit beside Sasha on the bed, not taking his eyes off the screen for the entire span of seconds. It was then that Sasha saw that he wasn't looking at a picture, but at the camera feature in self-view. "I look *really* hot as the Grinch."

Jesse's face was tinted green, with a deeper shade of green at the end of his nose. Furry green brows, big eyes with long black lashes, a tufted helmet of Grinch hair, culminating in a spout of green fur standing straight up from his head. The same furry jawline as Sasha had been given, but perhaps because Jesse read as male to the filter, the fur was multiplied, coating his face in a sexy layer of green hairs as distinct and defined as fronds of grass. It was like Grinch testosterone, with a certain feminizing effect: the tilted eyes, the red lips, the pointed Grinch cheekbones. It was an arresting image. Sasha sucked her breath into her chest.

It reminded Sasha of the time, actually, a few months before, when she and Jesse had dressed up as each other for fun. Sasha in Jesse's hoodie and baggy board shorts, Jesse in Sasha's pink satin Opening Ceremony dress that cinched at the waist; there had been something terrifying, but also sexy, about how Jesse had regarded himself in the mirror as a butch in a dress—the mix of horror and attraction to this female alter ego. It was like when Jesse was first beginning to grow breasts at eleven or twelve, how he'd promised himself that he would never take those breasts for granted, fondle them nightly, as though they belonged to someone else.

Jesse stared at his face on the screen, turning it this way and that, the left side of his face and then the right. He was ebullient, transfixed by his image, like Narcissus. His own face. It was like watching Jesse masturbate to an image of himself.

Neither of them breathed. For reasons she didn't understand, Sasha's abdomen wrenched.

"Fuck," Jesse growled, and he tossed Sasha's phone down on the bed. "Come here, I want you."

"Wait," Sasha said, gathering up courage like sweeping crumbs into a dustpan. It was now or never; the surreal moment of Jesse as Grinch had shaken the moment into a do-or-die scenario. Jesse's cheek already against hers was slick with sweat, dewy, a hot tongue pressed to a frozen pipe.

"What?" Jesse asked.

"What about what you told Faye?" Sasha said. "You know, about how I'm incapable of loving anyone but myself?"

Jesse laughed. "But that's what I love about you."

In the eerie, pre-dinner quiet of Bedroom 3, their hiking clothes tangled in the bed next to them, the sweat and cold air alchemizing into a frigid bundle of pheromones, Jesse rubbed the Chanel soccer ball necklace between Sasha's legs and slowly tried to insert it inside her kittycat. The ball was cold and clammy, its jagged rhinestone edges chaffing at Sasha's tender labia as Jesse pulled it in and out. Sasha winced. It didn't feel sexy, but beauty was pain, and pain beauty; what was sexy to Jesse should be sexy to her. And Jesse was into it, grunting and groaning as he scored his goal over and over again, pushing the miniature soccer ball in and out of the net.

"Can I Come Inside, my sweet WAG," Jesse recited like an altar boy.

It was clear that this was Jesse's dream rather than Sasha's; it was solidly in his section of the Venn diagram. There was something unsexy about what was happening, too on the nose. Getting fucked by a soccer ball was not the same as getting fucked by a soccer player. She could not let Jesse score without navigating her defense. She wanted to return to the moment about Faye, to get to the bottom of what Jesse had said about her.

"Stop," Sasha said when Jesse tried again to insert the Chanel soccer ball. "That hurts, you're going to ruin it."

She was no longer in the mood to pretend. She had to shatter the illusion that this was hot, that she was enjoying herself.

Vivienne plodded over to them and settled on Sasha's chest with the density of a dying star.

I visualize myself across from her with a pitcher's mitt, Jules recited, teleprompter-style, in Sasha's head, quoting the dykette authoress Robbie Sommers.

She doesn't like my sassy attitude? I don't care. Let her come to the pitcher's mound if she's got a problem with me.

Jesse placed the Chanel soccer ball on her bedside table. It rolled around for a few seconds before one of its rhinestones caught on the surface of a book and bolstered itself there, quiet.

"That's my girl," Jesse said, rubbing Sasha's back. "That's my girl."

He began kissing Sasha all over her face and neck, pressing his groin into Sasha's hip bone, rubbing against Sasha harder and harder, grunting. Vivienne scrambled out of the way, and Sasha could feel him cum on top of her, the pulse in his neck strong, his upper lip sweaty. She sensed him on the verge of speech, the hum of his throat revving up to say something.

"Shh," Sasha said. "Just touch me."

He forced a hand into her underwear and moved his fingers fast on her. Sasha clutched him, arching her back and drawing her legs up around his strong arm and clasping her arms around his warm neck. He revealed Pearly and the heart harness like a high-class waiter revealing a meal under a silver lid. She hadn't even known that Pearly had come along on this trip, tucked safe in Jesse's black duffel. He strapped her on, the heart facing out against his crotch, and slid his fingers into her, bicep twitching.

She loved the moment of elastic anticipation that occurred during the donning of a strap-on, the somber and serious moment of silence. Jesse plunged into her, filling her up inside, so full that it almost hurt, thrusting in and out, in and out, faster and faster. The pressure began to build up and up, and Sasha said, "You need to come." She kept telling him, "You need to come with me." He flipped her around and began grinding himself against her heel, calloused and dirty. Sasha felt him, wet and slippery, on her heel as he rubbed harder and harder, two fingers still yanking in and out of her, her toes jammed inside of him. Finally Sasha felt him liquefy, warm water dripping over her foot and down her calf, and Sasha could only remember, in the coital hallucinatory imaginary, that as Darcy had fingered Sasha's Chanel necklace, she had noticed the length and shape of Darcy's fake fingernails, at that point still intact, the palest of blue gingham—gingham nails, to match her top—on slender fingers with knuckles still white from the cold, and was taken aback by the extent to which they resembled the nails of a twelve-year-old.

Darcy had then leaned lazily in the pale winter sunlight and craned her neck backward, letting her black hair fall like a curtain closing, couching the fabric of her top under a layer of thick hair, the pulse ticking in her neck almost leaping out, so delicately that Sasha feared for a moment the skin would burst and blood would spout like a fountain. And even then, surely, Darcy would not die, would only stanch the hemorrhaging with a small gingham bandage.

Physical Education

 баре

They watched *Gossip Girl* after breakfast, a show that had shaped most of their adolescences. In pajamas and robes, hoodies and sweatpants, clutching mugs of lukewarm coffee in their dry hands, they sank onto the couch in Living Room 2 and stared bleary-eyed at the TV screen.

First there was Sasha's Upper East Side prep-schooling. Sasha and Natalya had started taking the Q train to the tony girls' prep school on East 84th Street when they were nine and ten, respectively. Each day an old maid had forced them to kneel on the carpet while she measured their plaid skirts with a ruler to make sure they were no more than two inches above the knee.

Then there was Jesse, who had watched *Gossip Girl* from his parents' ranch-style home in the northern Chicago suburbs, filled with longing for culture beyond field hockey trips to Phoenix and Orlando. Jesse wanted to sit on the steps of the Met, to live in a loft in Williamsburg and date a girl with huge boobs.

Darcy and Lou had watched in their California adolescences, just as they'd watched *The O.C.*, which they both proclaimed was a better version of *Gossip Girl*. They observed as West Coast anthropologists, parsing the differences between New York and California cool. The archetypal besties—Blair and Serena in *Gossip Girl*; Marissa and Summer in *The O.C.*—were comforting duos with their soothingly predictable roles: blond, effortless Serena/Marissa; brunette, snobby Blair/Summer. But while Blair and Serena feuded over early admission to Yale and did coke with the boys' school royalty, Marissa and Summer lounged poolside and tried their hands at surfing. Culturally, the difference was both aesthetic—Blair/Serena's prep, Marissa/Summer's bikinis—and tonal: the way the girls talked, the speed at which they sized each other up.

Miranda and Jules were both already adults in New York by the time *Gossip Girl* premiered in the fall of 2007, so their attachments to the show were thinner, less mythologized. Still, they remembered the cultural moment that it had engendered and were excited to revisit it, to see the show through the younger generation's eyes.

Because they were always casting themselves according to the available archetypes, it was decided that Sasha was obviously the lesbian Blair/Summer. Darcy was a Serena/Marissa. The rest of them fell somewhere in between, or else were the shows' male characters—Jesse and Lou were Chuck and Nate, of course, Jules was Rufus, and Miranda was Lily with undertones of Vanessa.

"Crazy how Blake manages to look like shit in every scene," Darcy sighed, already bored.

"I think she looks great!" Jules protested. Jules didn't have Darcy's refined sense of style—Jules saw a pretty blond girl and was happy; Darcy saw the Aeropostale-style low-rise jeans that were popular for about five minutes in the mid-2000s and was displeased. Sasha envied Jules's simplicity, her ability to appreciate the most basic pretty-girl things. It was refreshing to encounter someone with such an indiscriminate palate for femininity; everyone else in her life was so difficult to impress, not least of all Jesse.

Darcy made a disgusted face. "That skirt is fugly."

She was almost angry in her indignation, insistent that Jules see things from her point of view, but Jules would not relent.

Onscreen, Blair and Serena were walking down Park Avenue, Blair in a blue coat and headscarf and Serena in a cropped leather jacket.

"I think that skirt is cute," Jules insisted.

"That one's fine," Darcy relented for the leather jacket.

Sasha's phone flashed, announcing that she was receiving a call from her sister.

"Sorry," she said. "I'll be right back."

She stood shakily from the couch and entered the kitchen as she swiped her finger from left to right across the screen. Natalya rarely called her, preferring instead to send dozens of one- to four-word separate text messages in a neat gray row recounting her latest drama.

"Hello?"

On the other end, Natalya was crying so hard that she could barely get her greeting out.

"What is it?" Sasha insisted. "Who died?"

"No one died," Natalya managed. "Max broke up with me."

"Where are you?" Sasha asked.

The living room cohort burst into laughter, and then the sound of Jules saying, ostensibly about Serena: "Her voice is like *honey*."

"Home."

"Morningside?"

Natalya lived in a studio by Columbia, close to her job.

"Brighton."

"What? Why?"

"That's where Mom is."

"Can you put Mom on the phone?" Sasha asked.

"One sec," Natalya sniffled.

A few seconds later, Tsilia was on the other line. "Hallo?" she trilled.

"What's going on?" Sasha demanded.

"Your sister is driving us insane," Tsilia said. "She needs to go to the psych ward. And on top of this, your deadbeat uncle has trashed the apartment. I have so much to deal with. You should see what he did to the carpet in the living room."

Her parents had retained their apartment in Brighton Beach and rented it to Sasha's aforementioned deadbeat uncle, a brother of her father's.

"Mama," Sasha said. "What about Natalya?"

"What? Max keeps breaking up with her. She has no self-respect. She doesn't care how pathetic this makes her look— getting dumped all the time. She doesn't care about us, how we've been there for her. All she does is sabotage herself again and again. She will never be happy. She will never have a relationship like you have with Jesse—oh—your sister wants—"

The call was interrupted by a FaceTime request, which Sasha accepted. Natalya appeared onscreen, her hair pulled into a high ponytail and her eyes red and puffy. A few pimples dotted her forehead.

"Sasha, it's fucking disgusting in here," Natalya reported breathlessly. Sasha could see, in the background of the call, a vacuum cleaner propped up against the wall.

Sasha liked everyone better when they were in pain, especially people she loved. She wasn't a particularly empathetic person, and when her loved ones suffered she became hyperaware of the ways in which she was not filled with their pain, not beholden to it. This awareness gave her the strength to tap into something of a euphoric stoicism, offering endless emotional support and unlimited analytical processing.

"Who is that?" her uncle shouted from another room.

"Sasha!" Natalya said.

"He says hi. Show me around," Natalya said with a sniffle.

Sasha flipped the camera to give Natalya a quick panoramic view of the kitchen. Natalya immediately spotted Darcy's silver bag on the counter and asked if it was one of those Telfar bags, only she pronounced it "Teflar."

"Yeah," Sasha said.

Suddenly Jules was in the kitchen, too, opening the fridge.

"Who's that?" Natalya asked, the camera pointed straight at Jules.

"Jules, this is my sister; Natalya, this is Jules," Sasha said. Jules came around, a handful of chocolate chips in hand, to peer at Sasha's phone screen.

"Sasha's sister," Jules said, looking deep into Natalya's eyes. She didn't hold Jules's gaze, looking down after a few seconds into the wooden table. "Wow. You do kind of look alike."

Natalya blushed, imagining that Jules was flirting with her.

"Everyone thought we were twins growing up," Sasha said.

"Not anymore, though," Natalya said, rushing to distance herself from Sasha.

"Yeah, well, we dress really differently now," Sasha said.

Natalya didn't waste any time launching into her tale of woe. All she'd needed was an audience, and now that she had an eager assembly of Jules and Sasha, she was ready to lay everything out on the table.

Natalya *wished* she could be gay, she confided, glancing up at the two of them quickly to gauge their reactions before fixing her gaze back down. Natalya had even nursed a crush on a fellow therapist at her work, a long-haired futch who wore hoodies and baggy track pants. But the moment she'd had her chance to kiss the dyke, Natalya had chickened out. At most, she allowed, she was bisexual. Though, really, she feared she was just plain straight. This was Natalya's typical rotisserie of expressing, retracting, and then reiterating her point.

Natalya thought of herself as something of a rarity in the world of straight girls—she was pretty, fun, and normal, but most significantly, she was chill. Low-maintenance, no-frills. She didn't play games, she explained, didn't have unreasonable expectations surrounding monogamy, wasn't clingy. She loved sex. In fact—here she paused—*she* was kind of like the gay sister, and Sasha the straight one. Sasha with her makeup and aspirations of housewifery and antiquated gender roles. Natalya wore pants! She considered herself to be a jock (she'd played softball in high school). And while she'd been a sort of low-key sorority girl at Dartmouth, she was always the tomboy of the bunch, her sorority sisters plying her with mascara and blush before nights out partying. Left to her own devices, she was happiest in jeans and a ponytail, minimal makeup. She liked being outside and didn't mind getting cold or dirty.

Her desirability went without saying, because everyone around her had always affirmed it for her. Sasha could feel Jules stiffen beside her, assuming that responsibility, murmuring that there was nothing wrong with Natalya. A prick of resentment flamed in Sasha's chest, but she swallowed it down. Was Jules attracted to Natalya?

"I don't get what being a tomboy has to do with letting guys treat you like that," Sasha said.

Even the term *tomboy* felt flimsy and irrelevant to Sasha.

"It's hard to explain," Natalya sighed.

"Try," Jules urged.

"It's like"—Natalya took in a gulp of air—"my whole life I've felt like I didn't know how to be a 'real girl,' like the contestants on *The Bachelor* or whatever. I always thought that when I grew up I was going to be one of those girls, with their makeup and sparkly gowns, but then I never did. You know, those thotty girls who rag on their men and get bitchy when their guys betray them, who know what to say and how to be. I'm twenty-seven and still feel like I don't know how to be desirable to men, so I let them use me, treat me like their friends except when they want to have sex with me. I dunno—it's like I'll never *actually* be good enough, or woman enough, to be someone's girlfriend."

"Hmm." This was above Jules's pay grade—her eyes roamed the room as though she was looking for Miranda, and not finding her, Jules decided to take a stab at analysis. "And you think if you weren't straight, you wouldn't feel the same pressure to be a 'real woman'?"

Natalya sniffed. "Yeah, I guess that's it."

Jules slowly backed up, a can of seltzer fizzing in her fist. "Well, I'll let you sisters get back to it."

Jules wasn't invested in her sister's fake problem, for which Sasha felt relief.

"I texted with Mama after he treated me like garbage for the last time," Natalya said once Jules had retreated back to the living room. "I needed an adult woman's perspective, even hers. Mama told me something she'd told me a bunch of times, but kept forgetting she'd already told me: when Daddy is being mean to her, she asks if it has anything to do with her; he has to be honest, he has to tell the truth. And if it doesn't have anything to do with her, Mama says, 'I'm going to leave the room now so that you can deal with yourself. Come find me when you're over it and ready to apologize.' I wish I could do that."

Natalya didn't want to leave the room, though. After her last breakup with Max, a few years earlier, Natalya confessed that she'd sent a long document to Max called *M (As He Exists in the Mind of N)*, a compilation of all the notes she'd taken during their relationship and after it; she'd been destroyed by that breakup, sent soaring on the lip of a particularly dark wave, and after they said goodbye, she kept seeing M lookalikes all around her, teasing and tormenting her, a phenomenon she'd described in the document as always seeing "his weird, weird hair." Sending the document to M was part of the performance art, her final display of unwavering alertness. Her eternal presence.

When Sasha had hung up with her sister and was seated on the couch again, Serena and Blair bickering onscreen, she told the group about her mother's strategy for dealing with her father.

"That's such a straight idea of conflict and relationship," Jesse said. "That sense of *it either has to do with me or it doesn't; and if it doesn't, I can't let it touch me*."

"You're right, that's not an option for us," Sasha said sadly. "I could never leave the room, even if I wanted to. You'd always be right behind me."

Everyone nodded, and Jesse pulled her closer, interpreting her comment as affection even though Sasha was still deep in thought. *Weird weird*, Sasha repeated to herself as she watched Jules gather a cashmere blanket for Miranda, who was shivering on the couch. It was a phrase as loose and sad as the uncanniness of observing someone you've loved—still the same person, but also now different. The eeriness of the "weird" doubled, of the same word either ghosting or disfiguring its twin.

෨ ෬

Two hours later, they were drunk and high, warming up in the sauna. They had to wait forty-five minutes for the sauna to reach its full steaminess, which they hadn't quite bargained for, and so they sat, shivering slightly, while the sauna slowly progressed from a chilly fifty degrees to sixty to a mild seventy to a humid eighty.

Once the sauna reached eighty-five, Darcy and Lou immediately went topless, Darcy with her perfect, pert golden breasts and Lou with their sexy translucent top surgery scars. It was difficult for Sasha to picture what was happening beneath Darcy's bikini bottoms or Lou's booty board shorts beyond her presumption of porn-star loins. Jules had stripped down to a sports bra, and Miranda had kept a small tank top secured around her boobs, the tops of her small round tits gleaming with sweat. Jesse had removed her white T-shirt to reveal her little pecs. Sasha (irrationally?) thought that if she let everyone see her boobs, they wouldn't be able to handle them—not in a horny way, she wasn't worried they'd be too turned on, but that they'd be shocked, scandalized, appalled; her tits would be an affront to them, even an offense. She was sure that none of them had seen tits of her tits' shape and size. These were small-tit people; at the end of the day, that was the biggest difference among them.

The words *Hey, Gump, get a load of the tits on her* floated up Sasha's brain stem. Tom Hanks's army roommate in *Forrest Gump* calls this to him as they pore over pictures of Jenny in the porno magazine they're reading from a bunker in Vietnam. Though Jenny has chosen to expose herself, Gump sees the desperation in her eyes and tears the magazine up; Gump knows that she's miserable, exploited, that really she's a nice girl whose tits should be concealed, not revealed.

"I'm hot," Sasha pouted.

"Pecs out," Jesse, who had been waffling over getting top surgery, said with a self-satisfied smile. "Cute of me."

Murmurs of agreement spasmed through the sauna.

"You still thinking about getting the chop?" Lou asked Jesse.

"Yeah, maybe," Jesse said. "I'm in a prolonged gender moment."

Sasha was surprised to hear this—not that Jesse was having a gender moment, but that maybe Jesse thought that this, the gender moment, was why they hadn't been fucking and it wasn't Sasha's fault after all. Maybe it was the fault of the gender moment.

Darcy changed the subject to herself—how she wanted to get her tits done. Not an augmentation but a reduction, not top surgery but a sort of reverse puberty. She yearned to revert from average-sized tits to prepubescent ones that would be restrained comfortably by a training bra or, more often, remain braless and enjoy the breeze that floated up under a baby tee.

"You should do it!" Jesse said.

"I just can't decide if it's worth the money," Darcy hedged.

"That's gender-affirming surgery," Miranda put in. "I know therapists who'd advocate for you, if needed."

"Wanna see the tits I'm most jealous of on the internet?" Darcy asked, ignoring Miranda, grasping at her thigh for her phone before realizing she hadn't brought it into the sauna. (No one had except for Jules, whom Sasha had never seen part with her device.) "Oh, shit. Well they're really small. Like Hershey's Kisses."

"So you'd be even smaller than an A cup?" Sasha was hung up on the dimensions of Darcy's dream tits.

"Mmm, not so hung up on the cup size. I basically just don't want them to dangle like udders when I'm on top of someone."

Sasha relaxed with the assurance that a) Jesse was a breast guy and b) she'd never find herself on top of him (bottom politics aside, it was simply too exhausting).

"I'm such a stressed-out top," Darcy monologued. "If I'm not doing five thousand things, I get anxious that the other person is bored. Or not getting off."

"Sounds like a lot of responsibility," Miranda empathized.

"And it burns way too many calories," Sasha jumped in, trying to witticize her earlier, private thought—before worrying it made her sound like she harbored jealousy around Darcy's thinness.

"You don't feel guilty, letting someone else do all the work?" Darcy retaliated.

"Sasha has a different approach," Jesse said, prompting her with his eyes to rejoin the group.

Sasha couldn't think straight. All the liquid had soaked out of her pores and saturated the fabric of her clothes. This was worrisome, but a better option than disrobing in front of these microscopic dykes. The heftiest among them was Jules, the only one who surely weighed more than Sasha did, but Jules was ropy and muscular in that lean, aging way. Regaining her strength, Sasha took Jesse's cue and began to speak.

"You have to think of your body as the whole show. You're *lucky* to be with me! You're lucky to be seeing this!"

Everyone but Darcy—still morose from the perceived slight—laughed appreciatively, though Sasha sensed that they also understood that there was another reason they were seeing so little of her body, which mortified her.

It was now even hotter than she could have imagined. Sweat pooled under Sasha's track pants, thighs swishing in the soupy material, and streamed down her face. She gathered her hair out of her face and retied it in a tight, high ponytail. Jules took an enormous wooden spoon from the bucket of water positioned under a small faucet and poured it over the stove, sending a crackle and a plume of steam into the air. Miranda leaned back against the wall of the sauna and closed her eyes. Sasha felt dizzy and nauseated, but she didn't want to look weak or draw attention to the fact that she was still fully clothed by opening the door. *Courage*, she chanted silently in French Canadian, like a Sevigny.

She wiped away a patch of steam so that she could stare at Vivienne through the window. Vivienne was sitting upright, rapt, watching the glowing sauna with stock-still alertness behind the glass door of the house. Sasha wondered if she was peeing on the welcome mat.

I can't be here anymore, Sasha complained to Vivienne telepathically.

But, Mom, you're beautiful, Vivienne's eyes reminded her.

I know, Sasha relented.

Besides, Vivienne continued, *I'm your ESA and I love you. I'm on your side.*

A flash of tit in her peripheral vision snapped Sasha out of her reverie.

Miranda had pulled off her camisole to reveal small, round breasts with delicate, pointed nipples. They bobbed on her chest, light as air, like small apples in a bucket. Sasha tried not to stare, but she really wanted to understand the mechanics of boobs like that, how they were so round and so light. Sasha pictured Jules taking them into her mouth, sinking her teeth into the flesh around the nipple, and she felt a flush of heat between her legs that was almost unbearable.

You could bring boobs like that anywhere, Sasha reasoned. You could wake up in the morning and go to sleep at night without thinking twice about them. The gulf of misunderstanding between those with small tits and those with large ones was huge, as big as the Red Sea. It would take someone who'd had both to bridge the cultural divide. She twisted open her lip gloss, slick from being stashed in her cleavage, and applied it, deep in thought about tit theory as it melted onto her lips.

Sasha remembered reading an interview that Miranda July had done with Rihanna in Los Angeles a few years before. In the interview, July and Rihanna discuss Rihanna's fear of having a big vagina. The women debate whether the depth or the wideness of a vagina is more *problématique*. The two types of women, in July and Rihanna's conversation, are those with short vaginas and those with deep vaginas.

Wait, July says. *Deep's not an issue.*

Rihanna's rejoinder: *Deep is an issue, hello!*

July reveals that she's always felt "short-vaginaed."

Rihanna counters that July is lucky—that *if men can't feel the end, it's like, cannonball!*

July reflects: *Cannonball meant sailing into space—into something never-ending, like the cosmos. Men like to know that there is an end to the woman they're with, that she's finite.*

Sasha repeated aloud to the sauna what she remembered of the article.

"I like cannonball," Jesse slurred. Sasha registered this as meaning that Jesse thought being infinite was sexier than being finite; probably the thing that made him a lesbian above all else.

"Goddex bless," Darcy said, flashing two sloppy peace signs, but it was hard to know what she was talking about. The mood was devolving into a banquet of nonsequiters.

"Cannonball is your sexual gender," Lou told Jesse with a laugh.

Sasha knew from her graduate seminar on modern sexology ("my bullshit" as she called her PhD work, though it came in handy at times like these) about the nineteenth-century idea of sexual inversion. The understanding back then was that dykes were male souls in women's bodies. Before the 1920s, Western sexologists like Ulrichs and Von Krafft-Ebing insisted that queer sexuality was also a disorder of gender.

The gerrymandering of sexuality and gender—the idea that sexuality was totally separate from gender, that you could be gay without being masculine, straight without being feminine, that gender and sexuality were actually extricable—was recent stuff. The more recent debate had flipped back to some middle ground: namely, the idea that gender and sexuality were related, or at least in conversation. Which all came back to Lou's "sexual gender" comment.

Jules produced a bright red herbal bundle, tied tightly in waxy string, and singed the top of it by touching it to the fire. A sweet, rosy scent flushed through the sauna.

"This is blood sage," Jules announced.

"You mean dragon's blood?" Jesse perked up.

"It's white sage soaked in dragon's blood. An ancient healing tool."

"Dragon's blood is, what, a resin?" Lou used a hand to waft the smoke toward their nose.

"This stuff is sacred medicine," Jules said. "It'll cure your IBS, your arthritis—even some types of cancer."

"It cures cancer?" Sasha asked.

"It has well documented anti-inflammatory properties," Jesse lectured. "Indigenous peoples have been using it forever."

Sasha waved the bundle away politely, and it retreated for a moment to the small space beside Jules's left thigh.

Jesse's eyes fixed on the bundle, but he didn't move to take it. Jesse's nightstand was piled high with botany books. He was currently working his way through a book about Ashkenazi herbalism and was planning to feed Sasha an aphrodisiac nutmeg tea the next time he was horny. And in five to ten years, he'd rub fenugreek oil into her hair to induce lactation. Or would that only make her hair even thicker and shinier? He'd have to do some more research.

With considerable effort, Miranda twisted the quasi-floral valve above the faucet, and a rush of water landed in the bucket below. She watched it fill rapidly for a few seconds, turned off the water, and ladled some more water onto the coals, which roared and steamed wildly.

"I have a great story about lactation," Jules shouted at the top of her voice above the crackling, relieved to return to lighter things. She sat back down, the sap cast aside. "It was in the downtown New York performing scene in, like, 2007, there was a woman—a middle-aged woman—who lactated for years, well after she had children. She'd squirt her breast milk into the audience, spraying it from her tits like out of a fire hydrant."

"I've always wanted to be a wet nurse," Sasha said. "I plan to induce lactation even if I adopt."

"Grind those fenugreek seeds!" Jules yelled.

Darcy grabbed her own tits and stared off into space, stoned.

"They'd get so much milk," Miranda said dreamily, staring at Sasha's boobs.

"Can I be your wet nurse?" Sasha asked. "Like, if you and Jules have kids?"

"Of course," Miranda said, brow furrowed with integrity.

"She brought a nursing corset. Go get it, baby," Jesse insisted. Sasha demurred; her suitcase felt very, very far away. Darcy's and Lou's eyes both flashed with tepid interest. They were again attached, Darcy cradled in Lou's arms despite the extreme heat of the sauna.

"I want to see," Jules said, and that did it.

Sasha pushed the sauna door open, tumbling out into the dark night. The sweat on her body immediately turned to ice water, pulverizing her into action, and she dashed into the house, startling Vivienne, who was now sleeping on the welcome mat, eager not to abandon her post. Sasha hurried upstairs, dizzy and excited, and rifled through her suitcase to find the nursing corset. It was folded in half, the top empty cup spooning the convex one underneath to create a single tit impression. Vivienne stumbled up the stairs a beat after her, panting into the room. Sasha held the corset up to her chest, remembering what it felt like to unhook one of the cups and let one tit spill out. She wondered if she should put it on, surprise everyone in the sauna with a striptease. Was that a normal thing to do, or would she regret it in the morning? She started to take off her sweaty shirt, but Vivienne was glancing at her disapprovingly. Vivienne was right. She'd only embarrass herself.

Downstairs, the door slammed shut. Sasha jumped. The sound of footsteps in the living room grew closer and closer as they stomped up the stairs. Darcy was behind her in the hallway, trilling that she was grabbing her scrub. Sasha spun around with the nursing corset over her racing heart.

"It's coffee and chocolate," Darcy revealed, disappearing into Bedroom 2 and reemerging a few seconds later with an olive jar of thick, grainy paste. Sasha recoiled perceptibly.

"Wait, that *is* hot," Darcy said, staring at the corset in Sasha's arms. "Can I see?"

Sasha held out the corset tentatively, and Darcy grabbed it, pressing the fabric to her chest. She unfolded it completely and examined the width of the back, pursing her lips to the side as she considered its size against the outline of her own body.

"Mm, not sure this would work on me. Excited to see it on you, though!" she said, handing it back to Sasha.

Sasha bundled the corset in her fist. She was glad she'd decided against putting the thing on and giving Darcy the satisfaction of scrutinizing her torso. Without waiting for Darcy, she ran down the stairs and across the yard, seething the word *bitch* all the way across the frozen grass.

When she returned to the bath of humidity, Jules was brandishing her cell phone and playing a loud video of Flo Rida's 2012 hit "Whistle."

Darcy slammed into the sauna just behind Sasha, still holding the olive jar.

"What are you watching?" Sasha had forgotten how much she liked that song.

"Kittykat," Jules bellowed. "The emcee for the NoHomos— the BEST drag king troupe in Northampton."

Sasha leaned over to get a view of the screen. There was a tall, buff woman with long blond hair, a face full of makeup, and a short skirt that showed off her muscular legs—*A man's legs*, Sasha thought. This was Kittykat? Kittykat was dancing alongside a sporty-looking ginger dyke—a drag king, Sasha understood—in baggy gym shorts and a jersey. The whole thing was hopelessly 2012. Kittykat leaned down to the drag king's waist and took the whistle hanging there into her mouth. She blew loudly, like it was a blow job. The crowd went wild. Kittykat turned to the camera directly and grinned.

Sasha screeched. It was Jules.

"Is this real?"

"As Kittykat, I was almost like a wet nurse to the kings." Jules laughed. "Basically fed those boys from my tits."

Sasha widened her eyes and pursed her lips really small in order to imagine this.

"Were you *femme* back then?"

Jules let out a manic cackle. "No, I was in drag, too!"

"Were y'all together during this stint?" Lou wanted to know, and both Miranda and Jules laughed lightly, not exactly answering the question.

In one video, during a drag king's performance of "Afternoon Delight," Jules-as-Kittykat leans down and licks whipped cream off his neck. In another video Jules wore a cheetah-print minidress and white go-go boots. Her fingers—which sported amazingly long and red shiny fingernails—gripped the microphone as she shimmied and gyrated to "Love Shack," a group number that she performed with the kings. Darcy stared at the screen with vague dissociation, applying her scrub slowly to her upper arms. The sauna filled with the smell of olives and chocolate.

"I should audition to be a drag king," Sasha announced with what she hoped was gravitas, but it came out of her mouth sounding more like a wisp of an idea. It was maybe even offensive, though she couldn't quite articulate why.

"*You* as a drag king?" Darcy lobbed at Sasha.

"I don't think you'd be a hyper-masculine drag king," Jesse jumped in, trying to mediate. "I think you'd be a little sissy boy with womanly curves, and you'd sing in a cute baby voice. You'd be a gay prince or something. You'd be a boy dressing up as a girl singing the *Riverdale* cover of 'Milkshake.' You'd be wearing your own boobs as a boy."

"Wearing my own boobs?"

Jesse explained that it would be Sasha's boobs, but she'd be a boy who had put on those boobs to perform "Milkshake." Darcy put in that she'd seen Kelis once at Villa de Gucci, and

Jules yelled, with much exasperation, "Where the fuck's that? The Amalfi coast?"

"It's a spot in the Ukrainian Village," Lou explained. "Not as scene-y as, like, Dimes. But still sort of scene-y."

"Oh, sure, sure, I've heard of Dimes Square," Jules acquiesced, pacified.

"Can I see the video again?" Sasha asked.

Kittykat was dressed in a purple-and-gold cheerleading uniform and white platform sneakers. The uniform spelled out *CAT* across the chest.

Miranda looked away pointedly, her face inscrutable.

"We're going to make all your dreams come true," Kittykat yelled to the crowd.

Jules's performance as Kittykat was an embodiment of Sasha's erotic desire, a puppet of her *own* kittycat, which was oriented, like Kittykat herself, straight toward the drag kings.

Jules was loving every second of this trip down memory lane; her reverie unrelenting even though everyone else's fascination had more or less faded. Sasha could tell that Jesse and Lou were trying hard to stay focused on the screen as the dutiful young kings they were, but Darcy and Miranda had turned away. Sasha wondered if Miranda was bored, but that wasn't it—she looked like someone who was trying to pass her pain off as indifference, setting her face to neutral with considerable effort.

"Oh, come on, stop," Miranda said when Jules went to click on yet another video, shifting on the wooden bench, her tits gleaming with sweat. "No one wants to watch any more of these."

Jules's big finger tapped the two parallel lines of the pause button.

"Your outfits are spectacular," Jesse said to defuse the awkwardness. Miranda's annoyance had implicated all of them.

Jesse grabbed the nursing corset off Sasha's lap and began frantically liberating the dozen or so tiny hooks on the back. Early in their courtship, Sasha and Jesse played a game with this very corset called hook-and-eye. Jesse would scurry around undoing the buttons and hooks of Sasha's nursing corset, and just as soon as she'd undone them, Sasha quickly did them up again, making her desire to get Sasha naked hot in a Sisyphean way.

Jules grabbed the open corset from Jesse and placed it over her sports bra, as though to spite Miranda. The cups drooped, unfilled.

Miranda said, with a hint of warning in her voice, "Jules."

"Kittykat was famous for her air kisses," Jules said.

She snapped her fingers at Lou until Lou's eyes met theirs, and as Jules narrowed her eyes in a sultry, steely gaze, Lou let out a good-natured laugh. Jules jutted her chin up and twisted the corners of her mouth into a smile that bordered on scornful. Then, not breaking eye contact with Lou, she curled her lower lip up into a pucker, forcing her top lip to conform to the shape of a kiss, and released a tiny air kiss accompanied by a nearly silent *pop!*

"Ha ha," Lou said, pretending to grab the kiss from the air and clutch it to their chest, head bobbing awkwardly. "Jules— that was really good."

"Lemme try Sasha," Jules said, and began the same show of forcing Sasha to lock in with eye contact.

Sasha burned under the tight rope of Jules's gaze, which twisted her body into a self-conscious contortion, her wrists coiled into a hand bouquet.

Jules smiled with half her face, shot her eyebrows up almost imperceptibly, cocked her jaw at Sasha. Sasha withered.

"Sasha hates eye contact," Jesse noted.

The kiss that Jules produced for Sasha was slower and better formed, the lips coming together in a precise pucker and the *pop!* cleaner and more satisfying.

"Jules," Miranda said again, and Sasha writhed with the discomfort of having to choose between maintaining Jules's gaze and aiding Miranda. Sasha patted her cheek to show Miranda that the kiss had landed there, and not her lips, and then cast her eyes down to the floor of the sauna.

"You as a sexy wet nurse," Jules slurred to Sasha, ignoring Miranda and looking over at Sasha with a mixture of attraction and curiosity, "reminds me of the best downtown New York performance I ever saw in the early 2000s. It was by this woman named something Diva, god, I wish I could remember her name. And she'd kept herself lactating well after she had kids, and her art was squirting the milk from her tits out into the audience—can you believe that?"

Everyone exchanged an uneasy glance at Jules's drunken repetition.

"That's it," Miranda said. "I'm done."

She stood, gathering her small breasts in one hand and pushing back her curly black hair with another. Her legs were slim, glistening with sweat. She looked unreasonably pretty as she sauntered to the door of the sauna, not yet opening the door, testing Jules.

But Jules wasn't looking at her. Jules was unhooking one of the cups of the nursing corset so that one sports bra–clad mound of pec showed through.

"Imagine if I did that," she said. "Lactate into the crowd."

With one big hand, she grabbed the meat of her pec through

the sports bra and squeezed the flesh out through the open flap of the nursing corset, shaping a cone of Lycra. She aimed the cone at Miranda first, then Jesse, then Lou and Darcy, like a titty water gun, and then, finally, at Sasha.

"C'mon," Jules said to Sasha, shaking the Lycra cone-pec at her. "Wanna see if I can do it?"

Sasha let out a mechanical laugh. An awful, static moment of silence followed, and Darcy released a loud laugh of her own. Soon they were all laughing, laughing at Jules and themselves, except for Miranda, who was still perched by the door of the sauna. The humidity of the sauna made her hair stand up in angular puffs and scraggles. Her faint mascara was smudged, her face was blotchy, and her eyes shone with rage. She looked, admittedly, a lot like Adriana from *The Sopranos*.

"Honey?" Jules asked dopily, letting her pec go. Miranda shoved her way out of the sauna and trekked, her naked back steaming in the cold air, across the yard to the house. They watched as Vivienne greeted her, curled tail aflutter with excitement, and then as Miranda wrapped herself in a cashmere throw, disappearing from view into the kitchen.

"Everything okay there?" Darcy asked Jules, though it was fairly obvious it wasn't.

"She has issues with the drag stuff," Jules sighed.

"Why?" Darcy insisted.

"I loved that fun gender for you," Lou said supportively.

"I mean, it was so long ago, too," Jesse said.

"It's all—" Jules held her hands out before letting them drop onto the damp wooden bench by her sides. "It's just a lot."

Jules began to lather her arms and legs with Darcy's coffee and chocolate scrub. The scent was now that of old seasonal lattes, tepid and slightly sour because of the body odor coefficient. Jules passed the olive jar to Jesse, who scrubbed the mixture onto her chest and along the ridges of her clavicles, and Lou, who did the same but also doused their thighs with goop. A few of the coffee grounds sprinkled to the floor of the sauna. When the jar came around to Sasha, she waved it away.

ॐ ॐ

Miranda was on the couch, her face shifting into a bemused portrait of lines and curves as she apologized lightly for her behavior. Everyone hastened to reassure her that she was *fine, totally fine.* The mass reassurance took on a high-pitched frenzy, culminating with Jules giving Miranda a big, slow hug and Lou tousling Miranda's hair affectionately.

Sasha wondered about that hug between Jules and Miranda. The bulky shape of Jules wrapped around Miranda called to Sasha's mind Dwayne "The Rock" Johnson. Jules was so strong, gripped Miranda so tight that her biceps bulged. Surely not everything that had transpired could be sorted out with a hug—particularly a self-conscious, rollicking hug. It wasn't a hug that worked through issues or changed perspectives; it was a hug that was meant for an audience—the four others who were gathered reverently, watching anxiously to see if all could be forgiven.

It had been a long day, they agreed. Miranda thanked them for understanding.

"Did you take a bath? With the stuff?" Jules asked Miranda quietly.

Miranda jolted at Jules's question, recovered, and then turned to address the group. "I had a minor vaginal procedure last week. So after sweating, they recommend bathing."

Sasha aspirated on her seltzer. "Was it a rejuvenation?"

Miranda forced a laugh. "No—something else. We're pretty sure it's nothing."

It was difficult to remember that Miranda had so recently been glamorous and shiny with sweat in the sauna, tits out. She'd rinsed off and put on her dignified cashmere bathrobe, wool socks. She was no longer tits-out Complicata but back to her baseline Simplia, still a persona but a tame one, a respected queer therapist with a healthy sense of boundaries and a good deal of self-awareness.

Sasha rinsed off in the shower and put on the baby blue bed-coat her grandfather had brought her grandmother, suffering in her twenties from a life-threatening kidney infection, in the hospital in Leningrad in 1965. Family lore had it that Sasha's grandmother, bloated and waterlogged far past her usual size—here the relatives would hold their hands far from their bodies and jiggle them cartoonishly, evoking a seal or a manatee—had screamed at her grandfather for bringing her such an offensively large offering.

"You're a horse thief from Odessa!" she'd shouted, high on painkillers, and because it was true they'd both laughed.

Sasha at twenty-five was the approximate size of her distended grandmother at twenty-three. The water was boiling. Jules sprang up and began making hot toddies, each with a generous splash of whiskey and a wedge of lemon. She hummed the Fiona Apple "Hot Knife" song that they'd all been singing the other night.

I Can Hear the Bells

༄ ༄

Sasha wanted to find a pair of '90s pink velour sweatpants like the ones her bimbo dentist wore under her white dental coat. The first thrift store they entered was cluttered and hot, giving Sasha an immediate headache.

Vivienne heaved herself on a colorful woven rug like a beached whale and groaned loudly, settling in for the long haul. They'd brought her along because Sasha didn't want her to be scared all alone in the house. Vivienne hated being alone, but she wasn't particularly patient.

"No dogs," barked the woman behind the counter.

Sasha informed the woman that Vivienne was an emotional support animal. "Do you want to see my letter?"

The woman scoffed but didn't push the matter, so Sasha dropped Vivienne's leash and began browsing.

The six of them were the only patrons. The shop owner was a woman perhaps in her sixties with frizzy gray hair, stationed behind a counter teeming with beaded purses and scarves and sunglasses. Every so often, she'd push her way through the pile that blocked her vision from her customers and shout a fact about the item they were perusing.

Lou was in the market for skintight tan pants to go with their deer jacket. They were tall and skinny, so Darcy picked out some vintage jockey-esque pants for them. For herself, she immediately pulled a white ribbed bodysuit with little shorts and a ruffled polyester collar.

"That's so hot," Jesse said.

"Right?" Darcy held the bodysuit up to her body. "I might try it on."

"Sasha, you should try it on too," Jesse urged.

"I don't want to," Sasha said.

Darcy took the bodysuit behind the dressing screen and disappeared.

"C'mon," Jesse was saying. "I feel like you'd look so good in that."

"It's not super stretchy," Darcy called over the dressing screen. "Sorry, Sash."

Sasha looked at Jesse, expecting him to say something along the lines of, *Well, that won't be a problem, Darcy, because my girl happens to be tiny*, but he said nothing, just looked helplessly back at Sasha and then at the carpeted floor.

Darcy emerged in the bodysuit, twisting this way and that in front of the mirror. It fit, of course. Her legs gleamed long and thin, her slim hips barely wider than her waist. Her legs were so cellulite-free they looked plastic, long femurs embraced by the lightest suggestion of flesh. Darcy was the kind of person whose wardrobe wasn't dictated by what fit or even what she looked good in (her body looked good in everything, and everything fit), but—luxury upon luxury!—by what she *felt like wearing*.

"Wow," Jules said, and Lou stopped browsing the rack they'd been browsing to come admire Darcy.

"I don't know," she was saying, spreading her legs like a spider—one bare foot pressed against the wall of the dressing room—to show off the way the bodysuit snapped at the crotch like a doll's outfit. "Not to be practical, but like, where am I going in this?"

Sasha migrated stiffly toward a rack of dresses.

"That one's rare," the woman behind the counter noted when she saw Sasha pawing at it. It was printed with a peacock pattern and had long, feathered sleeves. "Most of the dresses we get from the sixties are small, under a size six. You should try that one. It's nice and big."

Sasha stared at her. "I'm a size six."

The woman behind the counter let out a distracted *hmm*.

Sasha sank down to the rug. Vivienne was sleeping with her tail unfurled in relaxation against the glass counter. She stroked Vivienne, whose eyes squinted open. There was some goop in her eyes, which Sasha gingerly pulled out with her fingernails and fed to her. Vivienne lapped up the delicacy eagerly and went back to sleep. Sasha was eye level with a tray of vintage rings. They came in all different colors—pink, blue, orange— and sizes. She beckoned Jesse over. He came and sank down next to her.

"You should get me an engagement ring here," she said, both of them balanced on the scratchy rug, like kindergarten.

Jesse rested one hand on Vivienne's stomach and the other on Sasha's shoulder, balancing on the toes of his sneakers.

"Not a bad selection," he said. "I'll keep looking."

"You could use one of these as a template," Sasha pressed.

Jesse peered at the rings again.

"And then do the rest of the design with that lesbian gemcutter you know from Instagram?"

"I guess," Jesse said. Sasha could tell his heart wasn't in it.

"Can we see the rings?" Sasha asked the woman, eager to exact her revenge.

The woman let out a deep sigh and began to crumple to the ground, using the base of the chair she'd been sitting on to maneuver herself to the ground, shoving aside vintage purses to access the tray of rings.

"Anything else you want while I'm down here?" she grumbled.

Sasha scanned the selections. One of the hats was interesting to her. It was a vintage rodeo-queen style, blue and white lace and a pale blue ribbon at the back of the head. So were the Barbie purses from the '60s. Sasha was about to point out the hat when Jesse said, "Hey, what's that up there, behind the counter?"

Sasha stood up.

It was a snow princess wedding dress, the wrists and hemline trimmed with thick white fur. A matching white fur cap—a cunty Russian cap, jauntier than her green Ushanka hat—dangled off the side of the dress, attached by a white ribbon safety-pinned to the rest of the garment. It was vaguely '50s style, a structured bodice intercepting a silky, swirly skirt, but the reference was vague enough to not read as costume.

Jesse told her she had to try it on; it was too perfect not to. Abandoning the rings, the woman used a big metal hook to shake the dress down from its hook high up on the wall.

Behind the dress, when it emerged and landed in a heap in Sasha's hands, was a row of old Chanel perfume bottles, some in their original packaging.

"Any interest in these?" the woman asked, gesturing with her metal hook at the perfumes.

"I'm good," Sasha said.

In the dressing room, Sasha took off her clothes while Jesse unzipped the wedding dress and shook it out for her. She detonated a quick prayer. They had to ram Sasha's tits into the corset and she sucked in while Jesse tugged the zipper up. The worst thing would be if the dress tore, but by some twist of fate, it didn't. The fur trim at the neckline cut horizontally across her chest and along the tops of her shoulders. It was a beautiful shape just under her collarbone, which gleamed as though she'd balmed it. She'd have to wear a strapless bra. The train of the dress, also fur-trimmed, flowed elegantly from her body like she was standing on a satiny pond.

She took a tentative step, and the dress moved with her. It was too long, so she worked hard not to trip. She pushed the dressing room screen aside and peeked out. Jules and Miranda were close by, engaged in a hushed conversation next to a row of long, crocheted cardigans. In a farther corner, Darcy, still in the body suit, her back to them, was rifling through lace collars, and Lou was a few steps from her, a huge pile of fabrics stacked in their arms.

Sasha glided out of the dressing room, Jesse scampering after her, and arranged herself in front of the gilded floor-length mirror by the front counter. The shopkeeper raised her eyebrows. Sasha studied her reflection. The dress pushed her tits up, somehow both flattening them and accentuating their shape. The material hugged her waist and flared out at her hips, making her look like a distant Kardashian relative. And the cut of the neckline and the fur trim across her chest—coupled with the bare collarbone—was delightfully sexy.

The shopkeeper's brain had now paired the ring conversation with the wedding dress.

"When's the wedding?" she asked.

The question directed the rest of the group's attention toward Jesse and Sasha, and for a second everyone was quiet.

"Hot damn," Jules said, pulling out her iPhone to snap a picture of Sasha.

Lou was like, "Damn, Sasha, you need that."

Miranda didn't want the shopkeeper to feel ignored, so she asked Sasha: "When *are* you planning to get married?"

"Next month," Darcy said, in step as always with the social pageantry, easily claiming authority over the moment transpiring in front of them. "I'm their wedding planner."

"Are you now," the shopkeeper said.

They all stood in front of the mirror, flanking Sasha's reflection, and stared into the glass. They were framed like a wedding photo. Jesse was to Sasha's immediate left, sweaty and proud. Lou was Jesse's best man, nodding solemnly into the frame, one hand in a frozen slap on Jesse's back. Jules was at the leftmost corner, distracted, a queer elder ordained to marry them and release a few doves into the night. On Sasha's right was Miranda, an older sister or cousin perhaps, smoothing out Sasha's fur trim with one patient finger, and Darcy hovered just out of frame, included but slightly uninterested, or maybe just not interested in being peripheral—a reluctant maid of honor, selected because of her regrettably longstanding relationship with the bride and not because of any particular closeness between them. And there was Sasha, in the middle, looking shiny and huge, like a snowball. Rage began to coil. *Juggy* was a word someone might have reasonably used to describe her. Self-conscious, she looked closer at the group's reflection. No one was looking back at her. They were each studying their own reflections, sizing up their fits and the shapes their bodies made in the mirror.

"Help me take this off," Sasha ordered Jesse, and he began to unzip her as everyone scattered away. In the dressing room, she put her clothes back on and hung the dress gently on its hanger. She carried it to the woman at the front.

"Can I keep this with you?" Sasha asked. "I'm pretty sure I want to buy it."

As she handed the dress over, she saw the price tag for the first time: ninety dollars. It was expensive for a dress she'd likely never wear, but cheap for a dress that she might get married in. The relative cheapness of the dress when considered as a wedding outfit gave her pause, confirming what she hadn't quite let herself believe: that the material was surely polyester, thick and saturated with the previous wearer's sweat, the fur trim matted acrylic and speckled with dirt and the odd sparkle from a neighboring garment. The dress not real 1950s vintage, but instead a cheap 2010s-does-'50s approximation, a costume made for some heifer like Sasha to feel a part of things.

Jules was buying Miranda an old-fashioned tan hat with a long, skinny brim and multicolored gromets punched in it—crazier than anything Sasha had ever seen her wear, but cute and safely adventurous, perfect for a friend's birthday party. Lou bought Darcy an oversized, blue pinstriped pilgrim collar that fastened in the front and had bungee cords so that it could be tightened for effect. Her head floated atop the huge collar like a bulb, sleek and luminous.

Sasha and Jesse, who had accumulated more things than anyone else, compiled their options and began to debate the purchases. Sasha's eye landed on a pair of hand-knitted baby shoes up on a shelf, rainbow sherbet–colored yarn with two big plastic daisy buttons at either ankle. The shoes mended her mood—the way they were so small and brightly colored, the way they were made for a baby.

She marveled over them. "These would be perfect for Vivienne. If they had two pairs."

"Actually," Miranda said, coming closer and examining the shoes herself, "they'd be perfect for a baby."

"Jules, you should buy them for her," Darcy urged, and Jesse followed along: "Yeah, Jules, show her how committed you are."

Jules laughed uncomfortably, brushing the comments off without accepting them. The shoes went back on the shelf.

"I'm gonna dress my baby like an absolute clown," Darcy announced, swiveling over to the register with her items.

Lou used their height to reach up on a shelf and pull down an old top hat, handing it to Jules. Jules plonked it onto her head and turned eagerly to her reflection in the mirror.

"Huh-hey!" she bellowed at her reflection.

They watched as a strange force of nature overtook her. First Jules's elbows jutted to the sides, and then she skipped to the left like an old-timey gentleman, clicking her heels as she went. She then galloped the opposite way, nearly felling a rack of scarves, her skips and hops maintaining the rhythm of country people at a barn dance.

The group screamed with laughter as Jules dance-jumped around the store. Miranda, especially, was taken by Jules's antics, shrieking and clapping her hands. She laughed so hard she doubled over, wailing. Vivienne waddled over to see what the commotion was about, and when Jules started skipping manically toward her, she scuffled out of the way and settled nervously by the door. Sasha, on her way over to comfort Vivienne and laughing so hard she could barely see, glanced over to see the shopkeeper's reaction. She was stoically focused on ringing up Darcy's playsuit.

"Oh my god." Miranda straightened up and wiped at her eyes, though there were no discernible tears there.

"That performance!" Darcy, now holding a paper bag, tipped a fake hat to Jules.

Panting, Jules replaced her own top hat onto the shelf whence it had come.

Slowly, they became consumers again. Lou was still searching for the perfect item to buy for themselves. Jesse suggested a men's flannel nightgown, long and blue plaid. Lou said it was perfect. "It'll make me feel like Father Time."

Darcy took a selfie of her and Lou in the mirror—her in the big collar and Lou in the flannel nightgown—and later captioned it *afternoon faggotry* for her Instagram story.

The shopkeeper was writing everything down in a notebook and adding up the totals on a big, clunky calculator. It was an arduous process. Sasha was beginning to sweat, her feet aching. When the shopkeeper was finally done with Darcy, she moved on to Sasha.

"Taking the dress?"

"Yes," Sasha said.

The woman bundled the dress in newspaper and shoved it into a big plastic bag.

On their way out of the store, an alarm sounded. Sasha hadn't realized the store was high-tech enough to have a sensor. She froze, assuming it was she who had stolen. She remembered the bags of nuts she'd stolen from Fairway in her youth, how many times she'd left the store exhilarated and not-caught.

"I must've forgotten to take the tag off something." The old woman scuttled over to them and began rifling through the bags.

Sasha shifted Vivienne from one arm to the other. It was hot and stuffy. She wanted to push the door open, but she feared that the woman would assume she *had* stolen and was trying to make a run for it.

The shopkeeper pulled out the baby shoes from Miranda's bag slowly, revealing them over the span of five horrifying seconds.

They still had the bulky tag on them. She stared Miranda in the face, her expression changing from wary to confused. Surely Miranda hadn't taken the shoes on purpose. Throughout their whole time in the store, Miranda had been this woman's favorite—polite, not bratty, gentle with the merchandise.

"Babe?" Jules asked, jokingly, trying to lighten the mood.

"I'm so sorry about that," Miranda was saying. "I must have slipped them into my bag by accident. Here—I'm not going to buy them."

The shopkeeper bowed her head and accepted the baby shoes, turning to place them back on the shelf.

"Wait!" Jesse said.

"Wait?" Sasha asked.

"I'll buy them."

"You *will*?"

Sasha stared at Jesse. His face was difficult to read, a mixture of pride and resignation. He wouldn't meet Sasha's eye; it was like he was doing this out of duty to her, but also for some reason unwilling to give the moment to her, to let her and him be happy about it together.

"You can just take them," the shopkeeper sighed, eager to get rid of the group and their weird energy.

"Are you sure?" Sasha asked. The old woman nodded, studiously avoiding eye contact. (Because she'd heard their conversation about the baby shoes earlier? Or because she knew that Sasha was being humiliated here, for reasons beyond Sasha herself?)

Now that the baby shoes were free, Jesse seemed unburdened by them, slipping the pair into his bag and leading the group out of the store, calling out an absent-minded "thank you!" behind them.

৩ ৵

They passed a novelty T-shirt and hoodie shop, which they appraised for a few seconds before dismissing as a little too on the nose.

"Hold *on*," Darcy said.

There was a mannequin in the window wearing a bright orange Home Depot hoodie, the word *Hermès* scrawled in place of *The Home Depot*.

Jesse groaned. "Okay, that's kinda perfect."

Lou squinted at the price tag. "Dude, it's like two hundred dollars. I'll make you the same thing for free if you find a plain orange hoodie at Goodwill."

The air was thin and frigid. Sasha announced that she was going to find a tailor for her wedding dress. The rest of them took off down the main street of Hudson to take a cold lesbian walk, Vivienne shooting Sasha a few desperate looks as Jesse yanked her gently away in the opposite direction. Finally she trotted off, and the group turned a corner, disappearing behind a rambling inn.

Sasha headed west, googling on her phone to find an open tailor. It was easy—there was a tailor a few blocks down, operating from inside another thrift shop.

At the second place, she found a hand-knitted sweater in gorgeous shades of gray, a bright blue Tommy Hilfiger bag, and a pair of devastatingly reduced Fendi sunglasses, all of which she bought before approaching the woman at the counter. This shop owner was slim and sweet, making easy conversation.

Sasha was chatty and breezy in the way she was when Jesse wasn't around, when he wasn't there to cover for her. The owner's name was Samantha, and she was probably in her midfifties, or maybe early sixties; it was so hard to tell with athletic women of that age. There was something butch about her demeanor; Sasha wondered if she was gay, though she was learning that outside of Brooklyn, many of the women who looked butch and rough around the edges were actually just rustic and into rockclimbing.

Samantha looked at the wedding dress and declared that it would be a fun project for her, though it wouldn't be cheap, she warned good-naturedly. She charged fifty an hour and it would take her at least a few hours, given the math involved in such an alteration. Sasha told her she'd talk it over with her boyfriend and be back the following day with an answer. But she knew she wouldn't spend the money. It was too embarrassing to spend that large a sum to flatter herself. She'd tailor the dress herself, or she'd never wear it.

Before meeting up with the rest of the group in a coffee shop, she slipped into the hoodie store and crept to the section where bright orange fabric was stacked in neat rows. She shuffled through a pile of them to find a size medium, unfurled it and held it in her hands. She kind of understood why it was two hundred dollars. The material was luxurious, the outside thick yet pliant, the inside coated in a fleece so soft, it felt almost perverted to stroke it. She held it up to her own body and subtracted her boobs.

The others were drinking lattes in a nearby coffee shop, Vivienne perched on Jesse's lap. Her butt waggled as Sasha walked in, braced against the cold in her green hat.

The *Price of Salt* audio book was playing from the car speaker. The narrator had an even, silky voice that Sasha soon grew tired of, and she willed the scenes to move faster. They were at the end of the book, but it was taking forever to actually end. Finally, they listened as Therese decides to go live with Carol in her new apartment on Madison Avenue and Carol gets a job as a buyer at a furniture shop in Greenwich Village. Jesse said he wished the book had included a description of the apartment Carol and Therese shared, the details of their life there, how they had decided to decorate and what the furniture that Carol buys looks like.

Miranda was hot and Sasha cold, so Miranda slipped her cardigan to the back seat for Sasha to use as a blanket. There was a clunky weight in one of the pockets, and Sasha maneuvered the cardigan around, slipping her hand inside. The cool glass rectangle of Miranda's phone.

She was sitting directly behind Miranda, leaning her body against the edge of the car. She used Vivienne to block her arm as she slowly slid the phone out of the pocket and pressed the button on its side. The screen was pregnant with unread texts, so many that they'd been sorted into categories: texts from Jules, texts from her best friend and podcast cohost, Odette, a few Instagram notifications (@mirandacsaraf had a follow request and a message from a friend who had shared a post), and texts from a contact named Niles A.

Sasha thumbed the circular button at the bottom edge of the phone, barely breathing. It opened immediately to Miranda's home screen, which was weird—why didn't she have a passcode? Elders. It was also weird to be on someone else's phone. She didn't know where any of the apps were, felt like she was from the past or from the future; so much about the experience of using technology was about using your *own* device, the way you personalized how things looked and how they felt; it was difficult to navigate an identical device that belonged to someone else.

The Messages icon was at the bottom of the home screen, and Sasha pressed it. The unread texts were lined up, still categorized: Jules, Odette, Niles A. The most recent text from Jules read, *went outside.* The most recent text from Odette read, *wait but do you ACTUALLY think he will?* And the most recent text from Niles A had been cut off: *Hi Miranda, I got your message. While I do*

She wanted more, but she knew that if she clicked it, the texts would be marked as read. So she swiped the screen until she found Miranda's Twitter app.

The sight of the blue and white icon filled Sasha with anxiety, but she soldiered on. In the upper corner, Miranda's icon, a small oval featuring her close-mouthed smile and the top of a blue cardigan. Her chest contracted when she saw the number of notifications that Miranda had accrued since last checking—the mentions, the direct messages. She clicked the mentions, hoping it wouldn't clear them all but resigning to the possibility that it could. The screen filled with snippets of other users' harassment.

Can we talk about how @mirandacsaraf and @odette_bettendorf haven't apologized??

Having a hard time reconciling with the smart, compassionate takes I've heard on @TwoBadTherapistsPod with the recent biphobia of @mirandacsaraf and @odette_bettendorf.

I get that @mirandacsaraf is technically bisexual but isn't she p much married to @TheRealJulesTodd? Doesn't that make her a "refugee" (in her own problematic language)?

@mirandacsaraf Girl, it's like you said: if bi folks have passports in the straight community and r accepted as full members of it, and have to prove themselves as queer—

Sasha clicked the phone off, and the screen went black. She felt immediate relief. When they stopped for gas a few miles later, Sasha slid the phone back into the pocket of the cardigan and handed it to Miranda with a quick thank-you. She gathered one of her parcels and hopped out of the car behind Jesse, who was heading into the gas station for some snacks.

"Carol loves her daughter so much," Sasha said, coming up behind Jesse, alone in a row of Pringles and SmartFood popcorn. She was truly moved by this part of the *Price of Salt* audiobook. "But she still loves Therese more."

"I'll love you more than our kids?" Jesse guessed at what Sasha was fishing for.

"Aww." Sasha held the plastic bag aloft. "I got you a present."

Jesse pulled out the orange hoodie. "Baby! I love it!"

"You do?"

"Yeah, I wanted it so bad. You spent all that money?"

"It was worth it." Sasha delivered a quick peck. "You showed Jules who's boss back there. In the store with the baby shoes. I'm excited to have your babies."

She selected a big bag of Cheez Doodles and placed them in Jesse's small cart with a sniffle, then looked up eagerly into Jesse's face. A nervous look rolled across his features. Sasha braced for impact.

"Baby," Jesse said gently, "can we not talk about marriage and babies right now? Can we focus on being young and happy?"

Jesse said it as though he was only kidding, but the words had maimed her. Ever since Sasha had decamped semipermanently to Providence, she'd been clutching Jesse's words from Fire Island about the ring like a baby blanket, rubbing the reassurance against her cheek at night. Lou was on the other side of the aisle buying a small bag of salted almonds. She wanted to reach over to them, to have them come help her.

"You deceived me," she said, because she wasn't sure what else to say. "You played along and made me buy the wedding dress, you made me believe you, and then you deceived me."

"I didn't DECEIVE you." Jesse laughed furiously. "I thought we were joking!"

Sasha said she hadn't thought they were joking. "I thought you were serious about me, I thought I could *depend* on you. That's why I got the dress."

She snatched the sweatshirt back from him and stood with it, panting, feeling like a monster.

The doorbell chimed and Miranda entered the gas station. She headed over toward Jesse and Sasha, a wide grin on her face.

"Is that the sweatshirt we saw?" she asked cheerfully.

"No," Sasha barked.

Miranda pivoted toward the kombucha.

"I am serious about you!" Jesse exploded. "But it's like you won't care about any of this till we're old and it's *over*."

"But you got me *baby shoes*," Sasha protested. "Surely you weren't just playing along, then? What kind of sick fuck buys a girl *baby shoes* as a joke?"

"As a joke," he insisted gently. "Or not a joke, a gesture; I thought it was cute of me."

It was true: he'd only gotten them for her on a whim, as a joke, to make up for Miranda's mistake. Sasha thrust the hoodie back at Jesse, where it lay limp in his arms.

"I don't want this if it's like, contingent on me doing what you want," he said.

"Give me a break."

"I'm serious! You can't just buy me presents and take them away when I have *feelings* about something."

"Grow up," Sasha enunciated. "It's a fucking hoodie. Take it or leave it."

They made their way back to the car, both angry, snacks abandoned. The heat was cranked and the *Price of Salt* audiobook was playing at a low volume. Jules, Miranda, Darcy, and Lou were waiting in their respective seats, scrolling on their phones. They all glanced up as Jesse and Sasha slammed into the car.

"Everything okay?" Lou asked. No one answered.

In the car they were both silent, staring at the two-lane highway, cars whooshing by in the opposite direction. Sasha hated this highway. She hated the risk of the car traveling in the opposite direction crashing headfirst into them.

In the driver's seat, Jules's phone chimed, and she took the call, mouthing, *It's Cate*, to Miranda.

"Yeah," Jules said into the phone, "I did think about it, and—"

She held the phone away from her ear, and Cate's indignant squawk came thinly from the speaker.

"Look, I'm driving, I've gotta go," Jules said.

"STOP! PRESSURING ME! ABOUT! THE HORSES!" Jules shouted to the windshield when she hung up with Cate.

I don't want to waste my time, Sasha texted Jesse. She didn't know what else to say. *I don't want to waste my time on someone who can't commit to me.*

Who are you? Jesse fired back, thumbs flying across his phone's keyboard. *Stassi Schroeder from Vanderpump Rules? Can you be real with me? Can you say what you want without all the histrionics?*

Sasha: *please don't get triggered*

The look Jesse gave her in return made Sasha feel embarrassed that her game was so transparent, her performance clear as day. To save face, she said aloud, making everyone look over again, "No, that's not what I mean at all."

"About *any* of it?" Jesse insisted. "You're not joking about any of it at all? You think *that's* what makes this better?"

He was speaking lightly because everyone was listening, but Sasha could tell the rest of the group was tired and annoyed by the burden of performing witness to this charade. They would have preferred silence, small talk, anything to this secondhand humiliation.

"No," she said stubbornly, though she didn't know if that was quite true. "It's time to *grow up*," she said, choosing her words carefully for maximum impact, "it's time to be an *adult*, to be *normal*."

She, too, was trying to be funny. But Sasha's tone was hysterical, and she knew that her statement was neither exactly fair nor exactly true. It was the same problem she'd had with her ex but in different words, and in a different register. *Conflict is not abuse* popped into her head—the Sarah Schulman book she hadn't read. She recalled Jesse saying that to her about Sasha's relationship with her ex: *conflict is not abuse*. But it didn't work as a catch-all salve anymore and she sat moodily in the front seat, legs oriented away from Jesse to show him that she was mad. She willed a single tear to drip down her face and turned slightly so that he could see it.

He either didn't notice or didn't care, didn't ask Sasha if she was upset and why. What he said, finally, was instead incredibly moody: "Why is right now never enough for you?"

Sasha's face flared with humiliation. Jesse had berated her in front of everyone. From the front seat, Miranda intoned, "You love each other very much."

Months ago, before Sasha left for Providence, Jesse had been obsessed with their future. Their relationship was like a new bar of soap becoming a slippery nub.

"I love you, Sash," Jesse said, adopting the therapist's language. "That's all I'm saying."

He doesn't love me, Sasha thought, gazing out the window like an army wife.

In the driveway, the Prius's passengers parted to let the feuding couple escape first. The rest of them fussed over the packages in the backseat and the trunk, arranging items so that each bag could be given to its owner.

Jesse went straight to the back porch and beckoned Sasha to come over.

"Look," he said, trying to make amends, "look who's on the porch, staring at us."

Two enormous stuffed bears were sitting on the porch chair, slumped in the same lounge chair, gorgeous and plush. Their paws were covered in lush caramel fur, with rosy pink fleece paw pads on the undersides. Red ribbons were secured around their thick necks, eyes and noses were sewn with thick reams of black thread, red tongues flopped in mouths, felt-lined ears lounged at the sides of their heads.

Jesse had bought them for her as a surprise. He'd paid attention to her one wish each Valentine's Day—that someone would get her a massive stuffed bear, a bear so inconveniently big that it would be difficult to find a place for him in the apartment. He'd listened when she'd explained how receiving such a bear would be reparative for her, a salve for her childhood wounds of near-empty Valentine's boxes in stuffy, windowless elementary-school classrooms. How she'd cuddle up to such a bear each night, Vivienne in the mix, and know that she was loved.

"You got those for me?" Sasha asked.

Lou came over to where they were standing by the glass

door and tapped the glass lightly to show that they, too, were excited about the bears.

"I found those on the street earlier!" Lou said. "I thought they'd be good for the performance."

Sasha looked up into their face, unblinking—at first ruefully and then finally getting it.

Lou had probably gotten the bears from a family that was throwing them away after an adoption that had fallen through; or maybe they'd had the baby shower too early, and the woman had miscarried or had a stillbirth.

She wanted to weep for the dead baby, the grieving couple. She could not accept what he was saying as the truth any more than he could make himself want what she wanted. But what did she want? For him to tell the truth?

That was the issue: there was no truth to be told. There were still games, still antics. She'd argued in her green-ribbon essay that antics were a way to express desire that couldn't be sated and had to be performed instead. That camp was pretending to do something while actually doing it (not Sasha's original definition, but one she loved). Like poetry, she operated under dream logic—the logic of association, images, feelings. Yet now she expected Jesse to tell her the truth?

PART THREE

Bimbo

Music is a green wave coming into me, love will feel like this when it enters, when I meet you, you will do this to me coming in.

Laurie Weeks, *Zipper Mouth*

also reminder that this is late capitalism, we all buy our genders, some are just more expensive than others

Bryn Kelly, Twitter

Can I Come Inside

୬ ୬

Sasha's mother had taught her that shaving above the knee was for sluts. It was what it was—a rule cloaked in neutrals. The winter of her courtship with Jesse, though, Sasha began to understood her desire for hairless thighs on totally different (yet equally slutty) terms.

Tsilia's implication about shaving above the knee was basic: any activity that took place there on the sultry, hairless thigh was slut activity. But what was actually slutty about Sasha was the way she forbade Jesse from touching the thighs she had so carefully shaven. She was slutty in her minxy refusal.

She knew that when a proper, practiced slut wanted something, she asked for it, and often the asking was hot. However, Sasha was new to slutdom and sensed that her brand of sluttiness had to be backhanded, furtive. Plus, she could never predict if she'd be able to trust herself to resist Jesse's roving hands, so she shaved as a backup plan, too. This also made her slutty—the way she made provisions for her faltering restraint.

That winter, Jesse's new tattoo—a dyke-jock anklet that featured a soccer ball, a basketball, and a blue star to commemorate the 1940s and '50s working-class butch-femme community in Buffalo, New York, as featured in the ethnography *Boots of Leather, Slippers of Gold*—was wet, oozing, and wrapped in a tube of plastic. Its reds and yellows and pinks and blues were not yet set in their black outlines, and as Sasha's toes brushed up against the new tattoo, Jesse winced. Sasha saw that she was strong, or at least pretending to be, and this show of stoicism endeared Jesse to her. Sasha kept brushing her feet against the fresh tattoo accidentally, yet Jesse didn't get angry at her—instead she just kept wincing and laughing.

When Jesse slipped an eager hand into her underwear that night, Sasha grabbed her wrist and yanked it away. "I have rules."

Jesse looked at Sasha like, *Are you serious*. She clearly was not sure what to make of this; her face adjusted, and she set it right again, replying, "Okay, tell me, then, what are your rules?"

There was nothing more gross, Sasha understood, than wanting someone else to do your desiring for you. Except she wanted more than that, she also wanted Jesse in turn to defer her desire to Sasha; that was the thing she found it urgent to impress upon Jesse and the thing she chose to explain first. It was about the *back-and-forth*, the exchange of their desire. There was only so much she could orchestrate, she admitted to herself. Ultimately, her desire to produce and direct Jesse's desire was ill-fated, or even worse: futile.

"But what do you want me to actually, like, do," Jesse said.

Sasha was unsure of what word to use—*pussy* felt awkward, and *cunt* was too weird, so impulsively she said *kittycat*, as a joke, making them both laugh—and she couldn't remember if she'd used the sexy whisper she'd perfected in the bathtub, or if she'd talked, as she tended to do, in an increasingly high-pitched refrain, explaining the rules of the game like it were Bananagrams. Jesse would ask, *Can I Come Inside?* Sasha would say, *No.* Jesse was to repeat this line of questioning while petting Sasha. She was not to come inside. But when Jesse wanted to come inside badly enough, she was to thrust her way inside, disregarding Sasha's wishes.

Sasha repeated the iconic lines that Jennifer Tilly says in *Bound*: "I know you don't believe what you hear," she coaxed Jesse, drawing his big hand between her legs, "but do you believe what you feel?"

The first night they'd played Can I Come Inside, she had been wearing a long, sheer pink nightgown with a black bra underneath. Jesse had started to touch her, and she ached with pleasure.

"Wait," Sasha said. "Have you thought about fucking me before?"

Jesse paused at the entrance, mouth hanging slightly open.

"Yes," Jesse admitted.

"How many times?"

Jesse smiled with half his mouth. "A few."

"And what did you think it would be like?"

"Mmm." Jesse eased his hand in and out of her, thinking about it. "I thought I'd make you come."

"Did you think you'd use your hands to do that?" Sasha grabbed Jesse's wrist and held it still, the vein throbbing inside her palm.

"Can I Come Inside," Jesse said, with some hesitation. Sasha could tell he was trying to get into it, the game, and not quite succeeding. There was something uncommitted in his tone the first time she said it, without conviction, and Sasha waited for him to correct himself.

"Can I Come Inside," he said again, stronger this time, "Can I Come Inside, please?"

The addition of the *please* was not entirely what Sasha wanted; she craved insistence, the proof of Jesse wanting her. But the fact that he was trying was important, and Sasha said, "No," then more firmly: "*No*."

She smiled.

"*Tell me all the reasons why you want to Come Inside.*"

Jesse balked, then laughed a little scoff of a laugh, and Sasha couldn't tell if he thought this was stupid or if he was turned on. This was demoralizing on one level, but thrilling on another—higher—level. Like all of the stupid antics Sasha was pulling those days, the game was flopping because of the way its underlying desire was floppy. Excessive. Instead it had to get acted out like a play—performed with the abundance of humiliation on both of their parts that always accompanies such a blatant performance of desire, the precise humiliation that neither of them had quite anticipated.

"I want to come inside," Jesse said finally, "because—because"—here he faltered, and when he next spoke, it was in a gruff and urgent tone—"I've got to get in there; I know it'll be so warm and perfect in there."

Sasha sensed, for a second, Jesse's embarrassment. This was not something she'd previously considered, that Jesse would be embarrassed to play her game; and it was not what she wanted, Jesse's embarrassment. What Sasha wanted was his desire. It was all wrong in that moment. She wished to die.

"Can I Come Inside?" Jesse asked again.

"No."

"How about now?"

"No."

"Can I Come Inside?"

"No."

"Now?"

"Remember," Sasha whispered, "you're supposed to force your way in there when you can't stand it any longer."

"I know, I know," Jesse said, but he still didn't thrust his fingers in. He kept touching Sasha and did not Come Inside.

No matter how many times she illustrated this idea in plain language, Sasha could not handle the material possibility that what she wanted most did not align with what Jesse wanted most. Sasha's goal was to extract Jesse's deepest fantasy, his darkest wish; Jesse was supposed to tell her every one of his perverted desires because she had already told Jesse hers. Jesse was now supposed to tell her something she hadn't heard before. But at that moment Jesse thrust his fingers inside Sasha, and the opportunity to speak was already gone.

How Strange, How Lovely

ଚ୬ ୬ଚ

MONDAY, DECEMBER 30

Vivienne woke before Sasha and Jesse. Her need to pee wasn't super urgent, so she nestled between them, curled into a ball with her back against Sasha's stomach (though in general she preferred to be big spoon, tucking one paw under Sasha's inner shoulder and wrapping her body around Sasha's back).

She couldn't fall back to sleep. Things kept waking her up— the sound of footsteps downstairs, the gentle hum of the wind outside, something scratching against the window. A smell was bothering her, too. She'd catch a whiff of it and lose it, then catch it again. Finally, she jumped down from the bed as quietly as possible, taking care to avoid bearing weight on the stiff joint in her left hind leg, and padded across the room to snuffle Sasha's suitcase. Most of the items carried Sasha's familiar scent—kinda like cotton-candy grapes, Vivienne mused, though she wasn't allowed to eat them. She groaned loudly. Sasha smelled like all the things Vivienne wasn't allowed to eat: chocolate, coffee, artificial sweetener, grapes. But there was something else, too, something wrong. She pawed through the suitcase until she found the offending item: the fur-trimmed wedding dress, crumpled in a heap halfway under the suitcase.

Oh, Sasha. How Vivienne's heart ached for her. Vivienne nosed at the dress until the whole thing flopped over, remembering Sasha trying it on in the vintage store, how they'd stood in front of the huge mirror and looked at themselves. Vivienne's nose twitched as she sniffed it, letting the old scent of it fill her nostrils and brush against her eyelashes. She had to. She knew she wasn't supposed to. But she squatted anyway, shame flickering up her brain stem.

Sasha sat up in bed suddenly and stared right at Vivienne.

"She's peeing!" Sasha accused groggily, snapping a finger at Vivienne.

The accusation was true; there was nothing Vivienne could do but let the last trickles of urine fall onto the dress—polyester, she noted, so the pee slid off in rivulets onto the wooden floor—and then approach the bed nervously, ears back, her body shaking with wags. She made eye contact with Sasha and radiated with kindness so that Sasha would understand that the peeing had been accidental, instinct rather than intention; she wasn't backsliding in her training, but instead expressing herself.

Sasha pulled her up by her armpits. Jesse let out a soft groan and shifted in his sleep.

Vivienne began licking Jesse's face to wake him up. The smell of Morning Daddy filled her stenotic nostrils (which would be enlarged the following summer in a veterinary rhinoplasty, a minor procedure that Sasha would refer to as "Vivienne's nose job") and she waggled, pacing back and forth along the mountain ridge of his body.

"Where's Daddy?" Sasha prompted, sitting up in bed and reaching for her cell phone, and Vivienne was like, *Mom, he's literally right here.* Sometimes Sasha treated Vivienne like an idiot, but it was honestly fine—Vivienne's job was to make Sasha happy, so she was willing to put up with minor indignities. Not every dog had so much ego power.

For the past ten hours, from the time they'd woken up in the morning until much later that evening, Sasha hadn't seen Jesse at all. Jesse and Darcy had been in the sauna, decorating its interior in preparation for that night's performance. Sasha spent the day in bed with Vivienne, scrolling on her phone and sometimes flipping through the copy of *The Well of Loneliness* she'd brought, trying for years now to get through. She could get into it, all the lusting and female masculinity, but found the WASPy prudishness frustrating. There wasn't enough sex, so she kept stalling.

With Darcy and Jesse in the sauna, and Miranda and Jules locked away in their respective offices doing work, Sasha still technically had Lou for company. But Lou was in and out of the house, checking on the sauna's progress and running out to buy last-minute props for the setup. Lou wanted to be helpful to Jesse and Darcy, which was where they fundamentally differed from Sasha. She wondered if she should be concerned that Lou seemed unfazed by this collaboration. She understood their blasé affect only as a personality disorder.

Lou had been tapped to man the iPhone and modulate the audio. Jesse offered that Jules and Sasha might watch the performance from just outside the sauna, through the window, but it was cold out, and Jules and Sasha were creatures of comfort. Over a lunch of leftovers (which Lou had brought out to the sauna rather than interrupt Jesse and Darcy's work) Sasha asked if she and Jules could watch together on Jules's laptop, and understanding that Sasha needed company, Jules had graciously acquiesced. Miranda, who had not bothered to feign much interest in the performance in the first place, had booked several appointments with clients that evening and would be shut away in her office.

"You'll protect me, right?" Sasha said to Jules, and everyone at the table—Miranda, Jules, and Lou—laughed.

"What are you afraid of?" Jules asked.

But Sasha could not articulate what she actually feared. Lou said gently, "Jesse loves you so much."

This helped, but she already knew this, and it was not exactly what she was afraid of, so she brushed away the conversation, bringing everyone's dirty plates to the sink.

And so, when the clock flashed eight, with the door to Bedroom 1 firmly closed and Vivienne gnawing a dried pig ear at the end of Jules and Miranda's four-poster bed, Jules opened Instagram on her laptop. They'd been notified that @reality___cheque had gone live. Usually Sasha appreciated the particular weirdness of social media language—going live, following, tagging, mentioning. Jules clicked *join*, and waited for the connection to go through. They were sitting together on the bed. Jules and Miranda were all over it—Miranda's fruity shampoo and Jules's butch cologne. The feeling of the mattress against her ass and lower back was titillating, how soft and steamy it felt to be in the older couple's domain.

In seconds, they were staring into Darcy's face. The self-aware close-up of someone showing that she's still getting her Instagram stream set up, though the lighting is already of course flattering. A look of concentration crossed her face as she tinkered with the technology, and she moved a little bit farther away once more followers joined the stream, evidently satisfied with the angle.

Darcy was dressed like a Slavic stripper. Her tan shoulders peeked out of a red satin robe and slashes of pink lipstick gleamed on her plumped up lips. Her hair was combed out and slightly frizzy; it was already hot in there. Jules's sauna—fuzzy pink rug, pearlescent candles, wooden slabs topped with cherub figurines, gems and jewels glued to every conceivable surface, pink and green ribbons swirling from the ceiling like vines, moss that Jesse had harvested (some of it airbrushed pink) draped artfully along the benches—filled their screen.

"Holy fuck," Jules said.

"Can she see us?" Sasha asked quietly.

Vivienne shifted her pig ear over to Sasha's thigh in order to provide emotional support, but Sasha yelped and shouted, "Fuck, her nails are so long."

(Sasha was one to talk—whenever she grabbed the goop out of Vivienne's eyes to feed it to her, Sasha's own long nails stabbed Vivienne.)

Jules shook her head absently, and Sasha saw that Jules was transfixed by the transformation—of Darcy, of her sauna. Jules's eyes flickered over the screen, her big pointer finger jabbing at the screen as she noticed each new detail. She guffawed and chuckled, a look of dumb amazement creasing her face, like a toddler on an iPad.

Darcy was admittedly beautiful, or at least looked that way through their screen. Sasha couldn't bring herself to look over at Jules to gauge how she was receiving this face. She had to stay focused on the performance, even if it annihilated her, because after all that was the point of her attendance: to destroy her enormous and ungainly self. She tried to enter a subliminal state, one where she was able to release her sense of self and experience the performance as an omniscient narrator, but she was called back into herself by the décor of the sauna, which she recognized immediately as *her*. The pink moss, the oversized bows, the airbrushed lace, the dolls. It was like a facsimile of her personal style, her aesthetic, an uncanny rendering of Sasha's Sasha-ness, which she could only understand, looking at the screen, as an awful parody.

She wondered if she'd see herself in this performance. She didn't want to make this all about her, but the basis of this performance originated in her work—she had every right to look for herself, for the sensibility that Darcy seemed to covet and deride, diminish and imitate in equal measures.

For the past few days, when Darcy and Jesse had gone to rehearse, disappearing for hours into the sauna and reemerging flushed and hungry, Sasha had waited for them to say something to her—an acknowledgment that she shared in what they were doing, that they might want or value her perspective. But they'd scampered off together with the glee of collaborators, of co-conspirators, without seeming to remember that this started with Sasha, and she didn't know how to remind them without seeming desperate. She'd been edged out of this, whatever these two shared, and it felt like a robbery.

Jules, Sasha, and Vivienne continued staring into Darcy's face. Vivienne could see what Sasha was seeing, and Sasha could see what Jules was seeing, because they were looking at the same screen. And what Sasha saw was Darcy's pristineness, her purity. She was not withered and horrible like Sasha but perfectly inflated, the pink and green blow-up doll Jesse had in her living room, a Niki de Saint Phalle original that Sasha bought for a large sum of money at an antique store because she liked how the blow-up woman's body was perfectly filled with air, every corner of it, not a single wrinkle on her plastic body.

I will know, Sasha had continually told Jesse over the past months. *I will know if anything happens between the two of you, and it won't take hours, or days, or weeks for me to find out—I will know* immediately, *I will feel it in my bones.*

Hello, Sasha typed into the chat box at the bottom of the screen before she could stop herself. Her hello appeared next to Jules's name, because they were on Jules's Instagram account. Because she had thousands of followers, Jules's icon featured a blue check mark, meaning she was verified as Jules Todd, the real thing and not a fake account. Jules's name and blue check floated up, buoyed by the many other comments below it: clapping emojis, hearts, balloons.

Jules flailed a hand out protectively, as if to tell Sasha not to type anything more. But she didn't actually say anything, so Sasha retained control of the laptop.

They were watching Darcy watch the comments flood the screen, smiling the empty smile of the adored—it was mostly empty encouragement, her friends expressing their joy at seeing her and saying she looked hot—and watching her face just be her face, every angle of it, the light streaking across her cheekbones and the teeth twinkling every time she parted her lips ever so slightly.

"I think we're ready to begin," Darcy said finally, after they'd stared into her face for a couple more slow seconds. She was inviting her audience to drink up her face, to see it under each separate pane of light. Her voice was syrupy.

Jesse was not in the frame; Sasha imagined that he was still scampering around the sauna, putting finishing touches on his set.

Darcy started reading from "The Girl with the Green Ribbon."

Sasha's mind skipped instinctively back to the sexual-inversion thing, landing on an image of Radclyffe Hall and her black pug, Joey, cast in microfilm.

She was trying to make this children's story sound sexy. It was well within her rights to call attention to herself, Sasha noted with displeasure. And it was within her rights to show off her profile, her nose as diminutive as a cat's. Sasha wanted to type again into the chat box, *Why won't you answer me, bitch* or maybe *Do you think you're too good to answer me?*

Neither of them were the first to make art from the green-ribbon story, nor would they be the last to examine how people might use each other's bodies as they see fit. The most famous example of the past few years was Carmen Maria Machado's short story "The Husband Stitch," which Sasha had quoted in her own ill-fated essay. Her favorite part of that story was the protagonist's telling her husband to use her body "as he sees fit."

The heterosexual "as he sees fit" is so different from the lesbian "as he sees fit." Specifically a lesbian telling another lesbian to do so—if only because it's less clear what that might mean, how she might see the fit of their bodies.

Sasha didn't say this to anyone, of course. But the best sex she ever had with her ex had taken place with her body stretched out on a table in the basement of their college's chapel, her head lolling off the end, the world bobbing upside down with zero awareness of its inversion.

There was a pause as Darcy went off set, and when she appeared again, Darcy was different: now two big blue eyes—each resplendent with long lashes—had been painted on either cheekbone underneath her real eyes, green and flickering. She was strung up in a wooden crucifix, arms perpendicular to her head. This must have been the terrible thing that Jesse had been building all week. (Jesus was a Jewish carpenter!)

"Pretty incredible how they transformed the sauna," Jules said.

Sasha didn't respond, because her throat wouldn't release.

"How are you feeling?" Jules asked.

"I'm fine," Sasha croaked, adding, "Darcy looks haggard."

Jules didn't respond, because Sasha was just being mean, and because Darcy was sexier than Sasha, it was kind of sad for Sasha to criticize Darcy, it only made her look undignified. This seemed to make Jules sad, and it made Sasha sad for herself. Sasha decided to remain silent. She must only watch.

A pair of gloved hands emerged from the bottom of the screen holding a suture. The gloves looked like the dishwashing gloves Jules kept under the sink, pink and rubber, but with ragged edges, rough-hewn by a scissor. The cheap ribbon Jesse brought from Brooklyn was stuffed through the needle in a perverted fashion, bunched up to fit through the needle's narrow eye.

The shape and size of the hands, the wrists with their big blue veins, made Sasha clutch Jules's forearm. Jules's skin was clammy and loose with middle age. Sasha twisted it between her fingers like wax. Jules pulled away absentmindedly.

"They're so close to us," Jules mused. "Think we'll be able to hear them?"

Darcy was still in the crucifix, her body straight up against the vertical beam and her arms tied to either end of the cross with green ribbon. She glanced over at the needle with a self-satisfied grimace.

"I'm going to be sick," Jules said suddenly. Sasha looked at the screen, but Jules turned the screen away, toward Sasha, at an angle that was impossible for her to actually see. Sasha grabbed the laptop back and set it a few inches from her face, and this must have been agreeable to Jules, because she didn't protest.

"Darcy, will you slap your thighs *really hard* so we can hear you?" a disembodied voice said, and a slapping sound came through the computer as the screen flashed to Darcy.

Jules and Sasha both screamed, Jules's scream surprisingly girlish. Jesse's hands had begun sewing Darcy's mouth shut, starting from the right corner, with the green ribbon, so that the right half of her lips was completely sewn shut in a series of neat green stitches. It was like the stitches Sasha used to sew into the tough skin of her palm with her friends, pretending to do surgery, but instead the stitches were inserted into the soft flesh of Darcy's lips.

"This is so fucking gross," Sasha said.

Jules was still stuck on the fact that this was happening, and so close to them, too. "It's not special effects, right? This is so cool."

Darcy's voice was muffled and strained as she read quietly with the unsewn half of her mouth. "Now that we're married, you must tell me about the green ribbon."

The left side of her plump, pink lips flapped with the strain of speaking. Sasha wondered how many other people were watching and who those people were, if they were screaming too, if it was the same people who attended Darcy's parties in east Williamsburg, that inner circle of Brooklyn queers; or random perverts from the internet; or the dirtbag left itself. And she wondered who *they* were, her and Jules, their eyes fixed on the screen. Where were the pink gloved hands, Jesse's hands?

They must have been waiting offscreen, twitching with pride, so happy to be included.

Darcy eased herself onto the ground, tilting her camera so that her entire ass was visible to the audience. She was wearing a pink camisole and a pair of pink lace underwear under the shirked red satin robe. She'd been freed somehow from the crucifix structure but her mobility looked stilted, her movements staccato. She lay prone on a pink towel. The pink of Darcy's outfit and the red of the rug looked nice together. Sasha had always appreciated that particular combination. Now, seeing it onscreen, it made her choke on her own spit.

Darcy pulled her lace underwear down to reveal a set of tanned butt cheeks, solid and firm as a volleyball. The supplicant. The word that immediately came to Sasha's mind to describe it was *sumptuous*, the same word she recently used to describe the maple cream that topped a decadent slice of cheesecake. There was also the bruise from falling at Kaaterskill, a galaxy of blue and pink and eggplant across Darcy's ass.

"Whoa." Jules pushed her lips together and bobbed her head forward in a sort of appreciative nod.

Sasha stared at Jules's profile. Her nose was longish and crooked, her eyes behind her glasses glassy and dark.

"Sumptuous," Sasha said aloud, wanting to type it into the chat box. But Darcy still hadn't responded to her *Hello* message and she felt embarrassed, and angry, scorned. She imagined what Jesse was seeing—the ass cheeks in real life, pore-less and supple under the soft glow of the candlelit sauna, like the most tender and beautiful bruised fruit, juicy and vulnerable. She ground down on her teeth until a tight pain buzzed at her temple, and then kept going.

The gloved hands returned, holding an enormous, hot-pink butt plug. Sasha wondered if butt plugs also came mostly in hot pink; it was a nice color, close to no human's flesh color, this vibrant, beautiful hue. The amount of caricaturization happening onscreen was nauseating. Must every object in Darcy and Jesse's universe be neon? Everything cloistered inside quotation marks (not gloves but "gloves," not a crucifix but a "crucifix," not a butt plug but a "butt plug"), exaggerated to the point of grotesquerie? Sasha reverted to grad school mode, trying to perform some scholarly calculus in her head that aimed to both distance herself from the material and digest it so that it could become part of her. By habit, she constructed each sentence beginning with *The way in which*.

The way in which this performance, the one she and Jules were watching right now, exerted an artistic deftness that her own writing lacked.

The way in which Sasha's essay on green-ribbon removal had forgotten completely about the potential for a green ribbon to be *acquired* and not just *removed*.

The way we make and remake each other, sometimes brutally.

The way we are made and remade by and for each other.

Sasha's green ribbon simpered around her limp ponytail. She contemplated pulling it out of her hair and choking herself with it.

Recently, Sasha had been addicted to looking at the Reddit community devoted to bimbofication. People posted nude selfies captioned, *I would love to be a bimbo, do you think I have potential?* People also posted pictures of celebrities who had apparently caught the Bimbo Virus, celebrities dollifying themselves with pink stockings, lip injections, false eyelashes, and hair extensions. The Bimbo Virus was about more than just plastic surgery. It was an aesthetic overhaul. Darcy was sort of bimbo lite, Sasha figured. She suggested "bimbo" here and there, but she didn't go so far with it, except in moments like this, moments of clear performance—which was maybe what made her, like Miranda, melm. This was a skill some women were born with and others spent their whole lives learning.

Jesse's hands pried apart Darcy's tanned ass cheeks and prodded at her opening. It was a deep, dark hole that the camera didn't quite capture in its entirety, the camera was too far away, and Sasha couldn't tell what constituted the hole's opening. It was an alien abyss. She had no idea what texture it might be or what it might smell like.

Jesse's gloved hands grasped the pink butt plug and slowly, gingerly, inserted it into Darcy's b-hole; it looked like it wasn't going to go, meeting some resistance as the tip of it rammed into her, but then it did, sliding in easily, and the glossy head of Darcy the bimbo bowed down. It was impossible to tell if pleasure or pain had reduced her, but Darcy seemed to shrink against the plug sticking out of her b-hole like the cropped tail of a French bulldog.

Jules was moaning that it felt wrong to watch this.

The camera moved, panning the body attached to the gloved hands, which became partway visible, a pair of thighs bending down to attend to Darcy's ass. Jesse's thighs shuffled across the screen, colliding with something sharp. Almost inaudibly: "*Fuck.*" He lifted one leg abruptly, whisked away the offending material, then placed it down again.

After shaking uncertainly for a second, the camera refocused on Darcy's ass. Jesse's hands began wiping down Darcy's ass cheeks, now slightly spread apart because of the hot-pink apparatus, with an alcohol wipe that they'd produced from a pile of supplies somewhere off camera. The alcohol made the butt cheeks glisten.

"Fuck," Jules said, "they're not going to tie that up too, are they?"

"Isn't she supposed to be the supplicant?" Sasha said.

"Oh. Yeah. I guess."

Jesse's hands disappeared, leaving the audience to ogle Darcy's ass shining with the alcohol, then Jesse's hands returned, this time with the suture, curving like a thin bow, and the same strip of green ribbon, pre-inserted into the eye and bunched in that way Sasha had found uncomfortable ten minutes before.

Jules said again, "I think I'm going to be sick."

Jesse's hands began toward the middle of Darcy's ass, piercing the right cheek of flesh with the suture. The bunch of flesh cocooned in the direction of the needle. The fire of pain moved through Darcy, her body ricocheting against the feeling of the needle puncturing her skin, the gloved hands slowly tugging the needle through the flesh and the wire thread attached to it slipping through behind it easily. The hands moved over to repeat the same procedure on the left cheek, and then they pulled the wire through so that the cheeks were sewn shut. The first stitch was complete, a bright green knot across the top of her ass. Jesse only punctured the first few layers of skin—there wasn't much blood, only a little pinprick of it oozing under the green ribbon. Darcy's body trembled; she let out a strained whimper.

The way in which it's an inversion of the original green-ribbon fable, where the ribbon gets yanked and Jenny's head tumbles off.

The way in which inversion is not reparation.

"It's over, I think," Sasha said. "You can look now."

Darcy, whose mouth was still sewn shut, let out a primal howl through the new hole that had come to form her new mouth. The hole puckered like an anus, alive with strain.

"Ew, ew, ew," Sasha shrieked.

"God, she's in so much pain," Jules moaned. "That's the worst part of it for me, imagining the pain she must be in. I can't look. What's happening now?"

Sasha scowled at Jules's sensitivity, but also Jules's blatant insensitivity. The worst part of it for her shouldn't be Darcy's pain, but Sasha's. Why the fuck was Jules even talking about Darcy's pain when Sasha's own pain—right there, next to her in bed—was so huge? Sasha's fury at Darcy's ability to eclipse her as easily and quickly as a big, stupid sunbeam steamed out of her mouth in short puffs. She clutched the bedsheets, aware that she was beginning to spin out. Jules threw a protective arm around her, then, and Sasha forced herself to relax against Jules's armpit.

The hands began to insert the green-ribbon-threaded needle into the flesh of the left ass cheek, gearing up to make another stitch, going right to left and then left to right; clearly the plan was to stitch up the entire ass crack, to reduce the bimbo to nothing but pain and a tight line of green stitches. Was this supposed to be reparative—the stitching like a surgery, holding broken flesh in place until it healed? Or was it wounding—puncturing the skin, making holes, ripping and pulling it like fabric? The hands eased the needle into the flesh, and Darcy screamed again, if you could call it a scream, it was really more of a prolonged, feral wail.

The body rocked back and forth, back and forth, so much so that the gloved hands had to steady her by the hips. It was not just an overtly sexual gesture but also a loving one, the steadying, loving and firm. It was as though the hands were plugged into an electric machine of desire, powered by some external source. These hands steadying Darcy's rollicking body sent a crater of grief into Sasha, and she sank deeper into Jules without feeling Jules's body, like Jules's body wasn't a body but a cave that she might disappear into.

Sasha tasted acid in her throat.

Jules and Sasha watched the hands get hungry in real time. Sasha dissociated quickly, letting the moment take on the hazy scrim of a TV show watched while half-asleep. The hands grew confident, active in the rubber gloves. They began to pet and rub Darcy's inner thighs, stroking with the frenzied energy of a teenage boy unleashed on his incapacitated crush. Darcy let out a deep moan.

"Whoa, whoa, easy now," Jules refereed uselessly.

Sasha's body was clenched up so hard that she could barely remember that she was in control of it. Her crotch was wet, her mouth dry. Jesse's hands were *heavily petting* Darcy's succulent inner thighs. She needed to wrench them away, to grab Jesse's wrists and twist them until they broke. Instead she grabbed at Jules, who didn't respond; she was like a big puppet, there for Sasha to manipulate with no material consequences. But it wasn't satisfying, it just made Sasha angrier, she slapped Jules's hands around and Jules laughed uncomfortably and Sasha let out a deranged shriek that made Vivienne's ears perk up and made her cock her head to the side.

The hands slid back and forth along the threads uniting Darcy's ass cheeks, like fingers strumming a guitar, hungry, toward her pussy and then back again. Because of the gloves, what came to mind was Darcy-as-kitchen-instrument, a sudsy ceramic bowl that Jesse was washing. Handling, really feeling it. No, it wasn't not happening, and then it was, maybe, and then it was not again.

"No," Sasha managed.

"I don't think—" Jules began, and shielded her eyes again.

The bimbo, wordless, arched her back again, her vertebrae rippling through her skin.

Two of Jesse's gloved fingers slipped inside Darcy, and although it only took maybe fifteen seconds, the hands jutted around inside her, a familiar yanking gesture, and she came instantly, you could tell by the way her back tensed and then relaxed. Sasha screamed, again startling Vivienne, who came to place her two front paws on Sasha's shoulders. When Jesse's gloved hands emerged from Darcy they were bloody. She'd started her period? Jesse's gloved hands took the two bloody fingers, pointer and middle on the right hand, and smeared the blood rather theatrically—*look, I'm making a porno!*—across Darcy's left buttock. Sasha levitated.

Neither of them—her boyfriend or that cunt Darcy—had considered hiding their betrayal from her. Their whorish need for attention had outpaced their consideration for Sasha. They were vile, she decided, deeply pathetic despite the comments that were now popping up at the bottom of the screen: *fuuuuuuuck* and *omfg so hot !!!!* and *im obsessed.* And worse yet, emojis of water droplets and red faces with sweat dripping down their faces. Purple hearts, pink bows, even a few lime-green clover emojis. The comments were like strobe lights at a party; she pressed a finger against the screen and pushed so hard that Jules had to gently pull her away.

"You'll break it."

"But—"

"Shh, I know." Jules awkwardly massaged Sasha's shoulders. Darcy's screen again.

"Look, they made a new hole," Jules marveled, pointing to the skin that gaped open between the green-ribbon stitches. Indeed it was a new asshole, one you could easily slip a finger inside, which one of Jesse's gloved fingers did at that very moment, suctioning it in and out.

"It's the pain, that's what's getting to me, I'm going to be sick," Jules said, but kept watching the screen, unblinking.

Oh, man UP, Sasha wanted to say to her, but instead she said nothing. Jesse's hands returned with a thin black rod, which they slipped underneath the tight stitches and pulled up violently while Darcy's body shook and quivered. The hands paused with the rod suspended in the air, and then they smacked her ass a few times with the rod, harder and harder *thwap*s that made Jules shield her face in her hands. The ass trembled under the rod, the end of the green thread rustling with anticipation, the boxer tail holding it all together, the tight green corset of the completed stitches bolstered against the impact.

Why wasn't Jules protecting her from this? Why was Jules sitting there, gape-mouthed like a dead fish, watching while Sasha got humiliated and betrayed?

Finally, after what felt like minutes of slapping, Darcy waved the rod away with her right hand. It was a pathetic wave, a flick of the wrist, a gesture that could mean only one thing.

"She's hit her point," Jules narrated with the authority of a news anchor, tentatively removing her hands from her eyes but keeping her hands cupped in little visors, ready to protect her again at a moment's notice.

Sasha was happy that Jules announced this. She had to admit that otherwise she might not have known what Darcy's gesture meant. The wave meant no, she couldn't take it anymore, and there was something soothing to Sasha about the way they rubbed up against this atomic boundary; this was the boundary that interested Sasha. Darcy's refusal.

She had no desire to cut a new hole into her flesh, but she

could have watched Darcy waving her hand in that small, determined way all day. She could have watched Jesse's gloved hands responding to the wave on an endless loop, settling the rod down and disappearing for a moment, selecting a more apt tool.

The hands removed the green corset with a pair of big yellow pliers, cutting them at their center, along Darcy's ass crack, and then pulling the green ribbon out of the flesh and tossing it to the side. The screen didn't let them see exactly where the discarded ribbon was cast. It appeared to dissolve into the air once it had been removed from her flesh. While the hands removed the stitches, Darcy quivered violently, grasping desperately at the towel around her waist, but the moves had become redundant, there were only so many ways to express pain and she had done all of them already.

When the stitches were finally out and her ass was red and dotted with blood from where it had been punctured, Darcy slowly tugged the pink butt plug out of herself. Did this mean the performance was done? Sasha wondered why Jesse's hands hadn't done this part. It seemed like an odd time for the hands to disappear. It was almost humiliating for Darcy to do this part herself, after all, the entire point had been that she was prone, harmed, a bimbo in distress. What sense did it make for Darcy to do this part herself? Sasha kind of wanted Jesse's hands to return, to not just attend to the pretty bulge of the butt plug but also be the ones to pry it out, to take responsibility for what they'd done.

A dark speck clung to the tip of the purple butt plug; the speck was shit, Sasha understood. She didn't say anything to Jules about it, as though out of some perverse respect for Darcy, and also she was basically catatonic now. Although Jules could surely see the shit, too. It was shocking, the shit. For a moment Sasha couldn't believe it was real—maybe a speck of dirt on Jules's computer screen, or a piece of moss from the set. But then Darcy's hand cast the plug away, and the speck was still there, and it was definitely shit. The plug bounced a few times on the red rug and then disappeared from the frame.

She was drenched in sweat, and her lips were still sewn shut with the thinner green thread. It seemed an insignificant pain compared to the butt sewing, but Sasha couldn't be sure; the lips, after all, were tender, their veins close to the surface, with none of the fleshy padding of an ass.

Darcy fired a ball of saliva through her mouth, still sewn up in its permanent pout. The glob of saliva hit the camera screen, and there was a moment of shaky pause while the situation got resolved. When she returned, Darcy grinned naughtily.

Darcy stuck a hot-pink nail, filed into a sharp point, into her new mouth hole. She pulled the nail in and out, in and out, faster and faster, fucking herself in her new green-threaded hole. It made a suctioning sound against her lips.

Jules and Sasha weren't in on the joke, but they laughed along anyway, with a degree of nervousness. The laugh brought Sasha no relief. It was even more agonizing to hear the sound of her own pathetic chuckle.

Sasha impulsively reached out and slammed the laptop closed, even though the performance wasn't quite done. Jules jumped a little.

"Sorry," she said. "I just couldn't take it anymore."

Jules's arm, arranged protectively around Sasha, felt like lead, a dentist's bib. The weight was nice but made it harder to breathe. Sasha shook the arm off. "Sorry."

"No, no." Jules took back her arm and placed it awkwardly on her side. They were still sitting side by side in Jules's bed, but now there was no occasion for their position. The performance was over, the laptop closed. Sasha threw the blanket off and stood on the rug. She peered out the window. She could tell they were finishing up—the clatter of equipment, the muted jangle of the items inside, the glow of the sauna's light within.

"Jesse fucked her," Sasha said.

Jules made a gaping, shocked face that annoyed Sasha. "When?"

"During the torture part. She kind of fingered Darcy."

"Oh." Jules blinked rapidly. "I must've been closing my eyes."

"Are you kidding me?" This came out more ragefully than Sasha intended. She softened her tone, adding, "How am I supposed to know if it happened or not if you didn't see it?"

"Did *you* see it?"

Sasha rushed toward the door and Vivienne followed her, flying off the bed and skidding against the wood floor before trotting after her down the stairs.

"Sasha!" Jules was behind her. "Where are you going?"

Sasha's chest rattled as she tore through the house. Without stopping, she snatched at the stretch of kitchen counter where Lou's duffel bag was crumpled, yanked out the gym class parachute, and flew out the glass door into the frozen backyard. She dashed across the grass, feet burning on the ice, Vivienne at her heels. It was past dusk already, that sickly moment just before the sun fully set.

She stopped short when she reached the door of the sauna. Vivienne stopped beside her, panting. Inside, where it was warm and glowing and safe, like a womb, Darcy and Jesse goofed around, bouncing around the sauna with the glee of a successful performance. Lou was happy, too, leisurely gathering their camera equipment. They were all tightly packed in there like canned fish. Darcy was again wearing the pink underwear and a big white T-shirt. Her nipples poked through the fabric authoritatively, twin boyfriend stealers. Sasha couldn't hear what they were saying, but they looked happy, enclosed in a microclimate safe from the harshness of the winter night.

Sasha dug her nails into her palms, creating two little fists, and let out a banshee shriek as she pumped her clenched hands into the sky. Because this was all she could do—scream and make noise, high-pitched and urgent, like an alarm system; this was the only noise she could make, the only way the anger could boil out. She unfurled the parachute with a quick flick of her wrist and took off running, the parachute billowing out behind her in a shock of wind. Not away, toward—she stayed close, stalking the perimeter of the sauna like a huntress, teeth bared and a foreign screech emanating from her vocal chords. She paced around the outside of the wooden structure in tight circles, dizzying herself, Vivienne prancing at her heels, the parachute rippling and the polyester shrieking in the wind, Sasha screaming as loud as she could manage, Vivienne whining and barking, Sasha making a racket, the parachute filling with intermittent puffs of air and then deflating around her body as she traced tight, small circles around the perimeter of the sauna, stopping every so often to catch her breath and pound her fists against the wooden barrel.

"AHHHHHHHHHHH!!!! EEEEEEEEEEEE!!!!" Sasha screeched.

Vivienne thought it was a game of chase, and in a way it was, the two of them racing around, screaming and wailing, Sasha's heels hooking into the frozen ground and tearing up clumps of dirt. She wanted to interrupt their good time, make them aware of the damage they had caused. She wanted, most of all, for them to stop looking at each other and attend to her.

She screamed until her voice broke and her throat was raw and her arms throbbed from grasping the parachute.

Then she stopped short directly outside the sauna door, which was coated with steam except for a single swipe, the size of Jesse's fist. He'd swiped a small window to see what the racket was about—inside the womb of the sauna it probably sounded more like a loud laugh than a scream. And through the shape of a clear asteroid, Sasha could see Jesse and Darcy at the window, wide-eyed, looks of panic creasing over their dumb, fleshy faces.

A pair of big, strong arms clamped just below her breasts. Sasha's body tilted back in a single stiff unit, like a big suitcase wheeled backward across the yard, a humid voice in her ear whispering again and again, "Shh, shh, honey, honey, it's okay."

"Ew, stop." Sasha tried to shake away the mouth and rub her ear against her shoulder to wick off the moisture, but Jules kept pulling her into the house, Sasha oriented backward, staggering to keep up with Jules's long legs. Jesse, Darcy, and Lou watched as she moved away; they grew smaller and so did Sasha, Vivienne staying close at Sasha's heels. Sasha panted wildly, wide-eyed, quiet as Jules navigated her back inside the house. She stared at the individual patches of velvet on the arms of Jules's coat, some oriented the wrong way, like Vivienne's fur after a roughhousing session with one of her uncles. Jules's face looked open and slightly red from the cold. Glasses fogging. Inside, they stood at the base of the staircase, observing each other, the parachute crumpled around their feet. Sasha hoped that there wasn't snot on her face and that her eyebrows were smoothed down, but the moment felt too tenuous to adjust herself, even aesthetically; everything had to stay exactly as it was, dangling here in this chrysalis until Jules initiated a change.

A peal of laughter erupted from the deck. Jesse and Darcy

and Lou entered together, still palling around, beatific, tripping slightly over the parachute but not pausing to consider it. Sasha compressed at the sight of them. Seeing her, her red, tear-streaked face, they sobered up very quickly. There was a moment of quiet. All five of them regarding each other— where's Miranda?—as Jesse took stock of the situation.

Jesse saw her, looking up with proud, glowing eyes, and took in Sasha's face. "Hey! What's wrong?"

"What were you doing out there?" Sasha demanded. "Why didn't you come inside?"

"We were reading the comments," Jesse offered quietly, her tone attempting damage control.

"Good reviews?" Jules took off her glasses and rubbed them against her shirt. It was the wrong thing to say for Sasha's purposes, but it was the socially acceptable one, so everyone responded gratefully.

Darcy piped up, a little nervously, that the comments had been really gratifying. "Yeah, good feedback from some people we really like."

Darcy spoke with one hand over her mouth, her words blurred and hesitant.

"'Some people we really like,'" Sasha parroted meanly, her voice snotty and try-hard.

"Baby?" Jesse stared at Sasha.

"I need to . . ." Sasha gestured upstairs.

Jules had started to edge up the stairs, clearly freaked out by what they'd just seen. Sasha pushed past Jesse and followed Jules. Vivienne's paws scraped the wood behind her, hustling to keep up.

Sasha was thankful that Jules led the way and didn't come face-to-face with Sasha's ass on the way upstairs. She fixated on the seat of Jules's jeans, which wrinkled and smoothed with every step. She was transfixed by the way they cupped and then released her ass, like a metronome.

What did Jules say about Jesse's ass in the Tommy Hilfiger snow pants a few days before?

She really fills those out.

They arrived back in Bedroom 1 without commentary. Jules shrugged off her velvet coat, the one she'd thrown on to go stop Sasha from screaming, and slung it onto the desk chair. Sasha wanted to shed a layer, too, copying her, but she had no layers to shed. She trod barefoot onto the plush cream rug.

They stood twenty feet apart, at either end of the cavernous room, the big four-poster bed between them. Outside, the lights of cars speeding down the country route, and then darkness. The hallway light was still on, and so was a lamp on one of the night tables. Other than that, the room was dim and shadowy.

A rap at the door made Vivienne whine and wag her little curled tail.

"Sasha?"

Sasha's throat closed again, but she eked out, "Go away."

Sensing that her skills were needed, Jules bolted toward the door. "It's okay," she called to Jesse. "Just give her a few minutes. I've got it."

Sasha's nervous system flooded with relief. Jules had saved her, kind of. Jules was a performer. Sasha had seen her perform on TV countless times, had listened to the messages Jules had sent her via the teleprompter. In Bedroom 1, against the closed door, Jules was still performing. Of course she was. Yet this time, there was no transcript. There were no words at the bottom of the screen, appearing a half second before Jules herself could say them.

Having successfully deterred Jesse, Jules walked into the

bathroom, taking a fresh paper cup from a stack in the cabinet and closing the door halfway behind her. Sasha sat on Jules and Miranda's bed, staring at the copy of *A Lover's Discourse* on one of the bookshelves, welcoming a floaty sense of déjà vu. It felt weird to be the one waiting for Jules, to follow Jules's lead. (*Every minute I wait for her to send a picture I become more femme*, a friend once texted Sasha while waiting for a potential lover to send their nude.)

Jules opened a different cabinet in the bathroom and produced a small flask.

"What is that?" Sasha asked.

Jules unscrewed the flask and used the lid, which resembled a cough-syrup top, to measure a tiny amount of liquid. It was stormy, purple-black, thick. *What's that.* The question itched at Sasha's throat. Jules took a long swig from the top, wincing.

"What kind of alcohol is that?" Sasha asked again.

"It isn't alcohol," Jules said, gulping hard.

"Then what is it?"

"Medicine. Iron."

She laughed, showing teeth stained blue-black from the iron.

Sasha's thinking at this point had become galactic, warped with pain and desire. She was seeing stars. Jules rinsed out her mouth with the paper cup of water and tossed it in the small silver trash can.

"What's up?" Jules said.

Sasha became aware of her desire to run her long, dark fingernails over Jules's jeans-clad thigh. To tease her, to turn Jules on and make Jules want her so much that Jules could not refuse her.

They settled on the bed next to each other. It was very quiet. Sasha didn't want to be the first to say something, so she said nothing. As though sensing the same thing, Jules got up and put a record on her hipster record player. It was the Beach Boys' *Pet Sounds*.

"Did you lose your virginity to this record?" Jules said. "I did."

"To who?"

"Suzy."

"Was that the first time you had sex with anyone, or the first time with a girl?"

Jules screwed up her face.

"No, my first time was with some boy. He was nice, actually—Danny Orland." A pause. "Is it *such* a trope to lose your virginity to *Pet Sounds*?"

"Not if you're an old-as-fuck lesbian," Sasha said, sniffing, aware that she was being mean. Though she said it lightheartedly, kind of self-consciously prissy, like the minx she was. After all Jules loved being old, much older than her, a spate of fifteen years which Sasha could tell they were holding in their minds always, a pregnant stomach between them.

"You never said if you and Miranda still have sex," Sasha said before she lost her nerve.

Sasha had the sudden urge to tell Jules that she was a gold-star lesbian but wondered if that was gauche, or maybe offensive. You probably weren't supposed to say that anymore because it was TERF-y. She said it anyway, trusting Jules's Gen X sensibilities. Obviously what Sasha meant was that she'd never fucked anyone but a dyke. And besides, how could she be a TERF when Twitter alleged she wasn't even a feminist?

A radiator ticked, then clacked. Was Jesse gone? And where was Miranda? Oh, right—she was working in her office downstairs, blissfully ignorant of all this. Sasha wondered if

Miranda heard her screaming. Sasha rolled the sleeve of her shirt between her thumb and forefinger. Jules remained, for once, inscrutable.

"Honestly, Darcy reminded me of Barbie tonight," Jules said, still not answering the original question. "How if she were a real woman, her waist-to-hip ratio would make her fall over. How she wouldn't be able to have any organs."

"'No girl's boobs are that big! No girl's waist is that tiny with such wide hips! And guess what. No girl's eleven inches tall, either!'" Sasha mimicked an imaginary humorless critic of Barbie. "Everyone always says that about Barbie like it's some major flaw. But who cares if she doesn't have organs? She's a fucking doll."

"Were you hot for Barbie as a kid?" Jules asked, then laughed: "No, you probably wanted Wreck-It Ralph."

Sasha had to admit that Wreck-It Ralph was sexy.

"The *other* thing about new holes and bodies without organs that it makes me think of," Jules continued, slowly sliding a piece of rolling paper from its sheath and reaching for her bedside stash of weed, "is this play I wrote as an undergrad in college, in a playwriting workshop. It feels like a hundred years ago. Anyway, the plot was that a girl had a 'foregina,' a vagina on her forehead, and so did her mother and her grandmother; they lectured her about how to keep it clean, massaging bananas into the hole and so on. The girl's boyfriend really wanted to fuck her in the foregina and she wouldn't let him; finally he wore her down and she let him fuck her in her foregina, and he became obsessed with it. He liked it better than her actual vagina. She got angry, said, 'No more fucking me in my foregina, it's my real vagina or nothing,' and he agreed. But one night she wakes up and he's fucking her in her foregina without her consent—he can't get enough of it—and she gets so angry that she takes a knife from the kitchen and carves a foregina into his forehead, making a new hole on his face, a big, gaping, bloody gash between the eyes."

"Do you identify with the boyfriend or the girlfriend?"

"Boyfriend, for sure," Jules said, "though when I was writing it, I guess I was supposed to be the girlfriend."

Sasha's own eighteen-year-old embarrassing story from college, she told Jules through the last of her tears, was that she trained to be an abortion doula in the fall of her freshman year of college.

"What's an abortion doula?" Jules asked.

Sasha explained, "It's someone who supports you through an abortion, who tells you you're making the right choice and rubs your arms then gives you shortbread cookies afterward."

One of the abortion doula trainers was a witch in a black plastic choker; the other was the type of kindhearted bobblehead that made Sasha recoil. They were humorless, made the group spend hours criticizing that Bill Clinton quote about how *abortion should be safe, legal, and rare.* And so on the third day of the training, Sasha decided to ask a very provocative question.

"If people could one day detect, like in vitro, that their baby was going to be gay, and they chose to abort that baby, would you still support abortion?" she'd asked the witchy one.

There was an awful silence, and then the witch in the choker retorted back at her, *Speaking as a bisexual, I certainly* hope *that never happens!*

Jules laughed. "Which part?" she asks. "Them identifying a 'gay gene'—ha—or people aborting their gay fetuses?"

"I don't know," Sasha said.

But something happened: the wires got crossed, and the

other women in the training—twenty-one-year-old liberal arts girls!—turned on her. They started a rumor that she *wanted* to abort gay babies, that she was a conservative infiltrator to the organization, a eugenics sympathizer or something nefarious like that, or maybe just a deeply provincial teen, the equivalent of a protester with a *Life Begins at Conception!* poster in the parking lot of the clinic. They ostracized Sasha, these cooler, older girls with nose rings and baby bangs. They made her feel stupid and worthless, and for a whole year she believed them, that she was unspeakably awful in a way she didn't even know, that in some way she'd been inadvertently exposed.

Later, she realized they'd willfully misunderstood her. It was only by misrecognition that she could be recognizable to them.

Jules reached over and placed a big, solid palm on Sasha's thigh. She was immediately turned on, her body curling over into Jules's, wanting to be closer. Their faces were close now, and Sasha could see the hairs at the center of her eyebrows, the thick, slightly greasy pores of her forehead, her dark eyes, the lines around her mouth. Sasha smelled her, too, that butch musk like the one Jesse wore a few times when they were starting to date, but then stopped wearing. She put her hand on top of Jules's hand. Sasha's hand was much smaller, she could still see the tops of Jules's fingers and the harsh tilt of her thumb beneath it.

Sasha fell forward, as though by accident, collapsing into Jules. Pressed into the shoulder of Jules's royal purple hoodie, she took a deep drag and closed her eyes. It was a sad smell, a smell of the past, a past that isn't quite gone. Jules arranged her arms around Sasha and pulled her in. The pressure of their bodies together made Sasha so wet that she wondered if she was somehow already coming. They stayed like that for a few minutes, and then she wedged her right knee into Jules's crotch, gently, again like an accident. Jules's big body gave in almost immediately, her groin warmly accepting Sasha's knee, sucking her knee into its microclimate, and Sasha felt Jules's wetness through Jules's jeans and through her own black tights.

She knew that in this moment, despite how much she wanted Jules to kiss her so that she could be plunged into something that didn't resemble Jesse, there was more to it than that—Jules was already receding, spotty, distant. Jules already didn't matter: the green blazer slung over the chair, the slim Adam's apple now bobbing up and down nervously, the long neck and the cocky head of dark hair, the glasses that Jules was removing and setting gently next to her on the comforter. They stared at each other. It reminded Sasha of that first night with Jesse, the hours of frisson between them cresting into one single, diluted moment.

Making one wrong choice after another had lead her nowhere, no closer to any self-knowledge or self-actualization; and this, the culmination of the wrongness, was nothing like momentum. She was stuck in the same wrongness that had dogged her for her entire life. Sasha was kind of on top, with Jules leaning back against the headboard, and she shifted until her thigh was planted firmly between Jules's legs. Sasha's face was buried in Jules's neck, and Jules moved, first slow then faster, against Sasha, grabbing her all over through her clothes, her shoulders and her back and her tits. Jules rocked and bucked her pelvis against Sasha's thigh, jerking up from Sasha's knee to her hipbone, rollicking faster and faster so that she was using Sasha like the arm of a sofa, rubbing her body against Sasha's leg so hard that Sasha wondered if her tights were going to rip from the friction. Sasha decided to be exactly what she imagined Jules wanted, giggling, tonguing her neck softly, making her gasp and stretch her neck out. Sasha produced a few soft noises of her own, to make Jules feel less alone in her pleasure, which she sensed would help Jules; she needed to know that she was bringing pleasure. Jules finished in a big gulp that Sasha felt, then saw, through her pants, a rush of wetness that made her tights sticky and the skin underneath damp; a dark circle on Jules's light-wash denim.

Jules's body relaxed, and Sasha glided one leg out from under her and rubbed her toe up and down Jules's denim-clad leg. At the same time, she swiped some "gloss on, gorgeous" onto her lips.

She thought of Andy Warhol's frequent refrain—*Can I just say* la la la?—when asked questions during interviews, hiding his face—and what Mary Woronov had written about him: "Andy was the worst . . . He even looked like a vampire: white, empty, waiting to be filled, incapable of satisfaction. He was the white worm—always hungry, always cold, never still, always twisting." Sasha felt like that white worm now, with Jules's hand at her crotch, incapable of being satisfied with her powers of self-expression.

Sasha couldn't meet Jules's eye, so she dragged a pointer finger gently down her left thigh. Jules let out a horny sound, which was the only way it could be described, really—a sound that was somewhere between a groan and a bray and a yawp, a desperate sound that made a bouillon of embarrassment dissolve in Sasha's chest.

The sound of footsteps resonated from the stairs.

"They're back." Jules rose to her feet.

෨ ෯

Sasha's new plan for dealing with Jesse was to ignore her. When she and Jules descended the narrow staircase, Sasha averting her gaze demurely and Jules fumbling behind her, flush with recent infidelity, Jesse was waiting at the bottom, her face desperately beaming up at the two of them. There was no reason for her to be so eager or so desperate. Jesse was supposed to own what he had done, because he had acted soberly and intentionally, and he'd done it because he'd wanted to, just as Sasha had acted on urges of her own. Jesse had done what she wanted; Sasha had done what she wanted. The whole point of a relationship was doing things you didn't want to do, sometimes, and not doing everything you secretly craved. Sasha had tried to explain this concept of sacrifice to Jesse before, who had never understood. But now that Sasha had also transgressed, she was beginning to get the appeal of thinking only about your own fucking self.

Sasha pushed past the waiting Jesse and made her way to the kitchen, where she began preparing herself a cup of tea. Miranda was there, too, wrapped up in a crocheted net of cream-colored yarn. Miranda looked at her hard and long, a questioning gaze, though Sasha also avoided her eyes. What had happened between her and Jules had nothing to do with Miranda; it changed nothing for her, made no difference in her life, and to involve her would be insincere, even cruel.

Miranda would not have understood that Sasha found herself zipping down the same axis of fate as everyone else. In the narrow sliver of time that Sasha had control over Jules, she had winnowed Jules down into a moment of Sasha's own creation. And in that way, even Jules was sort of irrelevant, making their encounter flimsy in the first place. If you really thought about it, it hadn't even demonstrably happened. Who could insist that it had? There were no witnesses, just two autopilots.

"What were you two *doing* up there?" Miranda asked the question with practiced neutrality, a bemused smile settling across her lips.

"The interview," Jules apologized.

Sasha had forgotten about that particular pretense until this very moment, but the answer seemed to please Miranda.

"Oh, that interview!" She pulled the fridge handle and selected an orange from the fruit drawer and addressed Sasha: "I feel like you really *get* Jules."

The orange slipped out of Miranda's hand and tumbled to the floor. She and Sasha stooped to get it at the same time, and Sasha emerged with it, absentmindedly performing a *Legally Blonde* bend and snap before placing the orange sadly on the countertop.

Miranda was positioning herself, of course, as someone who "got" Jules so well that she could be the arbiter of who else did or did not also "get" Jules. She peeled the orange in one strip of wrinkly skin, her fingers prying the rind from the flesh of the fruit.

Did Sasha "get" Jules?

Did Miranda? Did anyone?

In Bedroom 3, Sasha, Jesse, and Vivienne sat stiffly on the bed, at an impasse. Sasha rifled through her suitcase on the ground, and with her feet selected a sheer yellow nightie, her toes easing it up onto the bed with her.

"Don't look at me," she snapped to Jesse as she pulled off the dress she was wearing. Access to her body was all that she could give or deny.

If Sasha had been looking at Jesse, she would've understood that Jesse wasn't looking at all—he was only staring, wounded, at the door, fixated on making sure it remained closed. But Sasha wasn't looking, so she didn't know this, could safely imagine that Jesse was staring at her even though she'd instructed him not to.

"Are you not going to apologize?" Sasha asked as they got under the covers. She kept her body stiff and private, angled away from Jesse. If Jesse moved to touch her, she decided that she would flinch away like she'd done in the kitchen that fall, and this time she would make no excuses. But Jesse didn't budge.

"Baby," Jesse said. "I just got carried away. It was part of the performance."

Did he think that Sasha cared? And why sound so exhausted, as though he'd apologized even once before?

"I wouldn't be mad if it was you," Jesse said.

Sasha snorted. "Yeah, you absolutely would."

"I wouldn't. I'd understand that it was art. Like your writing—it's not *real*."

"I don't fuck other people in my writing."

"Well, maybe you don't understand art."

"*You* don't understand art!" Sasha yelled. "Art's not supposed to be cruel. It isn't!"

"So when *your* art is immoral that's fine," Jesse said snidely, "and when *mine* is, I'm the problem?"

Art had nothing to do with morality. Good art humiliated the artist, made her and her alone look pathetic. Good art didn't make *other people* (i.e., Sasha) look pathetic.

"I hate you," Sasha whispered as she turned away from Jesse and flicked off the bedside lamp.

She expected Jesse to come back with something, anything, but from her boyfriend's side of the bed there was only silence. She couldn't tell if he hadn't heard her or if he was pretending not to have heard her or—most brutally—if there was no pretense and he had heard her but just didn't care.

"Don't you trust me?" Jesse asked.

Trust was one of their buzzwords, but it didn't belong to just them—it grated against Sasha's sensibilities.

"No," Sasha said. "I don't trust anyone."

Jesse rose silently from the bed and stalked to the bathroom. Sasha glanced out the window. The road was empty, adding to her sense that no one else existed but the two of them. Sasha knew that Jesse felt her pain, and she felt Jesse's. So when Jesse came back from brushing her teeth, Sasha turned to face Jesse and started kissing her all over her cheeks, her eyes, her lips.

"There's a mattress spring in my rib," Jesse said, struggling away.

"Can we please lie here for five more minutes like this?" Sasha begged.

Jesse's eyes glossed over to the clock. "It's too late."

Sasha rolled onto her side, beginning to cry. She didn't want to cry, knew she was being pathetic. But sometimes even knowing that did nothing to stop her.

"You're so dramatic," Jesse said, somewhere between sweet and dead. "The kissing. The tears."

They were lying in bed facing each other, on their sides. Only the small lamp clipped onto the headboard of Bed 3 was on. A strange silence settled in. Jesse's eyes looked blank and small, like holes. Sasha didn't know what was in them. Her heart began to slam forward, propelling her toward the center of the bed, toward Jesse. She felt desperate and a little bit scared. Everything was different again, and she didn't know why and how it had gotten this way again. She always thought things were better for good, and then they'd get worse.

"It's easy for you to lie," Jesse observed.

"Yes," Sasha said, believing that honesty would win Jesse's favor. "It is."

Her heart slammed harder. Her vulnerability had done nothing. Jesse had never looked at her with such little care. She noted this somewhere deep, folded and smashed into some crevice. Sasha didn't know who Jesse was. She did not recognize his face.

And then Jesse said, in a quiet monotone, "Are you scared of me?"

"What?"

"Are you scared of me?"

Sasha said, "No, of course not, I'm not scared of you."

If she needed to, she quickly worked out, she could call out to Jules and Miranda in Bedroom 1, just across the hall, to come save her.

Sasha had the wild fling of a thought that Jesse might attack her, kill her. She could never tell if her paranoia was to be trusted or dismissed. The room was so quiet, and the only explanation was she was going to die there. She hadn't died before, but she was going to now. A fly buzzed against the window shade.

Sasha didn't know what time it was. Eventually, they must have fallen asleep. Jesse woke up at five in the morning to go to the bathroom. Hearing the door open, feeling Jesse crawl over her to get out of the bed, Sasha thought, She's going to kill me. She grabbed her phone and tucked it in her neck, her pulse beating out like an engine, and thought of the Etta James line, *I'd rather go blind than see you walk away.*

Things Fit Inside Other Things

ๆ ๐

They spent much of the day on their phones in various rooms, sheltering in place through the small universes of their screens. The weather was gloomy and nobody felt like going outside, so they retreated to separate corners of the house and scrolled. Technology was a world catered to its user, endlessly customizable and personalized; in that way it had the same soothing properties as journaling or scrapbooking. Jules was cordial to Sasha in the morning, wearing a neoliberal T-shirt while she made Sasha a cup of coffee the way she liked and pushed it toward her with the tenderness of an aged butler. Their tacit agreement was to move on with discretion and silence. Now Sasha looked at Jules with pity, as though Jules were a person who would never be enlightened. Sasha wasn't enlightened either, but Jules definitely wouldn't be, not while she was still sleeping with twenty-five-year-olds. At least Sasha still had a chance.

She and Jesse kept their distance, studiously avoiding each other in the hallways as they passed each other to swap in and out of the bathroom for their morning routines. In the kitchen,

Jesse burned a piece of toast and Sasha tossed it into the garbage without looking at Jesse, singeing the tips of her fingers and then, only after she'd turned away, pressing them into the cool tip of her nose.

Once Sasha began to see Darcy as a villainess, she couldn't unsee her that way. Every move Darcy was making now, in the downstairs of the house—one hand cupped around Lou's head as they lay together on the couch in a show of nascent adoration (Lou didn't care that Darcy had been penetrated by Jesse's gloved fingers, Sasha reasoned, because Darcy would never actually *date* Jesse—not that Lou and Darcy were even monogamous, and besides Darcy seemed determined to only show interest in Jesse long enough to ruin Sasha's relationship and not one second longer), one leg flung up—made it impossible for Sasha to forget the moment that Jesse had fucked her. She wore tight, cow-print jeans and a white wifebeater—oops, *ribbed undershirt*—with no bra as she scrolled absently on her phone, pausing every few minutes to squeal and call out to Jesse that *another*—yes, *another*—member of the queer elite had reached out to congratulate her and heap praise upon the performance (titled *Green Ribbon Girl: A Lesbo-Porno*)—casting herself deeper and deeper into the role of temptress, seductress, *her*. Sasha thought of Darcy as just *her*. There was no other Other woman that even mattered. Darcy was the Other one. There were only the two of them, Sasha and Darcy, and so even though Darcy was terrible, it meant she was also everything.

Sasha studied Darcy's face for signs of maimery, but there was less damage than she'd expected. Her lips were puffy and raw, yes, bulbous as fried worms, and in one spot beginning to crust over, but the wounds called to mind a beauty treatment—

lip injections—and in that way the violence done to them seemed reasonable, medical.

Sasha composed her strategy quickly and silently, scuttling around the house gathering materials. This—her stupid, half-formed plan—was to be the *punctum* moment of the trip. Whoever was able to determine the climax in a series of moments held the power. Darcy, and no doubt Jesse, believed that they'd already succeeded in producing the trip's *punctum*, that moment in the foreground when it all comes to focus. For that reason, it had to be Sasha.

Sasha went outside with Miranda and Jesse as Jules grabbed the lighter, rolling paper, and baggie of weed. She locked a stunned Vivienne inside behind her, and Vivienne swiped an indignant paw against the frosty door before settling on the rug. It was marginally warmer than it had been for the past few nights, but it was still very, very cold. Sasha's joints locked up instantly, her shoulders hunching. She loved the way cold weather shut everything down.

When the joint came to her, she took a long, dramatic inhale, letting the warm smoke fill her lungs and then blowing it out in a delicate puff. She twisted her neck from side to side to see if anyone had realized how delicate and perfect she'd rendered the puff. It was a tiny orb of smoke, rising up diagonally from her glossy lips into the night sky. Either nobody saw or nobody was impressed, and she watched as her fuzzy-edged cloud disappeared into the night.

If the others were surprised that she was smoking, that this was the first time she'd smoked on the trip so far despite the dozens of smoke breaks that had been taken, no one said anything; more likely, they hadn't noticed that she'd forgone smoking in the first place. Sasha always assumed that she was under surveillance, that others were scrutinizing her, an eternal spotlight focused above her head. But of course, this wasn't true. Actually, people barely noticed her.

She passed the joint off to Jules, trying not to cough on the leftover smoke in her lungs. Jules accepted it without making eye contact and took a long, beleaguered drag before handing it down to Miranda, who passed it to Jesse without taking a puff. Sasha didn't look at Miranda, either. She fingered the needle in her pocket, prethreaded with a strand of thin red thread.

The conversation had turned to the performance. Darcy and Jesse were still bathing in the digital glow of the positive reception.

"Now I wish I'd seen it," Miranda complained when Darcy read aloud a comment praising her and Jesse.

She was swaddled in her usual chunky orange knit scarf, and her short, unpolished nails drummed absentmindedly on the thigh of her jeans. Sasha had heard them—Jules and Miranda—in the hallway the previous night, after everyone had gone to bed. Miranda had said something in a low tone that almost resembled a whine, but wasn't quite a whine, because Miranda didn't whine, and Jules had let out a long, gravelly laugh. The sound of their bodies colliding, the squeaky floorboards beneath them shifting as their weight shifted into each other. In her bed, feet away, Sasha had gripped Vivienne's tail until she groaned.

"What was the matter?" Sasha asked. "Why did you have to work all of yesterday?"

"Nothing too exciting. A bad breakup."

"This is different than the client who was trying to cancel you?" Sasha wanted to know.

"Someone was trying to cancel Miranda?" Jesse asked, genuinely puzzled.

Miranda erased the space in front of her with a gloved hand. "Just some nonsense."

Jules gave Miranda a look that seemed to say, *You can talk about it.*

"It's one of those Twitter things," Miranda continued. Sasha could see that her hands were trembling.

Sasha slid the needle out of her pocket and held it up to Jesse, who had to squint at the object until she recognized it.

Sasha touched the tip of the needle to the outside of Jesse's hand, on one bulging blue vein roping around her knuckle, and Jesse yelped, yanking her hand away. "What the hell, babe?"

"I had a cyst removed last year, and it didn't heal properly," Sasha explained to the group.

"You *stabbed* me."

"I barely touched you." Sasha fought to stop herself from rolling her eyes.

"The cyst healed fine," Jesse said. "You're just obsessed with having no indents or wrinkles on your body."

Jules said the words *body dysphoria* in a knowing tone, like it was a thing she'd just learned about for the first time, perhaps when Miranda had said it about Sasha the other day as Sasha complained about needing a chin implant. But here, they were talking about dysmorphia, not dysphoria, so everyone graciously ignored her.

Jules had the joint again, and she puffed with great interest. Miranda was watching, too, her head a small orb inside the concentric circles of her scarf.

"Look," Sasha said, standing up, leaning over, and pulling her skirt down far enough to show them. "You can see the indent. It was supposed to close all the way, but it didn't. I can still stick my finger inside."

Jesse's face was murky. He was partially willing to do this. She could see Jesse wanting to be watched, and she could see Jesse hating her for being an exhibitionist. But Sasha knew she would accept the assignment. In the past, she would have grabbed Sasha's ass and said something like, *Mm, I love this buttock.*

"It's like a little dimple," Jules noted. "It's very cute."

"Blueberry dimple," Jesse intoned.

"I want Jesse to stitch it up," Sasha announced. "It's botched."

Botched was a word that Sasha's friends had used in upper school, prep school's term for high school, to describe ugly girls. The term had originated with describing their friends' mothers' bad plastic surgery—faces stretched beyond recognition from Botox, lip fillers that turned mouths into two distended sausages.

Miranda laughed a long, startled laugh. "With that?" She pointed to the needle, which was flashing silver in the porch light.

"Wait," Jules said, her voice bemused; she was neither really shocked nor really curious. "Is that needle sterilized?"

"No," Sasha said.

"Well, let's at least do this," Jules said, holding up the lighter and pressing down to produce a small flame. Sasha waved the needle into the flame a few times, coating it in heat until Jules put the lighter back in her pocket.

"*You know I'm the one who put you up there,*" came the sound of Lou singing Halsey's "Without Me," a pop ballad relentlessly played in grocery stores and gas stations, blissfully interrupting the sterilizing. "*Name in the sky, does it ever get lonely?*"

Lou and Darcy arrived onto the porch as Sasha extended her arm to Jesse, trying to get him to take the needle.

"What's this?" Darcy asked, all coy, one hand over her mouth. Sasha could see between her fingers that Darcy's lips glistened with a layer of ointment.

"Fuck, are you freaks serious?" Lou asked, seeing the needle. "You're sewing each other again?"

They accepted the joint from Jules and took a long drag.

"Can anyone help me with my emoji avatar?" Darcy asked the group at large, holding up her phone with the hand she wasn't using to cover her mouth. "I can't get it right—none of the options *look* like me."

Jules cast an obligatory glance at Darcy's phone. "Maybe that one?"

Darcy ignored her, continuing to swipe this way and that.

"Why do you think you're obsessed with it healing wrong, Sasha?" Miranda asked.

"My parents," said Sasha, meaning it as a joke.

Jesse asked what about her parents, and Sasha glared at her. "You know about my parents."

"Yeah," Jesse said, "but not, like, in that *specific* sense. I know your mom's obsessed with you being pretty."

"There's nothing wrong with being pretty."

"Do you know about this thing in therapy called 'reparenting'?" Miranda asked.

"She wants you to be doing preventative Botox," Jesse said, testing out how much private information he could get away with sharing to the group.

"That's right," Sasha said, rejecting the bait. "We all should be doing that, probably."

"No, we shouldn't," Miranda said loudly, as though demonstrating the mechanics of reparenting.

"So you *don't* think I need preventative Botox?" Sasha turned earnestly toward Miranda.

"Is that what this is?" Lou asked, gesturing to the needle in Sasha's fingers. "Are you doing, like, DIY Botox?"

"No, this is for Jesse," Sasha said.

Lou yawned. "You losers have fun, okay? I'm going to bed."

They waved farewell and slid through the door. Darcy remained on the porch.

"Faye does that with me," Jesse said once Lou was gone.

"Reparenting?" said Miranda.

"Yeah."

"What is that, exactly?" Darcy asked, smacking her glistening balloon lips together.

"So it would go like this," Miranda said. "We'd pick a moment to reenact, a moment where your parents really failed as parents. And I—or the therapist—would role-play as the *good* parent and attempt to do some healing around the incident."

"Can you demonstrate with Sasha?" Darcy suggested.

"That sounds boring," Sasha said.

"Sure," Miranda answered as though Sasha hadn't spoken. "So first we'd choose an incident."

Sasha insisted, again, that there had been no "incident."

"Faye's done that with me," Jesse repeated, "like when I told her about my mom crying when I cut my hair short and saying I looked like a cancer patient. Faye plays the role of my mom and tells me I look great—like myself."

Sasha scoffed. "Well, if reparenting is just flattery, then I reparent you all the time."

"Partners can reparent each other too, that's great," Miranda said.

"So why do you need Faye?" Sasha asked Jesse.

"Faye promises to keep me safe and holds me," Jesse said. "*You* don't keep me safe and hold me."

They exchanged a combative look. Sasha made her eyes big and sad to see if Jesse would take pity on her, and Jesse did, arranging her face into a goofy grin to show that she wasn't really mad. But then her gaze turned steely again and she looked away.

"Would you say my lips are shaped more like this, or this?" Darcy was asking, swiping through rows and rows of digital renderings of lips all shapes and sizes on her phone screen, still holding one hand up to her face.

Miranda glanced over. "That one," she suggested, pointing to a pair of wide, plush lips.

Sasha's heart was going like a big engine. She smoothed a towel down over the deck and kneeled on it, lowering herself all the way down to unbutton her skirt. The deck smelled like pine. It was unrealistically quiet, no cars on the road and no animals crying out in the night.

The hole, famously walnut-sized, was indeed now the size of a blueberry. It was to the immediate left of Sasha's tailbone. If she really tried, she could stick one fingernail inside the hole. And so she did, with three heads—Jesse's, Miranda's, and Jules's—pressed together above her in a concerned ceiling.

Jesse gamely poked the needle into her left buttock, barely pressing down, and Sasha shrieked. It was a high, piercing scream that reverberated in the quiet night, prickling the air around them, rustling tree branches overhead. She hadn't been expecting it to hurt so much. Jules screamed, too, a deep-voiced *ahhhh*. Miranda leapt from her chair. Jesse jumped backward. Darcy glanced up and smirked, though she wasn't paying attention. She was staring at her phone.

Attend to me, you bitch, Sasha thought. *Look at me, you pathetic fuckface.*

"I can't do this," Jesse insisted.

"Do it," Sasha grunted. "I won't scream again."

"I'm gonna go inside," Darcy yawned, but she didn't move. "Maybe take a bath or something. I'm chilly."

"Why don't we at least numb the area first, like with a piercing?" Jules offered when the door had shut. "I can go get an ice cube."

"Fine," Sasha said. She was annoyed and took an impatient elbow while Jules slipped inside.

"I'm out of the loop," Miranda was saying. From above, lit by the porch light, she looked like a sun with knitted rays, twinkling with mirth. She took a swig from an insulated thermos. "What exactly is the goal here?"

This was a stupid question, an irrelevant one, one that Sasha was frankly surprised a certified therapist would ask.

"Is this something to do with Darcy—the thing last night?" she asked.

Sasha didn't know how to answer that question. Of course it was something to do with Darcy and the thing last night.

"Look." Darcy showed Jesse her phone screen, and for the first time there was a hint of desperation in her voice that didn't sound like her. "I feel like none of the hair options quite look like mine."

Jesse shot a cursory glance at Darcy's phone before pointing to a shaggy haircut toward the bottom of the screen, which Darcy pouted at, dissatisfied, and Sasha felt relieved that Jesse wasn't attending to Darcy. But Jesse also wasn't attending to her. Jesse's whole presence shook with desperation to leave this scene, she was really already gone.

Jules returned with an ice cube cradled in a small washcloth. She transferred the bundle to Jesse, who crouched before Sasha again and pressed the ice cube gently into the slight hole. It hurt.

"We didn't sew your lips, so maybe your 'thing' can be, like, being really loud," Jules suggested.

It was halfway sweet of Jules to indulge her, but the

suggestion—being extra loud—was too embarrassing, made Sasha feel like a stupid child.

"Maybe your 'thing' can be actually watching this time," Sasha teased Jules, earning a guffaw from the older dyke.

"You sewed her *lips*?" Miranda's face was a picture of shock and delight, and there was something more wild and open about her features than there had been before.

"Darcy's, yeah," Jules said. "You should've seen it, babe. It was *nasty*."

Jesse pressed with surprising force, as if she wanted to hurt Sasha instead of soothe her.

"I'm kind of glad I didn't." Miranda smiled to herself, then giggled as though remembering a secret.

"Enough ice," Sasha commanded after Jesse had pressed the cube to her blueberry dimple for a good thirty seconds.

"So you want me to make a couple stitches?" Jesse asked.

Sasha forced herself to bear down on the towel and not slap Jesse. Jesse should begin without any heed for her feelings; Jesse should do what he wanted to do, not what *she* wanted. Sasha's frustration was as much at Jules and Miranda, not to mention Darcy and Lou, for their gaping obliviousness as it was at Jesse for her reluctance.

"Wait," Miranda said, but she was barely suppressing a laugh. "I feel weird about this."

"Go," Sasha commanded.

"Why do you feel weird?" Jesse asked Miranda.

Miranda let out a deep sigh, signaling that brave emotional honesty would follow. But when she spoke, she slurred her words, and Sasha realized that she'd been sipping something spiked and not an herbal tea, as she'd previously assumed.

"I don't know if I want to be here for this," she said. "It

feels—I don't know—I don't know if I'm up for this right now. I've had a really hard day."

Sasha craned her neck to look at Miranda. "You can leave."

Miranda bristled.

"Go," she repeated.

"What's your day been like, Miranda?" Jesse asked.

Miranda hovered above her chair but then sat back down unsteadily, drunkenly, but still weirdly upright.

"It—it—these people—" she stuttered, malfunctioning.

"The ones on Twitter?" Jesse said gently, and Sasha caught Jules glancing away to avoid eye contact with Miranda.

"Jesus Christ," Sasha snapped. "If you're gonna do it, do it."

"You sure you're ready?" Jesse asked.

Sasha didn't want her to ask if she was ready. Wasn't the whole point of the sewing, wasn't the whole point of what they'd done last night in the sauna, about just fucking doing it?

"Yes."

Jesse pierced Sasha's buttock quickly, and this time she willed herself not to scream. Her nervous system lit up with pain, her spine arching, her body contorting to find a home for the pain. It was halfway bearable because of the ice cube, and soon the needle was through, the stitch had been made. Sasha felt it pulled tight across the dimple, the two pieces of flesh strung together in a way both new and unnatural.

Miranda let out a deep, relieved sigh.

"This is reminding me of when I was a camp counselor and the girls would sneak out at night and pierce each other's ears," she said. "I think they used apples from the cafeteria to do it."

Sasha's rage felt boundless, it was shocking to her that there could be just more and more of it, like a endless spool of thread. What was happening was nothing like the fucking *Parent Trap* or like Jewish teenagers piercing their friends' ears behind a cabin called Strawberry Fields. She didn't understand how when Darcy did things, the same things Sasha herself did, they got metabolized as art. Yet when Sasha did them, the same things got processed by everyone—by the culture!—as frivolous, teenaged. She was reminded of something a critic had once said, attributing write-offs of *Sex and The City* to a denigration of anything stylized—funny, feminine, sexy, pleasurable—as inferior.

But Darcy was stylized, too, Sasha thought, defeated. Darcy was just stylized better.

It was only a day before that Darcy had gotten her ass sewn, yet time had expanded and folded up so many times since then that it might as well have been the previous year. This was already yesterday's news, already derivative. Sasha began to straighten up.

"I kind of want to do a stitch, is that crazy?" Jules said.

Jesse's face was set in frozen displeasure. She handed Jules the needle, which was still attached to the thread in Sasha's flesh, and Jules bent down to paw it clumsily. Why was it stressful when it was Sasha and not Darcy prone on the towel? Why was it cool and kinky, breezy and hot, when Darcy did it, but not Sasha?

Jules let her hand rest, for a second, tensed on Sasha's bare ass.

Sasha's body hardened in anticipation. Jules studiously dragged the tip of the needle gently against her ass. Like clockwork, Sasha's underwear grew soupy. She started to laugh, but she didn't want Jules to stop, so she buried her face in her arms and took a deep, dramatic sigh. She tried to peek at Miranda from the corner of her eye, but a hank of hair obscured her vision. Had Miranda seen Jules drag the needle? Whether or not she had, her face would look the same, but Sasha would've appreciated clocking the precise effort exerted to achieve neutrality.

Jules was devastatingly tender about her stitch, going at it so slowly, and rummaging deeper into her first few layers of skin, that Sasha bore down and clamped her buttocks tight. It hurt more than Jesse's stitch, but less than she'd anticipated. Was it too much to ask for someone to brutalize her?

Jules's breath released a plume of the blood-orange negroni she'd prepared earlier, her green blazer released a puff of weed-infused air each time she shifted positions. Behind her eyeballs, Sasha observed her own pain grow exponentially, red streaks like multiplying bacteria, a thousand red blobs stretching apart and then jiggling to a halt.

"I've never really understood why people are turned on by hurting each other during sex," Jules said, breaking the trance.

"Do you understand it now?" Miranda volleyed back.

"Well," Jules began.

The smell of Jesse's butch musk wafted toward Sasha. Her eyes still shut, Sasha could decipher Jesse's movements only through the intensity of the smell—he must be taking a step toward her now, sidestepping to the right, settling next to Miranda on the observation deck.

"Has anyone seen my phone?" Jesse asked.

Jules and Miranda murmured that they hadn't.

"Want me to help you look?" Darcy's voice floated into Sasha's airspace. She glanced up, surprised to see that Darcy had returned to the porch, swaddled in one of the blankets from the couch.

"It's okay, I can find it later," Jesse said.

"Do you want me to film this?" Darcy offered.

"What, Sasha getting sewn?" Jesse's voice replied.

"Isn't that why you wanted your phone?"

"No, that's okay."

"I was going to say no anyway," Sasha said.

"Wouldn't want anyone to make it into porn," Darcy said, making the same joke for the third time. Then there was the sound of Darcy's phone, set to the highest volume for the past twenty-four hours (dinging, chirping, and ringing as more praise reached her every few minutes), reverting to the "off" setting.

"It's like what you said last night, Sash, in your sleep," Jesse reminded her in a tone that was almost taunting. So different from the way Jesse usually spoke to her that she was, for a second, genuinely terrified.

"What?" Sasha asked, her eyes squeezed shut, the anticipation a strobing cone of darkness.

"You whispered it a few times," Jesse said. "It was: *Have you ever thought our lives are very dangerous? Have you ever thought our lives are very dangerous?*"

Sasha's eyes flew open. "I said that?"

"Your kink-lite manifesto," Miranda joked.

Miranda was so much smaller and thinner than Jules, just as she'd been at the beginning of the trip. This was right, to Sasha—Jules and her formidable body sheltering Miranda's as the latter bobbled unsteadily on her chair.

"To me it sounds like an immigrant thing, but maybe that's just 'cause my brain is broken," Darcy said. "My parents were always obsessed with telling me how dangerous life is."

Darcy and her polished stone villa on the Croatian coast calling herself an immigrant was a little much, Sasha thought.

"Aren't you German?" Sasha asked.

Jesse began to cut in: "Sasha, I think that's out—"

"Pssh," Darcy dismissed. "It's different in Europe. We're all a little this, a little that." Sasha scoffed, remembering Darcy's plan to celebrate Orthodox New Year. She struggled to a seated position on the towel, trying to ignore the throbbing in her ass.

Miranda's chuckle sounded from her bundle of materials, and they all looked over at her uneasily.

"Everyone there is traumatized," Darcy held forth. "My family—the ones who didn't leave—"

"Some more than others," Sasha, who had read in great detail about the Bosnian rapes at the hands of the Croatians, interrupted.

Miranda let out a peal of laughter and then shoved her face in her cashmere scarf.

"I think you're talking about two different wars," Jules soothed, still holding the threaded needle and perched on her knees. "The Yugoslavian conflict goes back to the fourteenth century, with the Ottoman Turks' campaign in the Balkans. It's important to talk about it within the context of the shifting borders of world history. Now, there are links, of course, between the Nazi conspiracy in the Second World War and the more recent conflicts in the Balkan region."

She set the needle gingerly onto the small iron table beside the ashtray. Sasha had forgotten that Jules knew anything about the world.

"See, you don't know what you're talking about," Darcy spat at Sasha.

"Your grandpa was a Nazi!" Sasha shouted over the sounds of Miranda's muffled hysterical laughter.

"Bitch, you're delusional," Darcy yelled back. "My grandfather was Bosnian!"

"Whatever," Sasha said. "Go write about it in your diary."

"Look at yourself." Darcy drew a flouncy border around Sasha with her fingers from her perch on the outdoor chair, tut-tutting as she enclosed Sasha in a sinister and lonely frame. "Look at how hard you're trying."

"*Shlyukha*," Sasha shreeched.

"*Jeb ice*," Darcy yelled back.

"What's everyone screaming about?"

The battle for authenticity was interrupted by the presence of Lou bursting forth through the door, Vivienne in tow.

"The Tito–Stalin split, I think," Jules observed drily.

"Seriously?" Lou wrinkled up their nose as though smelling Darcy's grandfather's rotting Nazi breath.

"I didn't want to talk about any of this," Darcy said. "It's my family—you can't just—"

Lou wrapped their arms protectively around Darcy.

"It's sensitive for everyone," Jesse said.

"I don't have a dog in this fight, I'm Persian." Miranda swiped a hand across the scene in front of her, as though erasing herself from the drama. Yet for some reason her voice wavered as though about to cry, and Jules moved instinctively over to comfort her. Only Sasha and Jesse remained separated from their respective partner, glaring at each other over the ash-strewn table.

Your whole family was exterminated by them, Sasha transmitted telepathically.

But they were in Warsaw, Jesse responded. *I think. Or was it Krakow?*

"Let's warm up," Jules suggested, and Sasha shrugged her tights back up, tears streaming down her face—nobody noticed, of course—and followed the rest of them inside.

ৎ ৯

Sasha felt the buzz of her hot toddy on the second or third sip, her head taking on a familiar weight that made her neck feel fragile. She tilted all the way to the left and then all the way to the right. Darcy and Lou had proceeded immediately upstairs after their outside bout, and Jesse still wasn't looking Sasha's way. For a moment the silence renewed each of the four remaining, forcing them into a quiet metamorphosis of mood transformation: Miranda's chest puffed out, projecting a bravado that was unusual for her; Jesse grew contemplative, his pulsating need to evacuate turned slow and moody; Jules was abuzz with nervous energy, unable to sit still, knocking her foot repeatedly against the base of the expensive coffee table; and Sasha had descended into her own universe of drunken catatonia, her mania replaced by a slowness that sent her deep into the recesses of the couch.

"How's the ass?" Jules asked Sasha, and Sasha murmured that she felt fine.

"I'm the only one"—burp, giggle—"that hasn't inflicted or experienced"—giggle—"bodily harm this week," Miranda said.

Sasha worked up the energy to reach out her hand, extending her fingers toward Jesse to make sure she was really still here and not deep within the couch's fibers. She didn't understand why he was ignoring her. She hadn't done anything worse than what Darcy had done, had just wanted her boyfriend to do to her what he'd already done to someone else. Her brain spun uselessly.

"How do people feel about shrooms?" Miranda asked, the word self-conscious in her mouth. "Seems like we could all use a little something."

"Like—mushrooms?" Jesse asked.

"Shrooms," Jules clarified. "Is that not what you guys call them?"

"No, it is. I just didn't know you had them."

"We're older," Miranda loudly reminded Sasha and Jesse once again, prophylactically mitigating her dorkiness, though

Miranda was not so very old, and for that matter neither was Jules.

We get it, Sasha wanted to say, *you are very old and we are very young.*

"Well, should we take some?" Jesse asked, unsure and possibly annoyed at the suggestion (though nobody got annoyed with Miranda; the annoyance bounced off Miranda and landed on Sasha instead). Jules galloped off to go get the mushrooms, eager to have a task.

"I already took a Klonopin earlier," Miranda sighed. "I should look up the interaction with shrooms."

"Oh, right," Sasha said. "You said you'd had a hard day."

Miranda stared down into her lap sadly. The thermos was beside her, on the wooden table, no coaster.

Jules returned with a baggie of gray-brown alien clumps in one hand and her daddy cigar in the other. She was quieter than she'd been in the past; Sasha wondered if this was due to Miranda's increased presence—if at any given moment only one of them could be loud, and because Jules had bellowed in the sauna, it was now Miranda's turn.

"Here," Jules said. "I recommend dropping a few into your hot toddy to start, more of a tea vibe. It'll make everything better."

Each drinker held out their mug, and Jules shook some of the mushrooms into their toddies. Sasha sipped gratefully, her head clouding more by the second, and she sank back into the couch cushion, a soft smile flickering over her lips.

Jules lowered herself into an armchair and brandished the daddy cigar. She lit it, filling the air with the sweet stench of smoke. After taking a few purposeful drags, Jules held the cigar out to Miranda, but barely extended, as though this were just a formality.

"I figured now's as good a time as any to break into it," she explained almost defensively, though nobody had challenged her.

"Are you going to share?" Miranda asked.

She laughed as she snatched the cigar from Jules, nearly knocking over her hot toddy. It dawned on Sasha that maybe this was the "real" Miranda, someone she'd never met. Sober, Miranda seemed determined to take up as little space as possible, or at least to adhere strictly to the boundaries of her physical body and personal space. And so in her drunkenness, unfamiliar and alluring, she would remain opaque yet insistently present.

When the cigar came to Sasha, she inhaled deeply, and Jules observed, "That's the first time you've smoked this trip."

The cigar slapped Sasha like a sopping towel across the face. After a coughing fit that filled her eyes with tears and constricted her throat, she settled into the feeling. In seconds, she was glitchy, her movements staccato.

"What if," Miranda said to Jesse and Sasha, in a stage whisper, "what if I played a *liiiiiittttle* practical joke on Jules?"

"What kind of joke?" Jesse asked.

Jules, staring glass-eyed into the distance yet in earshot of everything, let out a good-natured chuckle. You could tell she was playing along with Miranda, but cautiously. Jules wasn't as drunk or high as Miranda and felt the need, Sasha sensed, to maintain some sense of decorum. Especially in front of Jesse and Sasha, the ones they wanted to fuck. Was Jules embarrassed? Sasha's neck snapped from Jules to Miranda to Jules and then back again, trying to make sense of it.

Miranda was laughing hysterically as she answered, hardly able to get the words out. "Well, what if I gave her a taste of my pussy."

Jesse and Sasha looked at each other, Sasha's glance horrified and Jesse's mystified, both too uncomfortable to look directly at either Miranda or Jules. In all of their imaginings of what might happen upstate between them and the other couple—the two couples fucking in proximity of the other, Jesse and Miranda watching while Jules fucked Sasha; Jules and Jesse both fucking Sasha while Miranda watched; Jules and Jesse fucking Miranda as Sasha watched; or even Jules and Jesse fucking like boys, like an older daddy and his boy toy—this particular scenario, that of Miranda giving Jules a taste of her pussy, hadn't figured in anywhere. Moreover, Sasha hadn't prepared for this to go down while she and Jesse were at odds.

"Shit," Jesse said, laughing a little into her mug. Jesse didn't look over at Sasha, so Sasha wasn't sure if they were on the same page, or if Jesse was thinking the same thing as she was.

Sasha turned to see how Jules would respond. Jules looked stricken, but Sasha sensed that she was somewhat powerless, that what Miranda wanted was what they did, and Jules nodded solemnly; she was totally powerless. Even when Miranda was sober, she ruled their relationship, with a nod of her head or a look from the corner of her eye. Miranda's power was immense, so immense that Sasha couldn't help admiring it, coveting it.

Buzzkill, Sasha imagined Jesse was thinking about Jules. What an old butch buzzkill.

Sasha couldn't decide if Jules's submissiveness made her more or less attractive. She had a particular weakness for a submissive butch, one who let herself be ruled. But there was something depressing about Jules's captivity, which seemed more reluctant than intentional. There had to be strength alongside the weakness, a strength of spirit that in that moment Jules lacked. Sasha thought of a line from her beloved *Vanderpump Rules*, Stassi saying, *I want him to* want *to be my prisoner.* Having to force someone to play along was a humiliation beyond anything Miranda was doing.

Well, she's found someone who wants to be held captive by her, Sasha thought of Miranda.

It was odd seeing Miranda, this slightly older dykette, be so unruly. Jules winced nearly imperceptibly at the word pussy, then laughed it off, taking another long sip of her drink. When Sasha looked to her left, she saw that Miranda had shaken her caftan off, sitting on the couch in just a gossamer nightgown that revealed her small, pointed breasts. Things were happening faster than Sasha could control with her powers of observation and processing—Miranda taking the cigar and slowly, slowly edging the hem of her nightgown up until she revealed a crop of matted dark pubic hair and a deflated rose of labial lips. *How was this happening?* She wasn't wearing underwear. Sasha loved seeing other people's bodies in all their absurdity. It reminded her of a pervy childhood fantasy of being able to see her classmates naked—purely for scientific purposes—to examine the myriad ways a body could look. Sasha was filled with unlikely glee and admiration. Unlike her, Miranda knew how to do things, things like drive and identify plants and file her taxes. Miranda could spend nights alone in the house upstate without feeling even a whisper of fear. And now she was going to smoke with her pussy!

Sasha was struck by jealousy, though it was more of a protective instinct—the sense that Jesse was not supposed to be seeing this, although she of course was; Sasha felt the need to limit Jesse's view of what was transpiring, and she didn't know if it was due to her secondhand embarrassment for Miranda, and her over-identification with the wife in any scenario, or if it was her jealousy at Jesse seeing another woman's pussy open like that, glistening and proud.

"You sure this is a good idea?" Jules asked. The mood had tipped over. Sasha wanted to help Jules somehow but could not think of what to do or say. Sasha was aligned with Jules, as they were both on the side of caution and, though they hated it about themselves in equal measures, propriety. Miranda had always seemed like the proper one to Jules's gregariousness, but that wasn't the case at all. Her tameness when sober was a strenuous but necessary struggle, Sasha saw, because for her the alternative was a wildness that could hardly be controlled. In that way, she was like Jesse.

"Oh, stop it, of course I'm sure," Miranda said, edging the cigar into her cunt until it stuck out of her. It looked absurd coming out of those small legs, peeking out of her crotch like a dildo. Or, more unsettlingly, a dick.

"What about the minor vaginal procedure?" Sasha asked.

"Girls used to give themselves pelvic exams like this in the nineties," Miranda announced. "Look, it's a speculum!"

"That's true," Sasha said helpfully. "They made their own. It was the anti-gynecology movement."

"Lighter," Miranda commanded, and Jules handed it to her with an embarrassed laugh.

She lit the cigar, and the flame slowly began to lick at the edge poking out from Miranda's crotch. They watched soberly for three seconds. Sasha was pretty sure she saw Miranda tighten her pussy muscles around the pipe, imitating a suctioning mouth. And then Miranda screamed.

"Fuck, fuck, that *hurts*, that hurts so *bad*." Her words came out as a pathetic whine, so instead of being alarmed or worried about her, the group instead averted their gaze.

"Take it out, honey," Jules coached. "Jesus christ, you're going to hurt yourself."

Miranda slid the cigar out and breathed a dramatic sigh of

relief. She crossed her legs, shielding herself from view. "Ha ha ha," she laughed quietly to herself.

"Did you inhale the smoke through your pussy?" Sasha asked, attempting a joke.

Jules's face was an angry slab that appeared almost turned on by rage—because ultimately, wasn't sex drive just anger that Goddex had made you so horny?

"Pussy lung cancer," Sasha said, unable to shut up.

Miranda was waving the cigar around, as though using it to spell a cryptic message in the air. Jules looked deeply uncomfortable, avoiding eye contact with everyone; it was clear she wished that Jesse and Sasha were not present. A look of focus came over Jesse's face. He pried the cigar from Miranda's fingers and plugged it into his own mouth, taking a good long inhale while relighting it with Jules's red lighter.

"Ha!" Jesse said, exhaling a cloud of smoke that smudged his face before dissipating.

Sasha's heart was racing. She couldn't imagine that this was really happening, Jesse tasting another woman, taking great pains to show he was enjoying it—for Miranda's benefit? Sasha's? Jules's?—while Jules and Sasha watched like statues. It was the weirdest way for Jesse and Miranda to transgress in their respective relationships, much weirder than Jules humping Sasha's leg, and it registered in Sasha's body as a transgression she could access only through Jules's big body, sitting stoically in her armchair.

"I can't believe you're putting that in your *mouth*," Miranda marveled, euphoric.

Sasha sensed that Jesse had put it in her mouth only because it would have been awkward not to. Maybe to Miranda this was earning their keep, this was what it meant to stay with them; this wasn't Jesse's young gay male friends staying with their sugar daddies on Fire Island, having sex in exchange for a bed in an architecturally ambitious mansion; maybe this was what it meant to earn one's keep at a house in Hudson with two lesbian sugar mommies in their middle age, for whom this type of theatrically kinky behavior was very, very naughty. It had become Sasha and Jesse's responsibility to ease this painful moment between their elders—to mitigate the awkwardness emerging between Jules and Miranda, each facing an internal and external battle; to soothe the revelation of some lack or unspoken desire moving between Jules and Miranda; and to normalize the social discomfort of being implicated in another couple's perversions. Jesse was only doing his best to hold up his end of the bargain, and Sasha felt a rush of gratitude.

"It's just like what Bill and Monica did," Miranda mused.

Of course this was a pressure point for her—she'd been a teenager during the Lewinsky scandal, when Monica revealed she'd been fucked by Clinton's cigar. Sasha wonder if teenaged Miranda had crushed on Bill Clinton, who shared a certain obvious sexuality with Jules.

"He put out his cigar in her pussy," Jules said, her words dead on impact.

"No, he didn't." Miranda scowled. "She rubbed his cigar on her pussy to get off. It was unlit."

"Really?" Jules said on autopilot. "I always thought he put it out in her."

"That would've burned her pussy!"

"We didn't burn yours."

"That's because it went in the other way," Miranda explained patiently. "Not fire-first."

Jesse was still holding the cigar, but Jules and Miranda were looking at each other, in a silent standoff about the details of the Lewinsky trial.

"I'm pretty sure Miranda's right," Sasha said.

"Whatever," Jesse said, taking another inhale of pussy cigar.

Jesse's earring gleamed. She wore a small gold *S* in her right earlobe that she'd welded when they'd started dating to brand herself with Sasha's initial. But the earring, once the perfect thing, now taunted her. Sasha imagined Jesse thrusting into another woman with the *S* gleaming in the light that streamed in from the window above her bed.

"Omigod, you're really *smoking* my pussy!" Miranda laughed. The nightgown now covered her pussy but was, because of all the writhing she was doing on the couch, hiked dangerously north.

"Stop it," Jules snapped. "Give me that, Jesse."

She held out one big hand for the cigar.

In moments like these time tends to slow down, and that is no exaggeration. They all looked at Jesse to see how she'd react, then to Jules to see if her sudden strictness was a part of the performance, maybe even a joke which could end in laughter, or if she was really mad. Sasha stared at Jules's outstretched hand, the fingerpads rough and rounded, the knuckles aggressively tensed, a ropy blue vein cording down the length of it. Sasha imagined that as she was drooling over Jules's hand, Jesse was thinking that this interaction was getting stale. *Corny* really was the best word for it; the old butch buzzkill and the dykette who just wanted attention until she got it, at which point she'd protest and holler, unable to account for her desires. Wasn't that how they—Jesse and Sasha—had wound up here, in Hudson? They liked to imagine that they'd been invited as Jules and Miranda's desire incarnate, but when it came down to it, neither of them was able to claim it, to pursue them.

Miranda stared at Jules, her face a cross between crestfallen and puzzled. Sasha felt she could read on Miranda's face that she *had* wanted something from Jules (to seduce her, impress her, amuse her), but hadn't known precisely how to want it, and hadn't known the right way to accept it when it became a possibility. She didn't understand, as Sasha did, the right way to surrender, how to wear a green ribbon. Miranda's sex with Jules did not make her happy, Sasha projected smugly, and she did not feel created and destroyed by it. At best it was a mild salve. She didn't relish the promise of her own destruction at Jules's hands. Their sex did not take her beyond and into herself. She was sewn too firmly into her own irrevocable state of being.

Jesse wordlessly placed the cigar into Jules's outstretched palm.

Jules's phone went off in a series of rings and buzzes, as though she'd set a timer for the duration of the charade, and she swept out of the room with the phone pressed to her ear and the cigar clenched firmly in her right fist. Miranda sat back on the couch for a moment and closed her eyes tight before heaving herself up to follow Jules out of the room.

ᕮ ᕭ

Then again, maybe all Miranda had wanted was to destroy her pussy with fire. Maybe the small dildo she'd fashioned for herself, and then inserted into herself, was meant to both create and torch her—via her sex—into oblivion. They'd seen Miranda mark her territory. Despite herself, and despite the awkwardness that had transpired, Sasha felt a surge of true elation, not the uncomplicated joy of *having fun* but the thornier joys of seeing and being seen, recognizing and being recognized, envying and being envied.

What we are willing to do when we're young and newly in love is different from the sacrifices and compromises of middle age, Sasha mused. Perhaps the reason their queer elders had invited them here—and perhaps the way they'd already earned their keep—was the presentation of an alternative way of being. Their youth, their relative stupidity, made it safer for Jules and Miranda to be old and random in all the ways that Jesse and Sasha did not yet know how to be. Sasha turned these possibilities over and over, trying to work them out from the depths of her slightly drugged reverie. When she came to, Jesse was still beside her, slumped over in an identical catatonia.

❧ ❧

"I can't be in this house anymore," Jesse said after they'd sat on the couch without speaking for about half an hour. "I'm going crazy. I want to go home."

"Miranda was just drunk," Sasha said.

"It's not that."

"We've got just a few more days," Sasha said.

"I want to leave tonight."

"Let's just take a drive," Sasha suggested. "Go get the keys from Jules."

"Am I okay to drive?" Jesse said.

"You didn't have that much toddy," Sasha said.

"Okay," Jesse said like a robot. "Lemme go find the keys."

Inside the kitchen, Darcy smiled, their mêlée forgiven, and Sasha saw, quite plainly on her face—she wasn't attempting to hide it, and never had—how little she cared about what had transpired on the porch.

Sasha went to the fridge and took out the leftover tiramisu. There was a fly nestled in the surface, a dusty blanket of cocoa powder clouding its glassy eyes and shiny wings.

"Darcy?" she called out, conciliatory. "Want any tiramisu?"

"I'm good," Darcy called back.

Sasha made out the sound of Jules and Miranda fighting quietly in the small room right off the kitchen, where they kept random board games and towels they didn't feel like dealing with. Miranda was hissing something about "being upstate all the time now, playing wifey" and Jules was *shhh*ing Miranda while trying to keep her volume down. Sasha wasn't interested enough to listen in detail.

As Sasha was spooning a creamy hunk onto a dessert plate for herself, Jesse reappeared in the kitchen.

Sasha dropped her spoon on the wooden counter, leaving her serving of tiramisu untouched, and rushed to follow.

They got into the car. It was still lukewarm from Darcy and Lou's drive to town a few hours earlier.

"I lost my phone," Jesse remembered angrily. "Can you navigate?"

"Where are we going?"

"I don't know. I'm starving."

It wasn't that late—not even nine p.m., somehow—but Sasha knew nothing much would be open.

"Should we just go to the grocery store?"

"I don't care."

Sasha's ass ached as Jesse drove roughly, the stitch loosening with every bump in the road.

"You don't know what it's like," Jesse said, increasing their speed. "You have no idea what it's like. To be humiliated like that. To feel, like, implicated."

"What, you had secondhand embarrassment or whatever?"

Jesse shook his head. "You were just trying to impress Jules and Miranda. But it always ends up on me."

"*What* ends up on you?"

"In moments like that. Making everyone feel okay about

themselves. Not wanting to seem gross about Miranda. Putting my mouth on the pussy pipe. You don't get it. You're not—gay."

"You're right," Sasha said automatically. "I'm not. I don't know what it's like at all."

She didn't think this was true, even as she said it, though she knew she couldn't disagree with Jesse. After all, she did know what it was like—perhaps not to be butch but certainly to be gay, and she'd always been open about what it was fashionable to call her "invisibility privilege," or at least as open as one *could* be about being invisible. But it wasn't enough to be open about it. She also had to agree with statements like these, had to tell Jesse that he was right, and that she, Sasha, didn't understand what it meant to be a lesbian. An absurd conclusion to draw, but nonetheless, in this moment, true.

Once inside the grocery store, Sasha accidentally kicked a yellow onion that had fallen from its perch. It skittered across the floor. Jesse asked Sasha why she kicked the onion, walking ahead, away from her. Sasha trailed her, but she was walking fast. Sasha stopped short and let her leave, watched as she power-walked down an aisle and disappeared.

Sasha was alone in the bakery section. She sped down the main hallway, looking down long, empty aisles cringing under fluorescent lighting. Her stomach tangled. Each new aisle flooded out before her, large and still. Jesse wasn't there. She thought maybe she was the only one in the grocery store. Frozen bags of ice, bags of flour, rolls of paper towel, frozen-food shelves, rows and rows of jarred olives, jars of tomato sauce, carts of peaches, racks of spices.

Jesse had gone home, Sasha realized. She had left Sasha here with no car and no way to get home. Sasha didn't even know Jules's address, having always relied on others to navigate for her. She considered calling Jesse but couldn't make herself, then remembered the phone was missing. Sasha couldn't leave, but she also couldn't be outside. At least inside the grocery store it was warm. She couldn't think of how to get back to the house from here. She paced up and down the aisles, concentrating on how her feet looked against the grocery store linoleum. After what felt like twenty minutes of wandering, she caught sight of Jesse near the cash registers. Sasha knew he'd seen her, but Jesse kept walking. Sasha ran, half crying out, to catch up with him.

"Can you at least talk to me?" Sasha said, finally reaching him.

Jesse wheeled around to face her.

"Please talk to me," Sasha said.

Jesse moved from one freezer case to the next, examining the ice cream options. Sasha had forgotten that was what they had come for, a snack. Jesse picked up a bag of almond horns and asked Sasha if she would eat some of them the next day. Sasha said no, probably not. Jesse said he was going to buy them anyway. He also picked up a bar of dark chocolate and some mint chocolate chip ice cream. Sasha wanted to steal the almond horns, but there wasn't time. They were now proceeding together to the register.

The cashier's name tag read *OLYMPIA*.

"Hey!" Olympia said, ringing up the dark chocolate.

"Hi," Sasha said.

"Is it true?" she asked coyly, almost flirtatiously. There was something off about her manner, and Sasha wondered if they knew each other—but no, she was just high and had gay face.

"What?" Jesse asked.

"Is it true what they say?" she asked.

"What?" Jesse asked again.

"Is it true that black cats are bad luck?"

They looked at Jesse's shirt, which featured a black cat. Jesse laughed hollowly and said he didn't know. Sasha thought of the line from a hurt email someone had once sent to her eternally squabbling graduate seminar that fall, a line that went, *I DON'T UNDERSTAND WHY THE FACT THAT VIOLENCE BEGETS PAIN IS BEING ELIDED!* At the time, the line had struck Sasha as profound; now it seemed like it had been written by someone who understood neither violence nor pain.

"She's in love with you, and you won't even look at her!" the cashier said loudly. "She's a Capricorn, isn't she? And if she's not, she's anything you want her to be."

Jesse stared straight ahead, unwilling to take relationship advice from an upstate teenager, but Sasha felt the words settle heavily between them.

They walked outside and made their way down to Jules's car. It was windy, so Jesse shoved the ice cream inside the pocket of her puffer. When they got into the car, Jesse didn't turn it on, even though it was freezing.

"How do you feel?" Sasha asked.

Jesse shook his head. "Fed up."

"At *me*?" Sasha squawked, as though there was someone else who Jesse might be fed up with.

Jesse's head lolled back in exasperation, and she banged it a few times against the driver's seat, a series of dull thuds.

"Don't do that," Sasha said. "I'll walk home if you keep being like this."

"You see?" Jesse exploded. "That's what I mean. I can't live like this. I don't trust you."

"I don't trust *you*," Sasha fired back.

"Oh, please."

"You fucked her!"

Jesse let her head fall into his hands. "Does it matter if I did or I didn't?" he said. "Either way, I knew I'd be punished for it; you'd decided how it would be. Just like it always is."

What came to mind were lines from Betty and Theodore Roszak's book *Masculine/Feminine*: "She is stifling under the triviality of her femininity. The world is groaning beneath the terrors of his masculinity. . . . How do we call off the game?"

Sasha hissed that Jesse needed to stop "globalizing." "You're being such a drama king."

"That's just it," Jesse said. "I can't express a single emotion without you flipping it back around to center *you*."

"Please," Sasha said. "You make *everything* about you. YOU'RE THE MOST SELFISH PERSON I'VE EVER MET."

Jesse snorted, a sound stupid and embarrassing but still crueler than any he'd ever directed at Sasha.

"I didn't mean that," Sasha said, her blood running ice cold.

"Why'd you say it, then?"

"I don't know. I'm sorry."

"That's the problem! You just *say* shit. You don't even mean it. You don't even care how it affects me."

Jesse's eyes welled up, predictably.

"No, no, no," Sasha said, desperately backtracking at Jesse's sunken face. "I didn't mean it, you're not selfish. *I'm* selfish."

"Why did you say it, then?" Jesse insisted, sniffling.

"I didn't mean it."

"WHY DID YOU SAY IT, THEN?"

"I don't want to live in a world where people say exactly what they mean," Sasha insisted, as though maybe this argument would work where her apologizing had failed. What she meant was that she wanted whatever was the opposite of earnestness; but even this she'd failed at expressing.

Sasha tried to pull her into a hug, but Jesse resisted her.

"Well, I *do*!" Jesse yelled. "I just want you to tell me you love me and I'll never lose you. But you're so fucking repressed that you have to make up these games and say all this *bullshit*."

"You'll never lose me," Sasha said.

Jesse still wasn't hugging back.

"Never," Sasha said, though she struggled to say the word with sincerity. It was not what she felt, nor something she could promise.

"You make me feel like a pervert," Jesse said. "Like a little gay sicko. And then that's what I start to become. You tell me over and over again what I want, it *messes* with me."

Sasha's body flared with fear. For a moment she felt guilty for having spoken in such a tone, stricken almost with guilt.

"You took your big stupid hand and stuck it inside her," Sasha accused, back to her strongest offense, her most robust accusation.

"I'm so sick of *your* voice and *your* narrative," Jesse said. "Meanwhile, I do all the work in this relationship, I make all the meaning when we fight. You just stand there silently, mad at me. Think about how lonely that makes me. You're always abandoning me, abandoning me and terrorizing me with your feelings. You think you can say anything to me to work out your issues and I'll just sit here and take it."

How do we call off the game?

"You hold all of my reality," Sasha argued back. "I rely on you completely to tell me how to think and what to feel. And you're not taking that responsibility seriously *at all*."

This sentiment wasn't as comforting to Sasha as it had once been, and the hug was not comfortable either, the ice cream pressing against Sasha through her puffer. Jesse turned on the car and pulled out of the Hannaford parking lot.

Vivienne was going crazy in the foyer, jumping up and down behind the door. No one else appeared to be home.

"It's okay, Vivienne," Sasha cried, cradling the dog to her chest. "Mommy loves you, even if Daddy doesn't, and she will *never, ever* abandon you."

Jesse entered the house behind Sasha, reminding her of the moment he'd abandoned her in the grocery store.

"I thought you left me alone back there," Sasha accused. "I thought you left the store and went to the bus stop."

"I did," Jesse admitted. "But only for a minute. I left the store and I sat in the car. Then I thought to myself, 'What are you doing? You can't do this to her.'"

The scene unfolded before her. Jesse pushing the Prius's start button with an angry finger, backing a few feet out of the parking spot. Pausing there, the car half in and half out, unable to fathom his next move. All his stuff—including the lost phone—was back at the house. Through the big windows of the grocery store, he could see Sasha illuminated under the bright lights, pacing through the aisles, stopping at one point to ridiculously peek between two hefty bundles of paper towels, as though Jesse could be hiding there. And so he'd turned the car off, wiped his eyes with the backs of his hands, and went to find her.

"You got in the *car*?" Sasha shrieked.

"Yeah, but I didn't go anywhere. I didn't even turn it on."

"You're so scared I'm going to abandon you, but just look what you did!" Sasha swiped furiously under her eyes, surprised to find she wasn't crying.

"I'm sorry. I'm so sorry."

"I don't know if I can do this anymore," Sasha said.

Between them was a looking glass, or a pond, some shimmery reflective surface, and through it they studied each other for a few sickening seconds, the twin fear and loathing on the other's face. Finally, Jesse broke away, his face twitched, and they were no longer mirror images. He said, "You're a *demon*."

A laugh bubbled up in Sasha's throat, but she swallowed it back down. She didn't want Jesse to think she was uncaring, though *demon* was kind of funny. Recently they'd been discussing Jesse's upcoming Pisces-themed birthday party. Soon Pisces-themed had become Narcissus-themed, in homage to the ancient Greek who fell in love with his own watery reflection and spent his life staring into the shimmering pool eternally offering up an image of his own face. Jesse's face in this moment held a Narcissistic quality, as though he were contemplating not Sasha but his own image.

Sasha liked her own monster-face, though she didn't think she was really that bad, or at least that much worse than other people. After all, if they were keeping score, Jesse was the one who had walked away from her, Jesse the one who had slandered her to her therapist, Jesse the one who had looked at Sasha and said *demon*. And wasn't recognizing the devil in her just as bad as being one himself?

What had Sasha's mother said to her father?

It either has to do with me or it doesn't; and if it doesn't, I can't let it touch me.

I can look away? I can leave the room?

Ꮼ Ꮼ

Sasha's ass was already infected from the two stitches, one by Jesse and the other by Jules. It festered, raw and irritated, as she paced around the kitchen. Her heart pounded in her left buttock, bumping with pain as the blood rushed around her body.

"I need to find my phone," Jesse said.

"Wait, no," Sasha said.

"You haven't found your phone yet?"

Sasha jumped at Darcy's voice. She hadn't realized she was so close by, but there she was, on the other side of the counter with Lou, both of them oblivious to the drama that was still unfolding.

After scouring the house, looking into every crevice and under every couch cushion, Lou made the call that it was probably time to expand the search to outside.

The four of them stoically pulled on their coats, hats, and gloves, making their way across the frozen yard and into the woods. Jesse was on her hands and knees at the edge of the yard, a flashlight by her side, digging through piles of snow.

It enraged Sasha that Darcy and Lou were, in their newcoupledom, so impactless, that none of this was real to them beyond giggles and flirting and noticing each other. Darcy and Lou would get out of this unscathed.

"Here, have you tried Find My iPhone on someone else's phone?" Lou was asking.

"That's a good idea," Sasha supplied, and Lou handed Jesse their phone.

"Fuck, I can't log onto Find My iPhone without my Apple ID, which of course it sent to my phone," Jesse said. "Fuck! This is so frustrating."

"Does anyone have your location?" Darcy asked, sighing,

wistful for the New Year's Eve party at the Verso Loft that she should've been attending that night.

"No," Jesse said, at the same time that Sasha said, trying to be funny, "Now don't you regret not sharing your location with me?"

"It's definitely dead by now," Jesse added, not laughing. "Out here in the cold all this time."

"Doesn't your mom have your location?" Sasha asked.

"If the phone's dead, that wouldn't matter," Darcy said.

"It wouldn't show where the phone was right before it died?"

A wide beam of light appeared a few meters away, and Sasha screamed.

"It's okay, it's okay!" Jules said, shining the light up at her face so Sasha could see her, gleaming and dopey. "It's just us. We're here to help."

Beside her was Miranda, burrowed deep in her classic coat-scarf combo with a flashlight of her own, staring at the ground as though waiting for the phone to magically appear at her feet, and also as though the earlier events of the evening had not happened, because when Miranda was dressed in her utilitarian winter-archeology gear, she was a different Miranda to the Miranda who had prostrated herself before them in a thin nightgown.

"Are you feeling better?" Sasha asked Miranda, and Miranda shot Sasha a grateful, if mildly sedated, smile.

They'd all sobered up—Jesse and Sasha from their fight, and the others, Sasha assumed, from the previous two hours of lesbian processing. She even wondered if Jules and Miranda had fucked while she and Jesse were gone; Jules's face inside the perimeter of her hood had a freshly fucked sheen. Sasha checked her own phone absently; it was half past eleven.

"You can take my old phone, but it's just a shitty prepaid

mobile I used in Zagreb," Darcy offered, ever the proletariat, casting an uneasy glance at Sasha to gauge if Europe was still a sore spot.

"Miranda used to be an archaeologist," Jules broadcasted.

"Well, not exactly," Miranda corrected. "It was one dig in Iran during college, and I was part of a very large team. But I do know that an efficient way to find something is to divide the search area into quadrants, devoting one or two people to each quadrant. It dramatically cuts the time spent looking for any given thing."

She was relentlessly capable, Sasha mused, as Miranda went about measuring the area with the tape she'd handily brought along, her utility boots crunching through the sheets of ice under the thick layer of snow, dividing the area in which Jesse and Vivienne had been playing earlier that day into quadrants of about eight by eight. Miranda marked each quadrant with some sort of boundary—the toe of her boot dragged along the snow, a few sticks, etc.—and assigned them each a square: Lou, Jesse, Darcy, and herself. Sasha was to help Jesse, and Jules was to help Miranda. They all began digging in the snow, trading the four pairs of gloves they had between the six of them.

Lou and Sasha dug next to each other, stealing glances of *Can you believe this?* every few minutes. And again, Sasha began to wonder how Lou had felt about Jesse and Darcy's performance the other night. Where had Lou been, Sasha wondered, and how had they made sense of everything? Why had *Lou* not sewn Darcy up? But then: Jesse and Darcy had been planning the green-ribbon thing from the beginning; that was the ostensible reason for the whole performance, the big, storied moment (literally storied, too, disseminated in flashy fifteen-second morsels on dozens of audience members' Instagram accounts). Sasha fell to her hands and knees and started moving apart sheets of snow, not trying particularly hard to accomplish anything. Why should she look for Jesse's phone? It was full of congratulatory texts, probably, and effervescent DMs telling her how great she was.

"I'm freezing," she complained. "My hands are going to fall off."

"You can go inside," Jesse said uncharitably from her own quadrant.

"Alone?"

"You want someone to chaperone you?"

"I'll do it," Jules offered. "I can protect Sasha."

She'd forgotten that Jules was a fake outdoor butch, in reality indoorsy like her, while Miranda was the sturdy and adventuresome one, the one who didn't complain and the one who knew about archeology.

"Let's go," Sasha said. Jules followed her as they trod across the frozen ground, through the woods, and finally through the backyard, reaching the beacon of the warm house and stretching out their numb cheeks and chins to expedite the regaining of their speech faculties.

"It's midnight," Jules observed.

"Really?"

"Past midnight," Jules corrected, checking her big wristwatch. "Twelve fifteen, actually."

"Happy 2020."

"Any resolutions?"

"No, I'm already perfect."

"Ha."

"What about you?"

"Oh, you know."

"What?" There was something about the way Jules was

hedging that made Sasha curious. She was sure Jules would say something like, *Give back to the community* or *Get better ratings* or something. What goals could she possibly have?

"I'm proposing this year," Jules said, flicking on a light.

"What?"

"That's what we decided when we got together in, what, 2016? I'm proposing to Miranda in 2020. That was her deadline—my ultimatum." She let out a hollow laugh.

"I thought you were already married," Sasha said.

"Not officially."

"Why now?"

"As I said, it's something we've talked about for a long time," Jules insisted.

"You're doing this, like, imminently?"

"Maybe," Jules said. "I want it to be special, though."

"You got the ring?"

"It was my grandmother's. I got it re-embedded in a more minimalist, modern band."

"Wow." Sasha didn't try to hide her distaste for the words *embedded*, *minimalist*, and *modern*.

One afternoon not too long before the trip upstate, Jesse and Lou had gone to Sotheby's to look at jewels. A rich woman had died, and her extensive jewelry collection was being auctioned off. Jesse and Lou had charmed the girl at the consignment counter, and she let them try on big rings with strips of onyx, huge princess cuts studded with diamonds. They took pictures of Lou's hand decorated by flashing gleams, Jesse's neck ringed with a Chanel pendant.

Did you get my ring? Sasha had asked, and Jesse had answered, *Ha ha.*

"Yeah. All systems go."

Jules accompanied the dorky expression by taking off her gloves one by one and laying them precisely on top of each other on the table.

"You sound excited," Sasha told her, turning to make herself some tea in the kitchen.

Jules followed her. "What's *that* supposed to mean?" She kept her tone light and nonconfrontational.

Everyone handled Sasha with kid gloves, as though she were perpetually seconds away from an emotional breakdown. She'd rather they treat her as they treated each other, like adults.

"Nothing," Sasha said. "I wasn't being cunty."

"You sure?"

Jules's face flickered between anxiety and anger. Sasha called up the image of Jules fucking herself against Sasha's body, her thigh, her hip bone. She knew Jules was thinking about this, too, struggling to reconcile it all.

"I'm sure," Sasha said. "I'm really happy for you."

᦯ ᧒

It was Darcy who ultimately found Jesse's phone, they recounted breathlessly, after about twenty minutes of digging. She'd shrieked, holding up a sticker-covered phone case. Everyone celebrated, shouted with glee. This was a victory they could all celebrate, the end of the search, the return to the warm house. The phone's screen was glazed over with ice. It would soak in a cup of rice all night, and in the morning they'd turn it on to see what had been saved, and what lost.

The Girl with the Green Ribbon Around Her Neck

ৎ ৵

Sasha barely slept that night, lying as still as possible next to Jesse, her body curled around Vivienne's, which rose and fell with the occasional groan. When she took a long, deep inhale, Vivienne grumbled her approval and nestled her head in the space under Sasha's tits.

Bedridden with her tailbone cyst the year before, she'd texted Jesse on a whim at three in the morning, delirious with pain. She hadn't been expecting Jesse to be awake, but he was. They'd spoken on the phone until dawn, Jesse checking in every so often to suggest a new position that might relieve the pain.

"I'm always up for a long shot," Jesse had responded.

Now Jesse was right there beside her, and Sasha knew that if she woke Jesse up and begged for forgiveness, to try and make things right, Jesse would groggily acquiesce. Usually when they fought, Sasha dissociated and hid under the blankets until Jesse forced her out and apologized. But when Jesse wasn't conscious,

Sasha had to be the one to offer forgiveness. She wasn't up for the task.

The only place she could get a painkiller for her infected ass and spare herself the embarrassment of a trip to urgent care was from somebody else in the house. Luckily, Darcy had some Xanax, ostensibly for an anxiety condition (though Sasha had never seen Darcy display anxiety), and Lou had some Valium from getting their wisdom teeth removed the previous month. Sasha accepted the latter, not wanting to owe Darcy anything. She kept the pill on the bedside table, telling herself that she'd take it when the pain became insurmountable.

Jules was hastily throwing together a New Year's Day brunch for the six of them and Miranda's much-discussed bestie Odette, who was also in the Hudson Valley working at a retreat center that winter. The retreat center was stationed on the grounds of a summer camp, now off-season.

Everyone slept so late that the brunch effectively became a late lunch, and then an early dinner. Darcy, Lou, Sasha, and Jesse sulked around, resenting Jules for making this plan. Odette showed up around five with a cloud of blond hair arranged around her head in tight corkscrew spirals. Her white Subaru was parked outside. She wore glasses so thick that her eyes behind them looked watery and unfocused. She and Miranda embraced for a long time, even though it had only been a few weeks since they'd seen each other.

Jules's phone rang, and she stepped into Miranda's office to take the call.

Sasha sat grimly in a chair in the living room, trying not to put too much of her weight on the left side of her tailbone.

When Jules slammed out of Miranda's study, everyone startled. "Babe? Who was it?"

"My mom." Jules stomped over to the counter to refresh her mug of coffee. "They made it to Santorini. She wanted to wish me a happy new year."

Jules's mother had been pitying, Jules said, almost embarrassed to regale Jules with tales of the Mediterranean. Her mother had used a tone indubitably meant to retaliate against her and Miranda's rejection of the Todds' offer for their daughter and her girlfriend to join them. In reality, Jules and Miranda had wanted to stay in Hudson, spend the holidays with their friends. In a last-ditch effort to convince Jules and Miranda to join them, Jules revealed, her parents had offered that all *six* of them join the cruise.

"Isn't it crazy that they don't know that *we* had a way better time than *they* could ever dream of, and *they* pity *me*?"

Jules's eyes were hollow and ringed with gray circles. Her hair hung lank and greasy around her face, deflated from its usually greased helmet. The chain around her neck looked smaller, too, or maybe it had just lost its luster. She set cookies onto a silver platter in an unattractive, clumsy way, shortbread tilted against Italian rainbow cookie.

"They have no idea how much fun we had, we had more fun than they could ever imagine having," Jules continued to rant. "*Fuck* them and *fuck* their cruise."

"That's the spirit!" Darcy cheered.

"Wait," Sasha said, "we were invited on the cruise?"

Darcy was flipping through photos from Italian Christmas on her phone, deciding which ones to post. As Sasha watched over her shoulder, Darcy lingered on the shot of Sasha and Jesse in front of the mantle. In the picture, Sasha stood perfectly straight, her lips twisted into a demure smile. Jesse was pressed against her. Sasha saw that they had of course missed nothing on the cruise.

Darcy swiped to another photo and double-tapped the screen to zoom in on her own abs, and Sasha diverted her attention.

"Did you see that fucker's latest post?" Odette asked Miranda loudly.

Miranda groaned. "No, I've been trying not to look."

Jules tossed an arm around Miranda's shoulders. "It'll go away. People can't stay focused on anything that doesn't involve them for too long."

"Is this about the podcast?" Lou asked from the kitchen, filling the electric kettle with water.

"It's just some bullshit," Odette said. "People coming after Miranda for something she didn't even *say*."

"She didn't say it?" Darcy wanted to know, her back to them, eyes on her phone. "So they're hallucinating? Or making it up?"

Her tone was light, nonaccusatory, but Jules jumped in defensively.

"They're grifters," Jules said, now also with an edge to her voice, still disjointed from the parental phone call. "They'll say whatever they have to for likes and fame."

Sasha sat stock-still on her right buttock, riveted.

"Well, that's how *they're* the true exhibitionists, right, these internet people," Jules said. "They pull people along the same threads and lines of inquiry that interest them, or are simply *in* their best interest, all while paying lip service to the idea that you're somehow having a conversation with them. And then it piles up into a narrative, right, and then the facts get lost."

(*Shrug*, the internet giggled minxily, *lol i'm not even sentient*.)

Sasha wanted to hear Odette's answer, but she sensed that she didn't know Odette well enough to jump in and soak up the gossip, so she migrated over to the wall of thrifted dishware that Jules and Miranda had been collecting for years.

Jesse caught her eye. She was standing on the back porch, looking out at some waifish ducks that had assembled on the yard. Jesse pulled chunks of bread from a big sourdough baguette and tossed them to the ducks below. Each big hunk of baguette fell into the water with a loud splash, displacing a few inches of lake.

"You'll give them angel wing syndrome," Sasha said sadly as she slid open the glass door and joined Jesse on the porch. She stood beside him, and he instinctively reached to hold her waist.

"I looked up what they're talking about, with Miranda," Jesse said. "There are all these hashtags on Twitter about it. The bad therapist thing."

Sasha knew she could've looked, too, but she had been too scared, having been the victim of Twitter bullying all too recently.

"What is it?" she asked, bracing herself. "What did she say?"

"Shhh," Jesse told her. "It doesn't matter."

She pressed into Jesse, and they both stood, watching the ducks.

෨ ෝ

Odette was gone. They ate a disappointing dinner of grilled cheese sandwiches, prepared by Jules and insufficiently melted, so that the meal became regular cheese sandwiches. Nobody talked much—Miranda and Jules seemed done with hosting, ready to be on their own again, and after dinner retreated quickly to the living room, where they sat up talking, two mugs of tea atop coasters on the oak coffee table. Jesse and Lou posted up over hot toddies at the kitchen table, a candle flickering between them. Darcy retreated to Bedroom 2.

Sasha, no longer wanting or needing and falling victim to the January 1 evening blues, retreated to Bedroom 3 and promptly began to cry. *Fraternité*, Sasha kept repeating to herself like a metronome. *Liberté, Egalité, Fraternité*. She got into the bed, under the top sheet, her chest contracting and expanding with each muffled sob, the scope of her misery exaggerated to fill the entire bed.

She texted Sylvie from the depths of her despair. Sylvie was having a meltdown of her own, unable to decide if she should quit her job fact-checking for *New York* magazine and go to Dublin. At first Sasha urged her to go, but then she remembered that every time she'd run away from her own problems, they'd come with her. Sylvie told Sasha she'd read a piece of writing that Sasha had sent her, something she was working on, and she was surprised that Sasha quoted an essay of Sylvie's called "Deceptive Things." In "Deceptive Things," Sylvie claims, among other double takes, that "the regal butch drinking an egg cream is a stoned teenaged boy" and "the dog corpse on the sidewalk is a discarded mink stole." The point being that misidentification is also a sort of identification.

Instead of being flattered, Sylvie told Sasha that she should respect herself more as a writer. She told Sasha that she should either just be honest or suck it up, accept that she was a liar, and write fiction.

You want every tote bag to be a purse! Sylvie lamented, drunk at a bar somewhere in Morningside Heights. *Sometimes a tote bag is just a tote bag!!!!*

Sasha reached for the pill on the bedside table and washed it down with a mug of green tea gone cold and bitter.

ର ବ

It was gray and drizzling when Sasha woke up at five in the morning. Jesse was a mound beside her, rising and falling with big lumbering breaths. Sasha stayed absolutely still, the weight of all she couldn't do because they were still at odds—stroke her hair, press her cheek against her back, nestle one cold leg between her warm thighs—pressed to her like a wet shirt. She reached over in the hazy half-darkness and touched the short hairs at the base of Jesse's neck. When she stirred a little, Sasha removed her hand.

She dressed in the wedding gown and dragged herself to the bathroom. Vivienne lifted her head sleepily but didn't follow.

The sound of voices in Bedroom 2. Sasha paused on her haunches, straining her muscles into stillness.

Darcy yelping, and Lou stage-whispering.

Lou: "Shh, shh, you'll wake everyone."

A soft exchange followed that Sasha couldn't make out.

Lou: "—the Eileen Myles. In 'Peanut Butter.' Something about a wink and the vastly conventional step of the sun. I thought of it because whosever room this normally is has a copy of *Not Me*. Which at first was, like, funny. But sometimes the things that everyone else likes are actually good, and that's why so many people like them?"

Darcy: "Mmmm."

"Can I go find it?"

A body sweeping up from the bed and the sound of a single

book swishing past the ones flanking it. Something—a pair of eyeglasses? A trinket?—clattering to the floor.

"Here it is. 'I love / you from my / childhood . . .'"

"That's nice," Darcy said meaningfully as Lou continued reading the rest of the poem—about the sun's conventional path, about taking the ride. Sasha pictured Lou tucking their forearms behind their head, bristly armpits warm and inviting. She imagined Darcy snaking a hand up Lou's pecs and nestling into the crook of their shoulder. *My spot* is what she used to call that part of Jesse's body.

Sasha could tell that Lou, like her, was sexually oriented toward the future. They were both horny for it, always had been; they liked the implication of a future better than the future itself, sometimes; what was most delicious to them was the promise of what was to come. Darcy must be like that, too— that was how both of them (she and Lou) had skated through this trip unscathed by any of the destruction that Darcy had inadvertently wrought.

While the sauna heated up, Sasha haunted every room, a juggy ghost. She stood at the foot of Jules and Miranda's bed and watched the elders slumber, Miranda curled into fetal position and Jules flat on her back. In their bathroom, she stared into the mirror, her face a smudge against the glass.

She woke Jesse, told him that he needed to come with her, and pulled him outside. Vivienne scampered down the stairs with them but remained a blurry mirage beyond the glass door. The whole world tilted on its axis, as always, only this time Sasha tipped with it. The wedding dress, yet unaltered, trailed behind, collecting ice chips and bits of debris from the slick ground.

Sasha hesitated in the sauna before removing the wedding dress, revealing an undersized fake Dior bikini. Her tits puffed out the tops and sides like raw dough, and the material stretched across her ass, neglecting her outer butt cheeks. A bulge in the bikini fabric where she'd taped a cotton puff against her ass wound meted out a faint heartbeat. The wooden barrel was as hot as before, and just as before she felt no relief from it.

Jesse, resigned to this fate of sitting bleary-faced in the sauna at dawn, reached for the string securing Sasha's fake Dior bikini and tugged it. Not because he especially wanted to see her tits, but because he knew she needed him to try.

Sasha tried to slap him away from her back, but her hand was a flopping sea turtle, and in her uncoordination she ended up hitting herself.

"Come on, sexy girl," Jesse urged. "We're the only ones in here, it's just me."

Sasha removed the bikini top. Her tits flopped down and to the sides, unsupported. She tried to stand up straight, head spinning and barely catching her balance, so that they were not so saggy. She wondered why, after a whole year with Jesse, she still tried to maintain the illusion that her breasts were not, in fact, the way they were, which was—and there was no doubting this—the exact way Jesse had always seen them. There was nowhere to hide, no ledge to climb upon.

Sasha tried something new. She puffed her chest out and gave her tits a good shake, like a Hooters waitress. The wedding dress remained a wet heap on the floor, limp, the polyester saturated with steam. Jesse wiped some sleep from his eyes.

"Oh, sexy," he said.

Jesse tugged at the ribbon around Sasha's neck and began to pull. Its bow disappeared immediately. Under the ribbon, her neck was wet with a film of sweat, throbbing with veins, ropy with tendons.

"Can I Come Inside?" Jesse asked, coming to crouch over her, his shoulders broad. Sasha let droplets of her sweat drip into her eyes and slide down her face like tears, slithering down into her cleavage.

"No," she said. She was, at the end of everything, a dykette.

There was something new underneath her refusal; this time, she wanted to say: *Yes, you can Come Inside. You have finally relieved me of my trick, good job, blue ribbon, green ribbon, gold star!* She heard herself say those things aloud, and she knew the game was finally working because she'd ditched herself. She drifted lazily down a current of Jesse's desire rather than her own. Now she was drugged, hysterical, and wanted to laugh manically. So she did.

Jesse was clearly on a different page.

"Goddamnit, Sash," he growled, touching her. She faced the wall of the sauna, so close to the wood that she inhaled the tree they came from, the lotions and herbs, the caked-in old sweat. Her back to him, him coming at her from behind.

"What?" she gasped.

"Can I Come Inside?"

"No."

"You interview Jules?" Jesse asked.

"Who, me?"

"Yeah, you."

Jesse pushed deeper into her. "Can I Come Inside?"

"No."

"Can I Come Inside?"

"No."

"Can I Come Inside?"

"Tell me why you want to Come Inside," Sasha gasped, quaking.

"I want to Come Inside."

"Ask me again where we went."

"Where'd you go?"

"Inside."

Jesse grinned like a killer.

"She fuck you?"

Sasha's face pressed to the sauna's wall: "If I say yes, will you take your hand away?"

"No."

"Yes."

"Can I Come Inside?"

—

"Can I Come Inside?"

"You know how to play this game."

"I know how to play this game."

"You know how to play this game."

"I know how to play this game."

"I know how to play this game."

"You know how to play this game."

"I know how to play this game."

"I know how to play this game."

—

"I know how to play this game."

"I know how to play this game."

Jesse jumped up and yanked a lever jutting out of the wall. Water cascaded into a bucket waiting below; Sasha observed this as though it were someone else's memory. The bucket grew very full. Jesse pulled the lever back to its original position, and a few last droplets squeezed themselves from the faucet and plunked downward, trembling the surface of the pool. Sasha stared down into the bucket and saw nothing reflected there. She poked the contents with an inquisitive finger and discovered that it was freezing.

"Wow," she breathed.

Jesse lifted the bucket, his muscles straining with effort.

Sasha's heart flew on the wings of an eagle—this was the breaking point, the climax, Jesse would douse her with ice water and her makeup would run off and she would be exposed as a small, terrified bird. She would be seen for what she really was, which was nothing, not a bimbo and not book smart. Jesse would see that Sasha meant nothing to anyone. Jesse would see that Sasha didn't even look pretty without the little wings of eyeliner she drew each morning.

Her body clenched, anticipating, wanting it so badly that it scared her and made her question her ultimate desires. Did Sasha want to be tortured or did she want to torture Jesse? All she knew was that this was what she deserved, for the water to cascade over her and scald her with its iciness. The appropriate way for her to meet her end. To be carved anew, to become a cave into which Jesse must dump the bucket of water, rinsing it out like a festering wound. The bucket wobbled in Jesse's arms.

෧ ෨

In the shed, thirty or so paces away from the sauna, Jules double-checked to make sure her audio was working, fiddled for a moment with the tangle of wires sprouting from the video camera, and then sat down to run through the end of her live segment later that afternoon. This was the personal aside she included about once a week, after the news of the day has been properly analyzed.

The teleprompter began scrolling, and Jules read the lines as they were fed to her—lines she herself wrote, but didn't yet know by heart.

Hi to you all at home. You might notice that I'm not in my usual spot,

but don't freak out. I'm not being held hostage in some degenerate shed;

this is my backyard upstate, where I've spent the past week with a few friends as

well as my partner, Miranda. More on her in a sec.

A few days ago, my friends and I watched the movie *Boys Don't Cry*. Absolutely

heartbreaking stuff. There's this part in particular I keep thinking about. Where

Chloë Sevigny, who plays Lana, leads Brandon Teena into her little house in rural

Nebraska. She's ashamed of it, tells him, "Don't look at my stupid house." I've

seen the movie probably a hundred times, but this time, during that scene,

I found myself thinking about Miranda. And about stupid houses. And about the

raptness, the commitment it takes, with those you love, not to look at them. About the love

made visible by the choice to not look at someone's stupid house—the stupid myths and legends

that surround the bodies they're stuck in, the literal and figurative filth of their lives—but look

instead at them, straight at them, the rest of the shit not gone but invisible for that moment.

Well, folks, this is how that sauce is made.

It's not always very pretty, admittedly, but this is me, in my stupid house,

talking to you folks—people I've met and people I haven't—in your own stupid houses. And I want to let you in on a little secret: Tomorrow I'm going to propose to Miranda, quite literally my everything.

I'm going to say to her: I don't want you to be looking at my stupid house.

I want you to be looking at me.

❧ ❧

This was when Sasha noticed it. Bobbing at the top of the cold water like a dead goldfish, an oblong glimmer, and a flash of inspiration: a pink-and-orange emerald-cut diamond, a miniaturized sunset on a tiny golden pedestal atop a thin, gleaming band. Her color scheme. The shrunken universe floated through Sasha's eyes and singed her optic nerves, steaming her vision with pink and orange. Sasha gasped, staring into the pool of water, now saturated with the very essence of the gloaming.

She reached for her bathing suit top so her tits wouldn't be flopping around. Jesse's anger was and always had been a show, a joke, that aimed to catch Sasha by surprise. The anger is a decoy—she is what Jesse loves. She waited anxiously, pulling the wedding dress up around her body and preparing to be doused with the water, for the ring to cascade over her like a dykette baptism. She stretched her mouth into the shape it will make when the ring bounces off her head and into her hands like a ping-pong ball, the way she will seize it and squeal and say, *Yes, yes, yes!!!!*

But instead, Jesse tilted the bucket of ice water up, the gesture taking on the speed and rhythm of something impulsive. The bucket was lighter than Jesse expected; the force he used to lift it above his head suddenly shown to be excessive, the water sloshing over the lip of the bucket and onto the wooden floor as Jesse foisted it aloft.

He let it tilt forward, at first little by little and then in an increasingly Niagara Falls–speed free fall, and dumped it over his own head. He released it in a big rush, a clear blue liquid curtain, and the water pressed his short hair into his scalp and rushed down his dark eyelashes in a thin stream.

Jesse trembled as the cold water steamed off his body in dramatic plumes, vaporizing into the humid air of the sauna. A scent clustering in the air around a piece of fetid meat before dissipating, filling every conceivable space until it's undetectable. Jesse closed his eyes tight and small, a newborn. The oldness shaved off of his body. Emotions that no longer served him regurgitated and disposed of themselves, the bad memories drying up as the mood bled from deep plum to lavender to lilac. Sasha saw the dispersal of everything that was now lost, and what was stood to gain. She saw the room opened up around Jesse, in Jesse.

All this time, Jesse was clenched, orifices squeezed shut while this wave crested over his body, the lip of it skimming the top of his head and falling over his face in a transparent sheet. Jesse's face refracted by the water into a hypnotic blur that swiped away its distinguishing features. Her boyfriend reminded Sasha of a pair of structureless nude underwear, a second skin of fabric slipping through her fingers. Jesse's renewal shuddered through her body. Sasha stood watching, the wedding dress gathered around her waist and melting into the floor. She half expected Jesse to evaporate, but once the water had gone, gravity whisking it downward, he was still there, eyeing Sasha from beneath wet lashes.

Then Sasha remembered the ring. It bounced off Jesse's newly slick body, slaloming down the side of his nose, skipping into the divot of his collarbone, ricocheting off his left pec and soaring like Icarus toward the furnace, its coals crackling with red-blue heat. Jesse, noticing too, cried out, but was too blissed-out to take action.

Sasha crashed to the ground, a volleyball star, grasping point-lessly at the threads of water running every which way across the sauna floor, clutching the ground with her fingernails. One acrylic snapped clean off, leaving a purple-black crescent wedged in between the wooden boards, a portal to another world.

The ring sizzled once more, letting out a final gasp before the coals swallowed it like quicksand.

Have you ever thought our lives were very dangerous?

I can look away? I can leave the room?

For one moment, Sasha and the ring had glared at one other, twin flames. As the coals subsumed it, an awful tinkling digestion, she realized that the diamond was not pink-orange at all. The colors she'd seen in the pool of water were a trick of the light, taking on its sunset hues from the fire. Now that the ring was actually in the fire, rather than simply illuminated by its toasty glow, it was obvious that the ring was clear, a watery diamond so transparent that she could see through the prism. And she knew that this pretty, pretty object was not meant for her.

Acknowledgments

THANK YOU!

To Ruby Rose Lee and Miriam Altshuler, for believing in this book from the beginning and providing constant support and encouragement. I'm so lucky to have you both by my side. And to everyone at Holt and DeFiore, you're all brilliant at what you do. Thank you for handling this novel with so much care.

Scattered lines in this book first appeared in an essay entitled "High Femme Camp Antics," published at the end of 2020 by the *Los Angeles Review of Books*. Thanks to everyone who has published and supported my writing, including Wednesday Books and the Iowa Arts Fellowship at the University of Iowa.

To my friends and family in New York, Iowa, and beyond— I'm not worthy of your absolute perfection. Thank you for giving me yards and yards of material (literary and fabric), for reading so many early drafts of this book, and for being so funny and generous. Thanks for teaching me everything I know about everything.

To all the teachers and mentors I've been lucky enough to learn from throughout my life, especially my undergraduate and graduate advisors, Danielle Vogel and Melissa Febos: You are so special to me and your work is a gift to the world. Special thanks to Hannah Beresford, too, for providing transformative feedback on an early version of this book.

Thank you to all the members of my MFA cohort for always seeing both what was already there and what could possibly be. All my love and eternal devotion!

To all the writers, artists, scholars, and archivists whose work has documented our gay lives from time immemorial—you are the smartest, sexiest, brightest; you're why I want to write and literally why I'm able to.

To Lois, I'm obsessed with you. Thank you for letting me love you with such patience and grace. You are so, so wonderful. Perfect. My whole world.

And to Tess, thank you for making such a gorgeous home for Lois and me to live in. You make everything you touch better and sweeter and more beautiful, and I can't believe I get to be your girl.

About the Author

Jenny Fran Davis received her MFA from the University of Iowa, where she was an Iowa Arts Fellow. The author of *Everything Must Go*, a novel for teenagers, she lives in Brooklyn.